CHASING POWER

ALSO BY SARAH BETH DURST

Conjured

CHASING POWER

SARAH BETH DURST

BLOOMSBURY
NEW YORK   LONDON   NEW DELHI   SYDNEY

First published in the United States of America in October 2014
by Bloomsbury Children's Books
www.bloomsbury.com

Bloomsbury is a registered trademark of Bloomsbury Publishing Plc

For information about permission to reproduce selections from this book, write to
Permissions, Bloomsbury Children's Books, 1385 Broadway, New York, New York 10018
Bloomsbury books may be purchased for business or promotional use. For information on
bulk purchases please contact Macmillan Corporate and Premium Sales Department at
specialmarkets@macmillan.com

Library of Congress Cataloging-in-Publication Data
Durst, Sarah Beth.
Chasing power / Sarah Beth Durst.
pages   cm
Summary: Sixteen-year-old Kayla, whose telekinetic ability allows her to be a master
shoplifter with enough money to flee with her mother if her father finds them again, meets
Daniel, who has the ability to teleport and needs her help to find and steal an ancient
incantation that can help rescue his kidnapped mother—but may lead
to great danger for Kayla.
ISBN 978-0-8027-3755-7 (hardcover) • ISBN 978-0-8027-3756-4 (e-book)
[1. Psychic ability—Fiction.   2. Shoplifting—Fiction.   3. Single-parent families—Fiction.
4. Kidnapping—Fiction.   5. Mystery and detective stories.]   I. Title.
PZ7.D93436Ch 2014   [Fic]—dc23   2014005595

Book design by Nicole Gastonguay
Typeset by Westchester Book Composition
Printed and bound in the U.S.A. by Thomson-Shore Inc., Dexter, Michigan
2 4 6 8 10 9 7 5 3 1

All papers used by Bloomsbury Publishing, Inc., are natural, recyclable products
made from wood grown in well-managed forests. The manufacturing processes
conform to the environmental regulations of the country of origin.

For Rachel Bickford

1

Razor blade.

Thread.

Gum.

A ball of tinfoil.

A dull fishing hook.

Kayla checked each pocket in her jean shorts, knotted the straps of her bikini top tighter, and pulled on her favorite black hoodie. She frowned at her bare feet. She'd blend in better with flip-flops, but she could run better in sneakers, if anything went wrong. After a half second, she chose the sneakers. She believed in herself, but she also believed in the supreme idiocy of people and their tendency to interfere in the most inconvenient way possible.

Telling herself to think positive thoughts, Kayla applied kohl eyeliner around her blue eyes, then put on three necklaces: a hamsa hand, a blue-and-white glass eye, and a crescent moon with a pentagram. "Moonbeam?" she called as she yanked a brush through her black-and-pink hair.

When her mother didn't answer, Kayla poked her head around the Indian print scarf that separated her corner into an almost-room. Empty. Or, rather, not at all empty—Kayla and her mother rented a one-room cottage, and it was crowded with pots of herbs, baskets of polished stones, and piles of candles. Prayer flags were strung across the ceiling. Dreamcatchers filled the rafters, as did knots of red ribbons and mobiles of feathers and bones. Bits of mirrors caught and reflected the sun, and crystals split it into a thousand shards of light that danced over the room whenever the breeze blew through the open windows. Her mother must be outside.

Weaving between stacks of books and various baskets, Kayla crossed to the kitchen. She stepped onto a chair, then the counter, inserting her foot between the dishes piled there. Twisting, she stuck her leg out the window and ducked through the opening, shifting her weight until she was perched on a window box of herbs. She jumped to the ground.

Mildly, her mother said, "I wish you wouldn't do that."

Kayla grinned at her and plopped a kiss on the top of her mother's graying head. "Sorry, Moonbeam." Her mother was on her hands and knees in a flower bed. She had a pile of red ribbons beside her and appeared to be tying one onto each of the red-and-blue plaster garden gnomes. "Ooh, they look fancy. Special occasion? Garden party for garden gnomes?"

"I am allowed to be eccentric in my advancing age."

"You were eccentric when you were twelve. I know your stories."

"Ahh, but then it was a phase." Dusting the dirt off her sundress, Moonbeam got to her feet. She wore a shapeless multicolored dress, a dozen necklaces with eclectic charms that were knotted around one another, a half-dozen bangle bracelets on her arms, and rings on every finger except her ring finger.

Her bare shoulders were freckled, and her face was tanned but unwrinkled. Except for the gray that streaked her blond hair, she could have passed for Kayla's older hippie sister. "You know I should tell you to march inside and put on a shirt, or at least zip up your sweatshirt. Your breasts are not an art installation."

"But my belly button is a masterpiece that shouldn't be hidden from the world."

Moonbeam laughed. "Do I even want to ask what you have planned today?"

"Strut up and down State Street with Selena. Mock everyone and everything, and then return home feeling vaguely superior. Oh, and maybe eat a burrito."

"Lofty goals. Again, if I were a good mother, I'd ask if you planned to find a summer job. And maybe tell you not to smoke, drink, do drugs, or talk to strangers. Do we need to have the sex talk?"

"God, no. And I have a job."

"You do?"

"I look after you." Kayla flashed a grin at Moonbeam, and her mother rolled her eyes at her in a spectacular imitation of a stereotypical teenager, then ruined the effect by smiling. "Don't worry about me," Kayla insisted.

Moonbeam's smile faded. "I always worry about you." She caught Kayla's three necklaces in her hand and then dropped all but the blue glass eye. She held it in one hand and passed her other hand over it. Softly, she whispered to it, a string of lyrical words that flowed into Kayla's ears and then out again. Try as hard as she could, Kayla could never hold those words in her memory. They were a string of syllables that flowed through her like water between fingers, caressing her skin and then gone.

Her mother released the necklace. "Say hi to Selena for me," she said in a normal voice. "She's welcome for dinner, if she wants."

"She says we eat only rabbit food and horse feed."

"Tell her tonight it's birdseed."

"She'll be thrilled."

A honk blared from the street, followed by three short blasts. Kayla half stepped and half leaped over the cramped flower beds to the red wooden gate draped in hibiscus flowers. Moonbeam called after her, "Love you, Kayla! Be safe!"

"Love you too!" The gate creaked and a dozen bells chimed as Kayla opened and shut it. She hopped over the row of protective stones that Moonbeam used around the entire property, and she waved at Selena.

Selena leaned on her car horn once more for good measure, then waved back. She had the top of her red BMW convertible down, her shades on, and her bare left foot propped up on the door. Her toenails were painted with red glitter. She wore a matching red halter top and the same jean shorts as Kayla, except that hers were cut by a designer, not sliced with a pair of kitchen scissors, the same pair used to cut clumps of knotted fur off the neighbor's always-visiting dog. Everything about Selena was designer-perfect. She was half Guatemalan, half Kenyan, and 100 percent incredibly wealthy. "You know if you worked for me and you made me wait that long, I'd have flogged you."

Kayla hopped into the car and buckled her seat belt. "No, you wouldn't. You have people to flog your people."

"Yes. Yes, I do. I have floggers."

"And slappers, for anyone who doesn't deserve a full-out flogging."

"My slappers are fully employed slapping silly any idiot who thinks he isn't an idiot, which is basically everyone except you, me, and your mom. I've had to upgrade some slaps to flogs simply to meet the demand."

Kayla fetched the spare sunglasses from the glove compartment and slid them on. "You lead an odd life. Good thing you have me to add normalcy."

Laughing, Selena lowered her pedicured foot from the window, shifted into drive, and peeled out, roaring down the street. Wind whipped their hair behind them, Selena's natural black and Kayla's dyed black and pink. Sunlight streamed down on them. Kayla tilted her head back and let it soak into her. The sky was brilliant blue, and the palm trees looked so picturesque that it felt like driving through a postcard. "So what's the target today, Normal Girl?" Selena asked.

"State Street. Henri's."

"Again?"

"I like the challenge. Besides, I want a mochaccino."

"Okay, what's the twist?"

"No hands." Kayla shook her hands in the air, jazz hands. "I do it remote."

"Cash or prizes?"

"Both. And cash can be used to obtain prizes, so long as it's lifted cash."

Selena nixed that. "Too easy. No cash."

"Some cash," Kayla countered. "But can't be used for the primary target."

"Fine. Clock in under thirty minutes and I'll be impressed."

"Give me forty-five. I'll be relying on other people to determine whether I go with plan A, B, C, D, or improvise, and other people are notoriously unreliable."

"Indeed. They all need flogging."

The ocean came into view. Big, blue, beautiful. Windsurfers skimmed over the surface. Waves crashed as white foam on the sand. Brightly colored umbrellas dotted the beach, and the volleyball courts were full. Selena turned right at a traffic light and drove alongside the beach, down East Cabrillo. Ahead, a sculpture of leaping dolphins—the symbol of Santa Barbara—was surrounded by a flock of tourists posing for photos, the pier in the background. Competing radios blasted music, and Selena turned up the music in the car, a Spanish radio station.

Selena finessed the car into a parking spot outside a surfing store. The music shut off abruptly as she turned off the engine. "I'll be at the smoothie café. Signal if you need a getaway car, and I'll call you a taxi."

"You aren't coming with me?"

"Oh, sweetie." Selena twisted in her seat to clasp both of Kayla's hands. "You know how I love to watch you work, but when you finally land your little white tushy in jail, I am going to have plausible deniability and a café full of witnesses to vouch for me. And then I'll bail you out, because that's what good friends do."

"Your faith in me is humbling."

"Don't be humbled, Kayla. You are greatness personified. You are walking magnificence. The epitome of splendor. The penultimate paragon of awesomeness."

"You know that means second-best, right? Penultimate. Next to last."

"It does? It should mean better than ultimate."

"Doesn't."

"Huh. Someone should change that." Selena crinkled her forehead in mock concentration. "Such injustice should not stand."

"Not worth it. There are better causes."

"But the dictionary is a tyrant. Someone should challenge its authority!" Selena punched her fist in the air. Her bracelets clinked together. "Show it that it's people who control the words, not a book. You can't control the people's words! Set them free!"

Kayla climbed out of the car. "Enjoy your smoothie." She flipped up the hood on her hoodie and stuffed her hands in her pockets. Her fingers curled around a stick of gum.

"Hey, platinum bands only. None of this fourteen-carat crap."

"Don't worry. I won't embarrass you."

"See that you don't."

As Selena scooped up her designer purse and headed for the smoothie café, Kayla strolled down State Street. It was a beautiful day. The palm-tree shadows were as crisp as cutouts on the terra-cotta-tiled sidewalks. The white adobe faces of the buildings gleamed so bright that if Kayla hadn't been wearing sunglasses, she would have had to squint. All the restaurants had their outside tables set up with umbrellas open, and people were walking their stuffed-toy-size dogs up and down the sidewalk. One dog wore a bikini. Several motorcycles roared up and down the street, cruising in a clump, and packs of teenagers in all black had already staked out spots on the brick benches.

Kayla leaned against an archway next to an ATM outside the Santa Barbara First City Bank. She wondered what she'd do when she ran out of challenges on this street. Maybe convince Selena to drive to LA. Plenty of targets there. Moonbeam would flip if she left town, but what she didn't know couldn't disappoint her. Kayla pulled out a stick of gum, unwrapped it, and popped the gum into her mouth. As she chewed, she flattened the wrapper with her fingernails and waited for someone to approach the machine.

After a minute or two, a woman in a black suit-dress and stiletto heels strode up to the ATM. Rummaging through her purse, she pulled out her bank card. *Go time,* Kayla thought.

As the woman slid her card into the ATM, Kayla concentrated on the gum wrapper. She pictured it sliding over the pavement like it was a sail skimming the surface of the ocean, then she gave it a "shove" with her mind. The wrapper slid across the tiled sidewalk. Controlled by Kayla, it rose up the adobe wall of the bank. Kayla concentrated, and the wrapper angled itself beside the keypad of the ATM. Still leaning against the arch, Kayla watched the reflection of the woman's fingers in the silver of the wrapper as the woman typed in her password. Kayla then released the wrapper, and it fluttered to the ground.

The woman stuck her card back into her wallet. As she waited for the cash, Kayla shifted her attention to the wallet. She could "feel" the card poking out. It was stuck in the wallet's plastic credit-card sheath. She pulled at it, and the card wiggled, slightly. She concentrated harder, and it wiggled more. And then a sharp pain shot through Kayla's head and blossomed into little fireworks inside her skull.

Undeterred, Kayla drew the razor blade out of her pocket and sent it slithering fast over the sidewalk. It rose up to the woman's purse and dipped inside. Speed was essential. So was precision. Neatly, it sliced through the thin plastic sheath in the wallet to free the stuck ATM card. Kayla caused the razor blade to flip out of the purse and land on the sidewalk.

Free from the wallet, the card floated out of the purse nicely.

Sending it down the wall, she let it fall behind a rock border that edged a few brilliant orange flowers.

The whole maneuver took only seconds—less than the time it took the machine to spit out the money and the woman to count it. Completely focused, Kayla hadn't breathed. Now, she exhaled.

The woman walked away with her cash without glancing at Kayla. Ignoring her too, Kayla spat the gum into her hand and then sent it flying up to block the security camera lens above the ATM. The gum stuck, obscuring the camera's view.

As she strolled over to the ATM, the razor blade flew up into her pocket, and the woman's bank card flew into her hand. In front of the machine, Kayla pretended to draw the card out of her pocket. She stuck it into the ATM, punched in the woman's PIN, and withdrew the same amount as the woman had, $120. She pocketed the cash and then retreated, leaving the card in the machine. From a safe distance, Kayla called to the wad of gum. It fell off the lens, skittered along the sidewalk, and then jumped into a trash can.

Kayla despised people who dropped their gum on the sidewalk. No consideration for others.

Task complete, she continued to stroll down the street. Several heavily pierced-and-tattooed teens nodded to her, and she nodded back, but she didn't stop. She entered a coffee shop and used one of her new bills to buy a mochaccino with whipped cream and chocolate drizzle, and then she parked herself on a stool by the front window, directly across from Henri's Fine Jewelry and Watches. She pushed her sunglasses up on top of her head for a better view.

She'd never done this distance before. Happily, both the

door to the coffee shop and the door to the jewelry store were propped open, simplifying matters. She wouldn't have to wait for someone to open them. She took a sip of the chocolaty coffee, steadied herself, and concentrated. First problem: her target case was locked. Second problem: the jewelry store clerk was leaning against it.

Kayla focused on the case by the front door instead. The lock was easy and quick to pick. With practiced ease, Kayla shifted each tiny tumbler inside the mechanism until she "felt" it pop. She couldn't slide the case door open, of course—much too heavy—and besides, it wasn't her target. Instead, she repeated the lock trick with several more cases before switching her attention to the watch display. One by one, she unclasped each watch. The heavy Rolexes slid on their own off their displays. The clerk scurried over to fix them, leaving her vigil over the diamond case. While she was distracted, Kayla focused on the diamond case. She slipped three diamond rings—platinum bands only, per Selena—off their velvet display fingers and scooted them underneath a necklace stand, close to where the case door would open. Then, taking the ball of tinfoil from her pocket, she sent it out of the coffee shop and across the street, rolling like debris and pausing by the curb before hopping up it. She rolled it inside the jewelry store and tucked it under the lip of the diamond display case. And then she waited.

She took a few deep breaths and let her brain relax. Using her power felt like using a muscle—she focused, clenched, and then released. Her skull felt as though it were vibrating. As she steadied herself, the buzz of the coffee shop sank into her, soothing her. There were maybe a dozen people at the rickety wood tables, a few alone with laptops, others clumped around the tables. The coffee shop tried for an artsy look, with old vinyl records stapled to the walls and chalk signs with slogans like "Get Off My Unicorn" and "If a Tree Falls in the Forest, Call a Dryad." It had a shelf of used books and bins of specialty chocolates. You could also buy coffee-scented hand lotion. But Kayla liked it, even if it was trying too hard and even if the clientele thought they were too cool for school. All the self-absorbed people were too distracted by the glory of their own personalities to notice her.

Casually, she pulled a bit of thread out of her pocket and tied it to the fishhook. She kept her hands in her lap, where others couldn't see, and then sent the hook and thread out. The hook and thread snaked across the floor, nearly invisible against the bright patterned tile. The thread wound up the nearest stool. She let the hook snag the upholstery of the chair cushion while the other end of the thread dove into the pocket of a coiffed guy with a half-open shirt. She meticulously tied a knot over a loop of metal that she "felt" inside. When the customer stood, the thread, anchored by the hook, pulled out a car key with zero assistance from Kayla. She repeated this several more times, fishing out more keys, a five-dollar bill, and grocery lists from other customers. She left her finds on their chairs—she was just practicing—and commanded the thread and hook back into her pocket. As they hopped back in, she smiled to herself.

As usual, no one noticed.

After a moment's thought, she slithered the cash across the baseboards of the coffee shop. She pretended to drop a napkin and scooped up the five inside the napkin. Stuffing it into her pocket, she sat up in time to see a woman and a toddler walk into the jewelry store.

Perfect, she thought.

Watching, Kayla took another sip of coffee. She loved toddlers. She didn't know any personally, but every one she'd ever observed was a predictable ball of chaos. It was only five minutes before the little boy was yanking on the display cases, trying to open them. He succeeded instantly with the first case that Kayla had unlocked, a case of charms, and then, with delight on his face so clear that Kayla could see it from across the street and through the window, he repeated his discovery with several other cases, including the diamond ring case.

Clucking, the mother scurried after him, closing the cases as she went. Kayla immediately concentrated on the ball of tinfoil. It rose up and hopped into the corner of the open case door. The mother caught the boy just past the diamond ring case. When she paused in her scolding long enough to close the case, it didn't shut all the way, stuck on the foil. Finishing with the boy, the mother apologized to the store clerk, who had begun to relock the cases, starting with the charm case.

While the clerk was distracted by the mother, Kayla flipped the hidden rings out of the case and let them fall softly onto the carpeted floor. She hid them in the carpet pilings under the lip of the display case and then popped out the ball of tinfoil a few seconds before the clerk locked the case.

Carefully, under the case, she unwrapped the ball of tinfoil with her mind, and then she rolled the rings onto it. She folded the tinfoil around the rings and guided it out of the store. She let it tumble down the street and into a hedge of bushes half a block away.

Standing, she finished her mochaccino and tossed the cup in the trash. Putting on her sunglasses, she then sauntered out of the coffee shop and across the street. She didn't go anywhere near the jewelry store, but she did pass by the hedge and scoop up the tinfoil ball and stuff it into her pocket. Humming to herself, she strolled to a candy store. With her mind, she selected a lollipop from a rainbow-of-flavors display. She sent it flying up to the ceiling, out the door, and along the gutter on the roof. She then flew it directly into the hand of the toddler as he waddled out of the store, his other hand firmly gripped by his mother. Kayla watched as the toddler looked in surprise at the lollipop.

The boy wasn't flummoxed for long, though. Seconds later, he was waving the lollipop in the air, demanding his mommy unwrap it. Absently, she did, and he stuck it into his mouth.

Kayla grinned and checked the State Street clock. Twenty-five minutes. *Better than penultimate*, she thought. Humming again, she headed for the smoothie café and a soon-to-be-impressed Selena. She passed by the brick bench with the pierced-and-tattooed teens.

One of them was watching her.

He was tall with black hair that dusted over his eyes. Unlike the others, he wasn't pierced or tattooed. He wore a clean black T-shirt and black jeans with boots. Kayla felt his eyes on her as she walked by and for an instant, she thought, *He saw me; he knows.* But no, that was impossible. It was far more likely he'd noticed her pink-streaked hair or her bikini top, which was the point of both. Also, she liked both. She flashed him a smile as she passed.

He didn't smile back.

When she reached the smoothie café, she glanced over her shoulder. He wasn't there. She fingered her blue glass eye amulet and went inside.

2

In the window, the charms and crystals caught the moonlight, twisting it and turning it until it danced over the walls and the floor and across Kayla's bed. She sat cross-legged on her futon bed in a patch of dancing moonlight and rolled the tinfoil ball soundlessly from hand to hand as she listened to her mother breathe on the other side of the curtain. Almost asleep.

She heard her mother shift and the crisp sheets crinkle.

A deep exhale.

A slow inhale and then steady breaths.

Yes, asleep.

It was funny how roles reversed. Moonbeam talked all the time about how she used to listen to Kayla sleep, checking on her several times each night, reassuring herself that she was here and that no one had taken her in the night.

"No one" being Dad, of course.

And now it was Kayla's turn to take care of Moonbeam as best she could.

Kayla flicked on her lighter. She focused on the flame, and, with her mind, lifted it with a bubble of fluid from the lighter, spun it in the air, and lowered it onto the wick of a candle. It lit the walls with a warm yellow glow, and the scent of honeysuckle rolled out with the colorless smoke.

On her lap, she unrolled the tinfoil ball. The three diamond rings lay nestled in the creases. She lifted out one. It was platinum, per Selena, in the shape of two bulbous dolphins that met nose to nose to hold a lump of diamond. Extremely tacky. The second ring was encrusted with starbursts of tiny diamonds. Also overkill. The third was a classic engagement ring with a single stone propped almost aggressively up on spikes. It defied the concept of the word "subtle." Holding it up, she twisted it, and it caught the candle flame in each of its facets. She stared into the reflected flames, momentarily mesmerized. When the moment passed, Kayla slipped the ring into the pocket of her hoodie, which was draped over the chair that she used as a bedside table. The diamond could be useful, perhaps to cut glass or to cause a distraction.

On the other side of the curtain, Moonbeam tossed under her covers. Kayla froze, ready to snuff the candle, hide the rings, and flop back into bed as if she'd fallen asleep hours ago. But her mother settled again.

Kayla dumped the other two rings into a pouch, the kind used to hold herbs and other protective charms, the kind that Moonbeam wouldn't look at twice. She then pulled a backpack out from under her futon and put the pouch inside. The backpack held emergency supplies: dried fruit, granola bars, a bottle of water, a map of California, and a bus schedule, plus a few other trinkets that Kayla had lifted.

Next, the money. She slid a twenty into her hoodie pocket with the ring. She'd use it for food tomorrow, or maybe slip it into Moonbeam's purse. Tomorrow, she'd also deposit sixty in Moonbeam's bank account, a small-enough amount that she wouldn't notice the influx but enough to cover at least part of the electricity bill—they didn't use much with just the cottage, but it still added up. The rest went into a Ziploc stuffed with bills in the emergency backpack. She had several thousand dollars in her backpack so far. If Dad ever tracked them here, Kayla planned to grab the pack before they ran.

With a few thousand dollars in cash, they'd be able to run as far as they wanted. Across the country. Or maybe to another country altogether. She'd love to see France. Or Egypt. Or Thailand. And if they pawned the trinkets that Kayla had collected, they wouldn't have to start over with nothing.

She knew she was being paranoid. Dad wasn't going to find them. It had been eight years and no hint of any danger. But she felt safer with the backpack—and it was a lot more practical than Moonbeam's thousand charms and amulets, which couldn't even protect her from mosquitoes.

Kayla stuffed the backpack under her futon again and blocked it from view with a spare pillow. She straightened just as the curtain was pulled aside. Moonbeam stood in the gap in a loose nightgown that hung to her ankles, white and billowy so that she looked like a ghost in the candlelight. For an instant, Kayla's heart jumped, but she forced herself to take an even breath. No way had Moonbeam seen anything.

"Can't sleep?" Moonbeam asked.

"Just . . . you know." She winced inwardly at her lack of eloquence.

"Chamomile tea with honey? Alternatively, I could rub your back and sing you a lullaby. Loudly and off-key. Most likely, the neighbor's dog will howl."

Kayla unwound her legs from the covers and pretended she was stretching after just waking. "Tea works." She slid her feet into slippers, a pair of Minnie Mouse ones she'd rescued from a yard sale. She'd claimed she wanted to wear them ironically, but really she liked how fuzzy they were between her toes. She padded after Moonbeam.

She loved how the house looked at night, soft and safe. The windows were open, and a breeze blew the crystals and dream-catchers in lazy circles. The scarves and curtains rippled like waves. All the shadows overlapped like blankets that you could sink into.

"Were you having bad dreams?" Moonbeam asked.

"I wasn't having any dreams," Kayla said. "I was awake."

"One of the girls at work analyzes dreams. Yesterday she was telling everyone if you dream of a flounder, it means you're feeling indecisive. Who dreams about a flounder?"

"Indecisive people, apparently."

Moonbeam lit three candles in the center of the table. Warm light spread through the cottage. Shadows danced larger. The candles smelled like sandalwood, rosemary, and sage. "Who even knows what a flounder looks like?"

"Indecisive people who love seafood?"

"I wonder what indecisive vegetarians dream about."

"Vegetarians are naturally decisive," Kayla declared. "After all, they decided no steak, despite the temptation of steak tacos with fresh guacamole."

Moonbeam nodded as if that made perfect sense. "Ooh, let's make guacamole tomorrow. I'll pick up some avocados after work."

"Okay." Kayla perched on one of the kitchen stools and

rested her chin on her knee as Moonbeam filled a teakettle and set it on the stove. The gas clicked as it ignited. A soft blue flame added more layers and colors to the shadows. "Do you ever feel the urge to travel? See the world? Eat guacamole in Mexico? Or crème brûlée in France with a view of the Eiffel Tower? Or, ooh, *on* the Eiffel Tower with a view of all of Paris?"

Moonbeam fetched two mismatched mugs from a shelf. They'd made these mugs themselves during Moonbeam's pottery phase. Kayla had painted hers with hearts and stars—she was ten at the time. Moonbeam had painted symbols, amalgams of Celtic runes and Egyptian hieroglyphics. "Are you having itchy feet?"

"Not really. Maybe someday." *Yes*, she thought. "You and me, we could do it cheap. Stay in hostels. Camp. Backpack around. I heard you can get a train pass around Europe for not too much. Or maybe we could go to Asia. Or South America. See the rain forests and commune with the medicine men, or whatever you want."

"Aren't you supposed to be in some teenage rebellion stage and not want to be seen in public with your highly embarrassing mother?" Moonbeam brought out a canister of tea leaves.

"That's so eighties. But if you want, we can schedule in some time for me to cringe in between climbing the Eiffel Tower and shopping on the Champs-Élysées."

Moonbeam scooped tea leaves into a strainer. She didn't meet Kayla's eyes. "Are you so unhappy here? We have a nice life. It's a nice place. You have nice friends. You'd miss Selena."

"I don't want to move! Just . . . see more." Kayla shrugged, as if the suggestion was merely a thought and didn't make her want to leap off the stool and pack right now. "It would be educational."

"It would be unpredictable."

As the water heated, the teakettle shimmied on the stove. "Not if we planned it. Lots of guidebooks. Lots of maps. We could have a route mapped out for every day, if it makes you feel better. I promise not to improvise."

Moonbeam's mouth quirked. "Don't promise what you can't do." And then she sighed. "Oh, Kayla, can't you be happy with here and now? We're part of this place, and it's a part of us. We fit. It's familiar."

The teakettle whistled. Moonbeam poured the boiling water into the mugs. Kayla watched the brown tea seep from the leaves and swirl like paint in the water. In a soft voice, as if she were speaking to the tea, Kayla ventured, "It would be nice to not always be scared."

"Oh, sweetheart, I don't want you to be scared. But I want you to be smart. Familiarity is safety. We hide in plain sight—"

"Maybe I don't want to hide my entire life."

Moonbeam drew in a breath that shook, and Kayla wished she could suck the words back in. She'd never meant to say that out loud. It wasn't her mother's fault that they had to hide. She'd given up everything to keep Kayla safe. Everything she did was oriented around that one goal. And Kayla had just slapped her with it. "I'm sorry," Kayla said quickly. "Forget I said it. I'm tired. I didn't mean it. Maybe I did have some bad dreams. Not about fish."

Moonbeam sank heavily onto one of the other stools. "This isn't about travel. It's about . . ." She tapped her forehead. Kayla's power. She never named it out loud, as if she were afraid of even the wind overhearing. "You think I'm not letting you be yourself."

"What? No!" Kayla rubbed her forehead. Maybe yes.

"I know it must be so very tempting, and, Kayla, you should know I am so very, very proud of you for resisting. But you can't use it. Ever. He'd find us."

Drop it, her mind whispered. *You'll never convince her.* She didn't know what made her want to continue the conversation. Maybe it was the moonlight, making everything seem softer and easier to say. Maybe she was tired—tired of hiding and tired of lying. She thought of the boy with black hair who had watched her so closely. Sometimes Kayla thought it would be nice to be seen—to have at least someone recognize and acknowledge what she was. "But you use magic." Kayla gestured at the charms and amulets all around them.

"To protect us. Not to play. And I hide it under nonsense." Moonbeam gestured too, throwing her arms wide to encompass the entire house. "No one will see the real under all the fake. Or if they do, they'll think it's merely luck, that I don't know the difference. I'm hiding in plain sight! And you need to too. You have to be a normal girl, inside and out, home and away. Be what you want him to see. It's the only way to stay safe."

"I'd be careful."

"Of course you would. You'd try. But you can never be careful enough. Someday, someone might see, and someone might talk, and then word would spread of a girl who can move things with her mind. And your father will hear, and he will know, and he will come. And he will do to you what he did to her."

There it was, the mention of "her." Neither of them said the name of Kayla's older sister, Amanda, but it still hung in the air, caught in the summer night breeze that twisted around the cottage. Kayla wanted to say it wasn't healthy to always live in the past, to let fear consume their lives, to always hide and lie. But the word "her" clogged her throat. "It might not be like that. He might not even be looking for us."

"He is. He will. If there's one word to describe your father, it's 'determined.' But then, so am I." Her lips thinned, and for an instant, Kayla saw an expression in her mother's eyes that she'd never seen before. It flashed by so quickly that Kayla wasn't sure what to name it.

"What if I only use it here? Supervised. At safe times. Like now." Before her mother could reply, Kayla concentrated on the sugar bowl. The spoon was silver, too heavy, but she lifted a stream of granules. Sparkling like diamond dust, they arced out of the bowl and dove into Moonbeam's mug. Moonbeam's hands tightened so hard around the mug that her knuckles looked like popcorn, bumpy and white. It was tricky, controlling so many specks of sugar at the same time, but Kayla guided the last one into the mug without faltering. Exhaling, she sagged back onto the stool.

Silence. Outside, insects buzzed and clicked.

"Tell me you haven't been practicing that." Moonbeam's voice was quiet.

Kayla studied her mother's face, and her heart fell. She'd hoped for . . . She didn't know. Pride maybe? Surprise? Maybe she could even be a little impressed? Instead her mother sounded . . . tired. So very tired. "I haven't." It wasn't a lie. She'd done a similar trick with sand but never sugar. "It's just . . ."

"He killed her, Kayla. He killed my Amanda. Your sister. He took her from us, and I can't let him take you too. Do you understand? I can't lose you!"

And like that, the shadows felt darker, and the breeze felt

sharper. The candle flames twisted. Kayla wished she'd never started this conversation. The wild edge in her mother's voice . . . She didn't want to hear that. She was an idiot to think she could change her mother's mind. It was stuffed too full of fear.

"Promise me you won't use your power ever again," Moonbeam said.

"I've already promised you a billion times."

"You used it just now!"

"Once. As an example. Safely. No one saw but you."

Moonbeam hopped off the stool and hurriedly pulled at the open curtains. They bumped into crystals and snagged on dreamcatchers. "You don't know that. It's dark outside, light in here. The windows are open." She shook the curtains, hard, yanking them away from all the charms. A few of the lighter ones, ribbons with pompoms and sequins, tumbled into the sink as she closed the curtains.

"The window faces the garden. You can't see it from the street. If there are lurkers in the garden, we have worse problems—" Kayla cut herself off. She drew in a breath and tried to steady herself.

Leaving the charms, Moonbeam sat down again. She had unshed tears in her eyes. She wrapped her hands around the mug. "Promise me. You won't use it again, ever, anytime, for any reason." She looked so fragile in the moonlight, as if she were a puff of smoke that could dissipate. The tea in her hands shook slightly, the surface rippling, and Kayla could tell how much she needed to hear the words.

Kayla met her mother's eyes. "Of course. I promise."

3

She'd steal from every goddamn store on State Street before the end of the summer, Kayla swore. Or before the end of July. Restaurants too, especially the ones where the hostess glared at you if you used the bathroom and weren't eating there. She strode down State Street, her hood up, her hands jammed into her hoodie pockets, twisting the diamond ring around the tip of her pinkie. She'd steal from every man, woman, and child on the street who had a designer purse or sunglasses that cost nearly as much as a boat.

Last night . . . she *knew* how that conversation would unfold. She should never have started it. And she certainly shouldn't have demonstrated one of her tricks to Moonbeam. What had she thought that would prove? Moonbeam had spent the rest of the night "quietly" crying into her pillow, as if it were possible to do anything quietly in a one-room house. You could practically hear how many squares of toilet paper someone used.

Kayla had felt as if she were the pillow, battered and damp. She'd slept badly, racked with guilt, and she'd woken to an empty house. Moonbeam had already left for work. Kayla had found a note on the kitchen table, next to a bran muffin: *Please pick up a half gallon of milk, water the plants, and remember your promise.*

After that, Kayla had started to feel angry. And the anger ate the guilt for goddamn breakfast, which was a buttery croissant bought with stolen money, *not* a bran muffin.

Moonbeam was wrong. Kayla was careful enough. She was careful, clever, and damn good at what she did. Halfway down the street, she parked herself on a bench that was free of breastfeeding women, middle-class teens pretending to be homeless, and overworked business types shoveling burritos into their mouths on their lunch breaks. She could do her tricks, help her family, and no one would ever know. Even Moonbeam.

Kayla focused on the store in front of her, a trying-too-hard surf store that sold novelty surfboards with fake shark bites cut out of them and bikinis so tiny they would have embarrassed a nudist. The cash register was by the front, next to a display of designer sunglasses. That was her target, simple and straightforward. She needed only to distract the clerk for half a minute.

Scanning the store, she selected her unwitting accomplice: a man in khakis and a Hawaiian shirt checking out the suntan-lotion options. He was holding a shopping bag from one of the other novelty shops. She popped a receipt out of his bag and set it skittering toward the front door. She left it next to the door-frame to use later.

The man reached for a bottle of suntan lotion. *Go time*, Kayla thought. She focused on the cash register, causing the buttons to depress one by one. As the drawer popped out with a ding, she covered the noise by causing the receipt to block the sensor—the bell for the door rang at the same time as the ding. The kid at the counter automatically glanced at the door, and Kayla

mentally reached for the bills in the cash register. She caused
three to slide out and down the side of the counter. She then
stacked them together and rolled them into a thin, straw-size
tube. As the customer approached the cash register with his
bottle of suntan lotion, Kayla jumped the bills into the cuff of
his pants. The customer paid and then walked out of the store.

Outside, Kayla forced the bills to jump out and then roll
across the sidewalk to hit her own sneaker. She bent as if to
retie her sneaker, palmed the bills, and then stuffed them into
the pocket of her hoodie as she sat up.

A boy was sitting next to her.

Kayla jumped a half inch off the bench. He hadn't been there
when she'd bent over, had he? Maybe he had. Maybe she'd been
concentrating so hard she'd failed to notice him. His elbows were
resting on the back of the brick bench as if he'd been relaxing
there for a while. He was looking at the surf store, not at her. She
recognized him: smoky brown eyes, black hair, the kind of face
that Selena would have declared poster-worthy. He was the guy
who had been checking her out yesterday after the diamond heist.

She debated saying hi, casually. Any other day, she would
have. But today she was in too foul a mood to allow even for
gloriously gorgeous guys. He spoke anyway.

"Nice day," he said.

"It's Santa Barbara. We specialize in nice days."

"Live here long enough and you get used to it?"

She shrugged. "Something like that."

He tilted his head back as if soaking in the sun. Over them,
the palm trees fluttered. It hadn't rained in a while, and the stiff,
dry leaves sounded like muffled wind chimes as they brushed
against each other. "Here's the part where you ask me where I'm

from, since I'm so obviously not from a place with nice days all the time."

"Only if I'm actually interested in hearing the answer."

"That's not necessary," he said. "People have conversations all the time where they don't care the slightest what the other person says."

"I didn't know we were officially having a conversation. Really, I'm having a bad day, so if you're looking to make new friends in a new place, try me tomorrow."

"But I'm here today, Kayla."

Kayla stiffened. "You know my name?"

He smiled and didn't answer.

"Yeah, that's not at all creepy. How do you know my name?" She thought immediately of her father, then dismissed the thought. No way he knew she was here—or even knew her new name. It was infinitely more likely someone from town had told him. She did have classmates here, even if she ignored them. Kayla wasn't her mother; she shouldn't leap to paranoid conclusions. She'd let last night's argument affect her more than she thought.

"My name's Daniel." He stuck out his hand like he wanted to shake. She shook it because she didn't have a particular reason not to, plus she wanted him to answer her question.

"Okay, Danny, now that we're best buds, how do you know who I am? Have you been stalking me? Because that's not what friends do." She tried to ignore the prickly feeling that walked over her skin. He couldn't know what she did, what she could do. Also, you couldn't get more public than the center of State Street. She was perfectly safe. This had *nothing* to do with Dad.

"Daniel. Not Dan. Not Danny. And how about I tell you a story? You can buy me a coffee. It might take a while."

"I don't buy guys coffee. You seem to be unclear on how this works. You're hitting on me. I'm not obliged in any way to supply the beverages in this situation. Besides, I have to meet a friend soon."

Daniel stood. He blocked the sun, and the light framed him, obscuring his features. She wasn't certain if he was smiling or smirking. He looked a bit like a dark angel, dressed in all black with the sun halolike around him. "You'll want to make an exception for me," he said.

Maybe it would cheer her up to flirt with a cute guy for a little while, at least until Selena showed up. Still, she was not buying him coffee, cute or not. "Cocky much? That's not as attractive as you think."

"Actually, I was going for ominous. And I am not hitting on you. I need to talk with you, Kayla. It's vitally important. Life-or-death important." There was sincerity throbbing in his voice, but it still bothered her that he knew her name. She was the anonymous pink-haired girl, and she liked it that way. "I came a long way to find you."

Instantly, she knew: *Dad*. She wasn't paranoid. He'd sent this boy.

Kayla rose from the bench. Her heart beat so fast in her chest that she felt as though she'd swallowed a hummingbird. Her hands, shoved into her pockets, formed shaking fists. "Congratulations. Tell my father it's about time. I'm sick of hiding. And he's going to pay for what he did."

And then she pivoted and ran.

Her sneakers slapped the tiled sidewalk. She veered around shoppers and tourists and random people who seemed to all move at a snail's pace, clogging every inch of the available space.

Glancing back over her shoulder, she saw he was still standing there, next to the bench, watching her run down the sidewalk. She felt a burst of pride—she'd surprised him, and she was fast—but that was quickly squashed by the inner shout of, *What do I do?*

It was her mother's worst fear, the consequence of using her power that Kayla had dismissed so quickly just last night. She had to warn Moonbeam and then . . . How much time did they have? Her father wasn't here, only this boy. Was there time to pack? She wanted to swing by for at least her emergency backpack. Did he know where they lived? How did he find her? How much did he know? Would she be able to say good-bye to Selena? She could call from wherever they ended up, maybe, once it was safe. Selena would be pissed, but she'd understand. Dammit, Kayla was going to miss her.

Kayla rounded a corner onto Arroyo Street—and the boy stood in front of her.

He held up his hands. "I won't hurt you."

She glanced over her shoulder. He must have known a short-cut. She didn't stay to ask. Pivoting again, she ran back to State Street. She'd flag down a cop and claim—

He appeared in front of her. Just appeared. One second, not there. And then . . .

Before she could react, he clamped a hand on her shoulder, and State Street vanished.

Dark. Light. Blue sky. She felt her knees buckle, and a pair of strong arms hauled her backward. She pitched back and landed hard on her butt. She was on a slope—a slope composed of red tiles. Like a roof.

Exactly like a roof.

She was on a freaking roof.

The boy sat calmly beside her.

She was even with the tops of palm trees. The leaves tickled the lip of the roof. Below was State Street, bustling exactly the way she'd left it, minus her and Daniel. "What—"

"I'd have preferred a coffee shop, but you didn't seem to like that idea. This, at least, has a great view." He pointed to the ocean, which was visible from the roof. Sunlight glinted off the waves. "You and I have to talk."

She stared at the ocean.

And then she stared at him.

She sucked a deep breath in and then let it out. He'd surprised her. She'd never met anyone who could teleport. She didn't know it was possible. Okay, she could handle this. She was a natural improviser. She could roll with it, right?

Putting on her sunglasses, Kayla leaned back onto the roof as if she were sunbathing. Her hoodie was unzipped, and the sun soaked into her bare stomach. "So, talk." She tried to sound as if she were unconcerned and this sort of thing happened to her all the time. It was the best she could manage under the circumstances.

"Uh, okay." She heard him swallow twice, and she counted that as a victory of sorts. "I don't know why you think I'm here or who you think I am, but I swear to you that your father didn't send me. I don't know your father. I've never met him. I've never spoken to him. I'm here because . . . Look, can you sit up? This is a serious conversation, and I can't talk to you while you're sunbathing."

"I can listen and soak at the same time. It's called multitasking."

"You're doing it to annoy me."

"You think, Danny?"

"I think it will take longer for you to climb down from here than it will for me to tell the police who stole those diamond rings yesterday. They'll surround this building before you're halfway tan."

Her stomach flipped over and over. How did he know about the rings? Outwardly, she kept calm. She lifted her shades. "You may have my attention." She managed to keep her hand from going to her pocket, where one of the rings was hidden. "But I don't know what you're talking about. I didn't steal anything."

He laughed hollowly. "Come on, Kayla. You're a master thief. I've seen you at work, though I admit today you were a little sloppy. Anyone could have seen those bills roll across the floor. And that man could have easily felt them in his cuff. Not to mention you were lucky with the cash register. If the clerk had been less stoned, he'd have noticed it was acting possessed. Yesterday you were much smoother. Something got under your skin today?"

"You've been watching me?" She kept her voice level. Her instincts said to run. But she was on a roof, and he'd caught her before.

"You're very good at what you do."

"Thanks. Who the hell are you?"

"Daniel. Rest of it isn't important."

Kayla snorted. Out of the corner of her eye, she scanned the immediate area. There wasn't much she could use on the roof. Roof tiles and chimney were all attached, as well as too heavy. There weren't even any stray dead leaves. She had only her phone and the ring in her shorts pocket, plus the cash in her hoodie pocket. She'd left the house so fast that she hadn't prepared her usual supplies. She wouldn't make that mistake again, assuming she ever got another chance.

"I need your help."

"Really? You have a funny way of asking. Oh, and by the way, the answer is no." She got to her feet. It wasn't so far to the ground. She could dangle from the edge and drop. No matter what he said, it would be a few minutes before he could convince any cop to come after her, especially if she made dirt fly in Daniel's eyes first. While he recovered, she could easily plant the ring in another person's pocket . . . his, for example. Mentally, she reached for dirt at the base of a palm tree. She swirled a patch into a spiral.

"I would have asked your mother first for her permission, but wait, she doesn't know you use your special power regularly. Or that you use it to steal." His voice was mild, but the look in his eyes was triumphant. "It would be a shame if she found out, especially from a stranger."

She stared at him and then forced herself to laugh. "You think she'd believe I have a 'special power'? My mother isn't *that* gullible, no matter what she looks like."

"I think she would. Especially after your demonstration to her last night."

Kayla froze. The dirt fell back onto the sidewalk. "You spied on me."

His cheeks tinted pink, as if blackmailing her was vaguely embarrassing. "I had to be sure I was right. Too much is riding on this. I need your help too badly to take any risks."

"Yeah, you said that, and you have a lousy way of asking for it."

He shrugged. "I can't risk your saying no. You'd understand if you'd quit whining long enough for me to explain."

"Excuse me, whining? You threaten me. You—"

From the street, someone called up to them. "You! Kids! Get off the roof!"

Daniel grabbed her arm, and the sky went dark, light, and then was blue again. Kayla was looking at the ocean. Her legs shook, and Daniel released her. She sank into the soft sand as the world steadied. The waves folded into white foam and crashed onto the beach. Closer to the surf, kids laughed and people shouted. "Explain. Clearly. Fully. Including what just happened and why no one around us is freaking out."

He frowned at the people not far away, primarily girls in bikinis, a pair of boys playing volleyball badly, and two toddlers fighting over a shovel. "People see what they expect to see, which is why I imagine you've gone unnoticed for so long."

"Also I'm careful. And very, very good."

"Of course."

His voice was so bland that she studied his face to see if she could detect any sarcasm. But he was staring moodily at the waves. The wind brushed his hair over his eyes. He looked like at any moment he would spout bad poetry. "My mother has been kidnapped," he said. "She could be killed if you don't help me."

Kayla opened her mouth and then shut it. The waves crashed on the sand. Nearby, a child squealed, and a mother scolded him.

"You don't know me," Daniel said. "You don't know her. You have no reason to help us. So I'm giving you a reason. Help me save her, and I won't tell your secret to your mother, the police, or the tabloids, who would eat up the proof I have on my phone's camera—and backed up in three places you won't find—faster than you can imagine."

4

Kayla could distract him and flee. Sand to the eyes would do nicely. But he knew her secret, he knew where she lived, and he knew who her mother was. Not to mention the itsy-bitsy fact that he could teleport. She'd have to knock him out cold if she wanted to really run.

She took a deep breath and tried to *think*. He knew. But he needed her. "Correct me if I'm wrong, but here's what I have so far: Your mother has been kidnapped. You need my help to save her. And you figured the best way to secure that help was to blackmail me, promising your silence in exchange for my assistance, instead of, you know, just *asking* me."

Quietly, he said, "You could have said no."

"I could still say no."

"But you won't."

"You haven't told me what you want me to do."

He clamped his hand around her wrist, and the world blinked again: dark, light, and this time, green. As the vertigo faded, her eyes adjusted. She was facing a hedge of dark green leaves punctuated with red hibiscus flowers the size of her hand.

Garden gnomes lined the front of the hedge, and ceramic fairies were tucked underneath the branches. A breeze rustled the leaves, and a half-dozen wind chimes tinkled and tolled.

Daniel parked himself on her mother's favorite bench—the one Moonbeam had found at a yard sale, sanded down, and painted herself with symbols for a safe and happy home. Kayla clenched her fists and then forced them to unclench. *Stay calm, Kayla*, she ordered herself. *Keep control.* She could fly mulch into his eyes, bash him with a garden gnome, and hope he stayed knocked out long enough for her to run to Moonbeam's shop and tell her . . . Tell her what? That Kayla had endangered them? That she'd used her power less than twenty-four hours after promising not to and a boy had seen? She'd break Moonbeam's heart.

Crap. There had to be a way out of this. She had to try to salvage the situation. He needed her. That gave her the advantage, didn't it? She drew in a breath, steadying herself.

"Are you done?" he asked politely.

"Sorry?"

"Are you done running through all your options and deciding you should hear me out?" His hands were folded. His legs were stretched in front of him, feet crossed. He looked relaxed, as if he had all the time in the world.

"I did mention that cockiness is not attractive, right?"

"And that would be relevant if I were trying to pick you up. But I'm not. Please, hear me out." He patted the bench next to him.

She thought she heard a note of . . . maybe rawness, maybe desperation slip into that "please." It occurred to her that he might not be as calm, cool, and collected as he seemed. Kayla dropped onto the ground and sat on the grass, several yards from him and her mother's bench. "Tell me a story, Danny-boy. I'm all ears." She picked up a gnome by the ears and wiggled it, then set it down next to her.

For an instant, he looked disconcerted. He recovered fast, but not fast enough for her to miss it. *I'm right*, she thought. He wasn't as in control as he pretended to be. It was an act. She could unbalance him. "Five days ago," he said, "my mother was kidnapped."

"And you came to harass me instead of going to the police like a normal human being."

"I *did* go to the police. Would you let me finish?"

"Sorry. Carry on." She waved her hand like she was a queen granting an audience. She'd seen Selena make that gesture a thousand times. It never failed to infuriate whoever was demanding her attention.

Daniel glared at her, but he continued. "A few nights earlier—"

"Hotel California" piped up from Kayla's pocket. "One sec." She held up a finger as she took her phone out of her pocket and answered it. "Hey." No better way to irritate someone than valuing a phone call above their problems.

Selena. "I hate my mother. I hate my father. I hate myself. I am moving in with you. Except not really because I hate your food. And because my parents would say 'no,' and it doesn't seem to matter how ballsy I can be with anyone else—the second they frown, I fold. Apparently, with them, I have the backbone of an invertebrate. But I need to vent so I am coming over."

Kayla's heart sank. She did not want Selena mixed up in

this, whatever "this" was. She kept her face neutral and her voice light. "It's really not the best—"

The red gate bashed open, and Selena charged in. Phone held to her ear with one shoulder, she strode through the herbs and flowers. "Seriously, I brought ice cream, the comfort food of choice for people with relationship issues, and—oh, you have a guy. Hi, hot guy. I'm Selena, the best friend." She clicked off the phone.

Daniel stood. "I hate to be rude, but I am discussing a personal matter with Kayla, so I have to ask you to come back later."

Selena blinked at him with her heavily mascaraed eyelashes and then turned to Kayla, who rose to face her friend. "Who talks like that? Seriously, where did you find him and why did you not mention him?"

"He kind of just popped into my life," Kayla said.

"You could have texted. Texting is fast."

"Believe me, he moves faster than that."

Both Selena's eyebrows shot up. "If you're putting the moves on Kayla, you need my approval. She's a special girl, and I don't care if you do look like you walked off one of the nicer LA billboards . . . Actually, that's a plus, but do you have a brain, a sense of humor, and ready cash?"

Daniel looked so confused that Kayla nearly felt sorry for him. Nearly. "This is Daniel. His mother's been kidnapped, and he's trying to blackmail me into helping him."

Since her eyebrows couldn't shoot up any higher, Selena settled for another exaggerated blink before she scanned Daniel top to toe. "Did he try asking you to help?"

"Nope. Jumped straight to blackmail."

Daniel scowled at Kayla. She noticed he had a vein in his temple that popped up when he scowled, and she wondered if she was pushing him too hard. If what he said about his mother was true, maybe she should be kinder. "I told you this in confidence—" he began.

Selena waved her hand dismissively. "Kayla and I tell each other everything." To Kayla, she said, "What does he have on you?"

Kayla shrugged. "Everything." She tried to keep her expression as bland as possible. Keep him off balance. She wanted control of the situation first, then she could decide how to deal with it. Selena was helping just by being herself.

"Even that time in eighth grade when you wore boy's underwear to school and—"

"Not that," Kayla said.

"Skinny dipping?"

"No."

"The thing with the pencil?"

"No."

"Or the—"

Kayla shook her head. "This is serious."

Selena's mouth formed an O. "So you mean the *you know*." She tapped her forehead and then made a fluttering-flying motion with her fingers.

"You're going with *that* as the sign for it?" Kayla asked. Really, that looked ridiculous. She was a professional, if it were possible to be a professional telekinetic. At any rate, she took it seriously. "Shouldn't it be—"

"I think it's perfect. Mind equals pixie dust."

"Looks crazy."

"Well, it *is* a little crazy."

"It's not that kind of crazy. Unusual, yes. Impossible, maybe.

But 'crazy' implies a whole lifestyle choice that I don't think I've embraced."

"True. And the negative connotations of the word—"

Daniel vanished. One second he was standing in front of the bench, and the next it was as if he'd been deleted. A second later, he stood between Kayla and Selena, and they both jumped backward. "Stop. Just stop. Please. My mother has been kidnapped. I don't know how long I have before she's killed. This isn't a game to me. Or to her." The cockiness was gone. The casual attitude, gone. He looked scared and alone and desperate.

Around Daniel, Kayla met Selena's eyes. She'd known Selena since her first day in Santa Barbara, her first real day of school since Amanda died. She and her mother had been on the run for half a year, never staying more than a few days in any place, when her mother chose California, picked this cottage, changed their names, and inserted them into life here. Kayla had walked into school in the middle of third grade, targeted the girl who seemed the opposite of her in every way, and informed her that they were going to be best friends. Selena had laughed in her face. But Kayla had shrugged and said, "You'll see." Later, when Kayla used her power to remove the shoelaces from the sneakers of the worst bully in class (from several rows away and without anyone knowing how she did it), Selena had been sufficiently impressed to invite Kayla over to play. Eight years later, the two knew everything it was possible to know about another person. So they didn't have to discuss anything to know they agreed.

"She'll help you," Selena said. "But you have to tell us everything."

❧ ❧

Inside, Kayla served oatmeal raisin cookies that she was pretty sure did not have pot in them. The brownies were iffy. Sometimes Moonbeam made them with the "special ingredient" as part of her persona—no one would think the hippie chick who made pot brownies knew anything about real magic—and Kayla was always careful not to eat them. As she'd explained to Selena once, no one with mental powers has any business eating or drinking or inhaling any substance that messes with the mind. Besides, Moonbeam would have killed her. Or worse, cried. So Kayla served the store-bought cookies with Selena's ice cream and pretended that this was a normal conversation and she had everything completely under control. Selena and Daniel sat on the stools at the table. Kayla perched on the counter next to the sink and bit into her cookie. She could have been eating cardboard for all she tasted it.

Daniel didn't eat at all. "My mom's an assistant professor of anthropology at the University of Chicago, one year away from tenure. She's an expert in comparative anthropology, specializing in rituals and ritualistic items. In lay terms—"

"She studies magic," Selena finished.

"Yeah. Exactly." He sounded surprised.

"Being Californian doesn't mean being stupid," Selena said.

"I didn't say—"

Kayla shot Selena a look. "Can we not get sidetracked?" They didn't have forever before Moonbeam came home from work, and she'd rather finish this conversation before then. "The false eyelashes *do* make you look dumber."

"Crap. Really?"

Kayla handed her a mirror that was embedded in the belly of a Buddha. Selena held it close to her nose and frowned at herself while Daniel continued. "For years, she's been working on what she calls her secret project. She's never applied for a grant for it. Never published a single paper or given a talk about it. She kept every scrap of research in a single notebook, handwritten, no digital record anywhere. I always figured she was saving up for a big reveal that would shock all her colleagues and guarantee her tenure—she started late on the academic track and constantly talks about how much she has to prove because of it—but then the other night, I found her burning the notebook in the fireplace."

Out of the corner of her eye, Kayla saw Selena lower the mirror to stare at Daniel. Daniel took a sip of water. His eyes were misty, as if it were a struggle to stay unemotional. Kayla tried not to notice. She did *not* want to pity him.

"It was her life's work. It was the reason she took the path she did, studied what she studied, traveled so much, worked so hard. And she was destroying it. I tried to stop her, but she said it was endangering her. Us. She began talking about an incantation written on three stones, a very old and very powerful incantation. A man she used to know had one stone, and he wanted the other two. Her research could lead him to them, and she couldn't let that happen."

Selena held up her hand. "Ooh-ooh! Let me guess. I think I've seen this movie. Since he couldn't get her research, he went for her."

He nodded unhappily.

"And so you . . . came to Kayla?"

Another nod.

"Instead of calling the cops." Selena shook her head. "Look, I get that you guys are all 'magical' and stuff, but kidnapping is illegal. And no offense meant to Kayla, but finding people isn't her specialty. She doesn't even really like people."

"I like people!" Kayla objected. "Some people. You. And Moonbeam." God, what if this had happened to Moonbeam?

"I *did* call them," Daniel said. "They opened a case and tried to put me in foster care. But I'm not going to sit around and let some stranger pretend to mother me while I wait for the police to find her."

If it were her mother who'd been taken, Kayla would do the exact same thing. No way would she sit on the sidelines. She reminded herself she wasn't supposed to be empathizing. "Can't you, you know, hop wherever and save her?"

"Yes, if I knew where 'wherever' was." Jumping off the stool, he paced. There wasn't much room for pacing in the cottage. He circled between the cluttered coffee table and the kitchen. Piles of books teetered precariously as he brushed past them. "I need to have an image in my head before I can jump, and I don't know where he took her. All I know is what's on the note she left for me." He pulled a piece of paper out of his pocket and tossed it on the table.

Both Kayla and Selena leaned forward to look at it. It was written in blue ink in cramped but precise letters. Kayla read out loud: "'Find the thief. Ask the queen. Remember I love you.'"

She sat backward. She felt . . . She didn't know how she felt. Fixing her eyes on the crystals in the window, she watched them spin and swirl. The bits of mirror winked in the light, and specks of dust sparkled in the air. *Find the thief.*

"And you think this"—Selena tapped the note with a very long manicured nail, painted in stripes today—"is related to her kidnapping. You're sure it's not just a strange grocery list. Because there are some health food stores with bizarre items.

Like quail eggs. Or dandelion roots. Maybe 'the thief' is a type of lettuce."

"She left it for me," Daniel said. "She wants me to find the other two stones." His fists were clenched, and his muscles seemed coiled, like he wanted to punch everything around him.

Selena frowned at the note again. "I'm just not getting that from this. It could mean anything."

"But it doesn't," Daniel insisted. "I know my mother. It means—"

"Me," Kayla interrupted. "I'm the thief. It means me." She met Daniel's eyes. "How did you find me?"

"She told me about you once, your name and where you live and what you can do, when I first started to jump between places. Told me never to seek you out unless it was an emergency. She knew I'd understand what her note meant."

"She knew about me? How?" Kayla felt prickles on her skin. No one knew her. She had no past; she didn't exist before they moved here.

"I don't know. You can ask her when we find her."

They were all silent for a moment. A breeze blew through the window, and the wind chimes clattered and chimed. It smelled like summer flowers, sweet and light, with the bite of salt water underlying it. It didn't feel like the kind of day that belonged to a conversation like this. The sky should be dark and filled with fog. All this sunshine felt false.

At last, Kayla asked, "Who's the queen?"

Daniel looked as if she'd just stolen his favorite kitten. "I was hoping you'd know."

5

Selena propped her laptop up on Kayla's futon. She lay on her stomach and kicked her feet behind her. Her flip-flops dangled from her toes. "Queen of England. Queen of Hearts. Drag queens. Queen in a deck of cards. Queen, the band that sings 'Bohemian Rhapsody.' She doesn't want you to talk to Freddie Mercury, does she? Because he's dead, and that could be tricky without a séance. Hey, do séances work? I mean, if you can do"—she made her sign for telekinesis—"then why can't dead people talk?"

Across the cottage, Daniel perched on a stool with his face in his hands. He'd looked so crushed when she hadn't known the answer. He must feel so lost and alone and powerless and . . . *Stop it*, she thought. She was *not* going to feel sympathy for the asshole who decided to approach her by blackmailing her. She was going to help him find this so-called queen and save his mother—and then ditch him at the first opportunity.

Selena's fingernails tapped on the keys. It sounded like a bird pecking at seeds. "And speaking of the dead . . . we have Queen Victoria, Queen Isabella, Queen Nefertiti . . . Can you give us anything else to go on? Did your mom study a particular region?"

Without lifting his head, Daniel said, "She worked all over."

"Any chance she had a favorite? You said she traveled. Where?"

It was hard not to feel *some* sympathy. Kayla would be freaked and scared and furious too if her mother were kidnapped. Just imagining it made her want to drape the house in even more charms and amulets. She picked up a yarn doll that loosely resembled herself. It had stringy black-and-pink hair, and Moonbeam had said Kayla's name as she drove a pin into it—to tie the doll's protective charms to Kayla, not to harm her, she'd explained—and then drawn a few words on it. If Kayla looked at it out of the corner of her eye, she could see the shape of almost-letters on its body. She couldn't read them—Moonbeam had refused to teach her how—but she could sense them, which was more than most untrained people could do.

"Everywhere," Daniel said. "Europe. Asia. South America. Mexico. Guatemala. Lots of places in the United States— Appalachia, Louisiana, New Mexico . . . Anywhere that has rituals for her to observe. Always looking for that one big thing that would make her career. She specialized in this crap." He waved his hand at the basket of polished stones on the floor; the scarabs on the shelf; the quartz crystals and dreamcatchers in the windows; and the handwoven borders of tassels, herbs, and roots over the doorway. "I usually stayed in the hotel while she did her work. She'd hire a babysitter when I was younger, sometimes even a tour guide. Rarely let me come with her to any sites. Said I'd be too bored. She never mentioned any royalty."

"You are completely unhelpful." Selena typed more into the laptop. "Do you know how many queens there have been?"

Kayla looked down at the doll in her hand. "Voodoo queen."

Both Selena and Daniel looked at her.

"She said 'Ask the queen,' so it needs to be someone alive. And this is about a spell, so it needs to be someone magical. There aren't many living magical queens out there." Kayla waved the voodoo doll in the air. "But Louisiana has a voodoo queen."

Daniel shot off the stool. "I took her to New Orleans a lot."

Selena rolled her eyes. "I asked if she had any favorite—"

"Look it up!" Daniel commanded. He shifted from foot to foot so fast that he looked as if he were vibrating. His hands were clenched, and his muscles were tense. So much for his cool, relaxed attitude. She *knew* he'd been faking it. He was hiding fear. Maybe anger. "Find me photos, and I'll take us to the voodoo queen's front door. All I need is a picture; then I can jump."

Selena leaned over the laptop. Her black hair brushed against the screen. She frowned, a crease between her eyebrows. Kayla didn't doubt that she'd find what Daniel needed. She was faster on her laptop than Kayla was with a cash register. After a few seconds, Selena said, "Every hit is Marie Laveaux. But she died, like, a century ago, and so did her daughter, who inherited the title. Looking for her descendants . . . and bingo." Selena leaned back and rotated the laptop to show a picture of a beautiful black woman in a flouncy white dress, with a white scarf around her head and gold hoops dangling from her ears. She was seated in front of a blue door with a wrought-iron gate. She held drumsticks in one hand and a gris-gris bag in the other. "Queen Marguerite, distant relative of Marie Laveaux II and reigning voodoo queen of New Orleans." Under the photo were three words: *"Ira Reginae Dolorem."*

Kayla pointed at the Latin. "Any guesses what that means?"

Selena turned the laptop back around. "'The anger of the queen brings sorrow.' In other words, don't piss her off. Seems reasonable for a voodoo queen. Can't she shrink your head? Or is that another culture I'm maligning and marginalizing?"

"You read Latin?" Daniel sounded impressed.

"*Regina*, queen. *Ira*, anger. *Dolor*, sorrow. Again, smarter than I look." Selena typed some more. "She has a shop. Also, a very cheesy website stuck in the nineties. Actually has flame wing-dings." She faked a shudder. "But seriously, don't let her hoodoo you. She could be like Kayla's mom—the real deal hidden under the tourist crap."

Kayla tucked her voodoo doll back on the shelf and thought that Selena was likely right. "We'll be careful. Can you give us an address?"

Daniel turned the laptop around to face him again. "Photos are better. I use images, not words. The more precise the image, the more precise the jump. Also, the less draining. Hardest jumps are the 'just hop over there' kind where 'there' is some vague faraway spot."

"Hey!" Selena grabbed the laptop and turned it back toward her. "Working here." She typed more and then rotated it again. The photo was of a street in New Orleans with old-fashioned lampposts; wrought-iron balconies; and buildings with pink, blue, and green peeling paint. One had green shutters around the door, a yellow skeleton in the window, and a black sign over the porch that read VOODOO SPELLS AND CHARMS.

"That's it!" Kayla said. She opened a drawer and plucked out a pretty chiffon blouse. She pulled it on over her bikini top. *There*, she thought. *Slightly more respectable for seeing a queen.*

"Hold hands," Daniel instructed.

"Oh, no, thank you." Selena scooted back on the futon so fast she nearly flipped the laptop off her lap. "I don't have the special magic mojo. I'm here purely as technical and emotional support."

"But you're involved," Daniel said.

"In a peripheral kind of way." Selena wiggled her fingers to shoo them away. "Go on, you crazy kids. Tell Auntie Selena all about it when you get back."

"But we might need you," Daniel objected.

"Do you have any idea how much trouble I'd be in if my parents found out I went to New Orleans? Call me a coward, but I'm not risking it. When my mom's disappointed, she gets this little crease in her forehead that I think I can scientifically prove is perfectly designed to trigger the ultimate guilt trip. I'm talking the kind of guilt that has you believing you're scum of the earth. And she does it all without saying a word. It's like magic. Believe me, I've had enough of it lately."

Outside, the chimes sang, and the gate squeaked. Kayla jumped up. Out the kitchen window, she saw Moonbeam wending her way through the garden toward the house. "Speaking of mothers . . . ," Selena said, pointing out the window. "Looks like fun and games are over."

Kayla spun back to Daniel. Never mind his fear, anger, whatever. Moonbeam was home, and his problem would have to wait. "Can't go now. My mom's home. You have to—"

Before she finished her sentence, his hand clamped onto her wrist, and the cottage vanished in a flash of white, black, then gray. Humidity closed around her. Air squeezed her skin, and she felt as if she were breathing soup. As her vision steadied, she saw they were on a street made of cobblestones, next to an old-fashioned streetlamp, and across from the stretch of pastel buildings she'd seen in the photo, including the voodoo shop. The only differences from the photo were the two police cars parked in front and the police tape stretched across the door.

"Take me back," Kayla demanded. "My mother's home!"

Daniel strode toward the voodoo shop. "I'll take you home when we're done."

"Oh, no, you don't understand." Lunging forward, she caught his arm. "Moonbeam takes protectiveness to an exciting new level. If I'm not home when she comes home—"

"Your friend will lie for you," he said. "She seems resourceful."

"Selena is *not* a good liar. She embellishes. Seriously embellishes. You have to take me back. After Moonbeam's asleep, I'll come with you. I swear."

He peeled her hand off his arm. "After I talk to the queen."

That would be too late. Moonbeam was home *now*. In a few seconds, she'd find Selena and no Kayla and no decent explanation. "I'll scream to the police that you kidnapped me."

"Then you can find your own way home." Daniel's face was flushed red. "You don't understand how serious—"

Kayla cut him off. "Wait. Why *are* the police here?" Two police cars. And police tape across the door. Without deciding to move, she crossed the street, heading toward the shop. Daniel followed, hurrying to keep up.

He caught her shoulder, stopping her, just as two police officers emerged from the store. They removed the police tape as the door swung shut behind them. One of the officers held a notebook. Kayla sent a thought at it, trying to tug at the pages, but the policeman was clutching it too tightly. Pretending she was interested in a store window that advertised scented soaps, Kayla loitered with Daniel on the sidewalk as the policemen conferred by their cars and then got in and drove away.

Without a word or a glance at each other, Kayla and Daniel jogged in tandem toward the voodoo shop. Daniel tried the knob. Locked. He knocked on the door as Kayla peered in the window. Behind the skeleton, drapes blocked any view of the shop interior.

From inside, a woman's voice called, "We're closed! Can't you see?" She had a thick Southern accent that stretched each word like taffy.

"We're looking for Queen Marguerite," he called through the door. "Do you know where we can find her?" On the street, a few tourists glanced at them. Leaning against the shutters, Kayla tried to look casual. She felt her heart thump hard. Police tape and two cop cars. She had a bad feeling about this, even though they'd taken down the tape and hadn't exited with a body or anything like that.

"Not available, y'hear? Come back next week."

Daniel leaned against the door with his shoulder, as if he wanted to bash it down but was holding back. His body was tense. His fists, clenched. "It's an emergency. My mother's in danger, and we think she's the only one who can help."

"Queen Marguerite can't help nobody right now. She's helping herself. Kindly go away and come back when we're open again." A horse-drawn carriage clattered by. If they stayed much longer shouting through the door, they were going to draw too much attention.

She did *not* need this kind of delay. The faster they could resolve this, the sooner she could be back with Moonbeam and Selena. Kayla whispered, "Can you jump us inside?"

Daniel shook his head. "Not without seeing it."

"Then move." Kayla positioned herself in front of the door-knob and concentrated on the lock. The tumblers inside shifted and clicked, and the door popped open. She pushed it open wider, and Daniel stepped in. Squeezing in with him, she peeked over his shoulder.

The store had been trashed. Display cases had been broken, and shards of glass littered the wood floor. Dolls had been eviscerated; their body parts lay on the ground. Skulls had been shattered, and masks had been torn from the walls. Bottles had been smashed. Liquid oozed over shelves. Plastic bags of herbs and powders had been ripped open, and crosses were strewn over the floor, crushed.

In the center of the chaos, a woman was sweeping shards of glass with a twig broom. She was undeniably the woman from the photo, but much older. Wrinkles had crunched her cheeks and squeezed her forehead. Her eyes were sunken into folds of skin, and her lips were cracked as dried earth. She wore a full skirt and blouse, plus a multicolored scarf around her head, knotted at the nape of her neck. Seeing them, she glared. "Out! We're closed!"

"I'm very sorry, ma'am, Your Majesty, Queen Marguerite . . . but I have to talk to you," Daniel said. "It's life or death."

"Everything always is. Now, shoo!" She swung the broom as if to sweep them out, and Daniel stepped back through the door, driving Kayla outside too. The woman, Queen Marguerite, muttered under her breath, and Kayla heard a hint of musical words—she was uttering some kind of spell. The door slammed shut on its own, and Kayla heard locks click.

Daniel put his hand on Kayla's wrist. White. Black. Brown. They were inside again, on the opposite side of the shop, behind Queen Marguerite. "Daniel," Kayla whispered. Queen Marguerite was the real deal, despite all the crushed kitsch on the floor. Maybe they shouldn't bust in here.

"We don't mean any harm," Daniel said. "My mother told me to talk to you."

Queen Marguerite spun on her heels to face them, very quickly for a woman who looked as old as she did. "Back again?" Broom held like a staff, she scampered closer, and Kayla retreated, pressing against a wall. An antlered mask, hanging by only a frayed thread, pressed against her. Stopping a few inches from Daniel, the voodoo queen stared at his face, then her eyes widened, the whites standing out brilliantly against her dark skin. The tone of her voice changed. "Evelyn's boy. Well, well. Pity she involved you too."

"You know my mother? Involved me in what?"

"In this! Look at my shop! My life's work. My mother's life's work. This shop was her and my legacy, and now it's . . . it's . . . Words fail me. Your mother has failed me. She led them to me. Leave now. I abjure you and yours." She waved her hand as if to wave them away.

"How do you know my mother? Who did she lead here? Was it her kidnappers? Did they do this? Were they looking for the stones? Did they find them?" The questions poured out of Daniel's mouth like water from a pitcher.

"I have no children, no apprentice, no heir. Only this place! And now it's destroyed!" With a groan, she knelt in the middle of the mess. She scooped up several of the voodoo dolls and decorated skulls and rocked them as if they were broken children. "I can't help you. I can't help nobody when my heart is scattered like leaves in the wind." She squeezed her eyes shut, as if to block out the world.

Daniel bent to pick up a ripped pouch. It had almost-letters on the leather. "Things can be fixed or replaced, but people, like my mother, can never—"

Both Kayla and Queen Marguerite shouted, "Don't touch that!" With a sigh, the voodoo queen dropped the dolls and skulls and heaved herself to standing. "There's too much mixed-up magic. You'll end up cursing yourself or worse if you touch anything. Best leave it where it lies. Most likely, I'll have to condemn the place and see it destroyed. I'm sorry, boy. Nothing anyone can do about this mess—or about your mother—now."

"You can help!"

Queen Marguerite barked a laugh. There was no humor in it. "You don't want my help. It ain't worth nothing now. You don't want broken magic. I had this place chock-full of protections, and they tore through it all. They didn't like the answer I gave them, you see."

"What answer?" Daniel demanded.

"I told them their power wasn't right to find what they sought. They disagreed. They thought they had power enough. And indeed they are powerful. All my juju couldn't stop them. So perhaps they are right, and they'll find what they seek and the world will suffer."

"Who's 'they'?" Kayla asked. "Who did this to you? Who took his mother?" Picturing a gang with masks and guns, she wished she weren't involved in this. Given the level of destruction, she bet they had baseball bats or even sledgehammers. Possibly a steamroller.

"Don't waste my time with questions you already know the answer to. In fact, don't waste my time at all. I won't, and can't, help you. Best leave an old woman to her misery." She waddled toward a door at the back of the shop. After seeing how fast the voodoo queen had moved earlier, Kayla was certain the waddle was an act. It would be a mistake to underestimate her.

Jumping over the glass shards and trampled crosses, Daniel chased after her. "I won't go, not until you help me. My mother's life is at stake!"

Intercepting him, Kayla caught his arm. "She doesn't want us here. Remember: *Ira Reginae Dolorem*. We should leave and come back later, after she has her shop fixed. Maybe then she'll be in a better mood."

He shrugged her off. "I won't take no for an answer. Stay here. I'll be right back."

Kayla swore under her breath. This had already taken too long. By now, Selena was probably drowning Moonbeam in lies. The only question was how pissed Moonbeam would be when Kayla came back. *If* she came back. *If* Daniel didn't piss off the voodoo queen so badly that the woman broke out her real magic. She'd already done one spell with the door. Who knew how many tricks she had up her puffed sleeves?

Think, Kayla. Daniel wasn't going to leave until the voodoo queen helped them; the voodoo queen wasn't going to help them while her shop was trashed. Well, Kayla was uniquely suited to fix that . . . so long as her mother never found out.

She'd be careful. Queen Marguerite and Daniel were both in the back room, and all the shutters were closed. No one could see her. Really, it wasn't so different from when she cleaned the cottage while Moonbeam was at work.

Sitting on a stool, Kayla concentrated on the shards of glass. Shifting several at a time, she sent them skittering across the wood floor. Larger chunks she left alone—they were too heavy to move with her mind; she'd need a broom for those—but there were hundreds of little bits. Soon, she had them in a pile. She grinned to herself. See? Not so hard.

Switching her attention to one of the wall displays, Kayla scooted together the scattered herbs and powders. She divvied them up as best she could, treating them like the sugar grains she'd moved before. Sweat prickled her skin, and the humid, motionless air made her skin feel sticky and her throat feel thick.

She wondered how much she could do at once. A lot of the charms and dolls were light, as were the contents of the gris-gris bags. Reaching out in multiple directions, she brought the shop to life. Powders swirled through the air in little dust devils. Liquids retreated back into their bottles. Herbs dove into bags. She began to feel light-headed, as if she were about to float into the air. She'd never done so much magic at the same time. It was intoxicating.

Daniel popped into the middle of the room. "Kayla, she's— What are you doing?"

Charms tumbled from the sky. Herbs, the ones not yet in bags, scattered as they fell. Catching doll parts with her mind, she stowed them on a shelf and then sent the remaining items flying into a broken display case.

The voodoo queen charged in. She skidded to a stop and stared as the last bits of broken glass tumbled into a pile. Kayla held her breath. *Did she see?* she wondered. She couldn't have seen. Kayla had been quick. She waited for the voodoo queen to react, to say something, to say anything.

Queen Marguerite burst into laughter, the sound shaking her entire body.

Kayla looked from Daniel to the queen and back again. Confusion was written on his face, and tension was woven into his muscles. Kayla leaned against a display case and tried not to pant too obviously as Queen Marguerite wiped her eyes and bent over her knees to catch her breath. "What one destroys, the other heals. I admire the symmetry, that I do. And I thought you were only here because of his pretty face—oh, it is so glorious to be wrong!" Marguerite continued to chuckle. "Sit yourselves down and I'll make us sweet tea."

"But you said . . . ," Daniel began. He trailed off as Queen Marguerite waddled out of the room again. "She threatened to skin me alive. I thought she meant it."

"She seems to have changed her mind," Kayla said mildly.

Crossing to her in three strides, Daniel caught her hands in his. "You did this! I failed. And you . . . You're amazing. Seriously, amazing."

Kayla flushed. Queen Marguerite might have been impressed with her cleaning skills, but Daniel knew exactly how she'd done it. She was used to hiding her power; she wasn't used to being admired for it. He was looking at her like she'd transformed into a movie star. She wormed her hands out of his. "All I did—"

Her phone rang. Moonbeam.

Moonbeam wouldn't think she was amazing, if she knew.

All the euphoria from using her power faded. She stared at the phone for a solid half minute, and then she shut it off. She wasn't ready to lie to her mother yet. Especially when she didn't know what kind of nonsense Selena had already spewed. Better to claim the battery died than be caught in a (bigger) lie. "Moonbeam is going to flay me."

"I'm sorry." He sounded like he meant it, but that didn't change the fact that she was royally screwed. Suddenly feeling exhausted, Kayla cast around for a place to sit. She spotted a stool that hadn't been smashed. Sinking onto it, she massaged her temples. She hadn't moved so many things at once before. Her head pounded. Daniel was still looking at her with something akin to worship, which was nice, albeit disconcerting since she'd already decided not to like him.

"Did she curse you?" Kayla asked, partially to change the subject and partially because it would be good to know if he was about to die a horrible death.

"Almost. Popped out of there before it could take."

"You really have no people skills."

Queen Marguerite returned with a tray that held a pitcher of tea and three mismatched empty jam jars for glasses. A stack of Oreos was on a plate. She set the tray down on the corner of a broken display case, precariously perched. "Cleaning is thirsty work. You must have worked up an appetite." She was right; Kayla felt so drained she didn't want to move. While the queen bustled over to her shelves, Kayla flicked an Oreo off the plate. Concentrating, she sailed it through the air. Pinpricks of pain burst like fireworks in her head. She reached out and caught the cookie before she lost control. Wincing, she rubbed her head again. Probably should have stood up and fetched it like a normal person. She was tapped out.

Humming, Marguerite returned with several bones and a candle. She positioned the candle in the center of the room and patted her pockets as if looking for a lighter. Wordlessly, Kayla handed over her lighter. The queen lit the candle and began to waft the scented smoke around the room. Kayla took the lighter back and pocketed it.

"Excuse me, Your Majesty," Daniel said, all politeness and faux patience, "but we don't have time for a snack. We're looking for two stones—"

Marguerite held up one finger to silence him. It didn't work.

"Did the people who did this, who wrecked your place . . . did they find the stones?"

"You think I am the stones' keeper? Hah! Oh, no, no, dear boy. So naive, so sure of his wisdom and knowledge and power when he has none of those things."

Kayla noticed Daniel clench and unclench his hands. He tried again, keeping his voice smooth and even. "Can you tell me where the stones are?" All he wanted to do was help his mom. Still, Kayla thought, he shouldn't irritate a voodoo queen. He might be gorgeous, but he was seriously lacking in common sense. He really did need Kayla's help. Anyone with sense could see that underneath the tourist trappings and stereotypical "voodoo queen" act, this woman had real power and was surrounded by real magic.

Groaning, Queen Marguerite lowered herself to the floor next to the candle. She waved the smoke toward her. "I am not the end of your journey, child. I am your beginning. Sit and learn. You too, fixer girl." She shook the bones in her hands over her head, then to one side and then to the other. She rocked back and forth and began to utter words, flowing words that spilled into Kayla's head, whisked around her thoughts, and then flew out, leaving no trace of themselves in her memory. Moonbeam's kind of words. Magical words.

Light flared so bright that it whited out the shop. Kayla's eyes teared. As the light faded, she blinked fast. Streaks and dots flashed behind her eyelids, afterimages from the glare, and then her eyes readjusted to the normal, dimly lit shop.

Daniel began to speak again, to ask what she was doing, and Kayla caused a slip of paper—a stray price tag—to fly up over his mouth. She put her finger to her lips and let the paper fall. He subsided and sat on the floor across from the voodoo queen.

Queen Marguerite spilled the bones onto the floor. Leaning forward, she studied them. She then rocked backward. "Ah, me, you're all going to die."

Kayla felt as if she'd been punched in the stomach. She tried to suck in air.

Then Marguerite burst into laughter again. Laughing transformed her, making her look twenty years younger. "Oh, you should see your faces! Sorry, sorry, sometimes I can't help myself. I have been under a lot of stress lately, you know." Composing herself, she was again the regal voodoo queen. Her accent seemed to thicken, and her voice deepened. "Three stones; one death. But whose, no one knows."

Kayla swallowed. She wasn't convinced that was so much better. She didn't want to be involved in this mess at all if anyone was going to die. Maybe she should tell her mother the truth, and then Daniel wouldn't have anything over her anymore. But she knew what would happen if she did that. Her mother would insist they run, change their identities, and start new lives. She didn't want to leave everything and everyone she knew. That would be like a death too. And besides, what would happen to Daniel's mother if Kayla ran?

"You must find the stones," Queen Marguerite said. "This, the bones know. Your enemies already have one. You must seek the two others. Or what was begun will be done."

"Where are they?" Daniel asked, hushed.

"I will tell you a story. Centuries ago, a man named Fire Is Born was sent by his king to conquer the city of Tikal. He had with him three stones, powerful stones, that were given to him by a white man who appeared one day in a place no white man should be. This was centuries before the explorers arrived with their guns and their smallpox, but still, the white man found a way to bring his evil where it didn't belong. And make no mistake about it—the stones are evil." She poured herself a glass of tea, swirled it, but didn't drink. "The stones had been used to found an empire, but now that empire was falling and the man wanted a new one built, far away from the old, and so he gifted Fire Is Born with the stones."

Daniel fidgeted as if he wanted to interrupt, but he stayed silent. Kayla watched him, wondering what he was thinking, wondering how she ever thought he was cool and collected.

"Fire Is Born brought the young son of his king and the stones before Great Jaguar Paw, the king of Tikal, and offered him this: 'Complete the incantation with us, and you may rule, you may live, or you may die.'" She ticked off three fingers as she said "rule," "live," and "die." "Each stone carries its own power: of the mind, of the body, and of the earth. Combined, they promise ultimate power. Three cast the spell, and three faced their fate. One was granted invincibility, one was left as he was, and one died that very moment. Fire Is Born became an unstoppable warlord who created the Maya Empire; the son of his king became his puppet ruler; and the old king, Great Jaguar

Paw, died and was tossed into a pit with the bodies of his slain wife and children. Several centuries later, the stones were separated and hidden by Fire Is Born's descendants." She then took a drink from her iced tea, set the glass back on the tray, and dabbed her lips with a napkin. Rising, she carried the tray toward the door to the back room.

Daniel jumped to his feet. "Wait! What about my mother?"

Queen Marguerite halted. "I have told you everything you need to know. And more. Make no mistake: if the stones are used, there will be a death, as there has been before. Your enemies have one stone. Find the other two, and you will find your mother. I'd wish you luck, but you already have her beside you. And she will change everything. Such a delightful surprise." The voodoo queen smiled directly at Kayla, an unnerving smile— and then she vanished.

Both Kayla and Daniel jumped to their feet. "Should she have been able to do that?" Kayla asked. She pointed to the spot where Queen Marguerite had stood a second ago. She hadn't heard her say a spell, if there was even such a thing as a teleportation spell. She'd just disappeared, like Daniel did.

"Never met another teleporter before." He sounded shaken.

"I'd never met any until today. Lucky me." She scanned the shop, half expecting Queen Marguerite to reappear. The crushed skulls leered at her from the shelves, as did the dismembered dolls. She shuddered. "Can you take me home now? You promised, after we talked to the queen."

He took her hand, but he didn't look happy about it.

6

Daniel delivered her to the red gate. "I'll be by for you tomorrow at dawn."

"Whoa, wait, no way. I can't disappear with you again so soon! Moonbeam's going to eviscerate me as it is. Besides, I don't wake at dawn for anyone." As soon as she said it, she winced at how pathetically shallow it sounded, in light of his problems. But it was a lot better than saying she was afraid.

"I need you," he said. "You heard her. You're my luck." He flashed her a smile that would have been charming if she hadn't wanted to punch him in the mouth so badly for involving her in this. The smile faded, and he said softly, "We'd leave right now if I knew where to go." As he looked away toward the unseen ocean, his expression was as forlorn as a homeless cat's. But he didn't give her a chance to decide whether to punch him or comfort him. He vanished, leaving her wanting to scream. She shouldn't be wrapped up in this. It wasn't her problem!

Taking out her phone, she texted Selena, *Here*.

She waited for a response, a hint as to Moonbeam's mood or the lie that Selena had told, and she paced outside the red gate.

A few cars drove up and down the street. A neighbor dragged trash cans to the curb and waved at Kayla. Pasting a fake smile on her face, Kayla waved back. Selena still hadn't replied.

Stupid to just wait here, Kayla thought. She stuffed the phone back in her pocket. Shaking out her arms and rolling her neck, she took a deep breath. She could do this. She'd weathered Moonbeam's disapproval before. It wouldn't kill her.

She pinched her cheeks, then slapped them so they'd look pink, as if she'd been running. She opened the garden gate and dashed across the lawn, leaping over a bush and throwing herself into the house as she cried, "I'm sorry! I'm so sorry! I tried to call. My phone died. I'm here! I'm fine!"

Moonbeam and Selena were perched on stools, seated at the kitchen table. Both of them twisted around to look at her in surprise. Skidding to a stop, Kayla looked at Moonbeam, then Selena, then back.

Please, say something, Kayla thought at her mother. *Scream. Yell. Anything. Just get this over with.*

Rising, Moonbeam crossed to Kayla and kissed her on the cheek. "Just tell me you didn't have unprotected sex, and I will forgive you for not answering your phone."

Kayla felt her cheeks flush even redder. Her mouth opened and then shut. She looked at Selena for help.

"None of these charms work against pregnancy or STDs," Moonbeam continued. "Plus you're much, much too young anyway. Wait until you're thirty. Thirty-five. Then you'll have something to look forward to, after the novelty of voting and alcohol wears off."

Selena smiled sheepishly. "Sorry. Had to tell her about your date. How was that café? Did you get the calamari like I told you to?"

Kayla felt limp. A plausible lie! "Had the shrimp soup. It was delicious." She decided that Selena should be nominated for knighthood, and she took back every bad thing she'd thought about Selena's ability to lie. Clearly, she'd been practicing.

Moonbeam held Kayla's shoulders. "I want you to know you can tell me anything. Really, I'd prefer everything, but I'll settle for anything. You don't have to hide your love life from me. You're supposed to have a love life. Without sex."

"It was a first date! I didn't sleep with him. And I can guarantee I won't." She couldn't ever be attracted to a guy whose idea of asking for a favor equaled blackmail. But she supposed she couldn't say that if she wanted to keep the lie going . . . Oh, God, this meant she was going to keep the lie going. She had no easy excuse to tell Daniel.

Moonbeam broke into a smile. "Then you may have a cookie." She put her arm around Kayla and guided her to the table. "Milk or iced tea?" Kayla noticed that there was a spread of food out: cucumber sandwiches, cookies, milk, and iced tea, as if Moonbeam and Selena had been having a full-out British tea party while Kayla was off cleaning a voodoo shop in New Orleans.

"So, details, please!" Selena said. "Did you kick him to the curb? Swear to never see him again? Strike his name from your heart with a felt-tip marker?"

"I . . . may have another date tomorrow. Early." A tiny part of her wished she *had* been caught. She was about to get even more involved. And if she failed and the spell was cast, someone would die. Swallowing, she forced a smile.

Moonbeam poured a glass of milk and set it on the table for Kayla. "Uh-huh, and what is this mystery boy's name?"

"Daniel."

"Last name?"

"Mmm, I don't know."

"You might want to bring that one up in conversation before you get too far into the smoochy-smoochy." Selena puckered up her lips for extra effect. "Just a suggestion."

Moonbeam managed to look both disapproving and amused at the same time. "When do I get to meet this Daniel-without-a-last-name?"

Never popped into Kayla's mind. "Not yet," Selena answered for Kayla. "Introducing a guy to Mom is a big deal. Has to fit into the strategy just right. Do it too early, and he'll think you're too serious. Do it too late, and he'll think you're not serious enough. Maybe after the fifth date. Unless you have my parents; then all bets are off. But for you, fifth date."

"Oh, no, I've seen sitcoms." Moonbeam offered Kayla a cucumber sandwich. "I get to grill him and embarrass Kayla from the moment he drives up. Does he have his own car? Please tell me he doesn't ride a motorcycle. I think my heart will stop if you're on a motorcycle."

"No motorcycle." Kayla nibbled at the sandwich. Now that she was sure Moonbeam wasn't furious, she was hungry. "He's mostly on foot."

"Bet he has nice feet," Selena said dreamily.

Kayla shot her a look, then devoured the rest of the sandwich.

"What? Everything else looked nice, and feet are deserving of admiration too. Don't worry. I'll look and not touch. He's not my type. I like nonbroody." Selena hopped off the stool. "But speaking of feet, there are shoes that need purchasing. Moonbeam, can I steal Kayla for an hour or two, if she's not grounded?"

Moonbeam frowned. "Parenting teenagers should come with a manual. She *should* be grounded, but I want her to know she can trust me with the truth."

"Manual says let her go with a stern but loving warning," Selena suggested. Kayla found it disconcerting to be discussed in the third person when she was right there, but then again, Selena seemed to have the situation in hand. She owed her for this.

Moonbeam laughed. "Your friend is incorrigible."

"That's why I like her," Kayla said.

Moonbeam wagged her finger at Kayla. "I want you home and asleep by ten o'clock, especially if you have an early morning date tomorrow."

"Come on, Kayla, those shoes won't walk themselves onto my feet." Selena hooked her arm through Kayla's. Kayla waved over her shoulder at her mother and headed out the door with Selena at a brisk walk. Arm in arm, they crossed the yard and pushed through the garden gate. "Okay, all the details," Selena said.

"Need beach privacy."

"Really? That serious?"

"Seriously serious."

They got into Selena's car, and Selena shot down the street. She parked at the beach, took off her shirt and shorts so she was only in a bikini, and fetched two beach towels and her beach bag—designer brand, of course. Kayla left her chiffon shirt in the car so she was just in shorts and her bikini top—the picture of two girls with nothing serious on their minds. Pretending to laugh, the two of them sauntered down toward the waves as if they were just hanging out, enjoying the end of the day. They spread their towels a few feet from the wettest sand, away from everyone else. In the distance, the sky was turning a rosy pink as the sun teased the horizon.

"I owe you," Kayla told Selena when they'd finished setting up their tableau. "I thought I was dead for sure. You were brilliant in there."

"Clearly. I'm a genius with every mother but my own. But we aren't here to talk about me. Now spill."

Kayla told her every detail, from the state of the shop to the story of Fire Is Born to the queen's vanishing trick at the end. She concluded, "So, it's not over."

"Of course it's not over. Don't you know how these things work? The wise old woman gave you cryptic advice to start you on your quest. Now the trusty sidekick, who is far smarter than the heroine, finds the pertinent information our beloved lead needs. Or she at least checks Wikipedia." Selena pulled her tablet out of her beach bag and flipped the cover open. "So we know Fire Is Born had all three stones in Tikal in . . . AD 378. Hey, he was a real person! Siyaj K'ak', Fire Is Born, formerly nicknamed Smoking Frog, which is pretty much the least sexy nickname ever. Heartily approve the change. He conquered Tikal on January 16, 378. Wow, that's specific. Oh, it's the day the old king died. Or was killed. Also, it's the same year the Roman Empire fell, and probably lots of other stuff happened that didn't make it into Wikipedia."

"Any mention of the stones?"

"Nope. But maybe we can find you a treasure map or a video that depicts them being hidden." Her fingers hovered over the keyboard. "Just for the record, I'm kidding. Seriously, Her Majesty couldn't give you any more specific info?"

"I think she thought she was being helpful enough."

Selena snorted and continued to type. She squinted at her screen, tilting it to avoid the glare of the sunset. Across the ocean, the sun dyed the clouds a burnt orange. It deepened to molten gold as it touched the water. Its reflection stretched like a path of gold coins on the blue-black surface. Kayla thought it was appropriately dramatic for a conversation about ancient death magic. "No record of his death," Selena reported. "Ooh, maybe he didn't die. That would be übercreepy. But she said invincibility, not immortality, right? So never mind. You won't have to face a millennium-old Maya. Hello, silver lining!"

She appreciated that Selena was trying to cheer her up, but Kayla didn't feel like smiling. She thought of the disaster zone in Queen Marguerite's shop. If their enemies were so strong that the voodoo queen's magic couldn't stop them, what was Kayla doing wrapped up in this? She was a pickpocket with a few fancy tricks, not a fighter. "I shouldn't be facing any of this. She said someone would die."

"*If* they use the stones, which you're going to prevent. Come on, Kayla, you have never wimped out of a challenge in your life. And this is way bigger than shoplifting a few blingy trinkets. You have the chance to save a life, stop evil, and be a superhero without Spandex." She paused. "Seriously, don't wear Spandex."

Kayla hugged her knees to her chest. Everything about this felt out of her control. She didn't have nearly enough information. And she was dealing with a boy who had trust issues. "This is too much. Too serious. I should tell Moonbeam, and we should run. He can't teleport to someplace he doesn't know. He'd never find us."

"And I'd never see you again! No. No. Absolutely no."

The sun spread into the horizon as if it were melting into the water, an act that, while poetic, would not have been appreciated by the fish. "How do we even know he's telling the truth? Maybe his mother wasn't kidnapped, and he wants the stones for himself so he can become invincible and conquer the world." She felt guilty even saying it. She'd seen that lost look in his eyes and heard the desperation in his voice, even though he'd tried to hide it. Also, the very premise was absurd. Who even wanted to conquer the world? The world was way too messy.

"Then let's spy on him!"

"You can't spy on a guy who can teleport."

"Virtually spy." Selena typed quickly. "University of Chicago, right? Anthropology professor. Missing." She hit Enter with a flourish. Wordlessly, she pointed at the screen. There were local Chicago news articles, dated less than a week ago, about an anthropology professor who was reported missing by her son. Her name was Dr. Evelyn Sanders. There was a quote from a colleague talking about how she was on the verge of a break-through and how everyone expected great things from her, and so forth, so this was a double tragedy, for her family and for academia. "Come on, Kayla, do this. It's the decent thing to do. Plus it means I can live vicariously through you. Quit it with the reluctant hero crap."

Kayla sighed. She hated being maneuvered into things. She'd rather be the one doing the maneuvering, preferably from a nice distance. But Selena was, as always, right. Kayla couldn't walk away from this. Daniel and his intense, wounded-puppy eyes would haunt her. "Fine. But I still want more info. Search her name and the Maya."

The result was instantaneous. Dr. Sanders had written

several papers on the Maya, both ancient and contemporary. It took more searching to find accessible versions, and Kayla and Selena spent the next hour huddled together on a beach towel, reading through them, as the sky darkened and the stars poked through. Most of the papers detailed Maya rituals, comparing them to similar rituals in other cultures. They referenced various stellae and murals from sites in Mexico, Guatemala, and Belize. But one discussed unsolved ritualistic glyphs and was, unlike the others, dedicated to her son, Daniel. None of the other papers were dedicated to anyone. One paragraph in particular caught Kayla's eye. "Wait. There." She pointed at the screen and read.

Inside the Temple of the Great Jaguar in Tikal, there were several tiny glyphs carved high up in a shaft within the inner tombs, completely inaccessible to archaeologists. They'd only been viewed remotely by camera, and translation was near impossible due to the layers of dust on the stones. Because of the shape of the tunnels, no one had been able to maneuver a tall-enough ladder to examine them closely in person, but a few archaeologists believed the glyphs marked the location of a small hole, perhaps with valuables inside. One of the minor mysteries of Tikal was why and especially *how* they were put there. The only consensus was that they were installed when the pyramid was built, around AD 700. Kayla tapped the laptop screen. "That's it. The stones are there, behind the glyphs."

"Seriously? Centuries-old mystery, and you read a few papers and solve it? Way to take the wind out of my sails."

"You shouldn't feel bad. It's not obvious, unless you're me." She felt a bubble of excitement inside her. She was sure this was it.

Selena frowned as she reread the paragraph. "Yeah, I still don't see it."

"Someone like me put them there." A telekinetic could have carved those glyphs or placed them in the shaft. No ladder necessary. "Queen Marguerite said the stones were hidden by Fire Is Born's descendants. A royal tomb could have seemed a pretty good hiding place. Slightly more permanent than under your mattress."

Selena pursed her lips into an O. "You might be right. At the very least, I think you should go there and check it out. He needs images, right? I'll send some to your phone. Just . . . be careful, okay?" For an instant, there was a flash of worry in Selena's eyes, but it faded before Kayla could answer. "Bring me back a souvenir."

∾ ⌒

Kayla slapped her alarm. Five o'clock. "I hate him," she muttered. She rolled off the futon and stumbled through the cottage to the bathroom. It was dark outside, but the birds were beginning to twitter and chirp, which made Kayla want to wring their feathery necks. "Stupid birds. I hate birds."

She showered and dressed in the dark in a tie-dye-camouflage tank top and khaki shorts, the kind with lots of useful pockets, plus sneakers. She stuffed her lighter in one pocket, a razor blade that she wrapped in tinfoil in another, and a spool of thread in a third. She grabbed her cell phone and put on her various amulets. Sitting on her futon, she untangled her hair by concentrating on the strands. It soothed her to separate the hairs and lay them flat. On the other side of the curtain, Moonbeam let out a groan. "Kayla?"

"Go back to sleep," Kayla whispered.

"Are you okay?"

"Sunrise date."

"Humph. And he thinks this is romantic?"

Kayla flopped back on her futon. "It's not."

"Definitely not."

"I plan to mention that." With a groan, she levered herself out of bed again and, after a moment's thought, took the emergency backpack that she'd tucked under her bed, as well as her hoodie. She then tiptoed out, past Moonbeam's futon. She heard the sheets rustle as Moonbeam sat up.

"Wait. Don't go." Reaching out in the dark, Moonbeam caught Kayla's hand. She clasped it tightly, her multiple rings biting into Kayla's skin. "Tell that boy another time. I don't want to fall back asleep and wake without you here."

Kayla extricated her hand. "I'll be fine. Don't worry."

"Do you have your cell phone? Charged? Your amulets? Why couldn't you have stayed a baby? I'd sit you in the middle of the floor, and you'd stay there. It was miraculous. And at night, I'd put you into your crib, your baby cage. Why is it socially unacceptable to put teenagers into cages at night? I'd feel much better if you were in a box."

"That's the kind of thing you shouldn't actually say out loud," Kayla said.

"You know I love you, right? I say it every day, but I wonder if you hear it. You are the smartest, funniest, sweetest, prettiest, most wonderful girl, and I'm lucky to have you in my life. Every day I am grateful that you are here and safe and with me."

And this was why no one should ever try to have a conversation before their brain was as awake as their mouth. "Go back to sleep. I promise I'll be careful." She wondered if that was another promise to her mother that she was going to break. For an instant, she wished she'd told Daniel flat-out no and then dealt with the repercussions. "I think you're great too, Mom."

Moonbeam lay back in bed. Kayla scooted out of the house before her mother could truly forbid her from going. She locked the door behind her and then bit back a shriek as someone touched her shoulder. She spun around.

Daniel, in black again, stood inches away. His face was shadowed in the predawn, and as shallow as she knew it was, she was struck again by his gorgeousness. He looked as if he'd walked off a darkened movie screen, full of angst and danger. It was, she had to admit, a little bit thrilling that a guy like this sought her out, that he needed her. No one had ever needed her power before. It was refreshing to meet someone who didn't want her to repress it, to repress herself.

She wondered if he'd been waiting for her or if he'd simply appeared. She supposed it didn't matter. "I think we should look in Tikal, specifically in the main temple." Kayla described what she and Selena had discovered, and then she pulled out her phone and showed him the photos of the Maya temple. She didn't have any of the interior, but there were plenty of the site itself. "Unless you have any better ideas?"

Daniel flipped through the photos. She expected a little discussion, but he tightened his grip on her shoulder, and then everything flashed white, then black, then sunlit dark green. The humidity felt like a bucket of water had been poured over her head. Her lungs contracted, and she gasped like a fish. Daniel kept his hand on her shoulder, steadying her, as the green and gray resolved itself in front of her and she faced the Temple of the Great Jaguar.

7

The Temple of the Great Jaguar rose in front of her, a gray shadow against the achingly bright blue sky. Moss and grasses stained the gray rocks. It looked as if the green wanted to devour the stone. Beyond the temple was the rain forest. Kayla heard birds she didn't recognize and a shriek that could have been either a monkey or a pissed-off parrot and . . . oh God, she was in another country! She was breathing air that tasted nothing like California air. It was thick with the scent of plants and so heavy with humidity that it felt like broth in her throat.

It was simultaneously so overwhelmingly real and unbelievably surreal.

Shielding her eyes from the blazing sun, Kayla squinted at the temple—a pyramid with a crownlike structure at the top. About two hundred steep stone steps led up the face of the ruin to a black doorway in the center of the crown. Other ruins were clustered nearby, including one shorter pyramid directly opposite the jaguar temple. Some of them had wooden staircases strapped to their sides. One staircase swayed as if it was going to break from its support beams and topple into the rain forest at any second. A few people climbed those stairs, moving slowly. No one was climbing the Great Jaguar Temple. But the doorway at the top beckoned to Kayla. Somewhere in there were the two stones!

Don't lie to yourself, Kayla thought. *You just want to climb it for the view.*

Kayla glanced at Daniel. His profile was severe and hard to read. He didn't seem as impressed with this place. Maybe it was old hat, compared to all the places he must have been. She tried to imagine what it must be like to be able to come and go wherever, whenever. That kind of freedom . . . It made her ache thinking about it. And yet here was Daniel, nonchalant, taking it all for granted. He wasn't even careful.

"You're lucky you don't get shot on sight, appearing out of the blue," Kayla said.

"The only people who notice are little kids. Adults like to come up with their own explanation for why they didn't see me before." He did seem to be right. There were other people— tourists, workers, and archaeologists—scattered across the plaza, as well as climbing the steps of various temples, but no one seemed to have noticed their sudden appearance.

It was decidedly unfair. Kayla was so careful about hiding her power. "So you just don't worry about it? Assume no one will think you're a witch and burn you at the stake?"

"People don't do that anymore."

"Yeah, until they discover the magic boy, and then it will be all, 'Bring the torches and pitchforks!'" Kayla drew in a breath. *Shake it off*, she told herself. She was here now, and it was more incredible than she'd imagined. Leaving him in the middle of the plaza, Kayla started walking toward the jaguar temple. "God, this place is amazing!"

He caught up to her. "Hey, where are you going?"

"Up, of course. And then in." She'd never thought she'd see the inside of a Maya temple. Or that she'd be only a few hundred feet from an actual monkey-filled jungle. She could hear the howler monkeys, even if she couldn't see them.

"Why not find a ground entrance?"

"Because there's one right there." She pointed up at the shadowed doorway. "Come on, Daniel, aren't you dying to see what's inside?"

"It's a long way up."

Kayla halted and gawked at him. "You're fine with popping into view in the middle of a plaza with people all around, but you don't want to climb a set of stairs? Are you scared of heights or something?" His face flushed red. "You are. You're afraid of heights. But we were on a roof in Santa Barbara."

"I'm not afraid of heights; I simply don't like the idea of falling. That roof was new and sturdy. Those steps are, by definition, ancient. Look how many rocks have already fallen." Daniel pointed to the clutter of stones that buried half the bottom steps. "They could crumble under our feet."

"So then you teleport us to safety."

"I can't jump if I'm convinced I'm going to break my neck. It requires confidence."

"Can you jump us to the top?" She'd rather climb up the steps herself, like the Maya, but at least she'd get her view. "We have to get inside the temple. That's where the stones are."

"You don't know that doorway leads into the temple. It could be for a shrine at the top of the pyramid. Makes much more sense to look for a ground entrance first. It will be safer *and* faster."

"But since we're here . . ."

"If you want to play tourist, feel free. I'm not going to waste time arguing with you. You climb up and see for yourself, while I scout for an actual entrance. We'll meet back here in a half hour." He tapped his watch.

"Uh-nuh, lousy idea. You're my ticket home. Besides, every horror movie begins with two idiots splitting up. You leave me alone, and I guarantee I will be eaten by a jaguar or used as a virgin sacrifice."

His mouth quirked into an almost-smile.

"Or *you'll* be the virgin sacrifice."

"You don't know that I'm a virgin."

"Of course you are. You haven't the faintest idea how to talk to girls. Bet you've never even kissed one." Kayla lifted her face, daring him. She was sure he wouldn't. Almost sure.

He held her eyes for a half second longer than usual, and in that instant, Kayla thought maybe he would. She noticed the softness of his lips and the steadiness of his breath. Then she pivoted to face the temple. She didn't even like this jerk. What on earth was she doing talking about kissing him? Especially when they had ancient Maya ruins to explore and two evil stones to find and steal. "Forget it. Meet you back here in a half hour." She added, "Chicken."

She strode toward the temple. Glancing over her shoulder, she saw only the empty plaza. He'd vanished again in plain sight. *Idiot*, she thought. He could see the danger in a few stone steps but not the danger he posed to himself. If he wasn't more careful, he could be caught by evil people with world-domination plans and forced to commit atrocious acts of atrocity. Or sent to a government research lab to be tested and dissected. Or forced to appear on TV talk shows. Moonbeam might be obsessively paranoid, but that didn't mean she was wrong. Daniel had a phenomenally rare, precious ability, and he was far too casual with it. Not that she cared. She didn't. After this was over, she was done with him. Except, wow, to be able to travel to places like this . . . She should just enjoy it while it lasted.

Deliberately pushing him out of her mind, Kayla hiked across the plaza. After a few minutes, she had to stop and stuff her hoodie into her backpack. She was starting to sweat, and she hadn't even begun to climb yet. Putting her backpack on again, she looped her thumbs through the straps and felt like a real tourist. She tried to commit every detail to memory so she could treasure it later when she was home and stuck on the same few streets day after day: trees draped in vines, thatched-roof shelters, broad stone steps like bleachers along the plaza, stone tablets deeply embedded in the ground on the walk to the temple. Most of the stellae had been worn smooth, but a few had remnants of glyphs that looked halfway between Egyptian hieroglyphs and bubble graffiti. How amazing would it be to know what they said? Maybe they were clues to the spell stones. Or directions to the fountain of eternal youth. Or a recipe for the world's best smoothie.

Reaching the steps, she looked up . . . and up and up. It was steep. And tall. Looking back over her shoulder, Kayla scanned the plaza for Daniel. He might have had the smarter idea. Then again, how often did one have the chance to scale an ancient monument that was the symbol of an entire civilization? Kayla could attest it didn't come up often within a ten-mile radius of her house.

She started to climb.

At first, the steps were narrow. Rocks had tumbled down to cover most of the stairs, but unlike what Daniel had implied, they seemed to have fallen decades ago, maybe even centuries.

All the fallen rocks were coated in moss, making them look as if they'd decayed. A quarter of the way up, the steps broadened and steepened. She had to lean into the pyramid and use her hands to climb. The stone was slick, worn concave from centuries of feet. She was glad she'd worn her sneakers. Selena always said appropriate footwear made a world of difference. It was practically her life code. Here, it was true. With the sun soaking into her back and shoulders, and wearing the right shoes, Kayla felt like a proper explorer.

The sky was full of noise. She heard shrieks, cries, and calls from a dozen different kinds of birds and animals. "*¡No subir!*" one of the birds seemed to call. "*¡No subir!*"

Halfway up, Kayla stopped and looked down. A man was at the bottom of the steps. He wore a khaki button-down shirt and shorts, and he was waving his pudgy arms in the air. "*¡Baje ahora! ¡No subir!*" he shouted up at her. *Oops, not a bird*, she thought. He switched to English. "No climb!"

She gazed across Tikal. She was even with the tops of the trees. Other temples poked through the thick green canopy. Mist curled around them. In the distance, she saw gray-green mountains. Pretending she didn't understand what the man meant, she climbed higher and faster. Sweat coated her shoulders underneath the backpack straps, and the back of her neck felt damp. Sun beat down on her.

Calves aching, she stopped to catch her breath about three quarters of the way up. Really, it hadn't looked like such a long climb when she'd called Daniel "chicken." Now, she was wishing for an elevator. Looking down, she noticed a man was climbing too—not the same man who had yelled at her to come down. This man wore a hat like Indiana Jones's that shielded his face entirely. The man who had yelled was at the base of the temple, with a cluster of people. From their gestures, they looked as if they were arguing. Maybe the man in the hat had been sent to bring her down. Or maybe he was another renegade tourist. Regardless, she couldn't let him catch up to her. Feeling exposed, Kayla climbed faster. Where was a helpful teleporting boy when you needed one?

At least she was almost there. She saw the doorway above her, wide as an open mouth. With a burst of fresh energy, Kayla scurried up the last few steps and ducked inside. She was instantly swallowed by shadows. She waited for her eyes to adjust.

It was a small room. A shrine. There was a stone altar in the middle, its surface scratched and stained. Carvings, faded and chipped, covered the walls. But what caught Kayla's attention was a black grate on the floor, locked down with a large combination lock.

She knelt next to it. Beneath the grate were stone steps, headed down into the temple. "Bingo," she murmured. "And I win a day of 'I told you so's.'" She reached for her phone to tell Daniel what she'd found—and realized they'd never exchanged numbers. *Stupid*, she thought. But too late now. It wouldn't take long for the man with the hat to finish his climb too. If she wanted to explore without interference, this was her chance.

Kayla concentrated on the lock for a moment. Pressing with her mind, she engaged the three cams inside, and the lock snapped open. She loved combo locks. So straightforward.

Lifting up the grate, she started down the stairs. Stopping, she lowered the grate back into place above her. She then reached her hand through a hole in the grate and reattached the lock. Let the man wonder where she went.

She took her lighter out of her pocket, flipped it open, and lit it. The flame cast dancing shadows on the wall as she walked down the stairs, and Kayla wondered if she was the first person who wasn't either an ancient Maya or a modern archaeologist to be here. She had to walk slowly—the steps were covered with sand and pebbles. She steadied herself with one hand on the wall. It felt chalky, coated in ancient dust. She hoped her touch wouldn't damage the intricate, orange-tinted murals. Chunks had fallen off or faded, but many faces, figures, and glyphs remained. Most featured the profile of a man with a sloped forehead, prominent nose, and plump lips. He wore an elaborate headdress and chunky jewelry like you'd find at an estate sale. Some of the carvings showed him seated in front of what looked like altars. Others depicted him in battle, spear raised, with victims writhing at the bottom of the scene. Kayla felt as if she were walking into the past. Studying the murals, she slowed— and thought she heard the scrape of metal on stone.

Halting, she listened.

She heard nothing. No scrape. No footsteps. It must have been her imagination. She was still alone, and anyway, the grate was locked. Reminding herself to breathe again, she continued down. The steps were even steeper than outside, and she had to feel each one with her toes before lowering her full weight. Some of the steps were partially crumbled, and at times, she had to cling to the wall.

The stairs led to a chamber—a tomb. She saw faces of long-ago kings on the walls, and she tasted air so stale that it could have been as old as those kings. Her lungs felt coated in old dust, the same as the walls. Lifting the flame with her mind, she scanned the ceiling, searching for the shaft that Daniel's mother had described. The ceiling was carved in intricate glyphs but there was no shaft.

Returning to the stairs, she continued deeper down into the temple until she reached a second chamber. Here, the walls were braced with wood posts, and she wondered how safe this was. Tons of stone surrounded her, held together by ancient mortar or maybe merely gravity. Moonbeam wouldn't be happy she was here. But then, Moonbeam wouldn't be happy unless Kayla were safely stuffed in a padded box.

No shaft in the second tomb either. Kayla returned to the stairs again.

Above her, Kayla heard a soft crunch, as if pebbles had shifted—a footstep? She wrapped her mind around the flame from the lighter and sent it up the steps. She didn't see anyone. Burning through its bubble of fuel, the flame died, leaving her in darkness.

In the darkness, silence spread through the tomb. It was the most complete silence she'd ever heard: no cars, no wind, no voices, no breath other than her own. Instead, the silence felt thick, as if a blanket were wrapped tightly around her. She listened to the darkness. Her heart beating faster, she flicked the lighter on again, cupped the fragile flame with her mind, and continued down.

She wondered how long the lighter could last—the fuel wasn't infinite. It occurred to her that she hadn't thought this through. She wondered where Daniel was and where he thought she was. Maybe she should have insisted he come with her. Or at least let him know she'd found a way in. On the plus side, he would be impressed when she returned with the two stones. *If* she returned with them.

The likelihood of the two stones still being in the temple at all was low. After all, one stone had already been found. The others could have been found, then chucked into the ocean or lost in the jungle or buried in the earth or stuck inside someone's closet. She wondered if that had occurred to Daniel. She hoped she didn't have to tell him the stones were lost. She might not like the jerk, but she didn't want to see the hope fade in his eyes. He'd looked so bereft when she hadn't known who the queen was. Like him or not (and she decidedly did *not*), she didn't want to see that look in his eyes again.

Kayla stepped into a third chamber, this one much smaller than the other two, about the size of a bathroom. Almost the entire room was filled by a stone sarcophagus. Its lid was covered in elaborate designs, including a man on a stylized throne, receiving gifts of food and animals. Above it, she thought she saw a shadow in the ceiling—possibly the shaft? Climbing onto the sarcophagus lid, she stood up and raised the lighter over her head.

"Yes!" she whispered.

Her voice was like a pebble dropped into a dark pool. It radiated out, echoing, until the shadows swallowed it. She froze again, listening for any other sound, but there was nothing.

This place fit the description from Dr. Sanders's paper perfectly: a chamber too small to maneuver a ladder and a shaft too narrow to fit a climber. She sent the flame from the lighter up, but it wasn't bright enough to illuminate all the way and it fizzled fast.

With her mind, Kayla reached up. She "felt" the walls of the shaft, and pebbles and dirt rained down as her mental touch loosened them. Higher, higher . . . And there they were, exactly as Daniel's mother had described: glyphs, carved in stone, high above her. She'd found them!

If she was right, the stones should be behind them. It occurred to her that she might not be strong enough to retrieve them. She might have come all this way only to fail as completely as the ladderless archaeologists. She felt along the glyphs, looking for a hole in the wall . . .

And the lighter went out.

Darkness closed around her so completely that it felt as if her eyes had been stolen. She flicked the lighter. Nothing. She tried again. Still nothing. It was dead. She didn't move. Rigid, she listened, as if listening could restore her sight. Her heartbeat felt loud. *Don't panic*, she ordered herself. *Do* not *panic*. She had her phone. Its screen could make light. Pulling it out of her pocket, she turned it on.

Low battery. She'd told Moonbeam she'd charged it. She must have forgotten to actually do it. After a moment of staring at its soothing bluish light, she turned it off. She'd save it for the climb out.

She didn't need light to do what she had to do. Taking a breath, feeling as if she were breathing in the darkness itself, Kayla concentrated on the glyphs. She ran the fingers of her mind over the surface of the wall, tracing the curves of the carvings. Dr. Sanders's paper had said the glyphs marked a small hole . . . but she didn't feel one. Her heart sank. She'd been so sure! But she only felt— ahh, there it was, a hole in the heart of one of the glyphs.

Concentrating, she burrowed her mind in through the narrow hole. Her skull felt squeezed. She touched cobwebs and . . . a spider skittered over her mind, and it felt like every inch of her skin was crawling with a thousand spiders. Shrieking, she yanked her mind back. She wiped hard at her arms and her legs. *No spiders on you*, she told herself. *You're fine.*

She took a deep breath and tried again. Reaching up, she touched the glyphs and dove into the hole. Cringing, she touched the spider and then felt through the cobwebs. Her mind touched a piece of rolled parchment. "Hello, you," she whispered to it.

Gently, Kayla guided it out of the hole and down the shaft. She held out her hands, and it landed as lightly as a tame bird.

It felt so very brittle, as if it would crumble into dust if she breathed heavily. Sitting on the floor, she pulled out her phone and used its light to study it as she slowly, carefully unrolled it. The edges crumbled, and the parchment cracked. She stopped, took a breath, and then continued until it lay open. It was covered in faint glyphs. Afraid it would disintegrate as she looked at it, she snapped a photo with her phone.

It certainly wasn't one of the spell stones. But maybe it was a clue to how to find them, like a map or a set of directions. Or maybe she'd stumbled on an entirely different mystery that would lead her to the fountain of youth and a very, very old Ponce de León. Or it could be a forbidden love note or secret plans to a battle station . . . At least she'd been right about one thing: there was no question that it had been left for someone like her.

Taking off her backpack, she stowed the parchment carefully inside. As she zipped it closed, she heard a voice. A man, speaking a spell. Melodious words flowed through her, filling the chamber, seeming to echo from every direction. Kayla jumped to her feet. "Who's there?" She held out her phone. Bluish light filled the chamber. She didn't see anyone. She spun around. "Where are you? What are you doing?"

Suddenly, the chamber flooded with light so bright that it stung her eyes. She threw her hands over her face. Just as suddenly, the light disappeared. White spots danced over her eyes for a long minute, and then they slowly, painfully faded. She turned on the phone again, but in comparison, her faint light only faded the darkness to a lighter black. Her heart thudded so hard that it almost hurt. As she peered into the empty shadows, she knelt to pick up her backpack . . .

And it was gone.

It couldn't be gone. She'd left it at her feet. It should be right here! Dropping to her knees, she felt around. She felt only floor. Jumping back up, she shined the phone in every direction. Dim light danced over the walls. He must have taken it. Whoever cast that spell must have used her temporary blindness to steal her pack with the rings and the cash and the parchment. *She* was the thief here. She wasn't supposed to be the victim. "Hey, you! Thief! Give it back!"

Kayla ran for the stairs. He couldn't have gone far. She pounded up the steps, higher and higher. The phone bounced in her hand as she ran, and the light jumped everywhere. Her side cramped, and her calves strained as she ran up, up, and up, past the second chamber, past the first. She didn't see anyone ahead of her. She didn't hear anyone either. But someone had been here! Someone had cast that spell and stolen her pack!

Above, she saw a square of daylight.

The grate was open.

She'd left it closed.

She heard a rumble, and the walls shook. She was thrown against a mural. The plaster cracked, and dirt rained down. Blocking her face with her arms, she ducked. Dust filled the cave, and she coughed. And when the rumbling stopped, she was in darkness.

8

Kayla spat out dirt as she felt for the stairs in front of her. Her hands hit rocks. Her mind was shrieking, *No no no no no no no!* Crawling forward, she felt rocks jamming the stairs. She took a breath to scream for help. And then she stopped.

Someone had caused this cave-in.

He could still be there.

She needed to find her phone. She'd call Selena. She'd know what to do, maybe have some miraculous solution for how to warn Daniel and tell him he had to pop her out of here. Or she could call 9-1-1 and explain she was trapped in a Maya tomb . . . except that they'd never believe her and there was no way she'd have cell service anyway.

Still, she could use the phone's light to help her search for another way out. Kneeling, she felt the rocks in the darkness. It had to be nearby, unless a rock had fallen on it and it was crushed, buried beneath the rubble.

Kayla tried to take a deep, calming breath, but the air was still clogged with dust, and she coughed so hard that she felt like she was going to expel her insides. Dust coated her arms, face, and tongue. Maybe there wasn't enough air. Maybe she was slowly suffocating.

Stop it, she ordered herself. This was a very large pyramid. There should be plenty of oxygen. She had to calm down and find the phone in the same way she'd found the parchment.

Lowering herself, she sat cross-legged on the fallen stones. She reached out with her mind and "felt" around her. She wouldn't be able to lift the phone when she found it—too heavy—but she should be able to locate it and then fetch it the normal way.

Slowly, she worked over the rocks on the steps. She skimmed over the rough surfaces and swept over the jagged edges. So many rocks. She didn't let herself think about what if it was crushed, what if it was underneath the rocks, what if she never found it, what if no one ever found her . . . *Focus, Kayla.* She pushed her mind farther and deeper, in between the crevasses of the rocks. Rocks and dust. Just rocks and dust.

In the distance, somewhere below her, she heard a shout. Her name. "Kayla! Kayla, can you hear me?" Daniel? That was Daniel's voice!

She wanted to cheer and cry at the same time. "Yes! I'm here! I'm up by the entrance! Daniel?" Leaping to her feet, she bumped against a rock. Tears popped into her eyes. Blinking them away, she cradled the back of her head.

"Are you hurt?"

"I'm fine, but the entrance is blocked! Daniel, be careful. I think it was intentional. Someone caused the rocks to fall!" Specifically the man who had followed her down here, cast that spell, and stole her backpack. Oh, God, the parchment! She'd bet large sums of money that the thief was the kidnapper, and she'd just handed him the only clue to the missing stones. Well, the only clue aside from the photo in her phone.

She had to find that damn phone.

"Stay where you are!" Daniel called. "We're coming!"

We? She heard other voices, speaking in Spanish. He wasn't alone. That meant she had to work fast. Kayla concentrated fiercely, running her mind over the rocks in all directions, until her skull felt as if it were squeezing her brain.

"Kayla? Shout so we can find you!"

She ignored him. It had to be here. It could have fallen out of her hands and tumbled down the steps farther than she'd thought.

"Kayla? Are you okay?"

Dammit. She heard footsteps on the stairs below her. What if they stepped on it? Fiercely, she looked—and she found it. Ten steps down.

"Wait!" she called. "Don't come closer!" She thought fast. "The rocks are unstable! I'm coming down to you. Don't move!"

The footsteps didn't stop. In fact, they came faster.

"Daniel, wait!" She hurried down the steps, holding on to the wall, hitting her toes on the fallen stones. Loose stones tumbled down around her. She slowed. Just a few more steps. She knelt, feeling in front of her. And then she felt a hand on her shoulder. She wrapped her fingers around the phone as everything flashed white then black then green.

∽ ∾

Kayla's garden.

She saw the red hibiscus flowers, the bench tucked against the enthusiastically green hedge, and the row of garden gnomes. From the house, she heard the door swing open.

"Kayla?" Moonbeam called.

Kayla spun toward Daniel, about to order him to take her somewhere else. Moonbeam couldn't see her like this. And she still had to show him the photo and tell him—

Before she could say anything, he vanished.

She heard Moonbeam's feet crunch on the walk, and she felt her heart sink into her shoes. Slowly, she turned. "Hey, Moonbeam," she began to say, and then she coughed. The cough shook her entire body, and she dropped forward onto her hands and knees. As she shook, she thought that this was probably not the best way to prove everything was normal and fine. She should have stayed in that temple.

Moonbeam raced to her side, and Kayla felt hands on her back and forehead, stroking her as if she were a baby waking at night. "Breathe, that's a girl. Nice and easy. You're okay. You're filthy. What happened? Where have you been?"

"Fell in the dirt," Kayla said. *Dirt . . . dirt . . . think, Kayla.* "We were dirt bike riding." She winced. Who went dirt biking on a date? Not to mention she didn't even own a bike. Master thief, yes; master liar, not so much.

"You were *what*? You don't know how to ride a dirt bike. Kayla, you are covered in dirt. What possessed you? Are you all right? Anything broken? Stand up. Let me see you."

Pushing off her knees, Kayla got to her feet. She turned in a circle, as if for inspection. "I'm fine. See? Just need a shower, and then I'll be right as rain."

"What sort of boyfriend drags you through the dirt, endangers your life, and then drops you home without staying to make sure you're okay? You could be hurt! Broken bones! Internal injuries! Concussion! Let me look at your pupils."

"I'm fine, I swear." She realized she was clutching her phone to her chest. She pressed the "on" button. The screen stayed dark. She tried again, holding the button down. She shook it. "My phone is less than fine." Kayla managed, somehow, to keep her voice steady. But her eyes heated up anyway, betraying her. She'd lost the parchment, nearly been killed, and the one thing she'd been able to salvage was broken.

Moonbeam's arms wrapped around her and pulled her into a hug. Moonbeam stroked her hair. "As long as you're okay, that's what matters. I can't believe that boy!"

"It wasn't his fault," Kayla said, pulling back. At least, not directly. Overall, yes, technically, it was. But she should have paid more attention to the man following her up the pyramid steps. She should have investigated the noises she'd heard. She should have held on to the backpack and not let some parlor trick with bright light distract her. As much as she wanted to blame Daniel, she had to take responsibility for those mistakes. "I wasn't careful enough."

"You're trying to cover for him." Moonbeam kissed Kayla's forehead. "Never cover for a boy. If they have faults, face them. Don't think you can change them or fix them or save them." Lightly, she brushed Kayla's hair off her forehead. "Don't make my mistakes."

Kayla felt a lump in her throat. What she really wanted to do was break down on Moonbeam's shoulder and tell her everything, including how terrifying it had been when the rocks came down and she was trapped alone in the dark tomb. But she didn't. Instead she dredged up a smile from nowhere and said, "I just want to fix my phone. And take a shower. Mind if Selena comes over?"

"She's always welcome," Moonbeam said automatically. "But Kayla . . . about this boy . . ."

Not waiting for her to finish, Kayla headed for the house. "I'm going to call her." She heard Moonbeam following her, but she didn't look back, even to hold the door open for her. Hurrying to the phone in the kitchen, she let the screen slam behind her. With shaking hands, she dialed Selena's number.

Selena answered. "Sorry, Moonbeam. Kayla isn't here."

"Really? You volunteer that right away?" If Selena had been covering for her, she would have instantly failed.

"Kayla! How did Operation Maya go?"

"Badly. And we're not calling it that."

"Operation Tikal? The Great Stone Quest?"

"Selena. Stop." She noticed she was squeezing the phone so hard that her knuckles were white bulges. She loosened her grip and tried to force a smile at Moonbeam, who was waiting between a stack of books and a basket of amulets. She felt as if she were grimacing instead and looked away. With luck, Moonbeam would think she'd merely had a bad date. Without luck . . . Moonbeam couldn't guess the truth, could she? She'd known that time when Kayla had sneaked out for a party on the beach. And another time when she'd failed a geography test and tried to hide it. But on the flip side, Moonbeam hadn't caught on about Kayla's extracurricular activities with the jewelry stores and ATMs on State Street. "I need you to come over and save my phone. I . . . sort of dropped it, and it has a photo on it that I really, really want to save."

"Tell me you didn't take any naked pictures of anyone."

"Selena. Please. Remember when you dropped your phone into the ocean and you said you found a miracle-working

phone guy? I need a miracle. Come on, please. Best Friend Code."
She hadn't said those words since she was about eleven. They'd
sworn a blood oath to each other after school one day under
Stearns Wharf, to always help when the code was called, not
unlike Batman with the Bat Signal. Selena mentioned it all the
time, but Kayla quit calling the code pretty much the same time
she discovered mascara and hair dye, leaving it behind with other
childhood things. Invoking it would get Selena's attention now.

"Seriously? Fine."

Kayla heard a sigh, a car door slam, and an engine purr to
life, then a *click* as the phone shut off. She put down the house
phone and then laid her poor lifeless phone gently on the
kitchen counter.

In the middle of the cottage, Moonbeam paced in tight
circles. She was working herself up to say something, Kayla
could tell. Kayla cast around for an exit strategy. She couldn't
leave; she was stuck here until Selena came. Maybe she could
duck into the shower?

Moonbeam stopped and faced her. "Kayla, this boy . . . If
he endangers you, then he's not serving his purpose. As much
as I want to approve—"

"You do?" Kayla blinked at her. She'd thoroughly expected
Moonbeam to forbid her seeing him again. She'd been positive
that Moonbeam had already started construction on the beach-
side equivalent of Rapunzel's tower. It would be guarded by a
fleet of garden gnomes.

"Yes, of course. Having a boyfriend will tie you closer to this
place. It will help make you part of the community and the
scenery, which will make you safer."

Kayla felt her mouth drop open. She didn't know what to say. So it wasn't about whether or not Kayla was happy; it was about hiding from her father. Everything was. "Moonbeam, he didn't . . . I don't . . . I . . . I need to shower."

Scooting into the bathroom, Kayla locked the door. Was there anything in her life untouched by fear of her father? She stripped off her clothes and dropped them to the floor. They set off a plume of dust when they landed. She turned the water on as hot as she could stand and tried to scrub away every speck of dust and every bruise. Not everything was about Dad. She was in the middle of a crisis that was happening right now, not eight years ago, and her life was in enough danger without the presence of an old bogeyman. Those rocks could have crushed her. She could have fallen down the stairs and cracked her head open. And all her "special power" couldn't have done a damn thing about it. She couldn't even hang on to one measly backpack.

When she finished, her skin felt tenderized. She'd made about twelve thousand mistakes today. So much for her supposed superhero status. She dried herself and dressed in clean clothes, transferring all the contents of her pockets, except her poor phone, which still lay on the counter. If she couldn't fix that phone, then she was useless. Worse than useless, because she'd led the enemy right to the parchment. He never would have found it if not for her. Instead of saving the day and Daniel's mother, she'd made everything worse.

Coming out of the bathroom, she blow-dried her hair by the kitchen sink, keeping the dryer blowing long after her hair was crispy so that she wouldn't have to talk. Beside her, at the table, Moonbeam organized a stack of coupons for the next supermarket run, though Kayla thought she wasn't actually looking at them. She switched off the blow-dryer only when Selena breezed through the door.

"So . . . how was the date?" Selena asked in her perkiest voice.

"She came home filthy and bruised," Moonbeam answered for her. "If I were a good mother, I'd forbid her from ever seeing that Daniel again."

Selena waved her hand in the air dismissively. "If you were a *typical* mother, you would. But since you're a good mother, you understand that making him forbidden would only increase the odds that Kayla will sneak out and see him for the pleasure of being her own person. As it is, by approving of him, you've actually shortened his shelf life." Sailing across the cottage, Selena scooped up the lifeless phone and pushed the buttons. "Ooh, yep, you broke it."

"Can your guy fix it?" Kayla asked.

Selena pursed her lips. "Yeah, see, here's the problem. I kind of alienated him a bit."

"How do you alienate someone 'a bit'?" As Selena opened her mouth to reply, Kayla interrupted. "Wait, don't answer that. I don't care. I just need it fixed."

"Got that. You called code. You *never* call code."

"I saved it for a serious crisis, unlike some people."

"Hey, shoes are serious."

"You wanted help with flip-flops!" Kayla said. "Flip-flops barely count as shoes. They're footprints with straps." Last summer, Kayla had been in the middle of a complex heist at one of the Montecito mansions, and she'd had to abandon it because of a cryptic text from Selena that called on the code. She hadn't let Selena forget it. Kayla jabbed her finger at her phone. "I *need* this."

Selena sighed, rolled her eyes, and then sighed again. "You have to come with me."

Both Selena and Kayla turned as one to look at Moonbeam. Moonbeam tossed her hands in the air. "Go on and fix it. And tell him it was malfunctioning before you dropped it or crushed it or whatever you did. The GPS said you were out of range, which never happens in Santa Barbara. Coverage is excellent within a ten-mile radius. I've tested it."

Kayla felt all her muscles clench. She should have known her mother would try to track her. "Hah! Okay, yeah, must fix that." She tried to read Moonbeam's face, to see if she was at all suspicious. She couldn't tell. Hopefully, Moonbeam blamed the broken phone. Grabbing Selena's arm and the dead phone, Kayla propelled her toward the door.

"And Kayla?" Moonbeam said. "I won't forbid you from seeing that boy. But please . . . before every action, ask yourself, 'Would I rather be home or in the emergency room?' Your choice, not mine. I trust you to make your own smart choices."

Kayla wanted to curl up into a ball. Being trusted was almost worse than being grounded. If Moonbeam ever found out what she was doing, flitting around the world, using her power right and left . . . Moonbeam couldn't find out. It was that simple. She'd never discovered the thefts; she wouldn't learn about this. "I'll try," Kayla promised.

Moonbeam smiled, so sweet and trusting that it made Kayla feel like the worst human being on the face of the earth. "That's all I ask." She kissed Kayla on the cheek, and Kayla waved as she followed Selena out to the garden.

Outside, Selena said, "Your mom is amazing."

"I know."

"I can't believe she didn't ground you."

"She wants me to have a love life." Kayla didn't say *why* Moonbeam wanted that.

"She wants you to be happy." There was a note of wistfulness in Selena's voice.

"Maybe." Kayla walked through the red gate, and the wind chimes sang a tangle of notes. A shockingly blue bird startled from a bush. It darted into the sky. "I wish she didn't have to be so afraid all the time. And here I am, making it worse." She got into Selena's car.

Selena hopped into the driver's seat and peeled out. Uncharacteristically, she turned the volume down on the radio. Wind drowned out the mariachi-like guitar riffs. "So, are you going to tell me what happened?"

"Yes. I nearly—" Her voice caught in her throat. She swallowed, and then she forced herself to recap events. When she got to the cave-in, Selena nearly swerved onto the median. "And that's why I need the photo. Someone wanted that parchment enough to nearly kill me. I at least deserve a look at it."

Selena nodded. For once, she didn't have a witty response. She drove faster down the palm-tree-lined streets until she squealed to a stop outside a rundown shop that looked plucked from the seventies. Its front window was stuffed with appliances from vacuums to tape recorders to electric tie racks. She parked the car, and Kayla got out. Cradling the phone to her chest like it was a sick baby, she followed Selena to the door.

At the door, Selena hesitated.

"What is it?" Kayla asked.

"You remember when I was coming over to your house to vent because my parents had flipped out about something, and then Daniel was there and we kind of got distracted?"

"Yeah, I vaguely recall getting myself caught up in some kind of perilous quest."

Selena took a deep breath. "Well, it was about him. Sam."

"Who?"

"The guy. The phone-miracle guy. The one we're about to see. Seriously, Kayla, did a rock land on your head?"

Kayla held up her hands in surrender. "You never said his name."

"Oh. Right. Sorry. Anyway, we were supposed to go on a date, and he came to the house and—"

Kayla stopped her. "You had a date and didn't tell me?"

"Can we skip to the important part? He met my parents."

Kayla's mouth formed an O at her doomed tone, ready to be sympathetic, though she wasn't sure exactly why it was warranted. "And I take it it didn't go well?" Admittedly, Selena's parents could be intense. Selena's father was kind—jovial and loud to the point of being overwhelming, but kind. And her mother was the most graceful, most intimidating person that Kayla had ever met. Not a hair out of place, ever. Taken together, they were so overpowering, they made you feel as articulate as a dishrag. "Did they intimidate him?"

"Worse, they disapproved."

"Oh. Why? What's wrong with him?"

Sighing, Selena seemed to deflate. "Absolutely nothing." She opened the door and gestured for Kayla to enter first. A bell rang as Kayla walked through the door. Selena followed. "Hi, Sam," she squeaked.

Sam looked like a surfer. Very blond. Very tan. He wore a muscle shirt and Hawaiian flower-print shorts. He had bare feet and wore an anklet made of shells. He was using a jackknife to clean out some unrecognizable gadget. "Whoa. Your Highness. I didn't think I'd be seeing you again." He got to his feet and looked at Selena with an expression that flashed from surprised to angry to wistful in a matter of seconds. It was an impressive display. Eyebrows raised, Kayla looked at Selena.

"I'm here for my friend Kayla." Selena gave Kayla a push forward between her shoulder blades. "She desperately needs her phone fixed, and, well, you're the best." Kayla heard a breathless nervousness in her friend's voice. Selena was *never* breathless.

"I can't take your money." Sam had a deep voice like a baritone opera singer. It was the kind of voice that Kayla knew Selena liked, the kind that thrummed in your bones when he spoke. "You know that. You know why." The words were loaded with that same mix of emotions.

Kayla looked from Sam to Selena and back again. Sam's eyes were fixed on Selena's face as if glued, and Selena was looking everywhere—floor, ceiling, walls, windows—except at Sam. Kayla felt like she'd walked into some kind of soap opera. She so didn't have time for this.

"You shouldn't be here. I can't fix it." Sam didn't look at Kayla or the phone. "You should take it to the mall. They'll either fix it or send it back to the manufacturer. If it's under warranty, they'll send you a new phone. Maybe even upgrade it."

Whatever was going on between them, it didn't matter right now. Kayla had other things to worry about. Hugging the phone, she said, "There's a photo on it that a friend of mine desperately needs. It's more serious than you could imagine."

Sam shook his head.

"Please," Kayla said. "Selena says you're the best."

"Genius," Selena clarified.

"You said that?"

"I'm a lousy liar. Ask Kayla."

Kayla nodded. "Back in fifth grade, she even stopped the school play because she couldn't manage to deliver her lines without breaking character. She was supposed to be a tree."

Sam sighed. "How dead is it?"

"It may have been in a cave-in," Kayla said.

"May have?" He arched his blond eyebrows.

Kayla shrugged and held out the phone. She felt as though she were delivering a family member for surgery. She couldn't explain why it mattered so much to her. She didn't owe Daniel's mother anything, and Daniel wouldn't blame her if they failed—no one could have predicted that light spell or the cave-in. If the phone wasn't fixed, she'd have a great excuse to end this craziness right now, before her life was in danger again. Daniel could try another way to find his mother. Or maybe the police would succeed. But she couldn't quit now. She had first-hand knowledge of how serious the situation was and how dangerous the people who had his mother were.

Sam took the phone. Examining it, he went behind the counter and pulled out a set of tools and a USB plug. "Not sure how long this will take."

"I'll wait," Kayla said at the same time that Selena said, "We'll go."

"No, thanks, I'm not letting that phone out of my sight." Kayla located a stool and perched on it. Selena shifted from foot to foot, looking as if she wanted to vanish like Daniel. Kayla had never seen her like this, even during the worst of middle school—like eighth-grade graduation when her mother's cell phone rang and she left just as Selena's name was called, telling another parent it didn't count since Selena was only ranked second. Selena had overheard. Even then, Selena had held her head high and gone home with Kayla as if she'd intended that all along. Or last fall, when a boy who'd had a crush on her started spreading rumors—she'd stood up to them, literally standing on a cafeteria table and systematically shredding everyone who'd spread the lies. She didn't embarrass easily. Kayla admired that about her. She was *never* breathless or embarrassed or whatever she was now. She always embraced her inner diva. Except around her parents. And now, apparently, with Sam.

Sam looked up from the phone. His gaze lingered on Selena before switching to Kayla. "You realize by bringing this to me, you're violating the manufacturer's warranty."

"Can you fix it?" Kayla asked.

"I can fix anything," Sam said. "Except her."

Kayla turned to Selena. "Selena?"

Selena examined her manicure and frowned at one fingernail. She was trying to pretend nonchalance and failing miserably. "Long story. Kind of boring."

"Short story," Sam corrected. "Not boring to me."

Selena winced. "Sam . . . I'm sorry."

Kayla didn't think she'd ever seen Selena apologize for anything. Ever. She looked slowly from Selena to Sam and back, feeling as if she'd tuned in after a commercial break and missed the show intro. "When my current crisis is over, I'll help fix this." She gestured at the air between Selena and Sam.

Sam frowned at the phone. He slid a tool into its side and

popped off the back. Holding it up to the light, he blew gently at its innards. "You can't."

"I can fix her," Kayla said confidently.

"In that case"—he picked up a tiny brush and gently cleaned the electronics—"this is free of charge."

Glowering at both of them, Selena waved her hands. "Hey, I'm right here. And I don't need fixing. I'm perfect in every way, in case you hadn't noticed."

Kayla ignored her. "What happened?" she asked Sam.

"I asked him out, okay?" Selena said. "And my parents said no. End of story. He's right; it was a short story. Can we please not talk about it?"

"Wait, *you* asked *him?*" Kayla said. "And you didn't tell me first? You tell me before you buy shoes. Where did you meet? What did he say? Why did your parents say no?"

"He fixed my phone, that's when we met," Selena said. "And he laughed at my jokes."

"Then her parents took one look at me"—he gestured at himself—"and no one was laughing anymore."

"Because you're white?" Kayla guessed.

"Because he doesn't wear shoes," Selena said. "And because he works here and barely pays his rent and can't afford a car that doesn't sound like it's murdering dolphins."

"Her Highness neglected to tell me that her parents are richer than God," Sam said. "When I came to pick her up, they looked at me like I was a bug smeared on the windshield of their Lamborghini."

"Bad analogy. Bugs don't touch the Lamb."

"Your parents like me," Kayla said. She'd never felt any disapproval from them, even though she lived in a cottage that was approximately the size of their master bathroom, even though she'd eaten her fair share of meals scrounged from the local restaurants' Dumpsters, and even though the closest she'd come to designer handbags was to the ones she'd pickpocketed.

"Yeah, but you don't have sperm," Selena said.

Kayla noticed a smile was pulling at the corners of Sam's mouth, and she decided that she liked him. Anyone who appreciated Selena's humor was a keeper. There weren't many boys who were more amused than intimidated by her. Or, really, any boys. "She's blunt," Sam commented.

"Always has been," Kayla said. "In sixth grade, she decided to catalog every one of my faults. She drew them up in a spreadsheet, marking off the frequency of behaviors that she found unlikable."

"What did you do?" Sam continued to fiddle with the phone, his hands working while his eyes were on them.

"I dumped sand in her bed."

Selena shuddered. "I can't stand unclean sheets."

Sam laughed, and the sound brightened the whole place. He transformed when he laughed, and Kayla saw the way her friend looked at him, as if she wanted to run into that brightness. He sobered. "So how do I convince her to confront her parents and tell them she wants to date me?" he asked Kayla. "Looking at her and listening to her, you'd never guess that she's afraid of anyone. But I bet she's never stood up to her parents in her life. Have you, princess?"

Kayla opened her mouth to defend her friend but couldn't. Selena never did break the law, stay out past curfew, or do anything to cross any lines with her parents. She was always talking about how she couldn't stand up to her parents; maybe she wasn't exaggerating. "And here I thought I was such a bad influence on you. I really have to work harder."

"I live vicariously through you. You know that." Selena had said that before, many times, but now Kayla thought her voice sounded a little sad.

Before she could reply, Kayla heard a familiar *bong*. Sam held up her phone triumphantly. "Fixed! You didn't break it. Just got dust where dust shouldn't be."

Kayla jumped off the stool and ran to the phone. She snatched it out of his hands and scrolled through the photos. The last one was the parchment. Immediately, she e-mailed it to herself and Selena as backup. "Thank you, thank you, thank you, Sam! I'll convince her to date you." Grabbing Selena's arm, Kayla propelled her out of the store and back to the car.

Selena got into the driver's seat. Hugging the phone, Kayla jumped into the car. "You're right! He works miracles!" She couldn't wait to tell Daniel.

Gripping the steering wheel, Selena stared straight ahead. "I wish you hadn't promised him *me*."

"Why not? You clearly like him. Also, why didn't you tell me? Can we get back to that?" Kayla asked. "I tell you everything. In minute detail. You even know the disaster that was my first kiss. Not to mention my first period. And of course the teeny tiny secret of my"—she made the ridiculous gesture for telekinesis that Selena had invented—"you-know-what that could get me killed if my father ever found out."

"I wanted to tell you, but . . . I like him. Really like him. And I didn't want to be teased about him, not until I knew if it would work. But then it didn't, and it was my fault, and I wanted to tell you—was going to vent to you, in fact, as you recall—but you weren't alone, and then after that . . . I was embarrassed, okay?" She said all this in a rush, as if the words were happy to escape. "I should be stronger, but I'm not. I'm not like you, master thief turned superhero. So I can't be with him. And you can't fix it because I *won't* disappoint my parents. They worked too hard for me to have all I have. They want me to have the opportunities they didn't and . . . I don't want to talk about it." Peeling away from Sam's store, Selena cranked up the radio so Kayla couldn't argue with her.

Looking again at her precious phone, Kayla studied the photograph. She'd fix Daniel's family first, and then she'd tackle Selena's. She could do it, she was sure.

She just wished she knew how to fix her own.

9

Selena parked in front of Kayla's house, and the music shut off abruptly with the engine. Before Kayla could say anything, Selena popped out of the car. Kayla stepped out too and spotted Daniel. He was leaning against the red gate, clearly waiting for her. He peeled himself away from the gate and crossed the sidewalk. His hands were jammed in his pockets, and his eyes drilled into Kayla. He didn't even glance at Selena.

He halted in front of Kayla. "Are you okay?"

"Yeah. You?"

"Sure. Yeah." A muscle twitched in his jaw. *Stormy*, she thought. She'd read novels where the guy had "stormy" eyes, and she never knew what that meant. But he had them. The colors in them reminded her of clouds closing over the sky. "Actually, no," he said. "I nearly got you killed, and I'm no closer to saving my mother. The police have no leads. They think maybe she walked out on her own. They're saying—" He cut himself off and gulped in air. "But I know she's still out there, and I know she's in danger. If you don't believe me, I don't blame you." He looked so very lost.

"Of course I believe you. Honestly, it's not like the whole cave-in and . . ." She trailed off as she suddenly realized that she hadn't had a chance to tell Daniel any of what had happened. "We should go inside. I have a lot to tell you, and I'd rather not do it out in the open."

"Your mother's home."

Kayla hesitated. She really wanted to be someplace she felt safe while they talked about this. The beach wouldn't work with him dressed like he was. She turned to Selena. "I hate to ask, but we need someplace private . . ."

"One condition." Selena held up a manicured finger. "I don't want to talk about Sam."

"Who's Sam?" Daniel asked.

"Exactly," Selena said.

Kayla glanced at the gate. If they stayed here too long, Moonbeam was bound to notice them. And Daniel needed to see what she'd found. "Fine. For now."

Selena hopped back into the car and turned on the engine. The music blared again. "Come on, guys, to the Bat Cave!" She patted the seat next to her.

"Shotgun." Kayla jumped into the passenger seat.

Daniel hesitated, then climbed into the backseat. It was more like a half seat, and he had to pull his knees up to his chin. Selena drove off, and the wind mixed with the music.

Crossing Santa Barbara, Selena took the curves fast, skimming the coast and then heading up into the hills near Montecito. Kayla felt the wind in her hair. The wind tasted like the ocean and like sunshine, so very different from the taste of dust and humidity in Tikal. Cradling the phone, she hoped the picture was worth what she went through to get it.

Selena's driveway wound up one of the hills. Palm trees lined either side, in between manicured flower beds. At the gate, Selena leaned over the side of the car door and punched in her combination. Kayla politely looked away, even though she could have broken the combo in less than a minute. The gate slid open, and Selena drove in.

Every time Kayla visited, she thought she should hear trumpets. Arriving at Selena's house felt like arriving at the palace for a ball. Her house was much more of a palatial complex than what Kayla called a "house." At least four buildings were visible from the driveway: the four-car garage, the maintenance shed, the guest cottage, and the house itself. Behind, there was also a pool house, a screened-in gazebo, and a Victorian-style doghouse for a dog that had died two years ago. Selena zoomed into the garage, parked, and hopped out.

The garage was the most spotless garage in existence, which Kayla thought was either because Selena's family had so much other space to shove their stuff or because Selena's mother prized neatness and had the money to buy it. It held beach chairs, a trash can, a tool bench with various tools, and four sparkly cars, including a Lamborghini and a Hummer.

Getting out of the car, Daniel whistled softly, admiringly, at the array of vehicles. "Are her parents home?"

"Selena wouldn't have brought us if they were," Kayla said quietly. "Her parents are firm believers in the study-more, socialize-less approach to life, even though Selena is always top of the class in everything. They have high expectations."

Outside, the driveway was pink cobblestones, and the gardens on either side were perfectly maintained with hibiscus and bird-of-paradise flowers every few feet. There was none of the overflowing green that Moonbeam favored. Each plant was neatly corralled in its own circle.

"You live here?" Daniel asked.

"Shut up and don't judge me." Selena strode toward the front door.

"She's a little sensitive about it," Kayla told him. "Rich-person guilt. Also, there's this guy—"

"No Sam!" Selena shouted.

Kayla shut up.

Daniel craned his neck as they entered the mansion. As much as Selena hated that kind of reaction to her house, Kayla couldn't blame him. It was worth some unabashed ogling. The foyer alone was impressive. It featured floor-to-ceiling mirrors and its own fountain beneath a crystal chandelier, as well as a grand staircase with an oil painting by Georgia O'Keefe on the wall. As a kid, Selena used to try to coax ducks to walk inside and use the fountain like they did at a hotel that her parents once took her to. She'd leave a trail of birdseed from the front door, and it was a constant battle between her and the maids to see how long the seed was allowed to dirty up the marble tiles. As far as Kayla knew, her parents never noticed.

"What do her parents do?" Daniel asked.

"Her mom founded some high-tech computer start-up that majorly took off, and her dad's a surgeon. I like them. Selena has a few issues with them."

"And the guy?"

"Reading between the lines, I'd say they're less than impressed with his career ambitions. Frankly, I don't think they'd be impressed with anyone. But they *do* want her to be happy, so if she—"

Selena shot a glare at Kayla. "This is exactly why I didn't tell you. Just drop it." She clomped through the house as if she were angry at it. Kayla followed behind with Daniel. She hadn't been here in weeks. Mostly, they met at Kayla's or at a café somewhere or on the beach. Selena didn't bring people home often, despite its being large enough to house their entire school. In fact, she was one of the only rich kids who didn't host keggers the second her parents were out of town. She never even had slumber parties. Her parents didn't approve of them. Kayla wondered how many things Selena hadn't done out of fear of disappointing her parents. She was good at making it seem like she made her own decisions. Before Sam, it hadn't seemed like such a big deal.

Instead of heading up to her princesslike room, Selena led them into the basement. She switched on the lights. Kayla's basement was a crawl space infested with about three billion spiders. Selena's basement was a game room, complete with billiards table, foosball, and Ping-Pong—all of which looked pristine, as if no one had ever played them. Absently, Kayla sent the foosball puck across the board with her mind. It slid into the opposite net with a clang. Selena shot her a glare. "Sorry," Kayla said.

Selena marched to the mammoth TV, which rivaled a movie screen, and sat next to a bank of computers, cable boxes, and stereo equipment. "Give me your phone." Kayla handed it over, and Selena messed with a few wires and plugs. Soon, the photo of the parchment was displayed on the giant screen.

Daniel sucked in air. "What—"

Kayla pointed at the screen. "This is what I found in the tomb. Luckily, I took the picture *before* some guy said a spell that flooded the chamber with light, stole the parchment and my backpack while I was blinded, and then caused the stairs to collapse when I chased him."

"Do you think it was the kidnapper? Or someone who works for him? Or just a coincidence? Do you think my mother was near . . ." He trailed off and gulped in air like a fish. "Why didn't you tell me?" Anguish filled his voice.

"Maybe because you snatched me out of there and dumped me home without giving me a chance? Anyway, this is why I believe you." She crossed her arms and stared at the image. It had three rows, each with glyphs and a series of dots. Above the glyphs . . . She squinted. "Are those letters? Selena, can you zoom in?"

The photo blurred and then steadied, closer in.

"Up," Kayla instructed.

Selena scrolled up, and then all three of them crowded in front of the wide screen to peer at actual, recognizable letters above the Maya glyphs. "I think it's Latin," Selena said. She scooted over to the computer and typed.

Daniel read out loud, *"Lapides tres, mors una."*

"'Three stones, one death,'" Selena said.

All of them stared at it again. "Guess that settles it," Kayla said. "It's not a smoothie recipe." Selena zoomed out so they could see the full parchment.

"Freaky," Selena said. "No way any Romans paddled to Guatemala a millennium before the Spanish. Are we voting aliens?"

"We're voting someone like me," Daniel said. "Queen Marguerite said a white man came where no white man should be. He'd seen an empire fall, she said."

Selena whistled. "Sweet. Wonder if he wore a toga." In a

more thoughtful voice, she added, "Guess the date wasn't a coincidence. Rome was falling then. Same year as the Battle of Adrianople, which did not go well."

Peering at the photo, Kayla said, "I think it's a map."

"Ooh, a treasure map? Should I get my eye patch and parrot?" Squinting at it, Selena frowned. "Nope, I don't see it. Totally doesn't look like a map."

Kayla pointed to the three rows of glyphs and dots. "Three stones. Three rows. Maybe each row is directions to finding one of the stones."

"Ooh, yeah, I like that theory," Selena said.

Daniel was looking at Kayla, not the parchment. "I can't believe you thought to take a picture of it. If you hadn't, we'd have nothing. Again, you are amazing."

Kayla felt her cheeks heat up in a blush. "Yeah, just born that way, I guess. Really, the parchment seemed fragile, and I thought it could be dust by the time I found you. I didn't expect to be robbed, then buried."

Selena pointed at a stylized face with a sloped, prominent nose and regalia on his head. "Okay, each row starts with the same image."

Kayla recognized the face from the murals inside the tomb. "Safe to assume that means the Great Jaguar Temple. I think that guy's the king."

"After that . . . look, these four glyphs repeat," Selena said. She was right. The same four glyphs repeated in a random order on all three lines, separated by dots. One glyph looked like a table on top of two clouds. Another looked like two clovers with a spout on top. A third was a snail with wings. And a fourth was a face looking at a wall with two clouds underneath.

"Any idea what they mean?" Kayla asked.

"Four glyphs on a treasure map? I vote they stand for east, west, north, and south." She typed fast and then opened and closed several browser pages until she stopped on one. "Yes, I am brilliant. You can all worship me now. I will accept sacrifices." She pointed to the computer screen. The glyphs were defined as four directional glyphs, exactly as Selena had predicted.

"I was the one who said it was a map in the first place," Kayla reminded her.

Selena graciously nodded. "You inspire my brilliance. Now what about the dots?" Each row had about fifty dots.

"Number of steps?" Kayla proposed.

"Miles?" Daniel said, simultaneously.

"The ancient Maya couldn't have measured in miles," Selena objected. "That's an English thing. Even though the English use kilometers now. It's basically just us. Because we're ornery."

"The marks have to mean something," Kayla said. "If the glyphs mean direction . . ."

". . . then the dots have to mean distance," Daniel finished.

"Exactly."

"Okay, so how did the Maya measure distance?" Selena typed and read, then typed more and read more. "Everyone's obsessed with how they measure time. And astronomy," she complained. "This might take a while. Help yourselves to snacks." She waved in the direction of a kitchenette and bar behind the billiards table.

Kayla frowned again at the photo. Each row ended on a dot. "Also, what do we do at the end of the trail? Highly doubt the stone will be just lying on the ground."

"X marks the spot?" Selena didn't look up from the computer.

"I think the key is those dots. If you're right that it's distance, then we need to know the units of measurement . . ."

Daniel was staring intently at the dots. "What if they're jumps?"

Both Kayla and Selena looked at him. Selena quit typing.

"The map was hidden where only someone like Kayla could find it," he said. "What if the stones are hidden where only someone like me can reach them? What if each mark is a jump?" He counted the dots. "Five jumps west. Twenty jumps south. Et cetera."

That . . . sounded completely plausible.

"How far can you jump?" Kayla asked.

"When it's a specific place I know or have seen a photo of, like Tikal, there's no limit. I just visualize it and I'm there. But otherwise, it depends how far I can see. On a flat plain . . . a few miles. On a mountain, maybe fifty? It has to do more with the topography than anything else."

"You've tested this?"

"Sure. Wouldn't you? Even tried jumping into the ocean once from shore. Nearly drowned. I was scooped out of the water by some fishermen. Interesting experience that I won't repeat."

Selena blinked at him. "I will avoid the cliché 'look before you leap' and just say it's a good thing you never tried to jump to the moon because your blood would boil and your brain would explode. Seriously, you didn't think the ocean would be full of water?"

Ignoring her, he said, "The tricky part with a jump like this—to a place I don't know and can't really see—is that it's draining. A thousand times worse than jumping to a place I know or have seen a photo of. I can hop around to familiar places all day and feel fine. But jumping to a spot on the horizon . . . there's just so little visually to focus on, you *feel* the miles as you jump. Makes it almost as exhausting as actually walking there."

"But is it doable?" Kayla pressed.

He studied the photo of the parchment. "Sure," he said at last. "And unless our ancient jumper had terrible eyesight or something, the jumps should be the same distance now as then. Unless you're in a city where your sight lines are blocked by skyscrapers, basic geography doesn't change all that much."

"So we go back to Tikal and start jumping? That's the plan?" Kayla asked. Her stomach clenched and unclenched. Was she really doing this? The man who caused the cave-in could still be there. Or worse, he could have already figured this out and be on his way to find the stones.

"You need beverages and snacks," Selena said. "Can't jump around in a jungle without water." She scurried to the minibar, found a nylon backpack from a technology conference, and filled it with water bottles and packets of pretzels. She shoved the bag at Daniel. "Oh, and let me print the photo for you. Multiple copies." She crossed to the computer and started to print. "You'll each carry one, and I'll keep one here." She handed them both the pages and also gave Kayla back her phone. "Give me your phone number, Daniel, and I'll text the file to you too." He gave them both his number, and Selena forwarded him the photo. "There. Now you don't have to worry about theft again. Just about cave-ins and other murder attempts." Selena hesitated. "You guys . . . You don't have to do this."

"Yes, I do," Daniel said gravely.

"Okay, yes, your mother, but Kayla . . ."

"I'm not going to live my life in fear," Kayla said. "I'm not Moonbeam."

Selena took a deep breath as if steeling herself. "Do you need me to come?"

Kayla shook her head. "I need you here to deflect Moonbeam if she calls—*when* she calls."

She exhaled. "Oh, thank goodness. I'm seriously not the heroic adventurer type. I'd be the sidekick that gets killed off so the heroine can be extra-motivated. Also, my mom is due home soon. So what do you want me to say to Moonbeam when she calls? Your mom is seriously hard to lie to. I don't know how you do it so easily." Quickly, she added, "Not that that makes you a bad person."

"Tell her I'm with you. I needed some beach therapy."

"And if this jaunt of yours takes longer than a trip to the beach?"

Kayla felt her face heat up. "Then tell her that I slept with him and I'm not ready to face her yet but I'm okay and not to call the police and not to run and hide." Cheeks blazing, she turned to Daniel. "All right. Let's go."

"Wait!" Selena said. "That guy has the same map. We figured it out in about seven seconds. He could too. What are you going to do if you see him again?"

"I doubt he can teleport," Daniel said. "We should have the advantage."

"But he has the parchment. Combine that with a topographical map . . . If you know the number of jumps and the contours of the land, it's not impossible to figure out. Just need some serious math skills. And then a plane or a helicopter. Kayla, you need a plan for what you do if you encounter him again."

Kayla pointed to Daniel. "He's my plan. No splitting up this time. I stick close to him, and if we're in danger, we jump out of there. I don't want more rocks on my head, thank you very much."

Selena nodded, appeased. "Much bravery in running the hell away." She pointed her finger at Daniel. "If you get my friend killed, I will personally have you drawn and quartered. I am dead serious. I know how it's done, and I have the horses to do it."

Impulsively, Kayla hugged her. "You are the best friend ever."

Selena patted her on the back. "Just the most bloodthirsty. Now go."

Kayla stepped away, and Daniel put his hand on her shoulder. White. Black. Green. And they were back in Tikal on the plaza in front of the temple. Heat slammed into Kayla. She felt as if she'd been shoved underwater. She gasped for air, and after a minute her breathing adjusted.

A man ran toward them, shouting in Spanish. He'd broken away from a group of men and women, mostly Guatemalans wearing khakis and holding shovels, who were clustered around a ring of vans. The site was crawling with people, many more than last time.

Kayla felt Daniel's grip on her shoulder tighten as the man switched to heavily accented English. "You! Not dead?" He called to people behind him in rapid-fire Spanish.

"Don't vanish," Kayla ordered Daniel.

"Are you sure?" Daniel asked.

"They've seen us. We can't!"

The man skidded to a halt in front of them. Others joined him, and Kayla watched their expressions switch very quickly from relieved to angry. She caught a few stray words tossed back and forth in Spanish. The workers had tried to rescue them, she gathered. They'd been presumed dead. A portly man jogged over to them. Sweat beaded on his forehead. He had a mustache that sagged as if from the heat over his mouth. It looked like a limp woolly caterpillar. He appeared to be Guatemalan as well, but he spoke to them in unaccented English. "What was this? Some kind of trick? You are in very big trouble. Very big. Damaging, irreparably, a national treasure. The cost of the rescue." He ticked off the items on his pudgy fingers. "Do you have any idea how many men were sent in after you? Do you have any idea how much bad PR you caused?" He continued to rant as he and the others propelled Kayla and Daniel across the plaza. On the opposite side of the plaza, where they were headed, Kayla saw a helicopter and a large group of people. Some were doctors. Some were police. Many held cameras with impressively weighty lenses, and several held professional-grade video cameras.

"Oh, no," Kayla muttered. "Daniel, I can make an exception. Get us out of here!"

He didn't argue. The world flashed white then black then beige, and in an instant, they were back in Selena's media room. She was at her computer. She spun around in her chair. "Guys, I think you missed. You're supposed to be in the jungle, remember?"

"I think we may have caused an incident." Kayla dropped Daniel's hand and strode across the room to the computer. "Can you look for Guatemalan news? Anything about an accident at Tikal?"

Selena searched. In less than a minute, she found it. She switched it from her monitor to the TV screen and swiveled in her chair. Kayla felt her heart sink. The cave-in. The rescue operation. And one photo, in profile and in motion, of Daniel's face, the friend of the victim. It was plastered all over Guatemalan news.

"This isn't good," Selena said. "How many people saw you this time?"

"Too many," Kayla said. "But I don't think the news cameras caught us."

"People snap photos all the time," Selena said. "You could be online right now." She started searching again.

Kayla felt ill. Her stomach flopped. "What do we do?"

"We have to go back," Daniel said. "That's where the map starts."

"But the whole area is swarming with people." Kayla took several long steps away from him, in case he got any ideas. "If you'd just rescued me like a normal person—"

"There would have been news and cameras then too, celebrating your survival," Daniel said. "I thought I was saving you from that, as well as the rocks that nearly crushed your head."

"I can't be caught on camera in Guatemala. Or anywhere. You don't understand. I can't be famous. Or infamous. Or have any kind of image of me out there. There's . . . someone looking for me."

Daniel fell quiet. "Your father."

"Yes." She tried to think of the words to convey how absolutely serious it was.

Before she could, Selena did it for her. "This isn't a joke. She really does have to hide. Her father killed her sister."

Kayla felt her breath stolen out of her lungs. That wasn't something she said out loud, ever. To hear it stated so casually . . . "I don't . . . we don't talk about it much. And he . . ." She swallowed. "I can't be on the news. Ever. He could see."

Daniel clearly didn't know what to say.

Not wanting to see pity in his eyes, Kayla went over to Selena's computer. Reaching over her to type, she brought up pictures of Tikal. "I bet Fire Is Born's great-grandkid—or whoever he was—started from the highest point in the area for the greatest visibility. So, can you jump us to the top of the Temple of the Great Jaguar? Skip the people and their cameras entirely."

"Heights are . . . difficult for me."

"Really don't want to be splattered all over the side of the temple. If you can't do it, we'll think of another idea." Not that she had any other ideas.

"I think I can do it. The top should be more stable than the steps."

Kayla studied him. Was she willing to risk her life and her happily unbroken bones on an "I think I can"? He was tense, she could see, but also intense. She wasn't sure she knew anyone as intensely focused on a goal as he was. It wasn't very Californian. On the other hand, she didn't think she knew anyone in such a serious mess. "Selena, do you have a compass? We'll need to identify west fast, before anyone notices us and points their cameras."

"Maybe with the camping supplies."

"You camp?"

"No one camps, except for people who hate to shower and families whose teenagers don't like them anymore but who desperately wish they did. Follow me."

The three of them traipsed through the house. Nearly to the front door, Selena held up her hand, motioning for them to stop. Kayla listened. Beside her, Daniel held his breath, as tense as a compressed spring. Footsteps echoed across the marble floor.

"Selena, are you home?" A woman's voice. Selena's mother. Kayla caught a glimpse of her in the foyer mirror. She wore a soft gray power suit and black heels. Her hair was slicked back into a tight bun. Her makeup was flawless. She made Kayla feel grubby and unkempt just by glimpsing her.

"Camping supplies are in the attic of the garage," Selena whispered. "I'll distract her." She waltzed out into the foyer. "I'm home, Mama."

Her mother's voice drifted into the hallway. As always, Kayla thought she sounded like a distant aunt who was faking polite happiness. She had a musical, lovely voice, but it was never warm, not like Moonbeam's. "Come give me a hug," Mrs. Otieno said. "You don't look well. Are you sleeping all right? Getting enough exercise? I left you those Pilates videos. Tell me you tried them."

Kayla heard the rustle of fabric.

"Ah, *mi chica*, you worry me. Are the classes going well? Did you sign up for more, like we talked about?"

"Yes, I'm sleeping and I'm exercising and I signed up for the classes. I'm fine. You don't need to worry so much," Selena said, her voice sad, as if she already knew what her mother was going to say next. When she talked to her mother, she sounded muted, as if the force of Mrs. Otieno's personality dampened Selena's own. In the hallway, Kayla listened, hoping that this time—

Kayla felt Daniel's hand squeeze her shoulder, and the house flashed. They reappeared outside, near the garage. He started in through the garage door, passing Selena's red convertible before Kayla had fully gotten her balance. Looking back once at the house, she darted in after him.

Inside, she saw Daniel had found a set of pull-down stairs next to the tool bench. He lowered the stairs, and their hinges squealed and squeaked, proof that even in a mansion, not everything worked perfectly smoothly. He climbed the stairs into the attic, and Kayla hurriedly followed.

The attic was crammed with piles of bags, stacks of boxes, and furniture, but even with all the junk, it was well organized and dust free. Kayla thought there was something not right about this much cleanliness. Lives needed a little mess in them. But it served her fine now. She spotted the camping gear in one corner. Climbing over bags and antique chairs, she reached it the same time Daniel did.

Side by side, Daniel and Kayla dug through the gear. She pocketed a new lighter, a few prepackaged trail rations, and a bottle of bug spray. She was glad she'd picked shorts with lots of pockets. Daniel was already carrying the water and snacks in Selena's backpack. Inside a box, Daniel found the compass. Holding it flat on one hand, he held out his other hand to Kayla. She took it.

In an instant, they were back in Tikal.

10

The view from the top of the Temple of the Great Jaguar was breathtaking—and not only because teleporting made her innards feel as if they'd been dumped in a blender. She held Daniel's hand as her equilibrium steadied. Before them the rain forest stretched off in all directions, an ocean of green with crests of white clouds. "First jump, west," Daniel said. He pointed to a peak on the horizon. She thought she heard the blades of a helicopter whirl and looked down to see that the crowd on the plaza had grown.

White. Black. And then green.

They stood on a stone ledge. Greenery filled the mountainside above and below them. She heard birds call to one another in elaborate trills. A monkey swung from one tree to the next, the branches bowing beneath its weight. Turning carefully—very carefully—Kayla saw Tikal far behind them in the distance, the stone tops of the ruins rising out of the jungle. He'd done it!

With luck, news of their appearance and disappearance would be confined to local stations and newspapers. It might not ever reach California. And with more luck, there might not be any photos of her. She could still make it through this with-out Moonbeam discovering the truth.

Above Tikal, the helicopter was a speck against the blue. "Look, the rescue copter is leaving! They've given up on us." Or it could belong to their enemy. Kayla thought of what Selena had said—all the kidnapper needed was the parchment, a topo-graphical map, and a plane or helicopter. She dismissed the thought. Much more likely that it was a rescue helicopter. Or from a news station.

"Think I'll skip looking," Daniel muttered. He pressed against the rock face of the mountain, away from the edge, the back-pack squashed between him and the rock.

"Where next?"

"South." Daniel checked the compass, fixed his eyes on a mountain that was due south, and they jumped to another peak. This time, they appeared on a slope of rock. Kayla caught her balance on the rocks and scraped the palms of her hands. Winc-ing, she rubbed the dirt off on her shorts. She glanced at Daniel. His jaw was clenched, and his eyes looked wild. Gripping her arm, he jumped again.

After three more jumps, Kayla had to break the silence. "What if the landscape was different when the ancient jumper hid the stones?"

"Mountains don't change that fast."

They jumped again.

"Visibility can be different from day to day," she argued. "If it was cloudier or foggier then or now, wouldn't that make a dif-ference?"

He shot her a glare and then consulted the photo again. "South." He jumped them again. "I think it's safe to assume he'd have picked a clear day for greatest visibility. He obviously wanted someone to be able to retrace his steps—otherwise, he wouldn't have left a map. Our jumps should be the same distance."

Kayla shook her head to clear her vision. The air was clammier here, and the heat sucked at her skin. The trees were spindly, and a barbed-wire fence ran along a dirt road. "Just saying that this might not work right away."

"Or at all," he said. "You can say it."

She didn't say it.

On the next jump, they reached the shore.

Waves crashed onto gray rocks. Palm trees bowed out over the ocean, and the water was a frothy blue. The rocks were slick with seaweed and ran into the water—there was no beach here. In the distance, mountains jutted up, seemingly out of the water, and white birds arced over the waves.

"Can I catch my breath?" With each jump, Kayla felt as if she were leaving a layer of herself behind. Daniel released her hand, and she sank down onto the rocks. She hung her head between her knees and let the crash of waves soothe her like it always did. She tried to imagine she was home on the Santa Barbara beach with Selena. The salt air tasted almost the same. "How can you stand it? Every time we jump, I feel like I've been shoved through a colander."

"The more familiar the destination, the easier the jump. These kinds of jumps . . . hurt."

She heard the exhaustion in his voice. She lifted her head to look at him, to see if he was all right. He was looking out across the water, and the wind was blowing his hair back. His eyes matched the ocean, dark and churning beneath a clear sky.

She wondered what was going through his head. "What's your mother like?" Kayla asked. "Are you close to her?"

He sank onto a rock and pulled out a water bottle from the backpack Selena had given them. He drank and then handed it to Kayla. She drank and then returned it. "She's the only family I have. She's . . . Well, she looks the opposite of yours, no offense meant. She's more like Selena's mother, from what I saw, minus the pricey jewelry. She only wears power suits, and I haven't seen her without makeup in years. She's always working, even when she's not. She has her cell phone glued to her. Not much choice. Academia is cutthroat, and she started late. I'm proud of her."

"She uses you for her travel, you said."

"I don't mind," he said quickly. "It's a good way for us to spend time together, you know? Anyway, maybe when this is over, she won't go anywhere for a while. She's been promising . . . Look, she is what she is, just like yours is what she is. I don't go around thinking I can change her. But she's my mother, and I know she'd do anything in her power to save me if the situation were reversed."

"You don't need to get defensive," Kayla said. "She's your mom. She doesn't have to be flawless for you to want to save her."

He was silent for a moment. "We fought the last time I saw her. Total cliché, right? You'd think I'd be racked with guilt and want to find her to say I'm sorry. But I don't. I mean, sure I'll say I'm sorry. But I just want to find her."

"I get that." Looking out at the water, she thought about Moonbeam. Kayla always tried to protect her too. She shielded her from the stuff the neighbors said, she secretly paid off bills with money she stole, and she made sure Moonbeam took her vitamins. "I'm sure your mother's okay."

"You don't know that."

"Not to be blunt, but if she weren't alive, her kidnapper wouldn't have known where to find the parchment or that they should steal it from me." She tried to sound convincing.

Daniel nodded, and for an instant, his face looked calmer, happier. But then the clouds rolled in again. "You may be right. But what did he do to her to find that out?"

Kayla didn't have an answer to that. She wanted to put her arms around him and hold him until the knots in his shoulders loosened and the wounded look in his eye faded, but she didn't know how he'd react. "We'll get there. I promise, it will be over soon." She pushed herself to standing and ignored the dizziness. "Okay, let's continue."

∾ ∽

Jump after jump, they traveled across Central America. Kayla guessed they'd left Guatemala, but she didn't know where they were. Honduras? Nicaragua? Wherever. She tried to drink in as many sights as she could: a rickety dock stretching into a blue-beyond-blue lake, a banana tree with leaves like elephant ears, a woman with red woven scarves and a cell phone that she dropped when she saw them, a mountain so peaked it could only be a volcano, a waterfall that fell hundreds of feet into a churning lake . . . Twice, they materialized on mountaintops that were so windy they had to clutch each other to keep from falling. Once, they appeared in a street in front of a donkey laden with sacks and beneath a billboard for shaving cream. Yet another time, they found themselves in front of a bulldozer in a half-torn-up field. It roared toward them like an animal, and Daniel had to jump them away fast.

After fifteen jumps, Daniel began to look pale. After twenty jumps, he swayed in between each one. After twenty-six jumps, he dropped to his knees. His eyes looked glazed. Kayla collapsed beside him onto the damp ground. They were in the rain forest, on a plateau that ended in a bluff. He'd managed to jump them to a flat area between the trees. She was grateful they hadn't appeared *in* a tree. Around them, insects buzzed, monkeys screeched, and birds called. Shadows stretched between the leaves. Beyond them, the sun was low in the sky. It stained the clouds a deep golden hue.

Kayla realized she was shaking, her muscles vibrating. She hugged her arms to try to stop them. "Daniel, you okay?" Her throat felt thick. She swallowed and tried the words again. "Are you okay, Daniel?" They came out clearer the second time.

He was shaking harder than she was. She crawled closer to him. "Never did . . . so many jumps like that. Just . . . overdid it. You feel it too? Need to rest—" He toppled to the side.

"Daniel!" She crawled to him. Leaning over him, she clutched his shoulders. "You need a hospital. Jump us to a hospital!"

His eyes were wide, as if he wasn't even seeing her. She didn't know if he could hear her. "Please, be okay. Stay calm. I've got you." She wrapped her arms around him and held him as tightly as she could, as if her arms were all that was keeping him together. He shook harder, nearly convulsing. His breathing was fast, too fast, and his skin felt hot to the touch. He sweated against her, and his arms shook like branches in a high wind.

She didn't know how long she held him, but at last his shaking subsided into tremors, and then he stilled in her arms. His breathing slowed until he was breathing normally and slowly. "Daniel?" she whispered.

He didn't respond.

"Come on, talk to me, please, wake up. Please."

She rolled him gently onto the mat of leaves that blanketed the forest floor, and she looked around them. She had no idea where they were, or if they were near anything or anyone. She pulled out her phone—no signal. Of course no signal. She didn't even know what country she was in. Panic squeezed her, and she felt her heart thump faster and faster, as if it wanted to gallop out of her chest. "Help! Someone, please help!"

The birds and the monkeys fell silent. And then they resumed, as loud as before.

Soon, it would be night, and their only ticket out of here was asleep or unconscious or . . . He wasn't dead, thank God. But he wasn't in any condition to jump, and she had no way of knowing how long he'd be out. Lying down next to him, she listened to him breathe. Maybe he only needed to rest. He'd wake soon.

He didn't.

It grew darker. Shadows overlaid more shadows. The jungle shrieked and shook. Beside Daniel, Kayla pushed herself up onto her knees. Her stomach ached, and her tongue felt swollen and dry. Clouds of insects swirled around them, and she sprayed every inch of her and Daniel's exposed skin with Selena's bug spray. It smelled sickly sweet, and it didn't seem to deter the bugs. There were more and more of them as dusk fell. She looked directly up at the tiny patch of deepening blue visible through the canopy of leaves. A star already poked through.

Think, Kayla.

She'd never been camping before, at least not since she was a kid. Fleeing from home with Moonbeam, she'd slept in cars and barns and abandoned mobile homes, but she'd never slept out in the open. Certainly never in a rain forest. There could be snakes here. And jaguars. And more snakes. She needed a fire. As soon as she had the idea, she seized it as if it were a lifeline in a stormy sea. A very green, very insect-ridden sea. Animals would be afraid of a fire, wouldn't they? And it would keep the darkness at bay.

Sounds filled the darkening rain forest: cries and growls and shrieks and caws from animals and birds that she had no way to identify. Insects buzzed around them so loudly that they sounded like radio static turned high. She tried batting them away with her mind. It wasn't easy. Unlike the grains of sugar, the mosquitoes and gnats swirled in swarms. Plucking them out of the sky, she flung them away. She devoted a portion of her mind to that task and sent the rest of her mind out into the growing darkness to find dry wisps of plants that she could use as tinder. Focusing on two things at once kept her from panicking more.

On the undersides of fallen trees, she found bits of stringy bark and, beneath branches, she found a few dead leaves that hadn't been soaked. Concentrating, she made each leaf float to her lap and then she rolled them together into a loose bundle. Once she had a handful, she left it next to Daniel and lurched to her feet. She still felt shaky from all the teleporting, but after a few steps, her head cleared. Searching close by, she picked up every twig she could find. She was careful to avoid the bluff— last thing she needed was to fall and break her neck. She carted it all back to Daniel and then gathered some thicker branches. She'd never made a fire before, but the concept seemed obvious: start with tinder, then move to twigs, then to thicker wood. Clearing an area beside her and Daniel, she placed her tinder in a nice neat pile and pulled out her lighter. Her hands were shaking as she flicked the flame to life and held it to the tinder.

It caught and then it died.

She tried again. This time, she caught the flame with her mind and forced it to touch the driest bit of bark. It sparked a second flame, and she nursed it as it spread through the tinder. Carefully, she laid sticks against her tinder. It smoldered and then died.

She swore, loudly.

Daniel shifted in his sleep. Abandoning the fire, she hurried to his side. "Daniel? Are you awake? Are you okay?" He moaned—that was a good sign, wasn't it? She felt his forehead. He still felt too hot. Mosquitoes hovered angrily around both of them. Concentrating, she repelled them with so much force that she heard them smack in a swarm against a tree.

She turned back to the fire. Now, she was determined to light it. She knew it was irrational, but she felt as though if she lit it, then he'd wake and everything would be okay.

Again, she flicked on the lighter. But this time, she coaxed the flame onto the tinder and, as it grew, forced it to split into multiple embers. Then she took each new bit of fire and set it on the wood. Slowly, it caught. Ignoring the insects and the sounds and the darkness, she nursed the fire until it spread and grew.

By now, the sky had deepened to near black, and the forest around them had fallen into complete darkness. Night was louder than day, full of calls and cries and rustling. Under her coaxing, the fire roared higher. Sitting back, Kayla hugged her knees. Her stomach rumbled, and her mouth felt dry. She took out the trail rations that she'd taken from Selena's camping supplies and pulled out one of the futuristic-looking packets. Freeze-dried ice cream. Kayla tore it open and ate half, letting the chalky sweetness dissolve on her tongue. She chased it with a sip of water. Daniel continued to sleep, and Kayla returned to methodically flinging the mosquitoes away from them. It helped keep her from thinking too hard about where they were . . . or what she'd do if he didn't wake.

After a while, she lay down next to the fire. Hopefully, Moonbeam would assume she was spending the night with Selena. Of course, she'd call to check up. She always did. And if Selena didn't think to lie . . . Or worse, if Selena herself worried enough to call Moonbeam to see if Kayla was back . . . It would take an act of supreme luck for Moonbeam not to find out she was missing overnight. And if she did find out, she'd assume the worst. She'd call the police, and she'd prepare to run. She'd pack their most generic clothes, as well as the supplies to create false paperwork for new identities. She wasn't a good enough forger to create anything that would hold up in court, but it would be good enough to get Kayla into school and rent a place from a not-overly-scrupulous landlord.

Regardless, there wasn't anything Kayla could do about it right now. Curling up near the fire, Kayla closed her eyes and listened to Daniel's shallow breaths. *Please wake*, she thought. *Please wake*. She repeated it like a mantra until she too fell asleep.

She woke minutes or hours later. It was dark, and the fire was down to embers. For an instant, she lay still, unsure if she was asleep and stuck in a nightmare or not.

With her mind, she picked up the embers, spread them to new wood, and held them there until the flames spurted up again.

Across the fire, the orange glow of the flames reflected off two shiny disks staring out of the darkness. Kayla heard a low growl, and a jaguar emerged from the bushes.

Her mind scattered, and the fire sputtered. Carefully, she reached toward the flames again, growing them higher. She didn't move a muscle. She stared into the jaguar's eyes as it paced back and forth on the opposite side of the fire. Teeth poked out as it curled its lips back.

Her heart pounded hard in her chest. She wrapped her mind around one of the embers and lifted it into the air. The cat paced closer. She flung the ember toward the cat's face. She hit its nose, and the cat recoiled. She grabbed a second ember and threw it. The jaguar yelped. She continued to pelt it with bits of fire until it retreated into the shadows.

She heard it pacing in the brush. Leaves rustled, and twigs snapped. Tense, listening, she wished she knew exactly where it was, then it occurred to her that maybe she could "feel" for it, like she'd felt for her phone after the cave-in. Sending her mind into the darkness, she swept around their makeshift camp— and she felt it, close, very close. Kayla cast about for an idea. She picked up the bug spray and waited.

Snarling, the jaguar stalked closer. With her mind, Kayla lifted an ember into the air. As the jaguar stepped out of the bushes, she sprayed the insecticide at the ember. Fire whooshed, flaring like a firework, and she propelled the flame toward the cat.

Yowling, the jaguar spun and vanished into the darkness. She sat awake for a long time after that, listening hard, probing the area with her mind. She wished she'd realized that she could "feel" around her like this before the cave-in. If she'd known, that man wouldn't have been able to surprise her. She built the fire back up as high as she could.

Sometime, somehow, she fell asleep again. Her dreams were filled with jaguars and fire and rocks and darkness and Moonbeam crying until she melted like ice cream into a river.

11

Kayla woke to the cries of monkeys in the trees above them. Daylight poured into the rain forest. Beside her, the fire had died, and her hair lay close to the ash. A few embers smoldered. Her head ached, and her mouth felt as dry as paste. Groaning, she began to push herself up.

"Don't move," Daniel whispered.

She froze.

"Snake."

She breathed shallowly, every muscle rigid. "Where?"

"On your foot."

Kayla tilted her head to look down her body. Coiled on her left sneaker was a snake with black and red stripes separated by thin yellow stripes. "Jump me out of here."

"I can't. Not while it's touching you. It'll come too."

She reached with her mind and wrapped her thoughts around the snake. It felt smooth and dry. And heavy. Heavier than anything she'd ever lifted before. Its tongue flicked in and out, and it regarded her with flat black eyes. Gathering every bit of inner strength she had, she tried to fling it away with her mind—and pain blossomed in her skull. Her muscles spasmed.

She felt a sudden prick in her calf, like a shot from a doctor. Yelling, Daniel touched her, and the world flashed white then black.

Her vision didn't resolve. It stayed blurred. The world seemed to be dipping and spinning. She saw colors, so many colors, and she heard Daniel shouting at her. Her mouth tasted like copper, as if she'd sucked on a penny. She felt bile churn in her throat. Oh, God, she was going to be sick. Or faint. Or die. Her throat felt as if it were constricting, and she gasped. She flailed, trying to grab someone, anyone, to steady her, and she felt arms around her.

"Snake," she heard Daniel tell someone. "Coral snake, I think."

A woman's voice answered. And then she heard more words, sonorous and melodic. The words wrapped around her as darkness rose to claim her. She felt her body turn rubbery, and she melted into the floor. "Moonbeam?" she whispered, or tried to. She smelled incense, myrrh. And then there was only darkness chasing the pain.

She didn't know how long she floated there, in that dark sea. But her thoughts chased through it like fish. Moonbeam. Selena. Amanda. She kept seeing her sister, the once vague memories now crystal clear. Amanda, playing school with her: Amanda as the teacher and Kayla as the student. Their dolls were the other students. Amanda liked to be the boss. Other times, they'd sing together into microphones made from the cardboard rolls in paper towels. Kayla would be three backup singers at once. On her fifth birthday, Amanda made her a paper crown, and they had their own coronation ceremony, complete with imaginary knights and horses. The summer that Kayla turned six, Amanda taught her how to ride a bike. Kayla also remembered fighting with her over stupid things—toys that broke or lipstick that neither of them was supposed to wear—and screaming at her to play with me, talk to me, pay attention to me! And Amanda screaming back that she wasn't her mother or even her friend. But then they'd be together again, curled up in the same bed, Amanda reading a bedtime story to Kayla while Moonbeam looked on. Except she wasn't Moonbeam back then. She was Mom.

When Kayla woke, she was crying.

A woman held her, and Kayla sobbed against her plump chest. When she drew back, she saw it wasn't Moonbeam at all. It was the voodoo queen. Queen Marguerite pushed her hair away from her forehead. "Better now?" she asked in her deep drawl.

"Am I dying?" Kayla asked.

"Not anymore. Your boy did the right thing, bringing you to Queen Marguerite. She knows just how to leech that poison out of you. You're healthy as a mule now." Her accent thickened when she talked about herself in third person, as if she were deliberately trying to sound more familiar and comforting. It worked. Kayla felt herself relax.

"I heard a spell," Kayla said.

"There's a spell that encourages a kind of sleep—that's what you heard—and another that draws the toxins out. Requires a certain special herb, which you yourself preserved when you cleaned my shop, little fixer."

Kayla scanned the room, looking for Daniel. He was by a window, watching her. His expression was shadowed. He had bruiselike circles under his eyes as if he hadn't slept, and his hair stuck up at all angles. He didn't look happy she was awake.

Beyond him, outside the window, she saw an alleyway with cobblestones, garbage cans, stacks of boxes and crates, and the rear entrances to shops and restaurants. A cat perched on a crate. Kayla belatedly realized she was in New Orleans.

"I won't blame you if you quit," Daniel said. She knew how much it cost him to say that. He looked so very alone by the window, angled light spilling onto the floor at his feet. She wanted to say something, anything, but her throat felt clogged.

Queen Marguerite pounded her cane on the floor. "She can't quit!"

Both Kayla and Daniel looked at her.

Instantly, Marguerite schooled her expression into a laid-back smile. "You may have done a nice cleaning job, but saving a life, well, that requires more. You owe Queen Marguerite, and I need my payment. You can't quit."

Kayla felt prickles walk up and down her spine and wondered why she cared so much. She thought she'd heard a note of real panic in Marguerite's voice. "I wasn't going to."

"Why not?" Daniel asked.

Kayla opened her mouth and then shut it. He deserved a real answer. He'd saved her life. Maybe that was why she wasn't going to quit? Or maybe it was because he wasn't really that cool, tough guy who'd blackmailed her. Or because when he talked about his mother, she saw herself. Or because he needed her. Or because with him, she could use her power and have it mean something. Or maybe it was because she'd hated how she felt in the dark temple when the cave collapsed and how she felt in the jungle when she'd woken with the snake, and she couldn't let that feeling win. "I don't like being afraid."

"I understand," Daniel said. He held her gaze, and, for a moment, Kayla felt as if they were alone together. The rest of the world faded away. Then he turned to face Queen Marguerite. "It's my mother who's in danger. What does it matter to you whether Kayla quits or not?"

Marguerite's smile faded, and she rose. "That spell shouldn't exist. Even incomplete, it causes a burden that no one should have to bear. But complete . . . it will change lives. *Your* lives, whether you want it to or not. People will suffer. Empires have risen and fallen with that spell. Cities have burned. It's an abomination. You need to find those stones, bring them to me, and I will see them hidden where no one will ever find them." She thumped her cane again. "I must do this! You children don't understand—"

"Then explain to us," Daniel said.

Abruptly, as if something had upset her, Marguerite walked to the window, clasped her hands behind her, and looked out. In a quieter voice, so quiet that Kayla had to strain to hear, she said, "I hate thinking of Evelyn all wrapped up in this again. She came so far in escaping her past. Your father was good for her. So different. Shame he died. If he hadn't, she might have stayed focused on the future, instead of turning back to the past." All trace of the affected persona was gone, and Kayla felt as if she was seeing a rare glimpse of the real Marguerite.

"You knew my father?" Daniel asked. "What do you mean 'wrapped up in this again'?"

"Oh, her history with those stones goes way back," Queen Marguerite said. "And it should have stayed history. Told her she should have left it alone. Smart enough to do anything she wanted, that girl. But no one ever could tell Evelyn what to do. Never could, once she got an idea in her head. Led her into trouble once. Looks like it led her into trouble again." Cutting herself off, she bustled back to Kayla and poured her a glass of orange juice. "You ask her about it when you find her."

"The more you can tell me . . ."

"It's not my story to tell. And anyway, it won't help you in your search." She tapped Kayla on the forehead. "Stay focused. Don't be distracted by the past. Eat food, and then go. You are running out of time. Your enemies speed toward your destination, and your mother needs you." She vanished before Kayla or Daniel could ask her more questions.

"Why do I feel like she knows more than she says?" Daniel asked.

"Because she obviously knows more than she says." Kayla pushed herself up to sitting. Stretching out her legs, she pointed and flexed her toes. Everything seemed to work okay. She even felt less tired than she had, perhaps due to the magic-induced sleep. "But so long as she wants what we want, it doesn't really matter." Pushing the blanket off her, she examined her leg where she'd felt the bite. Two red-brown scabs dotted her calf. She hadn't imagined it.

"Used to wonder what my mother would have been like if my dad hadn't died," Daniel said. "She switched to anthropology then. Got her PhD. If she hadn't done that, if she hadn't kept that notebook, if she'd never heard of the stones . . . What 'history' with the stones?"

"You can ask her when we find her." She put an emphasis on the word "when."

Daniel exhaled loudly but didn't say anything else.

Kayla looked around. Queen Marguerite had left her a tray with a few croissants plus a jar of blackberry jam. It was balanced on an upside-down barrel. The room they were in seemed to be for storage. It had shelves filled with jars, bins, and boxes, labeled with the names of powders, herbs, and roots. A few skulls sat on one shelf, decorated with feathers and black paint. Symbols from various religions were nailed to the door.

"We're in the back room of her shop," Daniel said. "It's impressive how much she's fixed already. Except for the missing glass on the display cases and a few broken shelves, it's like it never happened. I don't know how she did it in such a short period of time. I think there's more to Queen Marguerite than meets the eye."

"I think you saved my life," Kayla said.

"Couldn't remember a hospital well enough. But I knew here." Leaving the window, he crossed to her and took her hand. He caressed her fingers. "How do you feel? Really. Because I'll take you home. Right now if you say so. Forget what Queen Marguerite said. This is none of her business."

She smiled at him. He sounded like he meant it. "They're speeding toward our destination, she said. Can you jump again, or do you need to rest?"

"I'm all right. But you—"

"Let's get this over with. I'm rapidly losing my desire to travel."

"You're an amazing girl, you know that?" His eyes bored into hers as he held her hand, his hand so warm. She thought his eyes seemed damp, as if he'd cried, and she wondered how close she'd been to dying.

They jumped back to Central America.

∾ ⌀

Reappearing with Daniel next to the remnants of their fire, Kayla sent her mind through the camp, searching for the snake. It wasn't there. "All clear. But be careful anyway."

Quickly (and carefully), they reclaimed their supplies and continued on.

Rain forest.

A turquoise lake.

Gnarled trees with brown fruit next to a house made of blue cement blocks.

More jumps. And more. At last, they reached a field of yucca-like plants with green mountains in the distance. Here, they stopped. Kayla plopped onto the ground. Rubbing her neck and shoulders, she watched Daniel consult the photo of the parchment. He looked pale but not in immediate danger of collapse.

One jump left, if she'd been counting right.

She watched him breathe in, steady himself, and then exhale. She wanted to say something, but she wasn't sure what would help. She couldn't tell him to stop. Not when they were so close. "What's the first thing you're going to say to her when you see her?" Kayla asked.

"I don't know," he said. "Do I need a 'first thing'?"

"Guess not."

"Whatever it is I say, you don't need to be there to hear it. Once we have the stone, you're done. I'll tell the voodoo queen you repaid your debt."

"But she wants all three stones."

"I don't care what she wants," he said. "I want—" His voice cracked, and he looked at the mountains. Several of them had serrated points, as if they wanted to slice the sky. Clouds drifted in wisps around them.

"Daniel . . . this is going to work. We're going to save your mother." She didn't know when she'd switched from thinking he was the biggest jerk ever to actually caring about what happened to him, but she wanted, more than anything, to banish the hurt look that always haunted him. Saving his mother would do that.

"I know. And it's thanks to you. You're the bravest person I've ever met. Fear doesn't stop you." He looked at her with so much admiration in his eyes that she felt her cheeks heat up.

She changed the subject. "So, where are we? Do you have any idea?"

"Peru, if I calculated correctly."

"Seriously?" She might be lousy at geography, but she knew that was far from Guatemala. "Are those the Andes?"

"Yeah, I think so. The jumps have averaged about thirty to fifty miles each."

"Cool. Let's finish this." Standing, she crossed to him.

Daniel was facing the mountains again. "What if the stone's not there? What if this is the one that the kidnapper already has? Or if someone found it already and it's elsewhere? Or what if we're wrong about the parchment? Or if I jumped wrong? If I got even a single jump too long or too short—"

Kayla put her hand across his mouth. "Shut up and jump." She lowered her hand and held his arms. He put his hands on her waist. Looking into her eyes, he jumped—white, black, gray. Kayla stayed in his arms as the world switched and shifted.

Daniel loosened his grip but didn't let go. Kayla looked around them at the rocky mountainsides. Stiff plants like yucca clung stubbornly to the shattered rock face, making the rock walls look striped. Above, green vines and thick mats of leaves hung over the cliffs. Orchids were bright spots of color in the green and gray—bits of fragile beauty in a hostile landscape. All around them were mountains of rock and, in the distance, ice.

The air felt cooler and thinner. She took one deep breath after another. "Now what?" Kayla asked.

"I don't know." He wasn't looking at the mountains; he was looking at her. At last, he released her, as if he were letting go of a life raft, and he turned to see the view. They were on a mountain, above a valley with a winding river.

Kayla scanned the cliffs. She didn't want to admit out loud that he could be right—he could have easily miscalculated one or more of the jumps . . . Then she saw it. "It's there." Kayla pointed high, impossibly high, up on a mountainside on the opposite side of the river. There was a structure, clearly manmade, tucked under a cliff. No path led to it. It was simply embedded into the side of the mountain.

It looked like a one-room hut made of yellow and brown bricks. It was decorated with a stripe of stones laid in a triangle pattern and painted yellow and red. Two statues with elongated faces flanked the doorway, suspended on the sheer mountainside.

"I know where we are," Daniel said, hushed.

"Where?" Kayla asked.

"The tombs of the Chachapoya, the People of the Clouds. My mother wrote a paper about them last winter. I jumped her to Lima, and she hired locals to lead her through the jungle. She said she reached the tombs by dangling on a rope from above. No one knows how the Chachapoya built them so high up. Or why. But she was fascinated by them."

"Do you think she's been here before?" Kayla asked. She didn't voice the follow-up question of whether his mother had already found the stone.

"There are tombs like this throughout the eastern Andes. She was a lot farther south."

"Maybe she knew the stone was here but not exactly where?"

Daniel drew away. "My mother wasn't looking for the stone." His voice was sharp, as if she'd insulted him. "The Cloud People had rituals that she was studying. She studies cultures all over."

"Okay, fine. And that notebook she burned just had pictures of kittens. Can you jump us to the opening?" She shielded her eyes from the glare of the sun. "Looks like there's a ledge for the doorway. Just don't lean backward when you arrive. We can fall inside."

He didn't answer.

Kayla looked at him. He'd paled. His hands shook. He was breathing heavily, and not just because of the thinner air. "Hey, you can do this. You did it at Tikal. That's not so different."

"Yes, it is. It's like jumping onto a balance beam."

"Okay, yes, it's skinny, but—"

"The temple had a landing that was several feet wide. This has inches. If I miss . . ."

It *did* drop away to a sheer cliff beneath the tomb. It could crumble under their weight. "Keep hold of me," Kayla instructed. "If it seems at all unstable, then jump us back here, and we'll think of something else."

"Can't jump when all I'm thinking about is how I could fail."

"Then think of something else. Distract yourself."

His mouth quirked into a sad half smile. "You make it sound so easy."

"It is easy! You just jumped us across all of Central America. We're on a new continent! Don't you have any idea how amazing that is? How amazing *you* are? You can do this!"

He shook his head. "My mom thinks I'm a freak."

"What?"

"I heard her talking once, on the phone, to someone. A friend. Someone who knew. And she was saying how she didn't know what to do with me, that I was born as wrong as someone with a genetic disease and it was her fault for having me in the first place. I never told her I heard that conversation."

"You don't know the context," Kayla said. "Sometimes people say things for reasons you don't know." Still, it must have hurt for Daniel to hear his mother say that. Every time Moonbeam told her not to use her power, as if it were something shameful and wrong, as if *she* were wrong, Kayla felt herself shrink inside. "Anyway, she's right. You and me, we are freaks. But we're freaks who are going to do this!"

He was shaking his head. "It will be a self-fulfilling prophecy. I can't stop thinking about missing the ledge and falling. It's like trying not to think about a pink elephant when someone tells you don't think about a pink elephant—"

Kayla put her hands on his cheeks and drew his face down to hers. She pressed her lips against his and kissed him.

An instant later, he was kissing her back.

His lips were soft, and his hands held her as if to keep her from falling. He tasted like cinnamon and a little like sweat. She felt his heart beating against hers. Wind blew around them, and she heard birds call, their voices caught and spun away by the wind. She breathed with him, and they kissed as if it could anchor them to the earth.

Breaking apart, Kayla said, "Do it."

White. Black. Gray.

12

Don't move. Don't fall. Don't breathe. Her vision swam—she saw gray, only gray. She felt wind hit her back . . . Behind her was the cliff and open air. Forward was the tomb.

Pitching herself forward, Kayla pulled Daniel inside with her. He collapsed onto his knees just inside the opening and panted. "I. Hate. Heights."

"Noticed that." She untangled herself from him, then got to her feet. It was darker inside, shadows washing out everything. Slowly, her eyes adjusted.

The tomb was small and shallow. Just a single notch in the stony mountains, skinnier than Selena's walk-in closet. Along one side, bundles of sticks were lashed together with ropes— three of them, each taller than Kayla. Spears lay next to them, crossed as if ritualistically. Other objects filled the tomb: pottery, half-disintegrated baskets, frayed blankets, old ropes. One of the bundles was wrapped in burlap-like fabric and then lashed with braided ropes. At the top, the ropes had been sewn in the shape of a face: eyes, nose, and mouth.

Belatedly, Kayla realized they weren't bundles of sticks.

They were bodies, wrapped in cloth and sticks. Dead bodies. Mummies. "Great, more nightmare fodder." If she'd still hated Daniel, she would have added that to the list of things he owed her for. Instead, she merely looked away, scanning the tomb for the spell stone.

It was easy to find stones. Rocks of all sizes, shapes, and colors littered the tomb floor. The walls themselves were uneven stone, as if the tomb had been made by someone hacking away at the mountain with a pickaxe, which may have been exactly what happened. "Do you know what the stone looks like?" she asked.

"My guess? It's hidden in a way only you can find it." He smiled at her, a sunny smile, happier than she'd ever seen him. It made him look as if a halo surrounded him. She wanted to fall into that smile. It made her want to frolic through fields with him, and Kayla had never frolicked through a field in her life. *Oh, good grief, am I falling for him? How completely prosaic.*

"Quit looking at me that way," she snapped. "I can't concentrate."

He kept smiling. "What way?"

"Like you want to spin me around and sing Disney songs."

He held up one finger. "Spinning here might be dangerous. Could hit a corpse." He held up a second finger. "I don't sing. Much less Disney songs."

"Never? Not even in the shower."

"Not even in the shower. Unless it's a really good song." His expression turned serious, and he took her hand and kissed her knuckles. "Come on, Kayla. Save me. Save my mother. I know you can do it. *This* is why she told me to find you."

Taking a deep breath, Kayla closed her eyes and tried to

concentrate. Daniel was still holding her hand. She liked the way his palm felt against hers, the way his fingers curled so naturally around her hand, the way it made her arm feel warm all the way up to her shoulder. She'd thought she'd never want to see him again after this was over. Maybe she should reconsider that. *Stop thinking about him,* she ordered herself. She shook away his hand, opened her eyes, and sent her mind out.

Her mind ran over the rocks and the walls. It skittered over the corpses. The cloth wrappings "felt" brittle, and the ropes so dry that they were mostly air. She reached up toward the ceiling— and in the far corner, she found a fissure.

Her mind flew up the fissure. It was a thin shaft, not unlike the one she found in the temple. She touched the sides of the rocks. Several feet up, she felt glyphs, Maya glyphs, beneath a ledge. "Gotcha," she whispered.

"Do you have it?" Daniel asked.

"Don't get your hopes up. It could be another parchment." But her heart was pitter-pattering in an overly optimistic way. Reaching for him, she squeezed his hand, and he squeezed hers back. She reached up with her mind onto the ledge . . . and felt a triangular stone. "Yes!" She tried to pull it out. Immediately, her brain felt as if it were stabbed by sharp sticks. She stopped. *"Ow.* No, too heavy." Leaning over her knees, she rubbed her forehead.

Daniel's face was ashen. "So that's it? We came this far and fail now?"

Lifting her head, she gave him a withering look. "I swear you're more melodramatic than my mother. It just means that we have to get it down in a more clever way. Gravity will help. Things want to fall. We just have to convince the rock that it's one of those things." She scanned the tomb, looking for what she could use. "I need that rope." She pointed to the braided rope around one of the mummies.

Immediately, he crossed to the closest mummy. Ancient, priceless pottery crunched under his feet. She contemplated saying something, but . . . priorities.

"Here, cut it off with this." She flew the razor blade out of her pocket and dropped it into his open hand. He unwrapped it from the tinfoil, then sawed through the rope until he had a length of several feet. He tossed the rope to her. She lifted the razor blade and the tinfoil out of his hand, rewrapped it in mid-air, and flew it back into her pocket.

The rope was as light as she'd hoped, made of long-dried plant fibers that had lost most of their weight when they lost their moisture. She tied one end into a noose.

"You're going to lasso it," he guessed.

"Bingo. Give the boy a gold star." She laid her hands flat, the rope draped across her palms. Even as light as it was, it was still heavier than the thread she usually used. As she concentrated, bright spots of pain sparked across her mind. She exhaled, shook her head to clear it, and then tried again.

The rope rose up the shaft. She snaked it up, up, up, until it reached the ledge. Gritting her teeth, she looped it around the stone, then she released her mental grip on it and staggered backward as pain blossomed through her mind. Daniel caught her. His arms were warm and strong around her. She told herself to quit noticing that and get back to work. She shrugged him off and climbed over pottery and other artifacts until she was directly beneath the shaft. Using her hands instead of her mind, Kayla yanked on the rope. It slid to the bottom of the stone. She fixed it in place with her mind as she used her arms to pull the stone forward. It scooted to the edge, tottered, and then fell.

Hands up, Kayla caught it.

"You did it," Daniel said, hushed.

"Can't take all the credit. You got us here." She couldn't take her eyes off it. The stone was a carved triangle that fit neatly into the palm of Kayla's hand. It was a luminous black and had one smooth side and two serrated sides, as if it were meant to fit into a puzzle. Holding it up to catch the weak light from the doorway, she saw deep colors dancing within it beneath almost-letters that blurred if you looked directly at them. No question about it: this was it! She handed the stone to Daniel.

"You just . . ." He took it, fumbled it, and then clutched it to his chest. "This stone is immensely powerful." He looked flummoxed, as if he hadn't expected her to just give him the stone.

"So what? I don't want it. It's yours. You need it."

He opened and shut his mouth like he was a speechless fish.

"Why are you looking at me like that? Did you honestly think I wasn't going to give it to you?" Oh, fantastic. What did he think of her? "I'm a thief, not a jerk."

"There's something I need to tell you." He licked his lips as he hesitated. "I haven't been fully honest with you. But I . . ." He looked away from her, out the doorway to the white clouds that hung low in the sky, filling the valley between the mountains. "Thank you for this. My mother was right that I couldn't have done it without you. And I do, really do, think you're the most amazing girl I've ever met."

She felt a tightness in her stomach. She didn't know what was coming next, but she knew it would be bad. "That's sweet, but what weren't you honest about?"

"I'm not going to keep the stone safe," Daniel said. "I'm going to trade it for my mother." He said it fast, as if the words were escaping the confines of his throat.

Her stomach unknotted. That was it? "Good. That's sensible."

He blinked at her. "Really? You think so? But . . . Invincibility in the hands of unscrupulous people! You don't know who—"

"Look, it's your mom. You have to try to save her, and I don't think holding on to the stone is going to convince them to free her. Obviously you have to make the trade. All we have to do is figure out how to get the message to them." She considered it for a moment. In the distance, she heard the thrum of a helicopter, and that gave her an idea. "What about the news crew in Tikal? You could appear there, with the stone, and make the offer publicly . . . but then how would the kidnapper reply? Also, what if Queen Marguerite finds out you're offering up the stone? She wouldn't be happy. Still, I don't see many other options."

The look in his eyes was intense. "You are—"

"Yes, yes, amazing, I know. How about we leave this tomb? Rather not brainstorm with so many dead bodies around me, even if they're old and historical and all that."

He stepped closer, and she thought he was going to transport them. Instead, he kissed her. She felt her knees weaken as if her body expected to start floating. The kiss buzzed through her head, and every thought scattered as soon as it formed. The warmth of his body against hers, the softness of his lips, the taste of his breath were intoxicating. He kissed her as if this kiss would save him, as if he needed this kiss to live.

At last, they broke apart.

Kayla felt breathless. "You realize that relationships formed in reactions to intense situations don't last."

"Says who?" Daniel said.

"Don't know. Stole that line from some movie."

He smiled. "Thief."

She felt herself smiling goofily back at him. Her cheeks were stretched into a grin she couldn't stop. "Everyone has faults."

Before he could reply, a tremor shook the tomb. One of the mummies toppled to the side, and loose rocks rained down. *Crack.* A split ran down one of the stone walls, and a rock tumbled from the top. Before Kayla could even scream, the rock crashed into the side of Daniel's head. Shouting his name, Kayla dropped down next to him. "Daniel? Daniel!" There was blood on the side of his head, wetting his hair. "Daniel?" He was breathing. He wasn't dead. But he didn't move. "Daniel!"

The tremor stopped.

She heard a rustling from the tomb entrance and turned. In a climbing harness, suspended from a rope, was a man in khaki shorts and a crisp white shirt. He wore a tan Indiana Jones hat that shadowed his eyes. Swinging forward, he landed inside the tomb in a crouch.

Kayla began, "He's hurt! Please—"

The man rose to his feet, and the words died in her throat. Kayla felt like she couldn't breathe. She knew him. It had been eight years, but he'd featured in her nightmares many nights since then.

He looked older, of course. She should have expected that. Gray speckled his beard, and he had creases around his eyes. But there was no question that he was Kayla's father.

Every instinct, every bit of training, screamed at her to run.

There was nowhere to run.

She noticed he was carrying her backpack. "That's mine,"

she said. She didn't know why she said that. Why say that? Of all things, why that? She didn't want those to be her last words. Who cared about a backpack?

I'm going to die, she thought.

She should have stayed with Moonbeam. She should never have lied to her. She should have fled town as soon as Daniel found her. Now, Moonbeam would never know what happened to her. Selena could tell her where she went, but they'd never know why she didn't return. Kayla wished she could say she was sorry to both of them. She didn't mean to worry them or scare them or cause them grief.

She'd never felt fear like this. It clogged her throat. It froze her blood. It locked her muscles. She couldn't speak or breathe. But inside, every cell was screaming.

He tossed the backpack to her. As she instinctively caught it, he leaned over and took the stone out of Daniel's limp hand, and then backed to the ledge. He stepped out into nothingness and was pulled up on the climbing rope, the stone in his hand.

13

Kayla knelt beside Daniel. *Oh, please, please don't be dead!* She was shaking as she felt his head. He'd stopped bleeding. Red speckled the rocks and matted his hair. He groaned as she touched him—which meant he wasn't dead, didn't it? "Daniel, are you okay? Please be okay." She checked his pulse. It took her three tries to steady her fingers enough on his neck to feel anything.

Reaching up, he wrapped his hand around hers and opened his eyes.

"You're alive," she breathed. She wanted to grab him and hug him and then smack him for scaring the shit out of her, but she was afraid to touch him. Awake didn't mean well. "Are you all right? How do you feel?"

He pushed himself up to sitting and then groaned. He lay · back down. "What happened?" He looked around the tomb. "Where's the stone?" His voice rose louder. "Kayla, where is it?"

"Short version? You were hit on the head with a rock. My father swooped in, stole the stone, and left." Kayla tried to sound nonchalant, but her voice shook. "And there's no long version. It happened fast." So very fast. She felt her lungs constricting again. She sucked in air like a fish on land. He could have killed her. Nearly did kill Daniel. And then left her, stranded, which was not so different from killing her. If Daniel died, she'd die, trapped high on the mountainside, conveniently already in a tomb. Picturing it, she wanted to curl into a ball, pretend this was some hideous nightmare, and scream until she woke up.

All the blood seemed to run out of Daniel's face. He looked as pale as bone. "He was here? He took it?"

"I'm sorry. I didn't think fast enough." In retrospect, she could have thrown dirt in his eyes or used the razor blade to slice his climbing rope. Or . . . She didn't know. Her father, here! "I thought . . ." She'd thought she was going to die. She'd thought Daniel was dying. Kayla swallowed. It was hard to wrap her mind around the idea that her blood was still in her veins and she was still breathing in and out. She'd encountered her father; therefore, according to everything her mother had ever taught her, she should be dead.

"I'm the one who's sorry," Daniel said, his voice drained, beaten. He sank back against the rocks, as if he could fold in on himself. "He caught you by surprise. I should have told you who he was. I'd hoped . . . I don't know. I'm so very sorry."

Kayla felt herself go very still. The wind outside seemed to die, as if the world were holding its breath. Softly, she said, "You knew?"

"Your parents and my mother were childhood friends. That's how I found you. She told me once where you lived. Said I should know, in case of emergencies."

"Impossible," Kayla said. "My mother didn't keep in touch with anyone she knew before. She severed all ties. We started a new life. She never would have told anyone how to find us." But he'd known where to find her. And he'd called her Kayla, her new name.

He didn't argue with her. "You see why I didn't trust you at first? You're his daughter. I didn't know if you'd help me or side with him. That's why I didn't tell you. And later . . . I didn't know how to tell you."

"I kissed you." She'd let down her guard. She'd trusted him. She *never* trusted people. Only Selena. And Moonbeam, who had led this boy to her. And this boy, who had led her father to her. "I trusted you!"

"I'm sorry."

She felt as if her blood were burning, like lava about to explode out of her. Pebbles rose into the air around them. They whipped in a tiny cyclone. Other cyclones of dirt, dust, and rocks whirled around the tomb.

Daniel shot them a look. "Uh, Kayla?"

She didn't tamp them down. Instead she sent them shooting out the entrance to the tomb. They dispersed in the air, and debris rained down, far down, on the knotted green of the forest below. "Take me home. Now."

Again, he didn't argue. Reaching out, he laid his hand over hers.

Gray.

Black.

Red.

She was outside the red garden gate. For an instant, she felt cold as she saw her father's face flash before her. But no, he wasn't here. He was thousands of miles away in the mountains of Peru, and she was safe. Kayla snatched her hand away from Daniel and refused to look at him.

"Kayla . . . ," he began.

"Don't."

"When you're ready to look for the next stone, call me."

"I don't think it's overly melodramatic of me to say I never want to see you again." She pushed the gate open so hard that the wind chimes clanged. If Daniel called after her, she didn't hear. She strode through the garden, between the bushes and garden gnomes and ceramic fairies, and then into the house. Moonbeam was at the sink. Kayla ran past her. She stuffed the backpack under her futon and threw herself on top.

She started to wrap herself in the quilt like it was a cocoon. But Moonbeam threw it off her. "Kayla! Kayla!" Moonbeam gathered her up and hugged her close. Kayla wrapped her arms tightly around her mother.

"Moonbeam," Kayla said, muffled, into her mother's scarf. "Mom." Moonbeam's many amulets and pendants dug into Kayla's skin. Kayla felt as if something inside her snapped, and she was suddenly crying, giant ugly sobs into Moonbeam's shoulder.

Stroking her hair, Moonbeam rocked and rocked her.

At last, Kayla calmed. She breathed deep, and Moonbeam breathed with her. Eventually, Moonbeam pulled back and held on to Kayla's arms. She peered into Kayla's eyes and then inspected her. "Are you hurt? You're dirty." She spotted Kayla's hands, streaked with Daniel's blood. "You're bleeding."

Kayla tucked her hands in her armpits. "I'm fine."

"You didn't call. You didn't answer the phone. I didn't know if you were dead." Her voice was gentle.

Kayla closed her eyes. "Please don't ask me what happened."

"Kayla . . ."

"Please. Mom."

"Okay." Moonbeam was silent for a moment, and Kayla curled up on her bed. "Just one thing: Do you need a doctor?"

"No."

"Do you need the police?"

"No!"

"Then we'll talk later," Moonbeam said, "when you're ready."

Kayla felt her quilt being wrapped around her. Her mother tucked in the edges like she used to when Kayla was a little girl, and Kayla again felt tears spill out of her eyes. She didn't open her eyes, though. She listened as Moonbeam shuffled across the cottage to the kitchen. She heard the *clank* of the teakettle being set down on the stove and the *click-click* of the gas burner lighting. She heard the refrigerator open and close and then the cabinets.

She waited for the feeling of "home" to wrap around her. She wanted to feel safe. But she kept hearing the rock hit Daniel's head and seeing her father's face every time she closed her eyes.

At last, somehow, she slept.

⧫ ⧫

When she woke, Selena was seated beside Kayla's futon on a kitchen stool. She was frowning at her phone and typing as if she were stabbing it with her finger. Kayla sat up and looked around the cottage. The scarf separating her corner was pulled back and she could see the whole room, sunlight filtering through the windows, dust sparkling and spinning in the beams.

No Moonbeam.

Kayla tossed off the quilt and jumped to her feet. "Where's my mother?"

"No 'hello'?" Selena tucked her phone into her pocket. "You scared me too, you know."

"Sorry." Darting across the cottage, Kayla leaned over the kitchen sink to look out the window at the garden. There was Moonbeam, weeding. Her back was to the window. She was wearing a ridiculous floppy sun hat that looked more like an umbrella. She was barefoot, and a basket of weeds lay next to her. Kayla felt her rib cage loosen, and she could breathe again.

Her mother was safe. Dad wasn't here. He was thousands of miles away. Kayla breathed in and out, trying to calm herself.

"What happened?" Selena asked, quiet, serious for once.

Kayla turned. Her friend was standing close, next to her. Selena looked normal and perfect and beautiful as always. Without a word, Kayla hugged her.

Awkwardly, Selena patted her back. "Hey, hey, it's okay. Cry it out. No, wait, don't cry on me. Just tell me what happened. Did you find his mother?"

Kayla shook her head.

"Did you find the stone?"

A nod then a shake.

"Cryptic much? Okay, where is it? And where is he?"

"I . . ." She opened and closed her mouth. "I don't know." He'd been hurt. Was he okay? Of course he was. He'd brought her here. But where had he gone after? What if he'd had a concussion? What if he was lying in the gutter with internal bleeding, dying, and she'd just walked away? "I saw my father," Kayla said in the quietest voice she could. All of it spilled out, everything that had happened, from the kiss to the stone to the sight of her father taking the stone and leaving her stranded but alive.

"Oh, Kayla." This time, Selena hugged her back. "No wonder

you're a mess. Did you tell Moonbeam? I'm guessing no. You have to tell her!"

"She'd freak out," Kayla said. "And he isn't here. He doesn't know where we live." She had a sudden thought. "I'm not even sure he knows who I am. He didn't say." That thought was so glorious that it nearly made her dizzy.

"No 'Luke, I am your father' moment? That's a plus."

"Selena, this is serious." Twisting around, Kayla watched her mother weed. Moonbeam scooted over to the next flower bed. She was clearing space around select herbs. Kayla was sure they were for some kind of protective charm. After what had happened, Kayla wanted to drape herself in charms too. She wished she believed they worked.

"I know. But it's not doomsday."

"Close enough." She watched her mother sit back on her heels and wipe her forehead with the back of her gardening glove. Dirt streaked her cheeks. They'd sacrificed so much to stay hidden from Dad, and Kayla had just pranced blindly to him. She'd criticized Daniel for not being careful enough, when all the while, she was the one blind to danger. She should have grilled Daniel on how he'd heard of her, how he knew her name, how he found her. She shouldn't have trusted him at all.

"So what was he like? Giant monster with drool and twenty arms?"

Kayla shot her a glare. "You're really bad at the sympathy thing. Couldn't you fake it for a few more minutes?"

"He didn't kill you," Selena pointed out. "Look, I'm just saying, the worst has happened. You saw your dad; he saw you. You're still here. Let's move on."

"Luck. Sheer luck. If that rock had killed Daniel . . ." Kayla took in a ragged breath. "He would have killed two of Moonbeam's daughters."

Selena poked her shoulder. "But he didn't."

"I risked too much," Kayla said. "Moonbeam's right. I shouldn't ever leave."

"Not leave Santa Barbara or not leave this house? You know, you'd be safest if you tucked yourself under the table. No one would see you. I could pass you food every once in a while, like sneaking scraps to the family dog."

"Selena. He killed Amanda. My sister. Can you even imagine—"

"No," Selena interrupted. "And neither can you. You're not Amanda. And you're not little Katie anymore. You're all grown up now, and you're the most powerful, smartest girl I know, and I am not going to let you spend your life cowering in fear. The worst happened, and you survived. Get a grip. You're here, you're safe, and he doesn't know how to find you. He met you in *Peru*. You can't get much farther away without involving an ocean. Just don't visit Peru again. Problem solved."

"You're a terrible friend."

"I know."

"You're supposed to be all sympathetic. Instead you're just pissing me off."

"Good! Get pissed off! It's better than scared, right?" Selena said. "Who is he to make you feel scared? I ask again: Was he a multiarmed monster with drool? No. He's a man. A very, very evil man who did a very, very bad thing and will probably do more. But not here. And not to you. You are not helpless. You are not weak."

Kayla shook her head. "You have no idea what you're talking about. My sister—"

"—is not you! Look, Kayla, remember the time we snuck into that club and that guy cornered me outside the bathroom? What did you do?"

"Launched his cigarette ash into his eye and then set his shirt on fire."

"They were hosing him down with a fire extinguisher, and you kept dancing. Kayla, that's who you are. Not this. Snap out of it, girl. You're my strong, smart Kayla—far stronger than me. You were caught off guard this time. It won't happen again. If you ever see him again . . . which is a major 'if,' remember Peru equals far . . . you'll kick his ass. He's just a man with eyes, a throat, and other vulnerable spots. You're *you*."

Turning toward the window again, Kayla looked out at Moonbeam. She was digging with purpose, jabbing the soil with her trowel. Kayla noticed that the outer bushes were draped in ribbons and bells and charms made of roots and bones. Moonbeam wasn't gardening; she was placing more charms. Kayla swallowed. She didn't want to be like that. Living her life in defensive mode. Selena was right. That wasn't her. Kayla straightened her shoulders and lifted her chin. "I'm not going to live my life in fear," she declared.

"Good girl," Selena said. "One of us needs to be brave."

"I'm going to stop him, catch him, and see him behind bars."

"Whoa, wait, what?" Selena said.

Kayla marched toward her futon. She changed into fresh clothes; stuffed her phone, lighter, and razor blade into her new shorts; and pulled her favorite hoodie out of her backpack as she said, "I can take him. And I should. Once he's in jail, we won't have to hide anymore. Moonbeam won't have to be afraid. She'll be free. Finally. She'll be able to move on. She can't right now. Look at her. Fear of him rules her life. It dictates everything she does. It's transformed who she is. She wasn't always like this. I remember her before, when Amanda was alive. She was happy. She was fun."

"You can't go after him," Selena said. "Are you crazy? I just meant for you to stop moping. By all means, stay away from him. Tell Danny-boy to stuff his stupid quest and trust the police to find his mom, and you get on with your life!"

"If I let Dad get that last stone, if he does that invincibility spell, then she won't be safe, then I won't be safe, ever. It won't ever end. I have to end it."

"You don't even know what this so-called invincibility spell does! Maybe he casts it, and you don't ever hear from him. No harm, no foul."

"Sorry, Selena. I have to do this." Kayla marched out of the house.

Selena scurried after her. "You're right, I'm a bad friend. Can we start this conversation over? Something went wrong here."

Moonbeam looked up at the sound of the door. She had dirt smeared on her nose. "Kayla! You're awake."

Kneeling in the dirt, Kayla put her arms around Moonbeam. "I'm so sorry I scared you." She kissed her mother on the cheek. "Really, I'm fine, and I'll be all better soon. Everything will be better. I promise."

Moonbeam pulled back and studied Kayla's face as if trying to read her mind. "What happened? Where have you been? Are you sure you're all right? You can tell me."

"Someday, I'll explain it all, but I can't right now. There are some things I have to do first. I'll be back soon." Kayla stood. She felt stronger already. This felt right!

"Oh, no, that's not okay," Moonbeam said. "You can't leave again. You were gone all yesterday, all last night, and then when you came home—"

"Please, Moonbeam, trust me. Everything is going to be okay!"

Standing too, Moonbeam squeezed her hand. "Were you with that boy? Did he hurt you? Selena said—"

"I didn't sleep with him," Kayla said quickly.

Relief crossed her face. "Then where were you? And why didn't you call? You scared me, Kayla."

"I'm sorry, and I promise I'll be home soon."

Moonbeam was shaking her head. "No. Kayla, I want you to stay here. Rest. You need rest. Please, Kayla, I need to know you're safe, at least for a little while. We'll rent a movie. Make popcorn." She patted Kayla's shoulders and hair and cheek, as if reassuring herself that Kayla was still here and whole.

"Rain check?" Kayla said.

"I could ground you," Moonbeam said. "Don't make me ground you."

"This is important."

"What is? Where are you going?"

Kayla opened her mouth and then hesitated. She absolutely could not tell her mother the truth. It would plunge Moonbeam into a spiral of panic, and she was already freaked out. "Selena's going to take me shopping! She thinks the cure to a broken heart is retail therapy."

"Oh, it absolutely is." Selena nodded so enthusiastically she looked like a bobblehead. "I'm buying Kayla an entire new outfit, top to toe. My treat. But the offer is only good today."

"And then I'll be all better, and we'll have our movie night and eat popcorn until we feel sick and I'll tell you everything, I promise," Kayla said. "But please, Moonbeam, I need this."

Moonbeam frowned, then took one of the evil eye amulets from around her own neck and draped it over Kayla's. "Two hours. Any later, and that's it."

"I'll be back as soon as I can."

"You'll be back in two hours. You need to stay safe, Kayla. I need you safe."

Kayla couldn't think of a response that wasn't a lie, so she settled on kissing Moonbeam on the cheek again. She wouldn't be back within two hours. She then strode out the garden gate with Selena. Glancing back once at Moonbeam, she hoped she was doing the right thing.

14

"Park there." Kayla pointed to an open spot near the café, and Selena yanked on the steering wheel. She pulled up beside the car in front of the parking spot. Behind them, another car headed toward the same space. But Selena was faster, slamming into reverse and spinning the steering wheel. She slid into the spot before the other car could do more than aim its front wheels.

Selena hopped out and examined her parking job. She was mere inches from the curb. "Genius, if I do say so myself. You should really listen to me. I exude brilliance." The driver of the car who lost the spot flipped her off as he zoomed by. Selena blew a kiss at him.

Kayla headed for one of the benches. "Can you get us some smoothies, Genius Girl?"

"Sure, if you tell me you've reconsidered your suicidal and completely ill-thought-out plan and let me take you shopping, which was the first sensible thought you've had all day."

"I've reconsidered about seven times, and I'm back to yes."

"Well, so long as you're certain and have no doubts."

Muttering to herself, Selena headed for the café, and Kayla parked herself on a bench in front of the Santa Barbara First City Bank. She took out her phone and stared at Daniel's number.

Of course she had doubts. She was eaten up with doubts and fears . . . which was why she had to do it. They'd eat her alive if she didn't.

She texted Daniel. *Ready to try again. Meet me on State Street.* Staring at the phone a moment longer, she took a breath and then hit Send.

Fear wasn't going to stop her.

Closing her eyes, Kayla tilted her head back as if to soak in the sun, and she let her mind roam inside the bank. She drifted over the people at the ATM and others in line for a teller. She ruffled the deposit slips on her way to the counter. On the counter, she "felt" a vase with fake flowers and a bowl of lollipops. The teller was counting bills and then stuffing them into an envelope. Kayla felt underneath the desk—and she deliberately pressed the emergency button.

Nothing happened.

Kayla got up and sauntered across the street to the bait and tackle store. As she opened the door, she heard the sirens. Wails filled State Street. In seconds, the bank was quickly surrounded with police cars and armed policemen.

As distractions went, this one was definite overkill, but satisfying nonetheless.

The clerk at the bait store rushed to the window, and Kayla stuffed her hoodie pockets with fishing line and hooks. She wished she'd grabbed her backpack as well as her hoodie. Finishing, she joined the other gawkers on the sidewalk. Selena found her and handed her a smoothie. Kayla sipped it and watched the chaos at the bank unfold. *See what you can do? You're strong,* Kayla told herself. *You can face your father. No one can stop you.*

"Feel better?" Selena asked.

"Much," Kayla said.

They strolled to the car. Daniel was waiting for them, leaning against the passenger door. His hands were in his pockets, and he watched them approach with a wary expression, as if he expected to have to bolt. "Kayla—"

"Into the car," Kayla ordered.

Daniel obeyed, squeezing himself into the backseat. Selena jumped into the driver's seat. Glancing back at the chaos in the street, Kayla climbed in as well.

"Tell me you didn't rob that bank," he said.

"I don't need to tell you anything." Kayla opened the glove compartment, found another pair of sunglasses, and put them on.

"Even if she did," Selena said, "you are in zero position to judge. Better to be a thief than a traitorous, lying sack of slime. That's you, by the way, in case you're too thick to catch the insult."

Twisting in her seat so she could look directly at him, Kayla lifted the glasses and said, "I have not forgiven you. I will not forgive you. But I *am* going to help you find the other stone."

Daniel exhaled noisily. "Thank—"

Stopping him, Kayla held up a finger. "One condition. Instead of finding the last stone to trade for your mom, we catch my dad and then rescue your mom."

Selena started up the engine. Her music blared, drowning out any possible response. She wormed out of her parking spot and floored it down State Street, leaving behind the tangle of police cars and the knot of onlookers outside the bank. She turned at the pier and whipped along the coast, pulling into a half-vacant parking lot. The radio shut off. "You're down to an hour and a half left," Selena told Kayla. "Please don't make me lie to your mom again. She gives me these puppy eyes that make me feel like the most horrible person in the world."

"It'll be over soon," Kayla promised. To Daniel, she said, "Let's go to Tikal. The top of the Great Jaguar Temple, so we can avoid the irate archaeologists."

"Is that a thing?" Selena asked.

"It's totally a thing." Kayla flashed a reassuring smile at Selena, even though her insides were churning as if she was making the worst mistake she'd ever made. She hoped she wasn't.

He took her hand, and the world flickered white, black, and gray.

Rain pummeled them, hard, as if a bucket of water had been dumped on their heads. It poured down their faces and necks, instantly drenching their clothes.

Kayla yanked him backward into the shrine. Outside, rain poured so thickly that it seemed as if a screen had been pulled over the doorway. She took off the useless sunglasses and stuffed them in her hoodie pocket. "Now what?"

Daniel squeezed water out of his shirt. "It'll pass fast. It's only a thunderstorm. I've been in worse. Once, I jumped into a blizzard. Returned home with near frostbite."

"You know, we could jump back. Get a smoothie while we wait." Or she could get a smoothie, and he could wait outside or someplace else, not near her.

He shook his head. "You might change your mind."

"You don't trust me?"

"You hate me," he pointed out.

"Yes, I do."

"Besides, the rain will stop soon. Storms like this don't last. Once, I was in London and—"

"I really don't care."

He fell silent.

Shifting from foot to foot, Kayla watched the rain beat the stones. She couldn't see more than a few feet outside. It was shrouded in gray. On the plus side, at least no photographers or reporters would be out in this mess. On the negative side, she was stuck at the top of the temple with Daniel.

She checked her watch. An hour and twenty minutes to change her mind and return home with zero repercussions. She could claim she was wet because she'd jumped off the pier in a moment of wild abandon. Moonbeam would believe her, maybe.

Kayla studiously avoided looking at Daniel. Instead, she studied the murals on the walls. They were chipped and faded, damaged by time and weather, but she could make out a few glyphs, plus half a portrait of a long-ago king, the same one as on the parchment. Out of the corner of her eye, she saw Daniel kneel next to the grate that used to cover the stairs. It was warped and dented. The entrance was filled with rocks. He peered around the rocks, as if looking for a way through. Even a snake would have difficulty slithering through. Of course, since Daniel was a snake, he should know that.

She noticed she was clenching and unclenching her fists and forced herself to stop. If she wanted to do this, she had to play nice with him. She could deck him after it was all over. For now, civility. "Did you get in trouble?"

"With who?"

"Your mom. After the frostbite. What did she say?"

"Oh, she wasn't home. Plunged myself into a hot bath, and that fixed me. But still have some deadness to my fingertips here." He stood up to show her. Turning his hand over, he took her hand to touch the tips of two of his fingers. The skin was rougher to the touch, though it looked the same. She suddenly realized she was stroking his hand, and she yanked away.

He was looking at her as if he wanted to say something, maybe an apology or an explanation. She didn't want to hear it. Instead, Kayla stared at the rain and tried to will it to stop. The longer she stayed here, the more she thought she shouldn't be here at all. She should go home, apologize to Moonbeam, and forget about this idiocy. She didn't owe Daniel anything. He'd tricked her into helping at all. But the opportunity to stop Dad . . .

"Kayla—"

"Do you think it's going to stop soon?" she interrupted.

"How much trouble were you in?" he asked softly.

"A lot. She wanted to ground me. Only thanks to Selena she didn't. Certainly will if I'm late today. Assuming my father doesn't kill me first."

He was silent for a long moment.

Side by side, they watched the rain.

At last he said, "You know, you're lucky your mother cares so much."

Kayla heaved a sigh. She felt like she was deflating. She *was* lucky, and she was lucky that it wasn't her mother who'd been kidnapped by Dad. "I know. That's why it's impossible to be angry with her when she pulls her OCD overprotectiveness, which, given that my father nearly killed me, is beginning to seem much more reasonable."

Tentatively, he asked, "Do you . . . Are you sure that's what he wants?"

Kayla stirred the dust at her feet with her mind. She should be angry at Daniel for asking that. But instead the question only made her feel tired. She thought of Selena, asking if he was a monster, and she rubbed her damp arms. Rain battered the shrine, spraying inside. "I don't remember him very well. He didn't spend much time with me. I wasn't very interesting, I guess. All I wanted to do was play tea party or basketball or superheroes or board games or whatever he'd be willing to play with me . . . but as it turned out, I wasn't good at the games he wanted me to play."

"What did he want you to play?" Daniel's voice was hushed. He was treating her as if she were a wild animal that could turn vicious on him at any moment. She kind of liked that. She felt fierce.

"In one of the games, he'd throw a ball at me, and I wasn't allowed to move to catch it. It hit me in the face over and over. I didn't know what he wanted me to do."

"Sounds like he was testing you. You know, for—" He made Selena's gesture for telekinesis.

"I didn't have any power then. Certainly not enough to catch a ball. Anyway, I remember Mom saw once, when he was chucking a ball at me, and yelled at him for an hour. She was Mom then, not Moonbeam. After we moved to California, she became Moonbeam. Anyway, my dad played more with my sister, and I remember being jealous. Needless to say, all this negative emotion seriously messed me up after he killed her. I remember being convinced that if I'd been better at his games, she'd still be alive. Stupid, right? I was a kid. He was an adult. It's not my fault.

Blah-blah-blah." She looked at Daniel, studying his profile. He was staring moodily out at the rain. "What's your father like? You never mention him."

"He died when I was young," Daniel said. "He was a good man, I think. At least that's what everyone tells me. People like to say that."

"People like to say a lot of things. I think it comforts them to try to be comforting. You know she never even got a funeral? We fled, right after the police failed to do anything. It wasn't safe to stay. And so we left. We left everything. I wasn't even allowed to talk about her. No one could even know I had a sister; that might be one more clue for my father to find us." She felt so much bitterness swirl up into her throat that she thought she might choke. Maybe Daniel wasn't the only one she was angry at. Around her feet, the dust began to swirl in a miniature cyclone. She let it swirl faster and faster, whipping against her feet.

"No offense, but you had a messed-up childhood."

"And yours was peaches and sunshine? Father dead, mother absent. Any therapist would tell you that's why you're so reckless. You want to get caught. You want your mother to notice you. And that's why *you* want to save her, instead of the police, isn't it? She'll notice you if you save her. Did you even really tell the police? Or is this all a lie?" She sent the cyclone against his ankles. The sand and pebbles pelted him.

He glared at her but didn't move. "Defensive much? I haven't lied to you."

"Except about my father."

"That was an omission, not a lie."

"In case I haven't been clear, I haven't forgiven you."

He looked pained, but she refused to feel guilty. He deserved every second of angst. She created more cyclones. "But you hate your father more than you hate me?" he guessed.

"That sums it up nicely, yes. I want him stopped. I won't live in fear. That's my mother's life, not mine. He can't make me feel this way." She glared out at the rain and sent a cyclone into it. The dust was pummeled by the droplets, and the cyclone fell apart.

"If we meet him again, I can teleport him somewhere," Daniel offered. "Leave him on a mountaintop. Drop him in the ocean. Say the word."

Despite everything, she nearly smiled. That was the nicest present anyone had ever offered her. "You'll bring him to the police. That's my price for helping you. I want him behind bars for what he did to my sister. It's the only way my mom will feel safe, if she knows for certain he can't reach her. She'll never just take my word for it. It has to be visible." She let the other cyclones fall to the floor. "If he tries to kill us again, of course, all bets are off and feel free."

"Deal."

They resumed watching out the doorway. Soon, the rain swept by as if it were a gray sheet that had been draped over the trees and then yanked away. Blue sky appeared in patches and then spread, the gray peeling away around it. A few minutes later, Kayla could see the distant mountains. Daniel wrapped his hand around hers. She flinched. "Sorry my touch is abhorrent," he said stiffly. "Do you want to stay here?"

She glared at him and let him take her hand, and the world flashed around them.

Rain dumped on them again.

"Guess we should have waited," Daniel said, squinting as he looked up. Water streamed over his face.

"Indeed," Kayla said.

"Sorry."

"On the plus side, I don't think it's possible to get any wetter."

Around them, the rain battered the leaves. It sounded like drums. But soon, it lessened to drips, the forest lightened, and the birds began to call to one another again. Kayla shivered. "Any idea what the stages of hypothermia are?"

"A few jumps, and then we'll jump somewhere to warm up," he promised. "I just want to get a little farther."

"Fine." Her teeth chattered like fake windup teeth.

"I said I'm sorry."

"And I gave a very optimistic, silver-lining response about not getting any wetter. If you'd rather I actually complained, I can do that, though I'll warn you that I can achieve epic-level whining, given the opportunity."

"It *is* called a rain forest," Daniel said.

"Was I blaming you?" Kayla said. "I don't think I was. I blame you for lying to me. I blame you for leaving me emotionally unprepared to come face-to-face with the man who personified fear and danger to me my entire life. I blame you for bringing me to his attention, endangering both me and my mother. But I don't actually blame you for the rain."

"Good to know," Daniel said blandly. The sky had cleared enough to see a few peaks in the distance, but they were shrouded in streaks of gray. More rain.

Kayla noticed that his lips were tinged bluish. He was shivering too. "I vote we dry off now, let the rain get even farther away, and then come back and continue after the rain stops. Are you familiar enough with this place to come right to this spot?"

He glared at the rainstorm that they seemed to be chasing and then sighed. "Fine. The weather changes visibility anyway. Should I bring you home?"

Kayla glanced at her watch. Only a few minutes left before Moonbeam started to worry. She could go back, and Moonbeam would never know she'd tried this. But if she went back . . . she knew she wouldn't leave again. It would be too easy to stay there and stay safe and let her father roam around Guatemala and Peru without her.

"Kayla, home or not?"

If she saw her mother, Kayla would lose her nerve. She had to stay strong. "Not."

"Are you sure?"

"I don't want to lie to her. I don't want to explain. I want to fix this." All they had to do was get to the end of this trail, find the stone, and capture her father. Then her mother would forgive all.

"Selena's house?"

"Her mother's home. I don't want to complicate her life more. Queen Marguerite?"

He shook his head. "Rather not tell her we lost the first stone. *Ira Reginae Dolorem*, remember? We can go to my home."

"Yours?"

"It's not like anyone is there," he said, his voice grim. He put his hand on Kayla's shoulder, and the world winked around them.

∽ ∾

It took a moment for Kayla's eyes to adjust. She saw shapes in the darkness: a flight of stairs, a mirror . . . Daniel flicked on a light. They were in a foyer. A mirror in a wood frame hung on one wall, and Kayla avoided looking at her bedraggled self. There was an umbrella pail and a coatrack next to the mirror. She didn't know anyone owned a coatrack. She'd thought those were reserved exclusively for restaurants or the 1800s. A raincoat, gray and tailored, hung picturesquely from one of its brass hooks. A few black-and-white photos decorated the wall, mostly houses and streets in Europe. One had a cat in silhouette on a London roof. Another was the Eiffel Tower. A third was an ornate church with a triple dome. None were of people.

It hit her that she was doing this. She hadn't gone home. She was going to let the two hours expire. Kayla exhaled. *You can do this*, she repeated like a mantra, as if she were the Little Engine That Could, if what the train wanted to do was toss its dad into prison.

Through one doorway, she glimpsed a perfect dining room with a china cabinet filled with delicate glass vases, Fabergé eggs, and plates with Native American designs. Around a corner, she saw a hint of a kitchen with a stainless steel refrigerator and an extensive spice rack. Directly ahead of Kayla was a flight of stairs with a deep red rug running up them. Daniel trotted up.

She followed. There was dust on the handrail, and she realized that no one lived here right now. Her life might have been turned upside down by this, but so had Daniel's. At least she knew her mother was okay and would be okay, even if Kayla got herself killed.

That was not as comforting as it should have been.

Upstairs, the hall was filled with antiques and knickknacks from around the world: an African mask on the wall, an Indian elephant statue on a delicate European end table in one corner, a Greek-looking sculpture of a horse. There were four doors: two bedrooms, a bathroom, and a closed door that could have been another bedroom or maybe an office. The first bedroom had a four-poster bed with a bedspread that looked like silk with tassels on the edge. The bathroom had a shelf with a replica of an Egyptian boat. She didn't see anything in the house that looked like Daniel lived here too until she reached his bedroom. His door was open and he was rummaging through a dresser. She stepped inside.

Daniel's room was covered in maps. They wallpapered every wall from floor to ceiling. He had photographs pinned everywhere. She walked up to one, a waterfall that cascaded from black lava-like rocks. "You've been to all these places?"

He tossed clothes onto his bed. "Not all. But a lot. I keep them for reference—you know, for future jumps. I like knowing I can go anyplace I want. All I need is a picture."

She walked along the wall. There were photos of cafés, of dirt streets and colorful houses, of children with wide eyes, of icebergs, of jungles, of lava-filled volcanoes. "Is there anywhere you haven't been?"

"Wyoming."

"Really? Why not?"

He blushed. And then he shrugged. "I like to keep one place that I've never been."

"Why?"

"That way it can't ever disappoint me."

"Oh, dude, you have issues," Kayla said.

He tossed her a plain black T-shirt. "You can wear this. And whatever else you want. Bathroom's down to the left. You can borrow my mom's underwear, which is a weird sentence that no guy should ever have to say."

"Why not choose someplace more, I don't know, exotic for your 'one place'?"

"Because my mother and I didn't go there." There was pain in his voice, raw and clear, as he mentioned his mother. "Years ago, she planned a road trip for us, across the whole United States. Said she wanted me to see how the pieces connected to each other, instead of jumping from point to point all the time. I would have seen Wyoming then. But she was invited to speak at a conference so she canceled. Never mentioned it again."

"I'm sorry." Dammit, she was sympathizing with him again.

"It's stupid. It wasn't like I was excited about Wyoming itself. It's just . . . She didn't seem disappointed when she had to cancel, you know? Forgot about it instantly, even though it was the only trip we'd ever planned that didn't involve her work or my jumping." He frowned at the photos, as if they'd failed him. "Work always comes first with her. She'd say it has to. Publish or perish. If she wants tenure . . . She likes to talk about how much better it will be once she has tenure. They can't fire her after that, so we'll be secure. It's a guaranteed future. She doesn't get that I'd rather have had that road trip."

Kayla wanted to cross to him and put her arms around him so badly that she took a step toward him before she stopped herself. "I'll . . . get ready to go." She fled down the hall. Cranking the water to hot, she let the steam fill the bathroom before she stepped into the shower. When she came out again, she felt like a thawed Popsicle. Pulling on a mix of his clothes and his mother's, she emerged, wringing her hair, and she dumped her clothes in the dryer in the hallway.

"Your turn," she told Daniel.

He headed for the bathroom, and she sat in his room, listening to the shower and looking at the walls. He had maps of everywhere in the world. On his neat-as-a-pin desk were more maps, street maps, and atlases. The bookshelves were stuffed with travel guides and, oddly, dozens of photo albums. Kayla didn't have any albums from her childhood. Moonbeam had deliberately left those behind. So Kayla didn't have any cute baby photos or anything. Or any pictures of Amanda. She wished she had at least one of those. It was too easy to forget what her sister looked like. Sometimes she wasn't sure that she remembered at all. It had been eight years. Kayla felt her eyes heat up. To distract herself, she pulled one of the albums off the shelf and opened it. But there were no cute baby pictures of Daniel inside. Just more photos of places. She flipped through. There were no people in any of the shots, except for what appeared to be casual passersby. She looked through more albums, and it was more of the same.

She checked his desk. There had to be a photo of someone— ahh, there. A photo lay on top of an old album. It was of Daniel and a woman. His mother. It had to be. She had the same black hair and stormy eyes as he did. She was wearing a pantsuit, and she stood stiffly, her arm awkwardly around her son's shoulders. Kayla guessed he was about three years younger than he was now. He had that gangly new-to-being-tall look. His mother was smiling stiffly. Kayla wondered if they'd been having a bad day or an ordinary day.

The old album was battered leather. She opened it, expecting more landscapes. And saw a photo of Moonbeam.

Kayla sat down hard on Daniel's bed and stared at it.

Moonbeam looked to be about sixteen. Her hair was short, curled around her ears, and had zero gray in it. She was laughing, and her face was unlined. Her arm was around a younger version of Daniel's mother, who was also laughing. Both were holding ice cream cones. Ice cream was dripping onto her mother's wrist.

She turned the page and there he was too. Her father. He was sitting at a picnic table with corn on the cob in front of him, as well as a bottle of ketchup. There was a lake behind him. Another photo had her mother and father. Her mother's arms were around his waist. He was looking directly at the camera and smiling.

"They were friends," Daniel said from the doorway. He was wearing jeans and no shirt. He wiped his hair with a towel. "The three of them. Inseparable, from what I can tell." He sat on the bed next to her. He flipped a few pages and pointed to a photo of two kids, about six or seven years old—his mom and her dad. Her dad looked very serious and very thin. His mother, also too thin, had a bruise on her cheek. "My mom and your dad were best friends since pretty much nursery school. My mom met yours in middle school and roped her in to make a trio. Your parents started going out in high school, but near as I can tell, there were never any jealousy issues. My mom was best friends with both of them." He turned to a set of high school photos.

"What happened?" Kayla asked. "Did my father just, snap, become a psychotic killer one day, or what?" She pulled a photo of all three of them out of the album. They were seated on bleachers. They had sodas and sunburns and were smiling at the camera. Other people's legs were in the shot, so they weren't alone, but they might as well have been. They were sandwiched together, their arms draped around one another—a clear trio.

She flipped the photo over. Someone had written their names in blue ink: *Evelyn, Jack, and Lorelei.*

"My mom never talks about the past. Yours?"

"Only time we talk about my dad is when we discuss how to hide from him. There aren't any happy stories about him." Kayla gently touched her mother's face in the photograph. *Lorelei,* she thought. Young Lorelei's thigh rested on top of Dad's. Her head leaned against his shoulder. "Looks like they were happy once." She took a breath. She knew they must have been. They'd married and had two kids. She couldn't imagine that her mother would have married him if she'd had any inkling as to what would happen.

From the hallway, the dryer dinged. Leaving the album on the bed, she fetched her clothes and dressed in the bathroom, being careful to transfer everything from her pockets. By the time she returned to the bedroom, Daniel had finished dressing.

"I should call her," Kayla said. She picked up the photo of the three of them. Her mother looked so happy. "I should make some kind of excuse so she doesn't have to worry. She must be so—"

Downstairs, the doorbell rang. They both froze.

"I shouldn't have turned on the lights," Daniel said. "Neighbors must have noticed. Let's go." He put his hand on Kayla's shoulder, and his bedroom vanished. The photo was still in Kayla's hand.

15

The rain had stopped. Sort of. It had quit falling from the sky, but it still dripped hard from the canopy of leaves overhead. Shaking off the drops, Daniel walked onto an outcropping. Kayla watched him check the view, then check his compass, then check the view again.

As she waited for him, she knocked drops of water out of the sky. If she concentrated hard enough, she could flick them aside seconds before they hit her skin. It was tricky to hit objects in motion, and it required pinpoint accuracy, like with the mosquitoes. But the more she practiced, the better she got. Soon, she was able to deflect several dozen drops at the same time. She played with flicking them away faster and faster until the rain spattered sideways.

She felt Daniel looking at her. "What are you doing?" he asked.

Releasing the drops, Kayla let gravity grab the rain. It spattered onto her face and shoulders. She wiped her face with her hands. "Ready?"

He held out his hand, and she took it. He hesitated, as if he

wanted to say something profound, or at least difficult to pro-
nounce. "What?" she asked.

"Do you think . . . Will you ever be able to forgive me?" The
expression in his eyes was so intense and so sad that she had to
look away.

"Probably not." She tried to sound cold. What he did was
unforgivable. It was the honest answer.

He was still holding her hand. His hand was damp but warm
and covered hers almost entirely. "Can you tell me, if you were
in my shoes, would you have done any different?"

She opened her mouth to list the thousand ways she would
have acted differently. But if she was going to be honest, then
she'd be honest all the way. "In details, yes. In essence . . ."

"But you still won't forgive me?"

"Probably not."

He laid his hand on her shoulder.

The wet green vanished and was replaced by a house with a
chain link fence. Kids were playing in the yard in the middle of
a mud puddle, stacking goopy mud cakes on top of a toy truck.
Mud streaked their shirts. Clean clothes waved like flags on
a line strung between the house and the fence. One of the boys
jumped to his feet, shouted in Spanish, and pointed at Kayla
and Daniel.

Glancing at his compass, Daniel jumped again. Now, they
were in the middle of a street outside an abandoned gas station.
Rusted cars littered the cracked pavement, and half of the station roof had collapsed. And then they jumped again. And
again.

Rain forest. Fields. More rain forest. A road.

"Halfway there." His jaw was clenched tight.

"Are you—" she began. He jumped them again, and her words were left miles behind. Again. And again. And again. Over and over, until her head buzzed and he started to shake. She grabbed his shoulders. "You need to rest." She forced him to sit on a graffiti-covered rock at the side of a road. A bus rumbled past. It was crowded with people and released a cloud of exhaust that made Kayla's eyes sting. "Memorize this place and then take us home to sleep," she ordered.

Gulping in air, he hung his head between his knees.

"Really? Again? Can't you stop *before* you drain yourself? We aren't going to get there faster if we get ourselves killed sleeping out in the open." She felt his head. Hot. *Idiot*, she thought.

It started to rain again. Hard.

She swore, not quietly, and scanned the area for any kind of shelter. Closest was a house, a rundown prefab white house with a neat little garden, cement steps, and a dirt yard that was rapidly dissolving into mud. It had a rusted swing that hung from a tree and a beat-up pickup truck on the side. "All right. Here's what we're going to do. We're going to ask the people in that house if we can crash at their place, and we're going to hope they're not murderers, rapists, or drug dealers who think we'd make excellent hostages."

In the yard, a dog barked. It was tied to a stake in the ground.

"Come on. Let's get away from the road." She helped Daniel to his feet. He swayed. "Oh, no, you don't. No falling down." She put his arm over her shoulder and half carried, half walked with him toward the house. He stumbled once, slamming down on his knee and nearly knocking her to the muddy ground.

Bracing herself, she pulled him back up. His knees were coated in mud.

Rain fell faster and faster. She blinked, trying to see. Using her mind, she knocked the drops away from her face. The house, which she'd sworn was close, looked like a smudge, and Daniel leaned heavily on her, slowing her even more.

At last, she got him to the gate.

Yapping, the dog was turning itself in circles by the time they reached the door. Batting away the rain, she saw the door swing open and a man without a shirt come out, holding a rifle.

Kayla froze and let the rain crash down on her like normal. Oh, God, maybe they should have stayed by the road. Spending the night in a ditch didn't seem so bad now. She tried to retreat, but Daniel slumped to the ground, unconscious.

"Come on, wake up." She pulled at his arm. "Danny-boy, we have to get out of here."

Leaving his gun on the porch, the man jogged through the rain toward them. He kicked the dog out of the way, hard enough to scoot the animal away from the gate but not hard enough to hurt it. Snarling, the dog cracked its jaws together but didn't move.

Opening the gate, the man said something in Spanish.

"I'm sorry," Kayla said. *"No hablo español. ¿Habla inglés?"* She wished Selena were here. Selena was fluent, at her mother's insistence—she had to be able to talk with her grandparents. Kayla only knew bits and pieces of what she'd learned in school. She could ask where the bathroom was and how to find a shoestore, but she didn't know the word for "help." She did remember "please." *"¿Por favor?"*

The man hooked an arm under Daniel's other arm, and together they half carried and half dragged him across the muddy lawn. At the porch, they lowered Daniel onto a chair. The dog yapped around them. Kayla held out her hand, palm flat toward the dog, and the dog subsided, stopping barking long enough to sniff her. The man nodded approvingly at her and then bellowed at the house. More Spanish.

A woman and two children crowded at the door. *"Díos mio!"* the woman said—Kayla caught the meaning of that just fine—and the woman bustled out. While the children watched, the man and woman carried Daniel inside and laid him on the couch.

"He'll be okay," Kayla said. "He just needs to rest." The woman began to efficiently pull Daniel's soaked clothes off him as the man brought towels and blankets. She stripped him to his underwear and then bundled him up as if she were swaddling a baby.

The two children watched with owl-wide eyes. Kayla tried not to notice Daniel had very nice muscles. She looked at the kids instead. She guessed the boy was around two or three and the girl was four or five. Both had thick black hair, brown skin, and wide black eyes. The girl wore a blue summer dress, and the boy was in shorts and a white T-shirt. The boy had his thumb stuck in his mouth. Kayla smiled at them. The boy scooted behind his sister.

The woman felt Daniel's forehead and clucked her tongue. She then bustled toward Kayla, who retreated. Stopping, the woman made gestures toward her clothes and the rain outside, and then she pointed toward a closed door.

"You're right," Kayla said. "It would be great to be out of

these wet clothes. At least I assume that's what we're talking about?" She followed the woman into a bedroom. Glancing back, she reassured herself that Daniel was safe. The two kids had crept closer to Daniel and plopped themselves on the rug to stare at him. The father was outside again.

The bedroom was tiny and cramped. A double bed mattress on a frame was jammed next to another mattress on the floor, presumably for the kids. Both beds were made up neatly, with hospital corners. Several crocheted animals were displayed on the pillow of the kids' bed. A crucifix was nailed above the man and woman's bed, and a box of tissues was encased in a crocheted doily on the windowsill.

The woman pulled a skirt and blouse out of a tiny closet and handed them to Kayla, then left her alone. Kayla changed quickly, drying herself with a towel. She took the various items out of her pockets, including the photo of her parents and Daniel's mother—it was damp but thankfully not ruined. Sitting on the edge of the bed, she studied their faces, so open and carefree. Kayla wondered if Moonbeam missed being the girl in this photo. She wondered if she remembered her or ever thought about her. Right now, Moonbeam was most likely freaking out. And her freak-out was only going to get worse. Judging by last time, Daniel wouldn't wake until morning. Kayla stowed the photo and her other belongings in the pocket of her borrowed skirt. She also checked her phone. It turned on fine. No coverage, of course.

A few seconds later, the woman scurried in and scooped up the wet clothes. Kayla trailed after her to the main room, where Daniel lay asleep and shivering on the couch, and to the other side, which housed a flimsy table, an old stove, and an ancient refrigerator. The woman turned the oven on and shoved Kayla's and Daniel's wet clothes and sneakers inside.

The woman spoke again, too rapid for Kayla to even guess what she said, and then she began to bustle around the kitchen: fetching a pot, filling it with water, pouring rice into it. Kayla mimed an offer to help, and the woman pointed to the children and made shooing motions with her fingers.

"You want me to play with them?" Kayla asked. "Okay, I can do that." She knelt down on the frayed carpet with the two kids. She smiled brightly at them. *"¡Hola!"* She pointed to herself. *"Me llamo Kayla."*

The kids stared at her.

She'd never spent much time with little kids, at least not since she'd been one. She glanced at the floor to see what they'd been playing before she arrived. They had a newspaper, in Spanish of course, and a pair of blunt preschool scissors in front of them, as well as a few broken crayons. As Kayla reached for the newspaper, the little girl clutched a clump of paper that had been scribbled on with green crayon. Kayla hesitated and then pointed to a piece of newspaper that hadn't been used. The girl didn't move as Kayla picked it and the scissors up. She waited for the kids to object. When they didn't speak or move, she began to cut a rough shape of a man out of the paper. She laid the paper man next to the boy and then began to cut out a girl. Pressing closer, the kids watched her as if she were making magic.

The man came back inside, the door banging behind him. He took off his shoes and squeezed out his socks. His feet were a darker brown than the rest of him, as if they'd been deeply stained by mud. He had thick muscles in his arms and a tattoo of Christ on a cross on his biceps. There were crosses around the house too, as well as several bouquets of plastic flowers. Pulling on a dry shirt, the man headed to the refrigerator and helped his wife prepare food while Kayla played with the children on the floor. The man kissed the woman on the top of her head, and they spoke together as they cooked.

It was so domestic that Kayla felt she'd dropped into the middle of a TV show. She wished there were subtitles.

The kids crept closer as she cut out more dolls. She picked up one of the paper dolls and made it dance. The children howled with delight. They joined in, and together they made the paper dolls dance in a performance across the rug and over the couch.

This is what families without magic—and without constant fear—do, she thought. It was . . . nice. Really nice.

By the time dinner was ready, the kids were climbing on her as if she were their best friend. She was reasonably sure that the girl was named Lucia. She wasn't sure about the boy.

She ate with the family, one of the best meals that she'd ever had, even though it was only rice and beans. The woman set aside some for Daniel to eat, pointing at the food and at him, and put it in the refrigerator for later, slapping her husband's wrist lightly when he tried to scoop more for himself. Kayla kept saying *muchas gracias* over and over.

She wished this were her family. This was what it should be like, what she could have had, if her father hadn't destroyed her family.

The woman tried to insist that Kayla take their bed for the night, but Kayla refused. Instead, she chose the mattress with the children. They wedged themselves around her, clutching their paper dolls, and she fell asleep to the sound of their breathing. It was the best sleep she'd ever had. She felt completely and overwhelmingly safe.

She woke in the predawn, the first to wake. Worming out of the tangle of children's limbs, she went out to the living room to find Daniel groggy but awake.

"You saved me again." His voice sounded rusty. He swallowed.

"These people did. They're amazing." The word didn't go far enough. They'd welcomed Kayla into their home, into their family. She went to the fridge and pulled out the leftovers that the woman had so carefully saved for Daniel. He ate them cold for breakfast while Kayla found their clothes. They were dry and folded neatly. The woman had even ironed them. Kayla and Daniel dressed silently.

"Ready?" he asked.

"Almost." Kayla dug through her pockets to see if she had anything to leave them. Not much in the shorts. But in the hoodie, she found a few rumpled bills . . . and the diamond ring. She left the ring on top of the money in the middle of the table with a note that said "Muchas gracias." "Now I'm ready."

The bedroom door squeaked, and Kayla looked over. One of the kids—the girl, Lucia—stared at them from the doorway. Her eyes were wide. She still held the paper doll.

For an instant, Kayla wished she could stay and she wished she were home with Moonbeam, both at the same time.

Kayla winked at her as Daniel put his hand on her shoulder, and they vanished from the kitchen. They reappeared on the side of the road by the rock, and then continued on.

～ ～

Three jumps left . . . An empty field.

Two jumps . . . A crowded street market.

One jump . . . A city.

They appeared in the middle of a street as an ambulance screamed past them. Yanking Daniel backward, Kayla tripped over the curb and landed smack on the sidewalk. Daniel crashed down beside her. Sirens wailed. Noise hammered at her ears: the blare of music; the screams of children; the revving of motors from cars, trucks, buses, and taxis.

Kayla jumped to her feet. She spun in a circle. A group of men, construction workers with hard hats and equipment, had noticed them. They were shouting as they pointed at Kayla and Daniel. "Daniel, I think we need to leave."

"Can't," he said. "That was the last jump. It's here."

She glanced at the falling-down houses around them, the closed stores with graffiti on the garage doors, and the shiny new apartment building half built across the street. Certainly nothing looked like it had been built in AD 700. She didn't see any temples, tombs, or anything. "I don't think so. I don't think it's been here for a long time."

One of the workers, with a lug wrench over his shoulder, headed toward them.

Kayla grabbed Daniel's arm. "They saw us. We need to go now."

Pulling away from her, Daniel stared at a new half-built skyscraper, at a leaning house with a corrugated tin roof, at a pile of garbage waiting to be picked up while flies circled around it. Cars and motorbikes roared past on the street, and the air smelled like exhaust and sweat and sour food and rotting meat.

"Daniel, it's not here! And we need to leave." There was nothing here older than fifty years. It was a city, with skyscrapers and streets and sewers, maybe subways. Hazy smog obscured the tops of the skyscrapers and smudged the view of the sun. The whole place felt wrapped in yellow.

The construction worker shouted to them, again in Spanish.

At last, Daniel seemed to hear him—and to hear Kayla. He grabbed her arm, and the world flashed around them, yellow then green. When her vision steadied, she saw they were on the sidewalk outside Kayla's house, near the garden gate. Daniel swayed as if he was going to faint. She grabbed his arm before he fell against the hedges. "Daniel, are you all right?"

"That was the last jump."

"I know. It's okay."

He glared at her. "It's not okay! How is it okay?"

"We knew one of the trails would fail. One of the stones was obviously found, or it wouldn't have ended up in my father's hands. We just have to try the third trail. But first you need to rest. Got it? Rest."

"My mother could be dead by now. She could—"

"Are you listening to me? There's a third chance! We'll try again, as soon as you've rested. We'll find it! It will be at the end of the third trail."

He leaned forward and, without warning, kissed her. She pulled away, and then she changed her mind and kissed him back. She let herself melt into the kiss and every thought faded. Reluctantly, she stepped away. She glanced at the red gate. She hadn't planned to return here, not yet. But they couldn't continue, not with him as drained as he looked. "Go home," Kayla ordered him. "Sleep."

He nodded. And then he vanished.

Kayla breathed in. Her lips still tingled from the taste of his. She wasn't quite sure why she'd done that. She *was* sure she did not want to walk through that garden gate and see Moonbeam.

So much for her grand plan to capture her father and come back all victorious. Now what was she supposed to do? It was one thing to be away from Moonbeam when she was convinced she'd be returning with good news and a full explanation. But this?

She thought of the family who had helped them, the way the kids' eyes lit up when she'd played with them, the way the little girl had looked at her when they left. She wished her family was like that.

Taking a deep breath, Kayla pushed through the gate and went into the garden.

16

Moonbeam's garden was a mess.

Her garden was *never* a mess.

Kayla picked her way over the flower beds. Weeds had been pulled and then left in piles to rot. The hedges had been half pruned and then abandoned, sticks and leaves strewn over the lawn. One of the garden gnomes had toppled over. A wind chime had twisted into a mass of snarled string. Kayla jogged toward the house. *Please be okay, please be here, please . . .* She flung open the door. "Moonbeam? Moonbeam, are you home?"

Inside was worse. Dishes were piled up in the sink. All the tidy piles of books and supplies had fallen over and against each other until the floor looked like a sea of junk. Kayla waded through it. "Moonbeam? Are you here? Moonbeam, I'm home!" She didn't know why she was shouting. It was a one-room cottage. If Moonbeam were here, she'd see her.

Going to her corner of the cottage, Kayla pulled open the scarf divider. Her corner was exactly as she'd left it. Her last outfit was strewn beside the bed. Moonbeam hadn't picked it up, not even to leave it displayed as an object lesson as she usually did. A book Kayla had been reading on the floor, a ribbon used as a bookmark—on a normal day, Moonbeam would have put it on a shelf.

She'd been taken.

Or she'd fled.

Or both, fled then been taken.

Had she packed anything? That would tell Kayla which. She sprinted to the bathroom. Both toothbrushes were still there. Hairbrush. Deodorant. Body wash. Vitamins, an entire alphabet's worth.

If Moonbeam had fled quickly, she might have left it all behind—but she wouldn't have left Kayla. Not willingly. She would have stayed until Kayla was back and then they'd have fled together. And Dad could have found her, waiting for Kayla . . .

She told herself to quit jumping to conclusions. Just because the house was a mess didn't mean anything terrible had happened. Maybe Moonbeam had overslept and been late for work. Maybe she simply hadn't felt like cleaning.

Kayla pulled out her phone. Hands shaking, she dialed her mother's work number. She crossed to her futon and sat on the edge as the phone rang.

"Envision Crystal and Candles. How may I help you?" Moonbeam.

Kayla choked back a sob. Her mother was okay. She was here. She hadn't been taken. Dad hadn't found them. "When I saw the garden and the house, I thought . . . Mom, I'm glad you're okay."

"Kayla? Kayla, you're home! Are you all right? Don't leave. Stay there. I'm coming home. Promise me you won't leave. Stay right where you are until I get there."

"I'll be here," Kayla promised.

The phone clicked off, and Kayla stared at it for a moment. Now that she knew her mother was okay, she wished she hadn't called. In about seven minutes, Moonbeam would barrel through the door and demand an explanation. Kayla wasn't sure she had the energy to lie. But she knew she didn't have the strength to tell the truth. She flopped onto her futon, put her hands over her face, and groaned out loud.

Moonbeam made it home in six minutes. She burst through the door and leaped over the heaps of books and crystals and bags of herbs. As Kayla pushed herself up to sitting, Moonbeam threw herself onto the futon and hugged her. Moonbeam didn't say anything. Just held Kayla tight. Kayla squeezed her eyes shut, suddenly wanting to cry.

Eventually, Moonbeam let go. Kayla drew in a deep breath.

Moonbeam looked at her as if examining her for a medical study. She checked her eyes, brushed the hair from her forehead, cupped her chin in her hands, and stared at her. "You nearly killed me."

"I'm sorry." The words didn't go far enough. They sounded hollow, even though she meant them. She hadn't intended to scare Moonbeam. She'd meant to make things better.

"Are you all right? Why didn't you call?" She stroked Kayla's hair as she talked. "You were supposed to be home in two hours! That's all! A shopping spree with Selena! Where have you been? Are you hurt? Did he hurt you?"

Kayla pulled back. "No, nothing like that. I'm fine. I—" Her mother looked so stricken. The words lodged in Kayla's throat. She didn't want to lie.

"Were you with that boy?" Moonbeam asked.

Kayla nodded.

"You couldn't call? Just once? Just to tell me where you are. Or that you're alive." There were tears, fresh in Moonbeam's eyes. They threatened to spill down her cheeks.

"I thought you wouldn't understand." There, that wasn't a lie.

"Do you think you're in love?" There was an edge to Moonbeam's voice.

Drawing back farther, Kayla looked at her, really looked. Her face was pale, more than simply makeup-less pale. Her eyes were sunken, and the circles underneath were so dark that they looked like bruises. Her hair was loose and snarled, the frizz matted in several places. "No," Kayla said. She'd never thought of Moonbeam as fragile before. Needing taking care of, yes. Needing protection and watching, yes. But not breakable.

"Good."

Kayla tried to think of what to say, a plausible lie that wouldn't feel like a lie, or at least words that would soothe her.

Moonbeam stood up. "Oh, Kayla, I'm so very disappointed in you. I thought I could trust you. You were my mature girl, taking care of me. But I suppose I was asking too much of you. You *are* still a girl, my little girl, who will make mistakes and learn and grow . . . exactly as you're supposed to." She didn't sound angry; she sounded sad, which was worse.

Kayla didn't know what to say to that. She couldn't promise it wouldn't happen again. "I'll be fine. I can take care of myself— and you. You can trust me to do that."

Moonbeam shook her head, and her hair rustled softly. "I'm supposed to take care of you, not the other way around, and I clearly haven't been doing a good job of it." She shuffled over to a basket. Setting it upright, she selected several pouches of herbs. "You won't like this, but believe me, it's for your own good. You need boundaries. Limits. You need someone to set rules for you and say enough is enough. And that someone is supposed to be your parent. Me. So from here on in, I will be the parent that you need, not the parent you want."

"Moonbeam?" Kayla stood, alarmed. "*Mom*, you're a wonderful parent. You're fine. I'm the one who screwed up. I should have found a way to call you. I didn't mean to worry you. There was just . . . It was . . . I can't explain yet. But please believe me, I'm doing the right thing. You have to trust me."

"You violated my trust." Moonbeam picked up the Kayla doll, and she dropped it into the basket of herbs. "Unless you can explain in much more detail?" She straightened the piles of books. She scooped up the crystals and positioned them on the shelves. She folded scarves and ribbons. Watching her, Kayla felt her heart sink. Her mother only cleaned this frenetically when she was seriously upset. And she only let the house get this messy when she was seriously worried.

"I . . . I can't explain. Not right now."

Moonbeam sighed as she worked. She piled various amulets and statues on the kitchen table, and then sorted them rapidly into piles that seemed random to Kayla. "I remember being your age. You feel like you're alone. You can't trust anyone. No one understands. But it's not true. You can trust me."

Kayla thought of the photo in her pocket. She wanted to ask about Daniel's mother and why Moonbeam had kept in touch, even going as far as to tell them Kayla's new name and where they lived, but then she'd have to explain how she knew.

"If you truly are dealing with something major, you need to

tell me so I can help you." Soon, she'd cleared a path from the beds to the kitchen and also the door.

Kayla wanted so desperately to tell her. Just dump the entire thing on her mother's lap and let her help. But Moonbeam wouldn't help. She'd want to run.

"For the rest of the summer, until you have a little space from what you are feeling, a little distance from this boy, I need you to stay here. You may come with me to run errands. If you want to accompany me to work, that's fine. But otherwise, I want you here. I *need* you here. For my peace of mind, as well as for your safety." Retrieving the basket of herbs, Moonbeam walked out the door into the garden. Kayla followed. Speaking softly, Moonbeam recited the melodious words that slid through the air and then vanished as she paced the perimeter of the yard, circling the house counterclockwise, tossing herbs at the hedges. Like green and brown snow, they sprinkled on the bushes, the gnomes, the ceramic fairies, and the circle of protective stones.

"Moonbeam—"

"The boy is obviously a bad influence on you, and Selena can't be trusted either. You convinced her to lie for you. Several times. I don't want you to see either of them for several weeks. One month. After that, we'll reevaluate." She continued to walk as she talked, reinforcing the protection ring around the house. Kayla had never seen her do this when it wasn't the solstice, and she'd never used herbs. It was always incense and candles. The fact that she was varying from her routine . . . She must be beyond severely upset. Kayla had to fix this.

Kayla hurried after her. "Moonbeam—"

"This isn't open to discussion, Kayla. I'm your mother, and I am, for once, going to act like it." Moonbeam completed the circle and wiped her hands on her skirt. The crushed herbs left streaks on the fabric, but she didn't seem to notice. "I need to return to work. I do have responsibilities. Rent doesn't pay itself. The food you eat doesn't magically appear in the refrigerator." She leveled her finger at Kayla. "You will be here when I get back."

"I have responsibilities too."

"Kayla. You're making poor decisions. You need some time apart from the bad influences in your life, to think about your priorities and your role in this family. This is for your own good. You need to focus and regroup."

Kayla felt as if she'd been slapped. The air was sucked out of her. Moonbeam never spoke to her with that tone of voice.

Moonbeam's expression softened. "I love you, Kayla. I wouldn't do this if I didn't love you. You know that, right?" She carried the basket back into the house, stowed it on a shelf, and fetched her purse.

"Wait, Moonbeam, I'm doing something important!"

At the door, Moonbeam spun to face her. She seemed to tower, her expression not at all like that of the mild hippie-like woman she portrayed. "Then tell me what you're doing! Convince me! I'll listen."

"Can't you just . . . trust me?"

"You didn't come home. You didn't call. You won't explain. No, I can't trust you. You're doing something I wouldn't approve of, otherwise you'd tell me. So the answer is no." Softer, she said, "I'm sorry, Kayla."

She was right, in a way. Moonbeam would never approve of what Kayla was doing with Daniel. But still, she had to do it.

"Just . . . please trust me for a few days more. I promise after that, everything will be fine. Better than fine. I just . . . can't tell you why. Moonbeam, before this, have I ever let you down? Disappointed you in any way?"

"Tell me this one thing and tell me honestly. Are you using your power?"

Kayla opened her mouth to lie. But the words wouldn't come out.

Sadly, Moonbeam nodded. "I'll be home with dinner." And then she left. Kayla trailed her into the garden, then slowed, watching as she marched out the gate without a backward glance, her shoulders stiff and her back straight. The chimes rang in her wake. Kayla sank onto the bench. How had everything gone so wrong so fast?

She took a minute to breathe, and then she *did* "focus and regroup." She wouldn't let this stop her. She couldn't. Not now. Not when she was so close to making everything better!

Marching back into the house, she pulled out her emergency backpack and added extra food and water. She then checked her pockets. The lighter had fuel, but the razor blade was dull. She fetched a new one. Prepared, she paced around the house.

Yanking out her phone, she texted Daniel, *Ready to look for next stone?* He probably hadn't had a chance to recover yet, but she had three hours until Moonbeam would be back from work. If he came anytime in that window, she'd be fine. If he didn't and Moonbeam caught Kayla leaving . . . she couldn't imagine what the fallout would be like. She'd never seen Moonbeam like this.

Kayla tried to call Selena, then sent a text and an email.

She then tried Daniel again.

No response from either.

After a while, she grew tired of waiting for them. There was only so long one could wrap oneself in misery and angst and gritty determination before it lost its luster.

She fetched Moonbeam's pruners and gardening gloves and set to work outside yanking up weeds and trimming the bushes. Sawing at a particularly thick weed, she pictured her father, standing with the stone in his hand, leaving her with Daniel injured. The weed was healthy, and the stalk resisted the pruner. She hacked at it with a trowel and then stabbed it with the pruners until it oozed white sap. After the weed fell, she stomped on it for good measure, completely aware she was stomping on her metaphorical father. It made her feel minutely better.

She could do this. She could stop him. She could fix everything. Kayla repeated that to herself as she attacked the next weed, then the next.

The chimes rang—someone was here! Carrying the pruners, she rushed to the gate and opened it. She felt a wave of dizziness crash through her, and she steadied herself on the hedges.

"Kayla?" It was Daniel.

He grasped her shoulders and propelled her backward to sit on the bench. She sank into it and then shook her head as the dizziness cleared. "Hey. Sorry. Just felt a little . . . I'm fine. Are you okay?" She studied him. He seemed worn down, but he wasn't shaking or anything.

"Yeah." He scuffed at the dirt with his toe. "Got your message. You really think we still have a chance? You think the third one is still hidden?"

Kayla shrugged. "My bet is that my father is on the third trail right now. It would be nice to get there first."

Daniel flashed her a smile. "Then let's do this."

Grabbing her pack, she took his hand. The world flashed around them.

Instantly, her stomach constricted and flipped. It heaved up toward her mouth. She dropped to her knees, holding her stomach as the world spun around her.

She heard Daniel's voice, calling her name, and then she felt as if her stomach lining were turning inside out. Spots danced in front of her eyes as she threw up again and again. She felt hands on her shoulders, and she was cradled as the rain forest dipped and swirled around her.

Another flash, and then the nausea swept away as fast as it had swept in. The world steadied. She raised her head. She was back in her garden. Her stomach felt empty. Her throat hurt. Gently, Daniel guided her to the bench again. "I'm okay." She pushed him away. "I'm . . . What the hell was that?"

"Just . . . breathe deep. I'll get you . . . What do you need?"

She looked at him. Her mouth tasted like sour peanut butter. Her hair clung to her sweaty forehead and cheeks. "I feel fine now. Completely fine. Gross, but fine." She tried standing. She didn't feel a bit dizzy or nauseated. Daniel hovered near her as if expecting her to collapse into his arms.

"I'll get you some water." He raced into the house and then came out again with a glass of water. She sipped it, swished the water, and then spat on the flowers. She drank more water. Her stomach felt achy and empty but she didn't feel at all queasy.

She looked down at herself. Gooey bits clung to her shirt. "Got to clean myself."

"I'll help you. You're not well."

She looked at him. "We aren't married. We're not even dating. That's definitely not in your job description. In fact, I'd rather you didn't get up close and personal with the contents of my stomach. That's just a little too close for me." Alone, she headed for the house. She felt fine. After changing her shirt, she washed her face and neck with a towel. She then returned to the garden and picked up her pack again. "Okay, let's go."

"Are you sure—"

"I'm fine. Let's go."

He held her hand, and again the flash— Nausea slammed into her once more and drove her to her knees. Her stomach heaved, and then they jumped back to the garden.

She was fine.

"Kayla . . . that's not normal," Daniel said.

Grimly, Kayla nodded. She stalked to the garden gate and opened it. Taking a deep breath, she stepped outside. Nausea. Dizziness. She stumbled backward. She was fine.

Daniel caught her arms. She sagged against him. "She did it," Kayla said. "I didn't think she could. Or would." Pulling away from Daniel, Kayla prowled in front of the gate. She glared at it as if it were to blame. "She spelled it. Me. So I can't leave."

"What are you talking about, Kayla?" Daniel asked. She could hear the worry in his voice, the tinge of fear. "Who did what?"

"My mother," Kayla said. "She's trapped me here."

17

Kayla paced in a tight circle, feeling like a caged animal. They'd tried jumping elsewhere. They'd tried climbing over the hedges. They'd tried Daniel carrying her through the gate. Fail, fail, and fail. Whatever spell Moonbeam had done, it was intense.

"It's over," Daniel said, sinking onto the bench.

"It's *not* over." Honestly, if he said that one more time, she was going to have to gag him. "It's just more complicated."

"I can't do this without you."

Stopping, she glared at him. "Yes, you can, at least up until the last part. You're going to go right now, do all the jumps except the last one, and then come back for me. By then, I'll have found a way out."

He nodded slowly.

"Just promise me that you'll be careful. Pace yourself. Rest between jumps. Go home and sleep through the night if you have to. Remember, I won't be there to drag you to safety if you collapse." Crossing to him, Kayla put her hands on his shoulders so that he had to look at her. "This is serious. You have the common sense of a dim-witted lemming, and I don't want you to plunge off a cliff and die."

A corner of his lips quirked up. "Hey, you do care."

She released him. "Moonbeam's shift tomorrow is ten to six. Come back then. And watch out for my father. Especially if you're near any rocks."

"He won't surprise me this time," Daniel promised.

"If you do see him, then jump him somewhere he can't leave. Like the tomb in Peru. And then we'll deal with him together, okay?"

"You don't trust me?"

"I don't trust him." She paused. "And no, I don't trust you either. But at least I like you. I hate him."

He smiled, and it was like the sun appeared between the clouds. "You like me?"

Kayla felt herself begin to blush, so she rolled her eyes and tossed her hair. "What are you, six years old? Yes, I like you. You're intense. You love your mom. You have that neat teleportation trick going for you. Just because you're a self-centered liar with a dubious ethical compass doesn't mean you aren't my type."

He blinked. "I'm not sure whether that was a compliment or not."

"Time is ticking, Daniel." She tapped her wrist. "You need to make the jumps before my father finds the end of the third trail." Kayla hesitated. She wanted to say more. No, she didn't want to say anything; she wanted to *do* and *see* and *run free*! She wanted to take his hand, jump with him, and leave this home that had transformed into a cage. She wanted to see the rain forest again, even with the mosquitoes and the jaguars and the rain. She wanted to see all the places on the maps on the walls of Daniel's room. Now that she'd tasted a piece of the world, she wanted all of it. Imagining not having it, Kayla felt her eyes heat up. "Just go, Daniel."

He vanished, and she gulped in air. She rubbed her eyes vigorously. She was *not* going to cry. Circling the property, Kayla searched for clues to the spell. She felt fine in the yard, so that meant the spell had to be tied to the perimeter in some way. She just had to figure out what was defining the border—in other words, she had to find her jail cell walls. And then break them.

Her first guess was the protective stones. Years ago, Moonbeam had carted stones from the beach to their house and set up a circle of them just inside the bushes. She'd said a spell over them and refreshed the spell every solstice, saying melodious words as she walked counterclockwise with a candle and incense. Today was the first time she'd refreshed them with the basket of herbs. Maybe the new spell had given them an extra boost. Kayla took her trowel to the gate and dug several stones out of the earth. She tossed them aside, creating a break in the circle, and then she tried to walk through.

Hands plastered over her mouth from the immediate wave of nausea, she stumbled back.

Guess it isn't the stones, she thought. Taking a deep breath of air to calm her stomach again, Kayla turned in a slow circle. What else could it be?

The yard was ringed with an unbroken circle of bushes. Over the gate, the branches were woven into an arch. In the front of the house, they bowed out to avoid the electrical line coming in to the corner of the roof. The hedge was so thick that you couldn't see the neighbors' houses. Maybe the spell was linked to the plants.

Fetching the pruners, Kayla attacked one of the bushes. She trimmed branch after branch, carving an ugly hole in its center. With her hands, she ripped at the leaves. They fell at her feet, carnage from the slaughter, until she had made a break in the wall of green. She then pulled over the bench and stood on it in order to destroy the tops of the bushes. She didn't stop until she'd made a gap as wide as a person.

Taking a deep breath, she stepped into the gap. Careful not to touch the sides, she inched forward. The neighbor had a fence on his property. If she could reach the fence and climb over it . . . She took another step, and her foot crossed over the roots.

Sickness slammed into her, fast, and she retreated.

She hadn't destroyed the roots. The circle wasn't completely broken. She dropped to her knees. The roots wove a thick mat between the bushes. Grabbing the trowel and pruners, she dug into the earth. She snipped the roots as she found them. She worked feverishly, as if the hedge would close again if she slowed.

She'd never truly believed that Moonbeam's magic worked. It wasn't like hers, obvious and visual. All the charms against sickness, theft, bad luck, ill will . . . Until today, Kayla had rarely felt sick, but she might just have a decent immune system. They'd never been robbed, but they didn't have much to begin with, especially compared to people like Selena. Bad luck? Ill will? She didn't know. She wondered what else Moonbeam could do and how powerful she was. If she could craft a spell like this, why did they even have to hide from Dad?

Maybe that's what Moonbeam had thought before Dad killed Amanda. Maybe now she didn't want to take any chances. Maybe Kayla was being stupid pursuing a confrontation and thinking she could handle it.

But she could, damn it. She could fix this! Fix her life and Moonbeam's and give them a future without fear! That was worth a little risk. She'd be careful and clever, like she always was. Dad may have been a match for a young innocent Amanda, but Kayla wasn't a little girl.

At last, Kayla had torn up all the roots she could find. It looked like a warthog had dug into their hedgerow. She stood up and dusted the dirt off her clothes. Time to try again. She strode forward—and again the nausea crashed into her.

Stumbling back, she dropped to her knees. She stayed on her knees until the vertigo stopped. Okay, so the spell wasn't tied to the plants. There had to be some way she was triggering it. Maybe it was her? Something was tying her to the house? She thought of the voodoo doll that her mother had dipped in the herbs. Maybe that had been part of the spell, not just part of the cleanup as she'd assumed. Where was the doll? Kayla jumped to her feet.

"Kayla?" Moonbeam called from the gate.

Oh, no, she's home! Kayla glanced at the chopped-up dirt, the mess of leaves, and the broken roots that looked like severed bones. She couldn't hide this carnage. Putting down the pruners, she met her mother at the gate.

Carrying a bag of burritos, Moonbeam smiled sunnily at her. "Arranged to take the rest of the day off! Got extra guacamole, the kind you like. Also, chips and salsa . . ." Her smile faded. "Kayla, what did you do?"

"Yard work?"

"You're terrible at it," Moonbeam commented.

"I won't do it again."

Moonbeam studied her for a second. In an even voice, she said, "Trying to escape isn't the best way to rebuild trust."

"Imprisoning me isn't the best way to be a mother."

"It's for your own good," Moonbeam said. "I can't send you to the corner for a time-out." She sighed and then headed for the house. Kayla trailed behind her. It took all her self-restraint not to scream at her mother to *let her go!* Right now, Daniel was jumping across South America with no one there to make sure he didn't fall off a cliff or drown himself in a piranha-infested river or pass out from exhaustion in the middle of a road.

In the kitchen, Moonbeam unloaded the burritos, paper plates, and plastic forks and knives. Kayla stowed her emergency backpack under her futon—it looked like she wasn't going anywhere today—and then returned to help Moonbeam set the table. Moonbeam nodded at a bag by the door. "I stopped by the library also and picked up some books and movies for you. See, I'm not an ogre. When you're older, you'll thank me for setting boundaries."

"How did you do it?" Kayla asked.

"Eye of newt, tongue of frog, and a little bit of pixie dust." Moonbeam mimed catching a pixie and shaking it like a bell.

If she'd wanted to make Kayla laugh, she'd picked the wrong day. "This isn't funny. I can't stay here!"

Moonbeam sighed. "This isn't open to discussion anymore, not unless you've decided to be honest with me. And even then, the punishment stands. You have to learn that there are consequences to your actions and decisions *before* they are so dire that they lead to tragedy."

She was talking about Amanda again. Glancing at the shelves, Kayla spotted the basket with the voodoo doll. She looked away quickly so her mother wouldn't notice. "I didn't even know you had this kind of power. For someone who hates magic, you're very good at it."

Moonbeam unwrapped her burrito. "When I was your age, I did more than dabble. It got me into quite a bit of trouble. Magic isn't the solution; it's the problem. Always."

Kayla thought of the stones. "What happened?"

"When?"

"When you dabbled."

A faint smile crossed her lips. "Once, I tried a love spell. The results were like a bad Shakespeare play."

"Did everyone die?"

"Comedy, not tragedy! Lots of mistaken identity and flowery poetry." Her smile faded. "But there were other times when people were hurt. Not killed. We always stopped short of that. All of us swore to never cross that line."

Kayla slid onto one of the stools. "Who's 'all of us'?" She thought she knew—the photo was in her pocket.

Jumping off her stool, Moonbeam bustled to the cabinets. She pulled out additional spices, and she filled up two cups with water. "People from my past. Point is, I don't use spells to make things happen anymore. I use spells to *keep* things from happening—to keep you safe." Reaching over, she touched the eye amulet around Kayla's neck.

Kayla had the sudden urge to tear the necklace off, but she kept her hands clasped calmly in front of her. "My father. Is that who you did spells with?"

"I said it was the past, Kayla. I don't want to talk about it." Moonbeam's lips curved into a cheerful smile, clearly forced. "Come, it's movie night! We'll eat in front of the TV. Pick out a movie."

Wishing she dared ask more, Kayla shuffled over to the library bag and made a show of sorting through. There was an assortment of old favorites plus a few newer titles. Kayla had never been less in the mood for a movie. "Whatever you want."

Moonbeam chose *The Princess Bride*, a movie they both had memorized. She fetched the quilts she'd made herself and then thumped the TV until it worked. After setting their dinner on the coffee table, she curled up on the couch next to Kayla.

Kayla pretended to laugh in all the right places, all the while thinking about Daniel and wondering what he'd found. And whether her father had found him. She picked at her burrito and, later, when Moonbeam made popcorn on the stove with copious amounts of real butter, the popcorn tasted like cardboard in her mouth.

At night, she listened to Moonbeam breathe and barely slept.

∽ ✑

Moonbeam left for work the next morning a little before ten. She kissed Kayla on the cheek and promised to cook her favorite fried tofu for dinner. Kayla dredged up a smile and made a show of selecting a book to read. As soon as Moonbeam was gone, Kayla sprinted for the shelves. She grabbed the basket that she'd seen Moonbeam with yesterday, and she pulled out the voodoo doll.

Hands shaking, she carried it to the sink. She dropped it in and pulled out her lighter. She flicked on the flame—and then flicked it off. This might be a very, very bad idea. For all she knew, if she set it on fire, she could spontaneously combust in reaction. She needed a safe way to neutralize the doll.

Luckily, she *did* know an expert.

Pulling out her phone, she found the number for Queen Marguerite's store and dialed it. An older woman with a thick Louisiana accent answered. "Voodoo Spells and Charms. Queen Marguerite, blessed be, at your service."

Thank goodness she was there. "Your Majesty, this is Kayla . . . from the other day? You know, the one who helped you clean your shop? And the one you saved from the snake bite?"

"Ahh, the fixer. Yes, of course, my dear, I remember you. What can I do for you? Have you plucked out the evil in your family's heart?"

"Um, not yet. But I have a little problem . . . I need to know how to disable a voodoo doll." She cradled the doll in one hand as she held the phone with the other.

"Voodoo dolls are much misunderstood. They're used for good intentions, not bad. For protection, not harm! Hollywood has misrepresented my religion—"

Kayla interrupted. "My mother dipped it in herbs and said words over it, and now I can't leave without becoming incredibly sick."

There was silence on the other end. At last, Marguerite said, "Your mother did this?" She had an odd note in her voice. Almost . . . hopeful.

"She's worried about me," Kayla said. "I can't . . . I haven't told her what I've been doing. She wouldn't understand. She thinks using magic is evil."

"Yet she used it to confine you?"

"Yeah, believe me, I noticed the irony."

There was silence, as if Marguerite was thinking or distracted, and then she said briskly, "You cannot destroy the doll. Not without harm to yourself."

Kayla felt her heart sink. She stared out the window at the hedges around the garden. She imagined never seeing beyond them. "There has to be a way. I have to escape. We . . . we found one of the stones, but the kidnapper took it from us." She couldn't bring herself to say it was her father. "We only have one chance left."

She braced herself for anger, but Queen Marguerite only said, "Then this time, you must not fail. And then you must retrieve two stones from your enemy. If they complete the spell . . . you won't like the consequences."

"I can't do any of that trapped here. How do I break the spell?"

"One who knows the spell can negate it."

"I don't think my mom's in the mood." Out the window, she saw Daniel appear. His legs were caked in mud from the knee down, but he seemed okay. He waved to her, and she waved back. "Do you know the spell?"

"As it happens, yes, I do. But I cannot break it over the phone. It must be in person. Bah, I hate house calls. For you, little fixer, I will make an exception . . . on one condition."

Kayla stopped herself from saying "anything." "What condition?"

"Bring the stones to me."

"Why? What do you want with them?"

"I want to hide them. Even alone, they cause too much damage. I want to ensure all three stones are hidden so well that no one will ever find any of them again."

"Works for me. So long as Daniel's reunited with his mother and my dad's safely behind bars first." Kayla rushed outside. "Daniel? Are you okay?"

"Send the boy to me. I can't jump to a place I've never seen."

"Can you jump to Louisiana?" Kayla asked Daniel. She waved the phone in the air. "I need Queen Marguerite. She can break the spell."

Without a word, he vanished.

Into the phone, Kayla said, "Daniel's coming for you."

"Ah, yes. Hello, Daniel."

Kayla heard the phone click off. Retrieving the voodoo doll, she paced back and forth in the garden. She had second thoughts. And third thoughts. And fourth. She'd had it drilled into her again and again: don't trust anyone. She didn't know Queen Marguerite, not really, though the woman had saved her life. And Queen Marguerite knew too much, including Daniel's mother.

Before she could truly reconsider, Daniel returned—with the voodoo queen.

Cane in front of her, back ramrod straight, and eyes narrowed, Queen Marguerite surveyed the garden. Her cane was black and curved, with a silver skull at the top. She caressed the top of the skull as her piercing eyes swept over the hedges, the bench, the gnomes, and at last Kayla.

"So, can you help her?" Daniel asked.

"Yes," Queen Marguerite said decisively. "And I will." She reached into the folds of her dress and pulled out a white cloth and a plastic pouch with white sand in it. "The doll, please."

Kayla hesitated for a moment—if her mother could trap her with this doll, then what could a real voodoo queen do? She reminded herself that Queen Marguerite was on her side and that she had little choice but to trust her, if she wanted to escape. She handed over the voodoo doll. Queen Marguerite wrapped the doll in the white cloth.

"Stand still." Marguerite opened the pouch and began to pour the sand in a circle around Kayla.

"What is this?" Kayla asked.

"One of nature's greatest neutralizers. Salt. It can help end an open-ended compulsion like this or stop an unfinished spell." Halting, Queen Marguerite looked at the salt critically. "It needs to be a solid circle."

Kayla shifted a few grains of salt with her mind, filling in fissures in the circle. She then checked all the way around. "I think it's good."

"You'll excuse me if I dispense with the sideshow fanfare and usual light show. Real magic comes from the mind, not the paraphernalia. They merely facilitate. Also, they make people tip more."

"My mother says the same thing," Kayla said.

"She does?" Marguerite seemed startled.

"Half the charms here aren't real." Kayla waved at the charms on the hedge, over the gate, and in the window. "They're for show."

"Well, then," Marguerite said softly. "Well, then, indeed." She surveyed the various charms, the garden gnomes, and the ceramic fairies. "Your mother and I have much in common. Regardless, best get you on your way." Carrying the doll, the voodoo queen walked in a steady circle counterclockwise around Kayla, muttering in the sonorous tone that Moonbeam used for her spells. The words spun around Kayla, through her head and around her skin, leaving no impression on either. "There, that should work." To Daniel, Marguerite said, "Don't break the circle. When you're ready, reach over it, touch her hand, and go. Once she's away, the compulsion will end, and she will be able to come and go freely without any side effects." To Kayla, she added, "And no one, not your mother, not anyone, will be able to use this doll against you—or for you—again."

"Thank you," Kayla said.

"Don't thank me. Just find the third stone," Queen Marguerite said. "And the next time I come, have your mother bake some of her brownies. That will be payment enough."

Kayla, who had been reaching for Daniel, dropped her hand. She felt cold in the pit of her stomach. "How do you know my mother?"

Queen Marguerite smiled. "Wrong question. Someday you have to ask her how she knows *me*. After all, who do you think taught her this spell?" And then she vanished.

Kayla looked at Daniel. She had the horrible feeling that she'd made a terrible mistake. Now the voodoo queen had seen where she lived; she could come anytime. She wanted to call Moonbeam, confess it all. "Catch your father, and that will fix everything," Daniel said. "Your mother will be safe. And so will mine." He held out his hand. Kayla took it. And the garden disappeared.

18

Kayla and Daniel were on a road.

The air felt thick and hot. The pavement was cracked, and heat rose off it in waves, as if it were the surface of a volcano. A signpost next to the road listed kilometers to Guadalajara. Focusing on it, she breathed in. And out. She didn't feel sick.

Daniel watched her. "Okay?"

"Yeah. Let's do this."

"You know your father could already be there."

"Or maybe he's still in Peru. But if he is there . . ." She dug her hands into her pockets and felt the fishing line and hooks. "I distract him; you grab him." If she sent the hooks into his skin, they'd hurt enough to surprise him, hopefully enough to keep him from casting any spells, and then she could use the line to tie him up or trip him or at least slow him until Daniel reached him. It was a simple plan, but sometimes those worked the best. She just had to be quick and not freeze in abject terror when she saw him. She took a deep breath to calm herself. "Ready when you are."

Another jump, and they were in front of a Catholic church on the outskirts of a town. Flies buzzed around them, and the air

smelled like car exhaust. The road was dirt and had deep pot-
holes in it, the kind that looked like they swallowed cars. Two
pickup trucks were parked outside the church. One had a gun
rack, and the other had a tarp covering its bed. She wondered if
either of them was her father's. She'd never thought about what
kind of vehicle a murderer would drive. "Be alert," she whispered.

The lawn of the church was cut short and dotted with crab-
grass. Fake flowers adorned a statue of the Virgin Mary beside
the front double doors. Except for the two trucks, the place looked
deserted. She didn't see any movement at all. Even the wind was
still.

"So we just trespass?" she asked.

"Pretend we're tourists," Daniel advised as he walked toward
the doors of the church. "People forgive a lot if they think you're
an ignorant idiot with money to spend where they live."

"Sounds like the voice of experience." Following him, she
thought of all the photos in his bedroom. He'd seen so much
of the world.

"Use it all the time," Daniel said. "Once, I jumped to the
Roman Coliseum. Scared off about a billion cats and nearly was
arrested, until they decided I was an idiot tourist."

"I want to see Rome someday."

"When this is over, I'll take you," Daniel offered. "I know
this great gelato place by the Trevi Fountain, tourist prices but
worth it. Best flavor in the world is *niccolo*. It's hazelnut. Do you
like ice cream?"

"Everyone likes ice cream. Have you forgotten that I haven't
forgiven you?" As she walked toward the church doors, she continued to scan the area. If her father were here, would he be
inside? Had he already been here?

"You said you liked me."

"That has zero to do with whether I ever want to see you again."

"Then I'll have to try to bribe you with ice cream." Catching her hand, he swung her around to face him. "Kayla, this is it. I can feel it. The stone is here!"

His smile was so infectious that she couldn't help smiling back.

"You are my good luck charm. If it weren't for you—"

"Let's see if it's here before you start praising me." Pulling him with her, she marched to the doors. Plaster saints watched them from alcoves on either side. Wreaths lay at their feet. Kayla tried one of the doors, and it opened. No lock. "Remember: if you see my father, don't hesitate. Jump fast. I'll keep him from saying any spells."

Inside, it was noticeably cooler. Cool air seemed to radiate from the stone walls and floors, and everything was bathed in red and blue shadows, cast by the sun through the stained glass. The pews were festooned with wilted flowers, and at the front of the church, the altar was draped in white-and-gold cloth. Kayla heard voices speaking Spanish from somewhere near the altar— two voices: a woman and an elderly man. She couldn't see them. Keeping to the side of the church, Kayla and Daniel didn't speak.

The stones on the walls bore names. She recognized the words for mother, sister, and grandmother on one stone and uncle and brother on the other. "Do you think it's with any of them?" Kayla whispered to Daniel. "Our Maya jumper seems to like tombs."

"Not a bad place to hide something," Daniel said. "Dead people tend to stay put."

There were dates beneath the names: 1879, 1900, 1898, 1903 . . . Abruptly, Kayla quit walking. "Daniel, look at the dates. This church . . . How old is it?"

He looked at her, his face stricken.

Retreating to the vestibule, they found a historical marker by the front doors. The church had been built in 1856. Daniel's shoulders slumped. "We should have realized the moment we saw this place," Kayla said. "Catholicism didn't even exist here until the Spanish showed up." Frowning at the dates, she didn't look at Daniel. She didn't have to see his expression to know he was looking like a wounded puppy again.

"I'm an idiot," Daniel said. "The stone can't be here. It's—"

"If you say 'it's over,' I'll smack you."

He didn't complete the sentence.

"We need to find out what was here before this church." Kayla glanced toward the altar. The voices had ceased. Where had those people gone? "There has to be someone we can ask. I heard a man and a woman before."

Across the nave, she spotted a priest. She pulled Daniel toward him. "Hello! ¡Hola!" She waved. "Really sorry to bother you, but we have some questions about the church. ¿Habla inglés?"

The priest shook his head, spoke a few words in Spanish, and then started to walk away.

Kayla and Daniel hurried to catch up to him. "Have you seen this man?" She pulled the photo out of her pocket and pointed to her father. Barely looking at it, the priest shook his head. "He'd be older now." She pointed to her hair. "Older. You know . . . Daniel, do you speak any Spanish?"

"Nada," Daniel said.

Again, the priest shook his head apologetically. Shrugging, he began to walk away again. This time, they let him. Maybe there was someone else around . . . that woman she'd heard?

Kayla and Daniel scoured the church—the vestibule, the pews, the altar. Except for the priest, they were alone. Going outside, they looked up and down the dirt road. No houses were visible. Wind blew dried-up weeds against a barbed-wire fence. The two trucks were still there. One could belong to the priest. She didn't know about the other one.

"What about your friend Selena?" Daniel asked. "She could translate."

"I don't want to endanger her."

"She wouldn't be in danger. All we need is a quick translation. One conversation. And she'd only be talking to a priest."

Kayla shook her head. "Until my father shows up and knocks the entire church down on our heads. This isn't her problem."

"She's already involved."

"With research. With supplies. Behind-the-scenes stuff. Actually coming with us . . . way too risky."

"Even if it could mean the safety of your family, that you wouldn't have to move, that your mother wouldn't live in fear? Even if it could mean saving my mother? She's supposed to be your best friend. Can't we just ask her? She might surprise you. She might surprise *herself*. She could be stronger than the two of you think she is."

He didn't wait for an answer. He touched Kayla's shoulder, and the world vanished around them. She opened her mouth to yell at Daniel for not being more careful—the priest could have seen them—and then saw Selena and her mother were on the couch, their backs to Kayla and Daniel.

Kayla clamped her hand over his mouth and pulled him down behind the couch.

Peeking out, Kayla caught a glimpse of Selena's face in profile. Her cheeks were streaked with tears. Mrs. Otieno's hair was down from her usual bun, and it curved around her face. She wore no makeup and no jewelry. She looked even more beautiful when she wasn't looking perfect.

"We only want what's best for you," Mrs. Otieno said, her voice throbbing with sincerity. That was what made it so difficult for Selena, Kayla knew. Her mother truly cared.

Selena shook her head and didn't speak.

Kayla held up one finger, asking Daniel to wait. She wanted to hear what they were saying. Creeping closer, she listened. She heard Selena gasp. And Kayla realized that she was reflected in the computer screen across the room. Selena's eyes were wide and appalled. Quickly, Kayla reached with her mind and pushed the power button on the TV. Both Selena and her mom turned their heads to look at it, and Kayla mouthed to Daniel, *Out now.*

The room flashed, and they were outside on the driveway near Selena's garage. As soon as her vertigo faded, Kayla began to pace in a tight circle. "She saw me!"

"Ring the doorbell and when she answers it, explain," Daniel said.

"That was a private moment! She's going to kill me! You don't know how touchy she can be when it comes to her mother."

"She'll understand. How could you have known she and her mother would be there?"

Kayla stopped pacing and glared at him. He had no idea what he was talking about. No way would she understand. "You have a friend like Selena?"

"No one has a friend like Selena. But talking early could solve problems later. Look at your parents and my mom. Maybe if they'd talked more when they were our age, then—"

"—my dad wouldn't have turned into a psychopathic killer?"

He winced. "Bad analogy?"

"Bad analogy," she agreed. But she did walk to the door and ring the doorbell. It echoed like church bells. Kayla fidgeted. "Let me do the talking."

After a few seconds, Kayla heard footsteps. One of the housekeepers opened the door. "Yes? Can I help you?" the woman asked in heavily accented English. "Oh, Kayla, hello!"

Daniel leaned closer to Kayla. "Or we could just take *her*?"

Kayla ignored him. "Hi, Camilla. Is Selena home?"

Rising on her tiptoes, Camilla peered over them at the gate. She frowned. "How did you get here? Who buzzed you in?"

Oops. She'd forgotten about the gate. Waving her hand nonchalantly, Kayla pretended to misunderstand the question. "Oh, we walked. Lovely day out. Hills are great exercise. Really, it's important that we see Selena."

Before Camilla could answer, Selena charged through the foyer. She spoke a few words in rapid-fire Spanish, and the housekeeper retreated. She then turned the full force of her glare on Kayla and Daniel. "Tell me I didn't just see you inside my house, spying on me." Coming outside, she shut the door behind her.

Before Kayla could say anything, Daniel said, "We came for your help. We've tracked the third stone to a Catholic church somewhere in Mexico, but we can't communicate with anyone there to find out what could have happened to it. Please, come with us."

"I thought you were going to let me do the talking. My friend, remember?" Kayla said.

"You were going to screw it up," Daniel said.

"I was not."

"Or sidetrack us," Daniel said. "Look, we appeared in your house to find you but got out as soon as we saw you weren't alone."

"Really?" Selena said. "Because I'm thinking I made a massive mistake showing teleporter boy where I live. Can I rescind the invitation, like with a vampire? I don't want you appearing here like that. Ever. You come only with permission. Or, like, never. Kayla, I can't believe you let him. I'm dying of humiliation."

"We really need your help," Kayla said.

"How much did you hear? Did you hear how I failed to stand up for myself? Did you hear how I caved on everything? How I said, 'Yes, you're right,' when she said I'm not trying hard enough?" Selena blinked fast, her eyes overly bright.

"Selena . . ."

She leveled a finger at Kayla. "Don't you dare give me advice. You're strong; I'm not. And now I'm mortified that you saw it. I can't believe you just appeared like that!"

Kayla wanted to tell her that she hadn't heard anything, that it wasn't embarrassing to care what your parents thought, that it was no big deal. But before she could decide what to say, Daniel said, "We need you to translate for us. It will be quick. There's a priest at a church who only speaks Spanish."

Selena sucked in air, as if trying to calm herself. "Fine. Sure. Whatever. What's the plan? Your father—"

"If he shows up, we'll take care of him," Kayla said. "He won't catch us off guard this time. I'll distract him. Send dirt into his mouth to keep him from saying a spell. Tie him with fishing line. Et cetera. And then Daniel will jump him to a police station. Done, and done. You'll be safe. We won't let anything happen to you."

"And the police are going to hold him because . . . ?"

"Because I'll scream and cry and freak out so badly that he won't get a word in edgewise. Once they look him up in their records, they'll know he's wanted in connection with a cold case, especially when I give them the place, dates, and names. They'll contact the detective who—"

"Kayla . . . ," Selena began.

"It's going to work," Kayla insisted. "I'm going to capture him. And we'll rescue Daniel's mom while he's in custody. He won't be able to stop us, due to being behind bars."

"Not to be a party pooper, but how will you know where to find her?"

Daniel answered. "Because before the police station, I'm going to threaten to drop him in the middle of the ocean. Or dangle him off a cliff. Either way works." He said it so matter-of-factly, as if he'd done this before. It reminded her of the day they'd met—he'd seemed so unflappable. Kayla wondered how he'd learned to shrug on cool like it was a jacket.

"At least you've given it some thought," Selena said. "Okay, when do you need me to do this?" She glanced at the house. "My mom has a meeting at her office tonight."

"We need you now," Daniel said. He reached out and placed a hand on Selena's shoulder. Before Selena could react, the two of them vanished.

A second later, he reappeared—without Selena—and touched Kayla's arm. The world flickered, and they were in the vestibule of the church. Selena was standing there, and she was pissed. "You left me!" she yelled. "You took me, and left me!" She poked his shoulder with her manicured index finger.

He flinched, then held his finger to his lips. "Shhh, this is a church. I can only transport one at a time."

"Then transport me back!" Selena shouted. "I can't do this right now. My mother's home! If she notices I'm gone—"

At the same time, Kayla said, "Daniel, you can't just—"

"The sooner you help us," Daniel said in a calm, reasonable voice, "the sooner I take you back to your mother."

"Do you have any idea how much trouble I'm going to be in? I'm already in enough trouble. I've been skipping classes. Mom noticed."

"You have?" Kayla felt her eyes widen. Selena had never skipped classes before. "Is it Sam?"

Selena ignored the question. "If she thinks I'm skipping out on her lecture about why she's disappointed in me for skipping out and letting down the generations who toiled in the fields so she could come to America and work hard and give me every opportunity, and so on and so forth . . . You have to take me back. I'll help you later. I said I would! Just not now."

"We need you now," Daniel said.

"You are an asshole," Selena said.

"But I'm an asshole who can teleport."

"Daniel, take her home now," Kayla said. "We can do this later. You can't—"

Daniel leveled a finger at Kayla. "Do you want to stop your father or don't you? Your mother lives in fear. And I don't know if mine lives at all. Selena can help her, help my mother, and get home before her mother even notices. All the mommies are happy. Just, for the love of God, stop the incessant arguing and do it!"

Selena and Kayla stared at him. "You're going to get struck by lightning for blaspheming inside a church," Selena commented. "Not to mention kidnapping, which this is. You're no better than Kayla's father."

"Don't. Say. That," Kayla said flatly. "He's no murderer." Daniel was only being logical. One conversation, and Selena could save not one but two families. Selena was being ridiculous to reject such a simple request. "Yes, Daniel shouldn't have taken you like that, but now that you're here . . . Selena, just . . . could you please be our translator?"

Selena's glare was strong enough to wither plants. "If things go wrong and you get me killed, *you're* the one who gets to tell my mother."

"Deal!" Grabbing Selena's arm, Daniel led the way through the church. Kayla followed behind. She told herself they weren't endangering her best friend. As she walked, she watched and listened for any sign that her father was here. She didn't see anything move or hear anything other than their own footsteps echoing on the stone floor.

Beyond the altar, tucked to the right of the pulpit, was a door. Daniel knocked. No answer. He tried the doorknob. Locked. Stepping aside, he gestured for Kayla. Kayla unlocked the door with her mind, and Daniel pushed it open.

The church was empty.

Kayla felt her shoulder unknot. She didn't know what she'd expected. No, she knew exactly what she had expected. A dead priest. She'd expected her father to have beaten them here, interrogated the priest, taken the stone (if it was here), and left. She'd expected to lose.

A voice, a man, spoke sharply in Spanish. They all spun around.

It was the priest. He was alive, fine, and not happy to see them standing in the doorway to his office. Selena began talking quickly in Spanish. She pointed to Kayla and Daniel, and the priest's scowl darkened. Daniel leaned closer to Kayla and said in a soft voice, "She wouldn't take revenge, would she?"

"She absolutely would," Kayla said just as softly, "if this didn't matter so much. Right now, she wants to get back to her mother, and she knows you're her only ticket back. She's probably just insulting us to the priest and telling him to pray for us to burn in eternal hellfire. Or something like that." Raising her voice, she said, "Selena, we need to know what was here before this church."

Selena translated.

The priest answered her, and the two of them chattered back and forth.

Daniel interrupted. "We need to know—"

Selena held up her hand, palm out. She resumed talking to the priest. After a few minutes, she spun around and said, "Okay, take me home. I have what you need." She grabbed on to Daniel's arm.

"Tell us," Daniel said.

"After you take me home," Selena said.

"Fine." Daniel and Selena disappeared, fast as a bubble popping.

The priest's eyes rolled into the back of his head and he pitched backward, fainting. Darting forward, Kayla caught the priest before he cracked his head on the stone floor. She lowered him, unconscious, safely down to the ground. She hoped that whatever Selena had found out, it didn't require them to return here. It wasn't going to be possible to explain this to the priest in any language. She hoped he woke up okay. She hated to leave him alone like this. Standing up, she looked around the church. Maybe there was someone nearby . . .

A woman was at the back of the church, probably the same woman the priest had been talking to earlier. *Perfect*, Kayla thought. *She can make sure he's okay.* Sunlight streamed from the door behind her, making her silhouette glow as if she were an angel. She had blond hair and wore a yellow sundress. Waving, Kayla caught her attention.

As the woman walked through the pews toward her, Daniel reappeared. He grabbed Kayla's arm, and the church, the priest, and the woman vanished.

19

A flash later, and she was in Selena's garage.

"You realize people saw your disappearing trick," Kayla said to Daniel.

"Doesn't matter," Daniel said. "We aren't going back there."

"We might, depending on what Selena learned. You want to be burned at the stake or dissected by scientists or treated as a freak show?"

"So long as we succeed, it doesn't matter. I can deal with the consequences later."

Both of them turned to Selena, and Kayla saw the anger from earlier drain out of her face—and her eyes fill with pity instead. "Kayla, Daniel . . . I'm so sorry, but the dates don't work. He said the church was built in 1853 and that it's on the site of an older church that was built in the 1700s. And that site was chosen by the Spanish conquistador Juan Rodriguez de la Cosa in 1530. Before that, he didn't know. But *I* know that the Great Jaguar Temple was built in the 700s, which is earlier than 1853, 1700, or even 1530, which means . . ."

". . . which means we're screwed," Kayla finished for her.

Selena nodded. "I'm really sorry."

"Thanks anyway." Kayla heard herself say the words, but her voice felt distant. She swallowed hard. "You'd better get back to your mother. She's going to wonder where you are."

"Kayla . . ."

"It's okay. We'll think of something. Go."

Selena threw her arms around Kayla's neck, hugged her, and ran toward the house.

Kayla felt as if she'd been stabbed through the gut. The stone was gone. They'd failed. Daniel didn't say anything, but his hand brushed against hers. She seized his hand and held it tight.

"It was all for nothing," Daniel said quietly. "The stone isn't there and hasn't been for centuries."

Kayla grasped for some shred of hope. "But it could have been there at some point. That explorer guy . . ." She tried to remember his name and failed. "Not Cortez but like Cortez. Casa? Cosa? Whatever his name. He could have picked that church site for a reason. Maybe there was a Maya temple there, or another ancient tomb thing. Maybe he found the stone."

"And then tossed it aside, used it to build the church, buried it, or gave it to someone. We have to face facts. Anything could have happened to it. Only plus is that if we can't find it, neither can your father."

Kayla had a thought. It wasn't very likely but maybe. "Unless your mom . . ."

"Unless my mom what?" There was a hard edge to his voice.

She plunged on. "Unless she knows what happened to it. From her research. Maybe we can look through her notes and—"

"She burned her notebook."

"Maybe she kept something. It was her obsession, right?

Supposed to be her big break?" She wondered again about his mother's history with the stones and how much she knew about them. Did his mother know the church in Mexico was a dead end?

He nodded.

"This is *not* over," Kayla told him. She looked up at Selena's house. "Can't be. Come on, Daniel, take us to your house."

He laid his hand on her shoulder, and once again the world flashed.

∽ ∾

Daniel's house was full of shadows. Silence had settled throughout. Kayla felt as though she should whisper. "Does your mom have an office?"

"Upstairs," he whispered back.

He headed for the stairs—and then suddenly switched directions and strode toward an open doorway. Kayla hurried after him. "Daniel, what's wrong—oh." Inside the dining room, the china cabinet door hung open. Plates and vases were shattered within the cabinet and across the wood floor. The centerpiece of dried flowers was strewn over the table. Curtains were torn down, and an oil painting lay smashed over the back of one of the chairs. Several African masks lay trampled on the ground. Hooks were empty on the walls. Pivoting, Daniel pushed past Kayla and ran to the kitchen. She followed.

In the kitchen, it was worse. Every drawer had been yanked out. Utensils and pots and broken dishes littered the floor. Boxes of cereal had been upended. The trash was knocked over as if a raccoon had pawed through it. He surveyed it all, jaw clenched, and then jogged toward the stairs.

"Wait, Daniel." She caught his arm. "Whoever did this could still be here."

He stopped. "Can you tell?"

"Maybe." She'd sensed the jaguar in the jungle and the stone in the fissure. She should be able to sense a person. Kayla sent her mind racing through the house. She felt the mess—the overturned furniture, the emptied bookshelves, the broken knickknacks. She reached upstairs. Clothes had been strewn on the floor. Beds had been sliced open. In the bathroom, the medicine cabinet had been ransacked. Bottles lay in the sink and on the floor. She stretched herself to touch Daniel's bedroom. Papers were on the floor. Oh, no, his maps! "Daniel . . ."

"Sense anyone?"

"Not yet, but—"

He charged up the stairs. Yanking open a door, he plunged into an office. Kayla lagged behind. His mother's office had been trashed as thoroughly as the kitchen, as badly as Queen Marguerite's store. Every book had been knocked off the shelves. Every desk drawer had been pulled out. The file cabinet lay on its side, its contents spilling out like guts from a stomach wound.

"Who did this?" Kayla asked.

He shot her a look.

"But why? And why now?" His mother had been kidnapped a while ago. Why not search the place immediately? Maybe his mother had been cooperating, then stopped. Maybe . . . Kayla didn't complete that thought. His mother was *fine*. She had to be.

Daniel pushed past her out of the office and charged into his bedroom. She followed him. In his room, the maps had been torn from the walls. The photos had been shredded. Kneeling next to one, he picked up the pieces. He made a half-hearted attempt to fit a few pieces together, and then he let them flutter through his fingers like snowflakes.

Trying to sound positive, Kayla said, "You know, this is actually a good sign. It means my father hasn't found the last stone yet."

Daniel shook his head. "But if my mother had it, why send me—"

"Maybe he thought she was lying to him. Or maybe he thought she'd left a clue, like we did. Maybe he didn't know she'd burned her notebook. I don't know." Kayla sank down on the bed. She felt an object under her and pulled it out. It was the photo album, the one she'd found the picture of her parents in. She hugged it to her chest. It wasn't damaged, probably because she'd left it here, tangled in sheets. Or maybe because Daddy Dearest didn't want to destroy photos of himself. "He's always one step ahead of us, isn't he?"

Daniel didn't answer, but he didn't have to.

She surveyed the wall. It looked as though it had been savaged by a mountain lion. Sheer destruction. Something had clearly changed for him to trash the place now and not earlier. "Do you think this was vengeance, like with Queen Marguerite— maybe your mother said something he didn't like?" As soon as she asked the question, she wished she could suck it back in. She didn't want to imply his mother was in more danger. Still, it was obvious something had changed. Maybe Dad had discovered the dead end at the church too and he'd come here for more clues, like they had. "Or maybe he was looking for something? Are you hiding anything?"

Daniel crossed to his dresser. His clothes had been rifled

through. He went to one of the drawers and began looking through it. "It's gone."

"What is?"

"My knife."

"You keep weapons in your room? Exactly what kind of childhood did you have?"

He shook his head. "It was an artifact—she told me it was valuable and to keep it out of sight. It was actually one of the last things we argued about. She's always been lousy at present giving. I told her that's the kind of present you give to someone when you don't know what to give them, when you haven't bothered to know them well enough to know what they want."

"Ironic if that's the one thing my father wanted."

He searched the floor of his room and didn't find the knife. Finishing, he strode out. Still hugging the photo album, Kayla trailed after him as he looked through each room. At last, he ended up in the kitchen. He kicked a cereal box.

"Daniel . . . ," Kayla said quietly, not wanting to intrude.

"Maybe they took it. Maybe they took other things too. I can't tell! Why take a stupid knife? Unless . . . Do you think my mother took it, when they weren't looking, as a message to me?" His face lit up. "Maybe she was trying to apologize. It would be like her. Fix the symptom, not the cause."

"Or she took it as a weapon, to try to escape on her own." She didn't think that was very likely, but he clearly needed some explanation to cling to. He was as much of a mess as his house.

"Yes!" He spun around, as if looking for answers in the wrecked kitchen.

"Daniel, come home with me." As soon as the words were out of her mouth, she wondered if it was a terrible mistake. She plowed forward anyway. "You can't stay here. Come with me. Meet Moonbeam. Maybe she can help. I think . . . this is over our heads now."

He shook his head and kept looking through the mess.

"Sure, she'll hate you for a while. But she'll get over it."

Stopping, he looked directly at Kayla. "Did you?"

"Did I what?"

"Get over hating me?"

She opened her mouth to snap out an answer and then stopped. "Yes," she said more slowly. "You're still an asshole, of course, but I guess I am too. Especially to Moonbeam."

Stepping over the pots and plates, he crossed to her. She wrapped her arms around his waist. He kissed her, softly and gently, as if she were something precious that he didn't want to break. "I don't want to be the cause of more problems in your life." He caressed her cheek. "I'll take you home, then I'll go to Queen Marguerite, try to get some sleep, and try to figure out what to do next."

"Do you trust her?" Kayla asked.

"She wants what we want," Daniel said. "Why? Don't you trust her?"

"She can teleport, and now she's seen where I live. That makes me nervous." She thought about all the protective stones she'd dug up. She didn't know if Moonbeam had noticed yet and fixed them, or if they even made a difference. Kayla fingered the eye amulet around her neck. "But you're right—so long as she wants what we want, I think we can trust her. Daniel, let's go. There's nothing for us here."

He didn't argue, merely took her hand, and in a flash, they were standing in front of the red gate. "Come back tomorrow,"

Kayla said. "By then, we'll have a new plan." Stepping toward him, she kissed him again. She felt as if she were melting into him.

When she stepped away, he was smiling, albeit sadly. She smiled back. "You're amazing, Kayla. Nothing can defeat you." And then he disappeared.

In his wake, her smile faded. "I wish you were right," she said to no one. They'd followed all three trails. All three had failed. She had no idea what to do next. She had no more backup plans. And so she walked through the garden gate to wait for a brilliant idea. Or simply for tomorrow.

20

Moonbeam wasn't home yet. Kayla checked the work schedule on the refrigerator—she was due home in a few minutes. On the plus side, at least that meant Moonbeam wouldn't know she'd broken the spell and left. On the negative side . . . everything else was on the negative side. She crossed to her corner of the cottage and tucked the photo album under her pillow. Flopping onto her futon, Kayla stared at the ceiling, at the mobiles and prayer flags and dreamcatchers.

Could this really be it?

Rolling onto her stomach, she took out her phone and tried to call Selena. It rang. And rang. And rang until voice mail picked up. "Selena, hope everything went okay. Things are . . ." She debated how much to say. ". . . bad. Please call me." She hung up, rolled onto her back, and stared at the ceiling again.

Kayla had no idea what they were going to do next, but she still had to try. Even if she didn't know *what* to try. Her father was still out there, he still had Daniel's mother, and as far as she knew, he didn't have the third stone yet.

She heard the door fly open. "Kayla?" Moonbeam called.

Kayla sat up. "Hi, Moonbeam. How was work?"

"You're here." Moonbeam smiled sunnily. "I was half afraid you'd broken the spell, hopped on a bus, and traveled halfway across the country by now."

Trying not to flinch at that, Kayla faked a smile. "Still here."

Moonbeam dropped her purse on the kitchen table and crossed the cottage. She sat on the edge of Kayla's bed. "Kayla . . . I've been thinking . . . Maybe we've stayed here too long. I never meant for this to be permanent. It may be time we move someplace else."

Kayla jumped to her feet. "What? No!"

"You said you wanted to travel. You choose the place. Anywhere in the world."

She *did* want to travel. But not like this. And not now. "Not yet! I can't . . . We have lives here. Friends. You have your job."

Rising, Moonbeam picked up a plastic replica of the dolphin fountain from Stearns Wharf. She put it down, then touched a blue frame made of sea glass with a picture of Moonbeam and Kayla, then a clay vase with flowers from the garden. "Sometimes I'm tired of hiding too. Always living a lie. Never being myself."

"Starting new fake lives somewhere else won't fix that."

"At least it would be a different set of lies." Moonbeam smiled again, a sad half smile. "We pack only things that can't be traced to a location. Generic clothes that could come from a mall anywhere. Toiletries, again only generic. Make sure there are no price tags or store tags or anything that could be traced. When we're ready, I'll close our bank account. Take only cash."

"But . . . why? Is this because of me? To punish me?"

Returning to the bed, Moonbeam clasped Kayla's hands.

"No. Sweetheart, no, not to punish you. To keep you safe. Everything I've ever done has been to keep you safe."

For an instant, Kayla wanted to tell her the truth, all of it, but then the chimes over the garden gate rang. *She fixed them,* Kayla thought. And then she thought, *Maybe it's Daniel.* She rushed to the window. Between the dreamcatchers and crystals, she caught a glimpse of a boy with surfer-blond hair, coming through the red gate. Crowding at the window to see who it was, Moonbeam nudged her aside. "Who's that?"

"Sam." What was he doing here?

"Selena's boy?"

Kayla looked at her. "How do you know about him?"

"You were out, remember? We talked."

"I'll be right back. This conversation isn't over." Kayla crossed to the door.

Moonbeam followed. "Don't let him know we're thinking about leaving."

"Moonbeam—"

"This is serious, Kayla."

"Believe me, I know." Flinging open the door, Kayla sprinted outside. She wished she could run out the gate and keep running until she'd left everything that had gone wrong far behind her. But running away was what Moonbeam did. Kayla was supposed to be the fixer.

Seeing her, Sam stopped walking near the garden gnomes. "Hey. Nice gnomes."

Kayla skidded to a halt. "Hi, Sam. Thanks."

"Hi, Kayla's mom!" he called.

Glancing over her shoulder, Kayla saw Moonbeam pick up her gardening tools. Smiling broadly, Moonbeam waved at Sam and then began weeding enthusiastically in one of the flower beds, close enough to listen to every word they said. Kayla wondered if it was curiosity, or if Moonbeam truly didn't trust her anymore.

Sam looked like he'd come straight from the beach. He wore an orange bathing suit and a loose tank top with a palm tree printed on it. Sunglasses hung from his tank top. His feet were bare. "Sam, what are you doing here?" Kayla asked. "Did Selena send you?"

"Yep. Called me and . . . Well, she began to invite me over, told me she wanted to try again with her parents, but then her mother walked in, said phone time was over, and Selena switched midsentence to ask for another favor for you. I should have said no and insisted we finish the first conversation, but I can't say no to her. She has that way, you know?" He looked at the yard, at the flowers, at the bench, at the ragged hole in the hedge. "What happened there?"

"Badgers. What favor?"

He whistled low. "Seriously?"

"No."

"Huh. So what's your secret?"

Out of the corner of her eye, Kayla saw Moonbeam quit weeding. She was watching Kayla intently. "My secret?" What had Selena told him? Kayla faked a chuckle. "I don't have any secrets. Open book here. What you see is what you get."

He blinked and then shook off his confusion. "Your secret to reaching Selena. Look, I like her, and I think we'd be good together. I think she agrees, but those parents of hers . . . Ugh. Jailers are more lenient."

"They have high expectations, and Selena wants to please them."

"But—"

"Sam, what was the favor? Why did she send you here?"

"Oh. Yeah, she wanted me to tell you . . . Hang on, I wrote his name down." He pulled a piece of paper out of his swimsuit pocket. "Juan Rodriguez de la Cosa. She said to tell you he's buried in Seville, Spain, in a church called Iglesias de Santa Maria, along with a bunch of stuff he found in Mexico. Mean anything to you?"

Kayla felt her heart beat so hard in her chest that it was difficult to think. She sneaked a glance over at Moonbeam, who continued to yank out weeds, occasionally pulling out flowers too. "I'm helping her with her project. You know, for those extra classes she's planning to take at UCSB this summer. Thanks for letting me know."

"Sure, no problem. You think her mom is keeping her from calling me again?"

"Definitely. When her parents say 'no phone time,' they confiscate her phone. Listen, it's possible there's another reason she sent you here. She knows me, and she knows I'd tell you not to give up on her, despite her parents. Selena likes you. And she doesn't like many people."

He broke into a smile. "Then I'm the one who should be saying thank you."

"Just be patient. Selena likes being the apple of her parents' eyes. Going against them isn't in her nature. It's going to take . . . Well, I don't know what it will take."

"I'll wait," he promised.

She watched him saunter out the garden gate. Standing, Moonbeam dusted off her knees and crossed to Kayla. "What was that all about? You're helping Selena?"

"Her parents don't want her to date. I'm helping with her social life, under the guise of helping with her classes." At least that wasn't a lie. "Moonbeam . . . can we wait before we move? Just a few days. I want to make sure Selena's okay." Only sort of a lie.

Moonbeam's face softened. "You're a good girl, Kayla. A good friend and a good daughter, despite . . . lately."

"Mind if I call her? Privately?"

"Of course. Just don't—"

"I won't tell her anything."

As Moonbeam returned to the house, Kayla pulled out her phone. She tried Daniel's number first. No answer. Glancing back at the house, she dialed Queen Marguerite's shop. After two rings, the voodoo queen answered: "Voodoo Spells and—"

"It's Kayla. Is Daniel there?"

"He's asleep, poor dear. Exhausted himself."

"He'll want to wake up for this. Tell him I know where the third stone is." She kept her eye on the house. Moonbeam was in the kitchen, washing the garden dirt from her hands. She was watching Kayla.

The phone fell silent, and Kayla heard shuffling and the voodoo queen's murmured voice. "He's coming," Marguerite said into the phone. "And you must go at once. But be careful. Wherever the stone is, your father will be there. The bones say he is close to having all three." *Click.*

Using her phone, Kayla searched for and found a photo of the church, Iglesias de Santa Maria. A half second later, Daniel appeared just outside the red gate.

Moonbeam would see. But with luck, this would be it. She'd tell Moonbeam everything once it was over, and her mother would understand.

Kayla strode toward the gate as Daniel came into the garden. Reaching him, she showed him the photo, and then she looked back at the house in time to see Moonbeam charge outside. "I'll be back," Kayla called to her. "I'll fix everything. You'll see!"

The garden vanished in a flash of green, then white.

21

The air in Seville smelled like oranges.

Kayla looked around—they were on a cobblestone street. Sunlight streamed down on cute storefronts and restaurants. Trees in pots framed the entrances with fat oranges on skinny branches. A lemon tree boasted an oversize lemon that caused the trunk to arch nearly to the ground. Restaurant tables were set askew on the uneven stones, and tourists sipped wine and wrangled toddlers. Along the sidewalk, chalkboards were propped on easels with the day's specials written in multicolored chalk. Bicycles were parked in a rack outside a hostel. Several food vendors were lined up with carts along the street. Each had a line of a few people in suits and a few in flower-print summer dresses. She didn't see anyone who looked like her father. But then, the odds of his being right here at this exact moment had to be low.

"You think the stone is here?" Daniel asked.

"Selena thinks so." She explained about the message that came via Sam.

"You know your mother saw us leave."

"This is it. We're going to end this. The stone has to be here."

She faced the church. It was directly across the street, framed by more orange trees, as picturesque as a postcard. It had a tower with bells inside mustard-yellow arches. The front was crumbling white plaster, and the door was so ornately carved it looked like lace. The iron handles were elaborate swirls. A bronze statue of the Virgin Mary was by the front door. One foot of the statue gleamed like new from the loving touch of a million visitors, while the rest was tarnished. The entire church looked old, quaint, and totally like tourist bait. She couldn't imagine how a stone of immense power could lie undetected for centuries in a place that was probably featured on thousands of postcards.

Still, this was her idea—or Selena's, technically—and she didn't have a better one. Marching up the steps, she tried the handle. It opened easily, and she and Daniel slid inside.

In the vestibule, it took a second for her eyes to adjust to the dim light. Voices echoed around them, and she saw the other tourists as shapes at first. She forced her eyes to focus on them: an older couple speaking French, plus a family of five that included two little boys and a baby in a stroller. Not her father.

A man in a priest's cassock sat at a desk with a lamp. He had a guest book in front of him and a pile of brochures. Kayla picked up a brochure, and Daniel plucked it out of her hands and opened it. She reached for a second one, and the priest shook his finger at her and said, "*Uno, señorita.*"

"But he took mine."

He held up one finger. "One per family."

When the elderly couple came up to the desk to ask him a question, she reached with her mind and slipped a brochure off the pile. Joining Daniel at the back of the pews, she studied her brochure as he studied his. She wished she'd stolen an English version. As near as she could tell, it described every stained-glass window in the church but said nothing about any tombs. Useless.

"He's here," Daniel said.

Kayla lifted her head so fast her neck hurt. "Where?"

"It doesn't say. But he has to be here. Look, the church was built in 1464 on the site of a mosque." He pointed to the back of the brochure. "At least, I think that's what it says."

"Oh. I thought you meant my father. Queen Marguerite said he'd be here."

Startled, he looked up. "How does she know that?"

She scanned the church. There were names and dates on stones in the walls, like in the church in Mexico. But these dates ranged from the 1700s to 1800s. Not old enough. "She mentioned the bones. She must have done a reading. Or else she brought him here herself." She meant it as a joke, but once she said it, she started to wonder. She tried to remember exactly what she'd told the voodoo queen.

"Queen Marguerite saved your life on the condition that you'd keep helping me, not him. She's on our side."

Kayla nodded and pushed the worry away. It was a stupid thought.

"Most likely, your father figured it out through research like Selena did, then took a plane here and found the stone hours ago, while we were busy moping."

"You have such a bad attitude. A little optimism wouldn't kill you. My father might, but not optimism. Come with me." Stuffing the brochure into her back pocket, Kayla started forward across the nave. Inside the church, the air was stale and tinged with the smells of mildew and mold. Light filtered in through the stained-glass windows.

To the left of the pulpit was a wrought-iron door with an impressive padlock on it. Kayla beelined for it. She peered through the door. On the opposite side, there were stairs heading down—like in the temple in Tikal. "A thousand dollars says Juan de la Thingie is down there."

Daniel consulted the brochure again. "No idea where this goes."

"I vote it's a tomb entrance." Glancing back, Kayla saw that the priest at the desk was watching them. She'd have to distract him, as well as the tourists. The heavy door looked like it would scream as loud as a pissed-off cat. She scanned the area, considering her options. "Look casual," she ordered. She strolled under the pulpit, as if examining the woodwork.

The French man in the vestibule had coffee in a Styrofoam cup. He placed it down on a table in order to show his friend a map. His back was to the pews—and to his coffee.

Kayla pulled her razor blade out of her pocket, unwrapped it from the bit of tinfoil, and sent it across the floor, under the pews, and then up to the coffee cup. She sliced around the bottom, not deep enough to break through but enough to weaken it.

The man turned and picked up his coffee—and the weakened bottom fell off. Jumping back as the coffee spattered on his polished shoes, the man dropped the cup. Coffee splashed across all the tiles. The man swore, and the priest scurried over to him. His wife bent to help, and Kayla pushed the edge of her glasses. They tumbled off her face and landed in the spilled coffee.

Quickly, Kayla reached out with her mind toward the baby,

who was being pushed by his mother. A pacifier rested loosely on his bottom lip, as if he'd been sucking but lost interest. She popped it out of his mouth, and the baby began to shriek. The mother knelt next to the stroller. Simultaneously, Kayla flew her brochure across the church and smacked it into the face of one of the boys. He clawed it off and threw it at his brother. The two began to argue, loudly, in German, and the father tried to intercede.

In two strides, Kayla was back at the door. She focused on the padlock. Dots of pain sparked inside her head. The lock was old, and the cams moved reluctantly. She kept fiddling, forcing it to move. At last, it snapped open, and Daniel lifted it off the door. The door shrieked as it opened, but the baby's screams were delightfully loud and shrill and the two boys had begun a full-out shouting match, which the father was trying to quiet. Glancing at the vestibule—the French man was still gesturing wildly, the woman was on her knees searching for her glasses, and the priest was frantically running for paper towels as he shot murderous glares at the loud family—Kayla slipped inside with Daniel. They closed the door behind them. Sticking her fingers through the grate, Kayla tried to relock the padlock. Her fingertips brushed the iron, but she couldn't reach far enough through to move it into position.

"Forget it," Daniel whispered. "So long as the door's shut, they won't notice."

Kayla called the razor blade back to her pocket before retreating down the stairs into the darkness. It was blissfully quiet in the stairwell.

"Now what?" Daniel whispered. The dust seemed to soak in his words.

"Now we be very, very quiet." Pulling out her lighter, she

flicked it on and, with her mind, sent the flame ahead of them to light their way. Side by side, they followed the flame down the stairs. When it died, she sent a second flame after it.

The stairwell walls were coated with cobwebs and smelled like damp rock and dust, which added to the ambience. Not that this place needed more ambience. It was already creepy as hell. She half expected to see some sort of ABANDON HOPE ALL YE WHO ENTER HERE sign.

They reached the bottom of the stairs. Kayla pushed the flame ahead of them. Beside her, Daniel let out a low whistle. Kayla totally agreed. She'd expected a tomb, possibly a barren basement. But this . . . It was more like an underground cathedral, easily as large as the church above.

Kayla let her little flame fly up and around. Pillars supported a vaulted stone ceiling. Shelves lined either side, all filled with bundles of gray rags. Between them, lashed to the pillars, were bodies wrapped in more rags. Their dust-coated skulls stared out. The flame flickered over them, making shadows move, making them look alive.

Beside her, Daniel whispered, "So how do we know which one is him?"

She walked forward. Her footsteps sounded like muffled echoes in the vast chamber. "He was important, right? So his burial should be distinctive. Certainly labeled."

The silent skulls watched them pass. Kayla wished she had a better light. The single flame seemed so very lonely in the vastness of the crypt.

Several archways led off the main burial room. The flame dancing ahead of them, Kayla and Daniel explored the first passageway. The walls were gray, dusty stone, carved directly out of the earth, and Kayla wondered how old this place was. Certainly seemed old enough for their conquistador. They followed the tunnel to a chamber with an altar and shelves. The shelves held skulls displayed on stacks of bones. A rat skittered behind one of the skulls and then peered out at them with glittering black eyes. They didn't see anything that indicated the conquistador was here. Backing up, they tried the next passageway.

The second archway led to a chamber with a few shrouded bodies but also a boiler and an electrical box, presumably for the church above. They left quickly and tried the third. It led to a wall display composed only of skulls, hundreds of them, laid one on top of the other as if they were macabre bathroom tiles.

In a hushed voice, Daniel asked, "Who are they all?"

"The new denizens of my future nightmares," Kayla said. Her lighter flame swept across the eye sockets and then hovered beside a bit of wall. There was writing on it.

Daniel crossed to it and moved to wipe the dust. Faster, Kayla scooted the dust away from the letters with her mind. It had a date, 1630–1699, and then the rest was in Spanish. "I think they're monks," Daniel reported. "A hundred years after our conquistador."

Behind them, Kayla thought she heard a whispered rustle. "Did you hear that?"

"Hear what?"

Kayla sent her mind back behind them, trying to sense the shape of anyone following them, but there were too many corpses and too many statues. She cringed inside at the "feel" of dust and decay and death. She couldn't tell if they were alone or if an entire army was creeping up behind them—at least not without touching each body.

She heard a steady dripping, perhaps from a pipe. Maybe she'd confused that with footsteps. Of course, the last time she'd been in a tomb and thought she'd heard footsteps, she'd ended up getting trapped. "Never mind."

Following the flame from the lighter, they returned to the main chamber and continued on. At the far end, the crypt narrowed and became a corridor with an arched roof and unlit sconces on the walls. Here, instead of the wrapped skeletons, there were stone coffins. Words were carved into their sides— names and dates. Kayla and Daniel slowed to read them. The little flame from the lighter danced across the words and shed a golden glow around them. The tunnel ahead of them and behind them was wreathed in blackness. Kayla felt prickles on the back of her neck. She tried to send her mind back again; and again, she felt only skeletons and statues. She listened for other sounds and heard nothing. If anyone else were here with them, he or she was quieter than the rats.

Trying to keep her tone light, Kayla said, "If this ends in bugs, snakes, or a cascade of rats, we are going to have serious words. Very bad words."

The passageway ended in a chamber with three stone coffins, as well as shelves full of bodies wrapped in rags and ropes. A few arm bones stuck out of the wrappings. "Look at the inscription. That's him," Daniel said as he pointed to one of the coffins.

Kayla sent the flame toward it. There was a poem or quote in Spanish on the side, plus the name Juan Rodriguez de la Cosa, born 1489 and died 1543. Sculptures of Spanish knights were carved onto the four corners.

Opposite the coffin was an altar with a cobweb-coated goblet and several candles, as well as a warped and wrinkled old

Bible. An oversize crucifix hung on the wall. Beneath the dust, it looked gold. Kayla transferred the flame to one of the candles and then lit the second one. Warm amber light spread over the stone walls and ceilings, and the whiff of burning dust drifted through the crypt. Skulls leered from new shadows, and a rat ducked between two filthy vases on a shelf. Kayla and Daniel searched the chamber. There were candlesticks, pitchers, and plates, all tarnished and covered in dust and cobwebs, as well as a shield hung on the wall and a moth-eaten tapestry that was dull brown and full of holes. Wrapped bodies were stored on two shelves. Ornate boxes filled a third. Daniel climbed up to the boxes and opened them one after another. "Dust. Bones. Bones. Dust. Necklace, maybe gold. Surprised they'd leave this stuff down here where it could be stolen."

"You don't think it's in *there*, do you?" Kayla pointed to the coffin.

Daniel hopped down from the shelves. "Let's find out." He shoved at the top of the coffin. It didn't budge. Kayla joined him. Stone scraped against stone, echoing loudly through the catacombs. Pushing as hard as they could, they shifted the top about four inches.

"I'll try to feel it." Kayla took a deep breath and sent her mind into the coffin.

The dead conquistador was definitely in there. Her mind touched old bones. Retreating, she shuddered and then forced herself to focus again. His clothes had rotted away long ago, but he still wore a helmet and his sword, as well as a heavy belt that had fallen through his desiccated body and lay on his spine. She felt other trinkets: a necklace with a heavy amulet, a dagger, several coins . . . and then she felt a familiar triangle. It lay near his hand, or what was left of his hand. "Got it," she whispered.

Leaning over the side of the stone coffin, Kayla reached in, trying hard not to touch the skeleton, and her fingertips brushed the stone triangle. She grabbed it and pulled it out.

Beside her, Daniel sucked in air.

The stone looked very much like the first stone. It had two serrated edges, and if she looked at it out of the corner of her eye, she could see words that floated, blurred, on its surface. It was deep black with flecks of many colors within it, like a black opal, that glistened in the candlelight. She held it out to Daniel—and felt it yanked out of her hand.

The stone sailed across the tomb and landed in the outstretched hand of a young woman with blond hair and a wide-brimmed summer hat.

Daniel didn't hesitate. He dropped his hand on Kayla's shoulder, and the world flickered. They reappeared next to the woman, and Daniel grabbed for the stone before Kayla could even orient herself. The woman held the stone out of reach.

As if shoved by wind, Kayla and Daniel sailed backward. Ropes that had been tying together bundles of bones flew off the rags and wrapped themselves tightly around Kayla and Daniel, coiling around their legs as if they were flies caught by a spider, cocooned together.

The woman smiled.

22

It was the woman from Mexico. Kayla was sure of it.

The woman was tall and thin with shockingly blond hair and a model-beautiful face. She wore a sundress with a cheerful yellow flower print, and she carried a pink purse. She tossed the stone from hand to hand as she smiled at them. "Thank you so much. I really didn't want to stick my hand in that coffin. Honestly, why can't they put these things someplace nicer? Like a museum. Or even a closet. I don't think that's too much to ask." She had a light Southern accent.

Staring at her, Kayla eased the fishhooks out of her pocket. Holding them ready with her mind, she glanced at Daniel and nodded. He vanished, and the ropes around them fell limp. As Kayla kicked the loose ropes off, she sent the hooks flying at the woman's ankles.

Daniel reappeared behind the woman. The woman only had a mere instant to turn her head and see him, but it was enough. She kicked backward. Her high heel caught him in the stomach. He collapsed against a shelf of skulls, and the hooks embedded in one of the bundled corpses. Regaining his footing, Daniel charged at her.

She flicked her hand, and one of the skulls flew out of its shelf and smashed against Daniel's head. He staggered as the skull shattered. Quickly, Kayla stirred a tiny cyclone of dirt, intending to spray it in the woman's eyes.

"Stop," the woman said calmly. "Or I release it." She pointed above Kayla's head.

"No!" Daniel cried. Clutching his head, he'd fallen to one knee.

Kayla looked up and saw the stone coffin lid, hovering in the air above her. She let the cyclone collapse to the ground. The woman pointed at Daniel. "Don't vanish." And then at Kayla. "No more tricks."

Continuing to stare up at the stone, Kayla marveled at the woman's power. She'd never even imagined being able to move something that weighed so much. She couldn't even move it with her arms, much less with her mind. "Amazing," she breathed. "Who are you?"

"I'm not your enemy." The coffin lid lowered back onto the coffin. Stone hit stone with a heavy thud. "And I am sorry if I startled you."

"If you aren't our enemy, then give us back the stone," Daniel said.

"Oh, no, can't do that, but thank you so much for finding it for me. I am grateful." She did look earnestly grateful—her green eyes were wide and her soft lips were parted as if in breathless excitement.

"You're the one I saw in the church in Mexico," Kayla said.

"Who are you? What do you want with the stone? Do you know my father? Are you with him?"

The woman tossed the stone into the air, caught it, and then winked, as if this were all some delightful joke. "Come on, figure it out, Katie."

Katie.

No one called her Katie. No one knew to call her that. Kayla slowly stood up. Staring at the woman, she tried to force her features to match a memory.

"She looks like you," Daniel said quietly.

"Aw, I wanted Katydid to figure it out on her own." *Katydid*, her old nickname. The woman flicked her finger, and several rags from a mummy flew into Daniel's mouth, gagging him. He clawed at the rags, and the woman leaned over him and tied a knot with her hands. She then tied ropes around his hands and ankles. "Much better. Never a good idea to annoy people who are stronger than you. You really should work on your people skills."

"Amanda," Kayla said, tasting the name.

Amanda turned back to Kayla, and her expression changed, softening like butter. "Oh, Katie, I thought I'd never see you again. We looked for you, you know. For years, we kept looking for you." A tear welled up in one of her bright green eyes.

"I don't find that as comforting as you seem to think I should." Kayla's eyes flicked to the entrance. She wondered where Dad was, if he was nearby, if he was listening.

"Dad never gave up hope that you were out there somewhere. Some days I didn't believe him. Some days I didn't want to. After all, you left me."

"We thought you were dead," Kayla said.

"Dead?" Both her eyebrows shot up. Kayla noticed that her

makeup was perfect, delicate natural eye shadow over her eyes and pink shimmery lips. In comparison, Kayla was coated in dust and dirt. Amanda was not only alive; she looked vibrant. "As you can see, I'm not. Why on earth would you think that?"

"Dad killed you." She said it slowly, carefully, as if to someone hard of hearing. "That's why we fled. Left our house. Left friends. Left everything."

Amanda's beautiful smile faded. "Left *me*. Or Mom did. I couldn't believe it when Dad told me he saw you. I thought I'd never see you again."

"We've been hiding," Kayla said. "From Dad. Because he killed you. Because we thought he'd kill me. And you're . . . It was for nothing? We were afraid for no reason? Why did Moonbeam think you were dead?"

Gently, Amanda said, "She lied to you."

"No, she wouldn't. Not about this." Kayla tried to match this woman up with her memory of her sister. The memory was so frayed, though. She mostly remembered Amanda's laugh. It filled a room. She remembered they used to play dress-up with Moonbeam's hats and scarves and makeup. Or the afternoons they'd have tea parties—Amanda would write out invitations, and they'd set up Kayla's stuffed animals around a blanket. "You could be a fake. Maybe you're just pretending to be my sister, trying to trick me in order to steal the stone."

"I already have the stone," Amanda pointed out. For emphasis, she waved it in the air, and then she tucked it into her pink purse. "No further tricks necessary. Did you call our mother 'Moonbeam'?"

Stupid, Kayla thought at herself. She fervently hoped that Dad hadn't heard. "Mom said you were dead."

"She knew I wasn't. She knew Dad didn't kill me. Just as she knew he would never kill you." Amanda tilted her head—she looked like Moonbeam when she was thinking hard. "I can't imagine why she lied to you."

Kayla swallowed. Her eyes felt hot. "My whole life, ever since you died, we've been hiding from Dad so he wouldn't find us and kill me too. She *can't* have lied. I don't believe it."

"I'm not dead. Ipso facto, Dad's not a murderer." Amanda smiled sunnily.

Kayla shook her head. Moonbeam couldn't have lied. But Amanda was here . . . Kayla felt sick thinking about it. She sank onto the ground and hugged her knees to her chest.

Across the crypt, her sister plopped cross-legged on the dusty ground. Her dress poofed out around her as she sat. "Come on, Katydid, talk to me. Tell me about yourself. What have you been doing in the years since my supposed death?"

"You're really Amanda?"

"And you're really Katie."

"Kayla now."

They both stared at each other in silence. Amanda's smile faded as they evaluated each other. Without moving, Kayla slid the razor blade out of her pocket. She hesitated—she could use it either to cut the purse or to slice the ropes around Daniel. Glancing at him, she saw his eyes were fixed on the purse.

Hoping she was making the right choice, she snaked the razor blade across the catacomb floor. She let the dust hide it.

"Kayla. You were a lot smaller last time I saw you."

"You were less blond."

"You were less pink."

"It's my natural color," Kayla said blandly. She lifted the

razor blade up to the fabric of Amanda's purse, directly beneath the stone, and began to saw through the threads.

Amanda laughed, and Kayla felt prickles walk up her spine. She knew that laugh. Any doubt she had was swept away in the tinkling lightness of that laugh. This woman was truly her sister. "So's mine. If by 'natural' you mean chemically enhanced by products from a lab." Her laugh faded. "I thought I'd feel differently seeing you."

"Oh?" Kayla didn't know what to say to that. She never imagined she'd see Amanda. She felt as if the world had shifted under her, and the continents had rearranged. She'd walk out of here to find Spain connected to Australia and New Zealand in the middle of the Mississippi River. "I missed you. A lot." So badly that she thought sometimes that she'd die too, or that she should have died. She wondered a lot about why Dad had spared her and why Mom had been able to save her. For a while, she even blamed Moonbeam for not saving Amanda too. When they finally settled in Santa Barbara, she wanted so badly to have her sister there to share their new home and face the new school and learn the new city.

"I didn't miss you," Amanda said, and the words felt like a stab. "Not at first. You were always the one Mom loved best, you know? Because you weren't the freak in the family. You were normal. She didn't want a freak. But looks like she got one anyway." Amanda grinned but the humor didn't reach her eyes.

Kayla continued cutting through the fabric of the pink purse, creating a hole directly beneath the stone. "She doesn't like me to use my powers. Thought it would make it easier for Dad to find me. And kill me. Everything, *everything*, has been about keeping me safe."

"Think about it logically, Katie. Why would your own father want to kill you?"

Kayla opened her mouth and then shut it. She'd asked herself that question so many times. She'd even asked Moonbeam. But Moonbeam had only said that some people were sick in the head, and her father was sadly one of them. They got wrong ideas and couldn't shake them. "Because he's crazy."

Amanda shook her head. "Mommy Dearest is the delusional, paranoid one."

"She thought you were dead! She mourned you. Really mourned you. I did too. I had *issues* because of you. Because of your death. Which I guess is not your fault." Kayla shook her head as if to clear it. This was all insane. She couldn't be having this conversation. Amanda couldn't be here. She had to be dreaming. Or drugged. Or . . . She didn't know.

Amanda's voice was gentle, even mournful. "Katie. *Kayla.* She knew I wasn't dead."

Kayla felt cold. She hugged her arms, but it didn't help. "No."

"Yes. She tried to take us both with her, but I didn't want to leave. I wanted us to stay together, all four of us, as a family, like we were supposed to be. So when she woke me up in the night and told me we were leaving, I ran into the bathroom, locked myself in, and screamed for Dad. I thought that would keep her there. She wouldn't leave without me, her oldest daughter, her first-born! But rather than stay and be a family, she took you and left me behind. When I came out again, it was just Dad and me. And he was angry, so extremely angry, but you know what he didn't do with all that anger? He didn't kill me. He held me while I cried and said we'd be a team, him and me, and we'd be fine." Amanda's voice cracked on the last word, and she looked away.

"But . . ." Kayla trawled through her mind, searching for a reasonable argument or at least an explanation. "He nearly killed me in Peru. If Daniel had died, I would have been trapped. There was no way down from that cliff. I would have starved or dehydrated until I looked like a mummy."

"I didn't hit him that hard."

Kayla felt her eyes widen and her jaw drop open. "You? You hit Daniel with a rock *on purpose*?" A few things began to click together, logistical questions that suddenly had answers. She thought of how her father had rappelled into the cave. Amanda must have been above them, helping lower the rope . . . and sending that rock to hit Daniel's head.

Amanda shrugged. "It was necessary."

"What about in Tikal? Was that cave-in you too?"

"That was before I knew you were, well, *you*. And besides, you survived fine."

That last part was true, but Kayla was more inclined to credit luck than intent. "So you have telekinesis. Like me." Or not like her. Kayla couldn't lift a massive stone coffin lid into the air. "Do we have Dad to thank for that?"

"Dad doesn't have it. Only us kids. He didn't tell me who you were until after Peru. But he told me to be careful. Would a killer do that? And would a killer return your pack of supplies so you could have food and water? Nice rings, by the way. What on earth were you doing with them?"

"To pawn for cash, in case Dad returned to murder me. I didn't want us to flee with nothing. That's what we did after you were killed. Left with nothing. We were homeless for months. We slept in alleyways, warmed by garbage. We sneaked into people's garages and slept there, hidden behind lawn mowers. We stole food from their trash cans and from Dumpsters outside restaurants. Also, supermarkets. I wore clothes lifted from

Laundromats and bought for pennies at flea markets and yard sales and Goodwill." She'd been young, but she remembered it so clearly. Mom had explained it wasn't theft if you really needed it and if you planned to pay them back. Later, when Moonbeam got the job at Envision Crystal, she'd mailed cash to several places, anonymously of course. She had Kayla stick on the stamps, all the while lecturing on how stealing was bad. She might as well have saved her breath—and the stamps.

"Dad cares about you, even if he barely knows you. And he cares about me. For years, it was just the two of us against the world. He protected me. When kids at school decided to torment me because I was 'different,' he marched down to the school and yelled at the principal. Next day, the tormenting stopped. Of course, it may have helped that I scared the living crap out of the ring leader, Jessica Billings. Still remember her with her flawless skin and voice like a mouse."

As Amanda talked, Kayla whisked away the fabric beneath the triangle stone. She studiously avoided looking at it. Carefully, she guided the razor blade toward Daniel. She began to saw through the ropes that bound his wrists. "If Dad is such a hero, why did he kidnap Daniel's mother?"

"Evelyn's fine," Amanda said blithely. "She sends her love."

"Let her go, and you can have the stone."

"I already have the stone, and she's needed. The spell requires three casters. She understands that." Amanda rose. Dusting off her sundress, she shouldered her purse. The stone lay on the floor at her feet. Kayla kept her eyes glued to Amanda's face. "Speaking of which, it's time for me to be getting back. Dad will be worrying about me."

"Then Dad is planning on using the stones?"

"Of course. Who would turn down a chance like this? Invincibility!" Amanda stretched her arms out in a delicate curve, as if she wanted to embrace the world. Or do a pirouette.

She's crazy, Kayla thought. Screw loose. Bats in the belfry. One card short of a full deck. "You know someone will die if you use the stones, right? 'Three stones, one death.' One of the casters will die. Dad could die. Daniel's mother could die. You could die!"

"Oh, I'm not the third. I'm already powerful. But don't you think we've already considered the cost? It's worth the prize."

"Invincibility? Really? Stupid prize. Also, vague. What do you plan to do, start a new Roman Empire? Please tell me you aren't planning some comic-book-style supervillain plot. Are you planning to take over the world? Because that never works out well. And who's the third?" One of the ropes around Daniel's wrists snapped. She started on the next one.

"Don't insult me, Katie. You don't even know me, not anymore." As if she'd had a brilliant idea, she clapped her hands. "You should come with me! Talk to Dad. Get to know both of us. He has so much to teach you. He taught me. You saw how strong I am. That's all due to him." For an instant, Kayla imagined herself as strong as Amanda. She imagined being with people who encouraged, rather than suppressed, her power. Depending, of course, on who died when they cast the stupid invincibility spell . . . No, she couldn't do it. Obviously no. They'd kidnapped Daniel's mother!

"You should come with me and talk to Moonbeam," Kayla said. "She can explain all this, I know it." Moonbeam would be so happy to see Amanda. Her lost daughter, returned! And she could explain everything. This had to be some kind of tragic misunderstanding.

Amanda's smile faded. "I'm sure she can. You should ask her to explain. And once you know the truth, you should join us. Together, the three of us would be so powerful that we could do anything we want, live whatever lives we want, without fear. That's what power does, Katie. It takes away fear."

"I hadn't actually noticed that," Kayla said drily. "No offense meant, but have you considered therapy, in lieu of this not-well-thought-out and obviously insane plan to cast an ancient evil spell?"

"Our father was abused when he was younger. I bet you didn't know that."

Kayla hadn't known. She opened her mouth, then shut it.

"You don't know anything about him. How dare you judge him? He had to live with so much fear. He never feels safe. But these stones . . . this spell, it can give him safety. He deserves that. And he can use his power to protect others."

Was it true? Did it matter if it was? Casting the spell was still wrong, no matter what his childhood trauma. "Exactly why he needs therapy."

Amanda looked sadly at Kayla. "I suppose it was too much to expect you to understand. Perhaps in time you'll see." Bending down, she picked up the stone.

Kayla felt her stomach drop. She sawed faster at Daniel's ropes, and he struggled against them. She hadn't cut enough yet.

"Nice try," Amanda said. "But I'm older, stronger, and better than you, little sis." She tossed the stone in the air, and it hovered there. It trailed her as she walked out of the tunnel. Her skirt swished as she walked into the shadows, and darkness swallowed her whole.

23

Kayla chased after her. "Look, *sis*, I appreciate the dramatic exit and all. But . . ." Darkness closed around her, and she reached for her lighter and flicked it on again. She had to strike it twice before it caught—she was running low on lighter fluid. But she succeeded and cupped the flame with her mind and sent it forward. "Amanda?"

She saw a shape fly toward her. Cloth flapped in the air like bat wings, and the lighter flame illuminated the face of a skull, contorted into a silent scream. Kayla lost control of the flame, and it died, plunging her into darkness, as the skeleton crashed at her feet. Dust plumed up into her face. She heard whispers and rustles all around her.

"Amanda!"

Shaking, she lit the lighter again. One after another, the shrouded bodies flew from their shelves. Kayla screamed as corpses crashed to the ground, into the walls, and into her. She ran, knocking them away, her hands hitting bones and shrouds.

She heard a rumble. The ground shook. As she ran past, the statues of saints plummeted one by one from their alcoves. They shattered as they crashed down. Stone shards flew through the air, and Kayla ducked down, hands over her head. She dove behind a coffin. The flame died again as she huddled, curled into a ball.

In the darkness, she heard crash after crash. She prayed that the ceiling wasn't falling in on her or Daniel. It sounded as if the world were shaking apart. And through it, she heard the sound of her sister's laugh, filling the spaces between the crashes.

At last, it quieted.

Listening, she waited. Her breathing was loud and fast. Hands trembling, she flicked on the lighter. It sputtered but it worked. The dim amber light flickered around her—and she saw she was closed in on all sides, trapped behind the stone coffin.

She didn't know if Amanda was still out there or not. Switching off the lighter, she listened again. She heard a few pebbles skitter, followed by the light sound of dust raining down on stone. It could be the aftermath. Or Amanda could be in the catacombs, waiting for Kayla to emerge.

For a long time, she stayed crouched behind the coffin. Her brain felt slow, as if each thought had to wade through mush to surface. Her sister, alive. Amanda, working with Dad, seizing the stone, trapping her here . . . And she didn't know what had happened to Daniel. *Please, let him be okay.*

Distantly, she heard sirens. She flicked on the lighter again. It took her five tries before she had a flame. Tears pricked her eyes as she kept trying. Finally, the flame took. Lifting it up, she looked around her shelter, her cage. She wasn't buried in rocks, like in Tikal. Oh, no, this was worse. She was hemmed in by bodies.

She crawled to the closest shroud, and she pushed. Bones creaked and cracked like sticks. Pressing forward, she continued to shoulder through the corpses. They fell on either side of her, only to be replaced by more. "Daniel! Daniel, are you there?"

She thought she heard a voice. Was it his?

More bodies fell against her, tumbling toward her as she tried to push through. Retreating, she looked up. There were too many bodies pressing against the sides of the coffin. She couldn't escape that way. But maybe she could climb up. Gritting her teeth, she stepped onto the top of the coffin. She pushed a skull aside with her foot and then she reached up and grabbed.

Her hand closed around bones. She pulled, and the skeleton dislodged and fell on her, its face twisted to stare at her. Jumping to the ground, Kayla let the skeleton crash down. She stepped up on the coffin again.

This time, Kayla let the lighter flame die. She didn't want to see what she was touching. In the darkness, she clawed her way up through the desiccated skeletons, through the monks and soldiers and priests. She tried not to think. She tried not to feel. She just climbed.

At last, she reached up—and she didn't feel anything above her. She lifted her head and breathed. The air felt cooler. Pushing and kicking, she scrambled on top of the pile of corpses. She took out her lighter again and lit it.

The catacombs had been ravaged. All the shelves and alcoves were empty. Bodies were strewn throughout the hall. Most had been piled where she was hidden. Climbing down the pile, Kayla reached a patch of open floor. She felt coated in the dust of bones—on her skin, in her hair, under her fingernails. She wanted more than anything to run up the steps, out of the church, and keep running as far as she could. But she didn't.

"Daniel!" she called. She headed deeper into the catacombs,

toward the conquistador's tomb. She plowed through a sea of bones. Skulls littered the ground. Leg and arm bones cracked beneath her feet. "Daniel?"

Finally, she reached the tomb.

He wasn't there.

The tomb had been untouched. On the altar, the candles were still lit. Wax dripped down their sides and pooled on the candle holders. Shadows danced on the walls. The coffin sat quietly, undisturbed, and the Bible was untouched. A pile of ropes lay on the ground. He'd escaped!

She couldn't decide if she was happy or pissed.

Leaving the conquistador's tomb, she looked across the catacombs. She'd have to cross it, all of it, to reach the stairs. There wasn't a choice.

Wading forward, she began the trek. She weaved between corpses, climbed over stone coffins, and inched along the wall, trying to avoid the worst of it. Eventually, she reached the stairs. Ambient light from the church filtered down, casting enough shadows to see the outline of stairs. Letting the lighter flame dissipate, Kayla walked up the steps.

Close to the top, she stopped. The door had been yanked off its hinges. It dangled to the side. She heard voices. Multiple voices. Creeping up the steps, Kayla peered out. Pews had been ripped from the floor. Stones on the walls were cracked. The pulpit leaned cockeyed.

There was no question about it: her sister was scary as hell.

Police crawled through the church. A few of them were standing near the entrance to the catacombs. If they saw Kayla, there would be questions, a lot of questions she couldn't answer. Slipping back down the stairs, she sank onto the bottom step.

"Kayla?" The whisper echoed through the catacombs.

"Daniel?" She kept her voice soft and hoped it carried to him and not up to the police. "I'm here. By the stairs." A second later, he appeared beside her and pulled her close to him.

She wrapped her arms around his neck and buried her face in his chest.

"God, you're okay. I've got you. You're okay," he said. "What happened? I jumped as soon as she left the tomb. I tried to intercept her. I didn't know— What did she do? Are you all right?"

"Fine. I'm fine. Tell me she didn't get away with the stone."

"Chased her as far as I could. She chucked cars at me. *Cars*, Kayla. She's strong."

"Yeah, I noticed that."

"Lost her halfway across the city. She may have jumped into a cab. Or sprouted wings and flew. I don't know. Best guess: she's on a plane out of here. Probably halfway across the Atlantic by now."

"You couldn't intercept her at the airport?"

"I couldn't leave you," Daniel said. He stroked her hair, and she decided not to tell him what kind of dust clung to her. He added, "Plus I tried. I couldn't find her. For all I know, she went to a private airstrip. Or boarded a plane before I got there."

"Or hijacked one," Kayla said grimly.

"Possible. Your sister does lack subtlety."

"My sister is insane."

Flashlights flickered on the walls of the stairwell, and then the overhead lights snapped on. Strings of bulbs throughout the catacombs blinked and then blazed. Daniel put his hand on Kayla's shoulder, and the crypt disappeared as the police hurried down the stairs.

Gray. White. Yellow.

They appeared on the sidewalk across from the church.

News vans, police cars, and ambulances filled the street. Gawkers crowded the sidewalk. A few of them spotted Kayla and began to point. It occurred to her what she must look like, covered in dirt and dust from the crypt. Someone snapped a picture.

Retreating, Kayla threw her hands in front of her face. "We have to get out of here. Now."

One of the policemen noticed them. He began to head through the crowd as Daniel reached for Kayla's hand.

She pulled away before he could touch her. "We can't let them see us disappear. There are photos!" Pivoting, Kayla walked in long strides down the street. With Daniel trailing behind her, she wove between the onlookers. Too many people! Behind them, the policeman shouted at them to stop—or she guessed that was what he said.

Grabbing her hand, Daniel began to run. Together, they ran over the uneven cobblestones. Shouts grew behind them. Cars sped down the cross street. Kayla and Daniel turned the corner, running past a horse-drawn carriage and a vendor selling flowers and fruit. Shops were open beside them. A store with an antique birdcage in the window. A bakery. They passed racks of postcards and tourist knickknacks.

Yanking Daniel with her, Kayla ducked into one of the restaurants. She was out of breath but flashed a smile at the hostess as if she meant to be there. She walked faster, through the tables, toward the back. The hostess hurried after them, menus in her hand, but Kayla ran into the restroom, pulled Daniel with her, and shut the door.

Her heart raced. Her breathing was fast, too fast. She took a deep breath as someone knocked on the door. "Now what?" Daniel asked.

"Take us to my house," she ordered Daniel.

"You're certain?"

"Yes. It's time to talk to Moonbeam."

24

Seconds later, they were by the red gate, outside Kayla's garden. Dropping Daniel's hand, she pushed through the gate and bee-lined for the cottage. She threw her mind ahead of her and felt a shape inside—a woman. "Moonbeam? Mom?" When she didn't hear a response, she started to run. She shoved open the door.

Seated at the kitchen table, eating a brownie, was Queen Marguerite.

Around her, the cottage was in the middle of being packed. Piles of clothes were stacked on Moonbeam's bed. Baskets were stuffed with herbs and amulets. The kitchen dishes were out of the cabinets. Several half-full boxes lay on the floor, as well as an assortment of bags. All the prayer scarves and mobiles had been taken down from the ceiling and dumped on the floor—they looked like a pile of dead birds.

Seeing Kayla, the voodoo queen smiled. "Ahh, at last! Come in, honey. Bring the boy too. We have much to discuss, and I'm afraid time is not on our side."

Passing her, Kayla ran through the cottage, peered into the bathroom, and looked out the window. "Moonbeam? Moonbeam!

Where is she?" She pushed her mind through the house and yard, ruffling the prayer scarves and piles of clothes and stirring the loose papers. She didn't feel anyone else.

"You should sit, both of you. Have a brownie. They're delicious."

"Why are you here?" Daniel demanded.

Kayla reached with her mind for the open pepper container in the spice cabinet, and she swirled the pepper out in a cloud. It looked like a swarm of bees. "What did you do to her?" She drew the pepper swarm toward the voodoo queen.

"Me?" Queen Marguerite looked the picture of affronted innocence.

Around Kayla, the prayer scarves and mobiles stirred on the floor and then rose. Paper fluttered. Wind whooshed through the cottage. Kayla's hands clenched as she reached for more: herbs, sewing needles, her extra razor blades. "Tell me what you did to her. Or I swear I'll *make* you tell me."

Queen Marguerite scanned the array of items floating in the air. "Interesting. You've improved your control, my dear. Such range and precision. But you're aiming your wrath at the wrong person. I didn't do anything to your mother. Believe me, I'd never hurt her."

"I don't believe you, and I'm getting very tired of being played."

"Oh, lovey, you've been a pawn since the day you were born. But don't you worry. I am about to queen you. The only thing standing between you and the future you want is knowledge of the past, and I am here to give it to you." Beckoning, Queen Marguerite patted the stool beside her. Kayla didn't move and didn't drop any of her makeshift weapons. "Very well, have it your way. Be uncomfortable."

"Where is Moonbeam?" Kayla demanded.

"I don't know." Queen Marguerite looked for an instant as if she wanted to say more, but then she picked up another brownie and bit into it. "Mmm-mm, does your mother know how to cook. Always did."

"How do you know her?" Kayla asked.

"That's a better question," Queen Marguerite approved. "I am the one who sold her the first stone. I am the one who started it all, and I want to be the one who ends it."

Daniel laid his hand over Kayla's. "Calm down. I think we need to listen to her."

She met his eyes. Earnest. Intense. And as scared as she was. Slowly, she let the pepper and the herbs fall onto the floor. Sewing needles clattered as they fell. The scarves drifted down like feathers. The dreamcatchers tangled as they tumbled together. The razor blades landed on the coffee table and she put one of them in her pocket. Finished, Kayla crossed to the kitchen with Daniel. They both sat on stools.

Queen Marguerite smiled. "Good. Years ago, many years ago, before you were born and before I was born, my mother acquired one of the three stones. She was told that the spell required three casters to stand in a pool of water, drop their blood on the stone, and say the words—and the result would be ultimate power. She wasn't told it required three stones."

"But how—"

"She and two of her friends cast the spell, all hoping to gain power. And the magic came. It shook the ground and lit up the sky . . . but none of them felt any different. Without all three stones, the spell was incomplete. The magic was summoned but not directed. She spent the next several decades off and on, more off than on really, searching for where the power went. Once called, magic can't just disappear; it has to go somewhere. When I was born, she figured out where it went. Mystery solved, she put the stone away so no one could use or abuse it again. She didn't tell me that, of course. Not then. Not until after it was too late."

"Where did the power go?" Daniel asked.

Queen Marguerite held up one finger. "Patience. A story has to unfold at its own pace; otherwise it ends up muddled. Eat something, if you feel the need to move your jaw."

"Avoid the brownies," Kayla cautioned him.

Abruptly, the voodoo queen dropped her brownie. "Why?"

"She drugs them sometimes."

Marguerite eyed the brownies for a moment, murmured a few words, and then relaxed. "These are fine. Why on the good green earth would your mother mess with her brownie recipe?"

"It's part of her disguise. New Agey hippie chick, bakes pot brownies."

The voodoo queen shook her head. Her shoulders slumped, and all the attitude vanished as if in a puff of smoke. "This isn't the life she was supposed to have." Kayla thought she saw a true emotion on Marguerite's face: regret. "Your mother was the brightest light I ever met—"

Daniel interrupted. "Not to be impatient, but could you get back to the point?" Belatedly, he added, "Please?"

Nodding wearily, Marguerite set the brownies aside. It occurred to Kayla that she might have been eating for show, to pretend she was in control—like the way Kayla had with the cookies when she first met Daniel. Now, suddenly, the show was over.

She continued her story. "My mother wasn't the easiest

person in the world to get along with, and we fought often. One hot summer afternoon, after a vicious fight, I was working in the shop and a sixteen-year-old girl came in with her boyfriend and her best friend. They wanted a protective charm. They showed me the friend's bruises and the cigarette burn on the boy's arm." She paused, as if remembering. "I told them to go to the police, or a teacher, or someone else who could help. But they wanted magic. And I wanted to help them. I also wanted to upset my mother. I thought I could kill two birds with one stone, so to speak, and so I sold that girl the stone. I told her it required three casters to stand in water (to conduct the magic), drip blood on the stone (to bind it), and say the words (to summon it). I told her if she and her friends could make this spell work, no one would ever be able to hurt them again."

"Let me take a wild guess," Kayla said. "That girl was my mother."

"Not yet but she would be," Marguerite said. "My mother was furious, and when she told me what happened when the spell was cast with only a single stone . . . Well, I tried to get it back, but I didn't know where they had gone. Before I could find them, your parents and his mother activated the incantation."

Daniel objected. "But my mother never did magic. She studied it."

"Your mother used to do magic. She was addicted to magic." Her voice was sad. "All three of them were. They all had raw talent, and that drew them to each other . . . and eventually to the stone." She tried to smile but it ended in a grimace. She'd started the story as if it were any story, like the tale of Fire Is Born, but there was pain in her eyes, as if this tale meant something to her. Kayla found herself wanting to reach out to the voodoo queen, but she stayed where she was. Marguerite hadn't yet answered the most important question: Where was Moonbeam? "They were so full of fear. The lure of never being hurt again . . . I could not have thought of a better enticement if I'd planned it. Lorelei, your mother, wanted so desperately to protect her friends. But I never should have sold her that stone, not without knowing its true history, and for that, I'm deeply ashamed."

Kayla thought of what Amanda had said, about their father's childhood. And she thought of the photo she'd seen, of two thin children.

"After that, Lorelei and I grew close. I became her teacher— shared with her everything I knew about magic—and I thought . . ." She trailed off for a moment, as if caught in a memory, and then resumed. "But then Jack and Lorelei married, Evelyn escaped to college, and all three of them moved away from their families and from me. Soon after, Evelyn married a man with no magic at all who doted on her. I didn't see or hear from any of them again until years later when their children were born with powers of the mind. By this time, my beloved mother had passed away, but Evelyn—Daniel's mother—was clever enough to come to me to seek the answer why."

"Why?" Daniel asked, and Kayla echoed.

"Come now, children. Use your little brains." Queen Marguerite reached out and tapped both of their foreheads. "What do you and I have in common? Our parents all cast an incomplete spell. The magic was summoned but not directed."

Kayla blinked at her. "Our powers are a side effect? Like some kind of weird birth defect from our parents doing drugs?"

"Very like," Queen Marguerite said. "Once the spell was cast, the magic had to go somewhere. Since the spell failed to finish, the magic went into us, or into the seeds that became us. The magic is inside us." She thumped her chest for emphasis.

So Kayla was a product of a freak accident, a genetic mutation, a birth defect. There was nothing natural about her power. It wasn't a gift or a curse. It was a mistake.

Daniel voiced the thought out loud. "We're a mistake?"

"Some of the finest people I know were mistakes," Queen Marguerite said. "Don't you go thinking that makes you special. Or, more importantly, not special."

"What happened next?" Kayla asked.

"It was Evelyn who figured out why the spell failed. The incantation was meant to be performed by three casters *with three stones*. One stone for the mind, one for the body, and one for the world. The stone that my mother and your parents used held mind powers—telekinesis and teleportation."

"Hence, us," Kayla said.

"What about the other two stones?" Daniel asked.

"The stone for the body holds the power to heal and to harm. Cause diseases. Pestilence. The third stone is for power over fire, water, and wind. When the spell is activated with only a single stone, those powers manifest in the children of the casters. But combined . . . all those powers flow into one person and are magnified, creating a person so full of magic that he or she is invincible to all but the passage of time."

"Yikes," Kayla said. An understatement.

"Evelyn shared her research with me, and it was extensive. She traced the history of the stones back as far as Gilgamesh, who refused to use them with his friend Enkidu. And then to the first Roman emperor, who did *not* refuse to use them. The stones became Rome's secret treasure. According to Evelyn, the stones were nearly given by Julius Caesar to Cleopatra as tokens of love. Evelyn thought that's why he was killed. But their primary use was strengthening the empire. She believed the emperors used the stones individually to deliberately give power to their children . . . until one less-than-happy descendant used his power to set Rome on fire. Stories remember him as the emperor who fiddled while Rome burned. The stones disappeared for a time after that and then resurfaced at the end of the Roman Empire. The son of the last emperor—a man who supposedly had father issues bad enough to rival your own—stole the stones and used his power to bring them to Central America, where they were used by the Maya warlord Fire Is Born."

"The Romans didn't know the Americas existed," Daniel objected. "Even a teleporter shouldn't have been able to bring them here."

"Your mother's theory was he was aiming for Egypt, to finish what Caesar had started. She thought he must have pictured a pyramid but wasn't precise enough, and the magic brought him to the Pyramid of the Sun in Teotihuacán, which is only a little smaller than that famous one in Giza. Clever woman, your mother. Too clever, perhaps. In time, Jack—Kayla's father—learned of her research, and that's where your tale begins."

Kayla remembered the Latin on the parchment. They'd guessed right: the stones had been in Rome before Tikal. But their history didn't matter; what mattered was where they were right now. "My sister said they planned to use the three stones with three casters."

"Ahh, you met Amanda?"

"You know her?"

"Oh, yes." Her voice was grim. "She was the one who made

the mess of my shop. She didn't like my claim that her power wasn't right for the task. Or that I refused to help them."

"What task?" Daniel demanded.

"Why, finding the stones, of course! I refused to help them and told them they would fail." She said it slowly as if he were hard of hearing, then she continued in a normal tone. "Amanda didn't like that answer very much. She has a temper, that one. And determination. Despite my words, she wasn't going to give up. So when you appeared, I knew I had to help you find them first."

"You used us," Daniel said flatly. "You wanted us to find the stones and bring them to you so you could use the stones yourself."

Queen Marguerite tapped her cane on the floor. "Don't be dense, boy. I *helped* you. I hoped if I did, you'd deliver the stones to me, rather than to Kayla's father and sister—"

"So you could use them!" Daniel jumped in.

"So I could hide them a damn sight better than they were hidden! Who hides an evil spell and then leaves a map?" Queen Marguerite scowled. "No one should be able to cast any part of this spell ever. Even incomplete, it's dangerous! I made a mistake once, when I sold your mother that stone, and it changed her fate. I intend to make up for that."

"What about my mother?" Daniel demanded. "Did you intend to save her, or just the stones?"

Her expression changed, but she didn't answer. "Now that the stones are found and *not* by you, both Evelyn and Lorelei are in danger. All my plans and hopes have—"

Kayla jumped off her stool. "Moonbeam's in danger? Why didn't you say so sooner? Where is she? We have to help her!"

"Patience," Queen Marguerite said. "You have to know the past before you can see the future. Your father, Jack, believed that invincibility spell would fix everything that was wrong with his life. He still believes this, though his goals may have changed."

"But where—" Kayla said.

"He wants to complete the spell that was begun. This means two things." She held up two fingers. "First, if he succeeds, the power will leave the children and flow into one of the three casters, granting him or her full—"

"Our power?" Daniel demanded.

Queen Marguerite nodded. "Yes. You will lose your magic, one of the three will gain it, and one of the three will die."

Kayla felt as if it was suddenly hard to breathe. "But—"

"Second, in order to succeed, he needs to recreate the conditions of the original casting, which means he needs your mothers. I came here to protect Kayla's mother, Lorelei, but I was too late." Marguerite's grip tightened on her cane. "Lorelei gave up so much to avoid this kind of fate. As soon as she realized how obsessed Jack was, she wanted out. She tried to take both her children with her. But something went wrong, and she was only able to escape with one. With you."

"So Amanda was telling the truth?" Kayla felt as if her world were spinning. She wished there were something she could grab on to, something steady, real, and true. She grabbed on to Daniel's hand and held it tight. She wondered if Amanda knew about the result of the spell—that she would lose her powers if Dad succeeded.

"I don't know what that girl told you, but you can ask your mother yourself. Fixer girl . . . you need to find them."

Marguerite reached across the table and clasped Kayla's hands. "Before they complete the spell."

"Where are they?" Kayla demanded. Daniel echoed her.

Marguerite released her hands. "If I knew, would I be here? It's as I told you: Your father wants to complete the spell. He needs to recreate everything about that pivotal moment, and that means place as well. He needs the same water, the same people, and the same tools."

"The knife," Daniel breathed.

"He'll bring them to wherever they cast the original spell, somewhere that had special meaning to all three of them. Find that place, and you'll find them."

Kayla shook her head, as if she could deny any and all of it. Her mother had lied to her. Worse, her mother had started all of this. Her mother had bought the stone and cast the spell. She'd caused Kayla's power. And Daniel's. And Amanda's. And then she'd fled from what she'd done.

"You know your mothers best—you must know where their hearts once were," Queen Marguerite said. Her voice was raw. "Please. We have to find them, and we have to stop them, before one of them dies."

25

Out in the garden, Daniel paced in tight circles. "Louisiana? We know they must have been there because they found Queen Marguerite's store and the stone. Maybe they lived near there."

"You don't know where your mother is from?" Kayla asked.

"All she ever said was she didn't have a happy childhood. I didn't know *how* unhappy. Just that she wanted to escape it. We aren't a share-your-feelings kind of family. Don't you know where yours is from?"

"We never talked about the past. Ever. It was part of the rules to stay safe." Kayla tried to untangle a wind chime and failed. "Before I was eight, we lived in a bunch of different places. Pennsylvania. North Carolina. Texas. Florida. Dad and Moonbeam liked to move a lot. But I don't think any of those places were their home." Tossing the wind chime down, Kayla glanced at the house. *This* was home, the only place that had truly felt like home. Queen Marguerite was puttering around the kitchen, examining the spices. Kayla wished she could kick her out. She'd admitted to using them to find the stones. That placed her squarely in the category of "enemy." Or, at least, not to be trusted. "Do you have any other family to ask? Grandparents? Uncles? Aunts? Cousins?"

"She never talked to her parents. I think she needed to prove they had no hold over her. I never met them. I don't think they even know I'm alive."

"Well, aren't we nice and dysfunctional." Kayla kicked a garden gnome, and it fell over. It lay unmoving and unjudging on the lawn. Looking down at the ground, she noticed that the protective stones were still strewn over the lawn. She wondered if things would have been different if she'd left them in place. Maybe Moonbeam would have been safe. "Everything in my life is built on a lie. And now I find out the lie was based on a lie."

Daniel brushed her hand with his and then let it fall, as if he wasn't sure whether she wanted to be touched. She reached out and took his hand. His fingers closed around hers.

"I thought I knew my mother," Kayla said. "But maybe I never did. You know, I'd never even seen a photo of her younger until I saw your mother's album." A thought occurred to her, and she pulled out the picture in her pocket. A young Lorelei, Jack, and Evelyn smiled from a set of bleachers. "Where do you think this is?"

"Their high school."

Her heart sank. "Not likely they did the spell there. It's too public. Plus they needed water. To conduct the magic, or whatever Queen Marguerite said."

"Look, it says the name of the school in the background, on the building." Daniel took the photo and held it up so the sun hit it. There weren't enough letters visible to read the name. Just the words "high school." "It could be anywhere."

"Maybe there are clues in other pictures?" Kayla ran into the

house, and Daniel followed. Without a word to Queen Marguerite, she shot across the cottage to her futon. She'd tucked the
album under her pillow. Grabbing it, she sat cross-legged on her
bed. Daniel sat beside her.

Kayla flipped through the pages. She saw her mother smiling out at her from photo after photo. Many were taken in public places—a school, a Dairy Queen, a gas station. Or nondescript
places—a living room, a parking lot, a football field. Some were
taken in places that must have changed in the intervening years,
like on a lawn or in front of a grove of trees. But then she hit a
set of photos all from the same location: a swimming hole.

"There's water," Daniel said softly.

Her mother, so skinny and carefree, in a bathing suit,
and her father so young and handsome. And Evelyn, Daniel's
mother, lounging with them beside a tiny pond. The swimming
hole was nestled against a rock wall. Water trickled down
the face of the rocks. Trees, dripping with moss, surrounded the
pool. There was a sign in one photo: WATCH FOR ROCKS. NO SWIM-
MING. Daniel's mother was flicking water at the sign. In a second shot, Kayla's father had covered up the words FOR and NO so
it said WATCH ROCKS SWIMMING. Lorelei was laughing.

"They're trespassing," Daniel noted.

"That's good," Kayla said. "That means this is a private place."

Queen Marguerite drifted closer. "What did you find, lovies?"

Kayla clutched the album to her chest.

"Now, now." She clucked her tongue. "I care about your
mother's fate too. I'm coming with you. You could use my help,
my magic—"

"Sorry. Still don't trust you."

Kayla and Daniel grabbed each other, and the house flashed

around them. Red, then green. She thought she heard the voo-doo queen yell, but her shriek was cut off.

Daniel yanked her down. She knelt with him. As her vision cleared, she saw they were behind a rock, hidden. For once, luck was on their side. No one had seen them, and they saw no one.

Creeping forward, Kayla peeked out at the swimming hole. It was not the pristine oasis that it was in the old photos. Spray-painted graffiti filled the rock face. Old tires, cans, scrap metal, and other trash littered the water and the woods. The water itself was coated in a film of green algae. The bushes were thick knots of brambles around the pool. Humidity thickened the air, and insects buzzed loudly. "I don't see—" Daniel began.

Kayla clamped her hand over his mouth as a tire rose out of the swimming hole and then flew into the bushes. Another tire followed it, then a rusted barrel. *Amanda's here*, Kayla thought. But she didn't see her. Three people tromped out of the bushes toward the water: Moonbeam; a woman who had to be Daniel's mother, Evelyn; and Kayla's father.

Each of them held a stone. Kayla's father also held a gun.

He gestured with it, and Moonbeam scooted over the trash and waded into the water. The algae spread in ripples away from her. The hem of her dress was immediately saturated and pulled the rest of the dress down with its weight. She continued to walk in until she was hip-deep, and her skirt billowed around her. Daniel's mother joined her. Last, Kayla's father laid the gun on a rock and walked hip-deep into the water.

Daniel nudged Kayla and nodded at the gun. Kayla shook her head. Much too heavy. Besides, what was she going to do? Threaten to shoot her own father? She was here to stop anyone from dying, not cause anyone to die, even though she was sure her father was to blame. Reasonably sure. Sort of sure. She scanned the area for items that she *could* lift. Whatever she did needed to be subtle. Amanda was nearby, and Kayla had no desire to go up against someone who could toss tires with such ease.

In the water, Kayla's father drew a knife out of his shirt pocket. He was reciting words, melodious words that drifted and dissipated over the murky water.

"That's my knife," Daniel whispered. His lips were only an inch from her ear, and his breath tickled her skin. "We have to stop them."

"How?" she whispered back.

"Improvise."

He was right. Sitting here afraid to act simply because her sister was near wouldn't help anyone. She mentally grabbed the fishing line from her pocket, and she sent it into the water like a snake. She wound it around her father's ankles and knotted it. She then took one of the scraps of metal, a small sliver with a needle-sharp point, and slid it into the water too. "I'll distract him," Kayla whispered. "You jump to the mothers. Get them out of here."

"I can't jump both at once."

"Then I'll distract him a lot," she said grimly. "Don't jump them anywhere Queen Marguerite can find them. Or their stones."

Her father grabbed Moonbeam's wrist, and Kayla froze. Twisting her hand up, her father cut Moonbeam's palm. He squeezed her fingers closed into a fist and held them over the stone. Blood dripped onto the stone and into the water beneath, the red dissolving into the green. He then turned to Daniel's mother and began reciting more words.

The second he released Moonbeam and before he could cut Daniel's mother, Kayla acted. She jabbed the sliver of scrap metal into her father's leg. He flinched as it hit his skin, and the fishing line caught his ankles. He fell backward.

Daniel appeared in the water. He put his hand on his mother's arm—

And then he was ripped away from her and lifted into the air.

Amanda, Kayla thought. She threw her mind toward the trees, searching for her. She had to be near! Daniel was tossed out of the water and into the bushes.

Dammit, Kayla couldn't fight someone so powerful! She crept farther around the rock, trying to see what was happening, and she "felt" Amanda. She was only a few yards away, hidden in the woods. She wondered if Amanda sensed her too.

A second later, Daniel jumped to his mother again. This time, a tire hit him in the back. Splashing into the water, he fell forward. As Daniel caught his balance, Kayla's father twisted Evelyn around and held a knife to her throat. "Stop!" Dad roared.

Daniel froze, kneeling in the muck.

Instantly Daniel was lifted out of the water and tossed not-too-gently back onto land, only a few feet from where Kayla hid. And then Amanda stepped out of the woods with a smile. She held out her hand, and the gun flew into it. "Who do you think is faster? A disappearing boy or a speeding bullet?" In two strides she was next to him. Kneeling, she pressed the gun against his temple. "How about at point-blank range? Think you can disappear fast enough? Go ahead, test it."

"Don't!" Evelyn cried.

Finishing the words, Kayla's father took Evelyn's wrist. He cut her palm. She didn't flinch. She kept looking at Daniel. Blood dripped onto the stone.

Amanda stalked around the edge of the pond. "Katydid, I

know you're here too! Come on out! You don't need to be scared." *She hasn't sensed me yet*, Kayla thought.

Hiding behind the rock, Kayla barely dared to breathe.

"Kayla, run away!" Moonbeam shouted.

Her mind was running in tight circles. There were other things she could grab, more cans, leaves, dirt, small sticks. She had her new razor blade. But with Amanda here . . . Kayla couldn't out-magic her. Amanda outclassed her in power, and they'd lost the element of surprise. Blood dripped from Evelyn's hand, but she seemed not to notice, her eyes still glued to her son. Moonbeam cradled her hand to her chest. Dad was reciting words again, pre-paring to cut his own palm.

So Kayla did the only thing she could think of. She stood up, hugging the photo album, and walked toward the water. She halted at the edge. "Hi, Dad."

Her father broke off the spell.

Moonbeam's face paled so fast that it looked as if she'd been dunked in chalk dust. Every freckle and sun spot stood out stark on her white cheeks.

"What are you doing?" Kayla asked, casual, her eyes fixed on her father.

"Don't interfere, Katie. You don't understand. Amanda, sub-due the boy."

Amanda lifted Daniel up and chucked him against a tree. He slumped down silently, unconscious. Evelyn shrieked but didn't move, the knife back at her throat.

"My name's Kayla now." She kept her voice even, calm, friendly. Her eyes darted to Daniel. He seemed to be breathing. She'd help him later. Immediate problem first. "And you're right. I don't understand." Kayla opened the photo album. "Look at what I found in Daniel's house. It's you and Mom and Daniel's mom."

"How nice," Amanda said. "Let's get on with this."

Kayla ignored her. "Look how happy you all are. See this one? It's here." She gestured at the swimming hole. Her voice was shaking, but she continued. "Your arm is around Mom. You're happy." She turned the page and pointed to another picture. This one had Kayla's father with Daniel's mother. They were sitting on a picnic blanket. "So carefree and happy." She turned the page.

"Katie, I promise you'll understand after—"

"You look like you're going to prom in this one." They were in tuxes and gowns. The two girls had corsages on their wrists. There was an extra boy in the shot, but he stood a few inches away from the rest of them. All of them had awkward, frozen smiles on their faces. "I can't believe you went for a pink cummerbund. And who is that boy with the ruffles? Mom looks beautiful, though, doesn't she? Did you dance together? Slow dance? Cheek to cheek? Did you go to an after-prom party?"

"This is hardly relevant," Amanda said. "Why isn't anyone telling her to shut up? Oh, wait, yes, *I* am. Katie, shut up."

Still ignoring her, Kayla turned another page. "Ooh, look at this one. Graduation? I bet you guys tossed your hats in the air and then promised to stay friends forever, didn't you? I bet you promised that nothing would ever change between you." She lifted the album higher, holding it over her head, so that all of them could see. "Selena and I made promises like that too. Even shared blood once. Blood sisters, that's what we were. Is that what you were? Best friends? More? Well, there's blood now, but if you go through with this, one of you will die."

"It's the price that must be paid," her father said.

"Is that what these people would have wanted?" She shook the album. "Is that what *you* wanted? You didn't know about the 'price' then. You do now! One of you will die!"

A wind whipped against her, and the album was yanked from her hands. It flew into the murky water and was submerged. Algae closed over it as if swallowing it. Amanda waved the gun in Kayla's direction. "Nice try, Katydid, but you don't understand. You've been living a lie for years."

Kayla met Moonbeam's eyes and then looked back at her father. "Then enlighten me. Explain to me why it's okay to murder my mother, the woman you once loved. Or Daniel's mother, your best friend. Do they mean so little to you now?"

"Of course not," Kayla's father said. "They mean the world to me." He looked as if he wanted to say more. His eyes slid to Amanda and then back to Kayla. His expression was pleading, but he didn't say anything else.

"See, that's what I don't understand. If you care about them or even care about the memory of caring about them, why do this? Do you really need this power so badly?" She kept her eyes glued to her father's face. She had his blue eyes, she noticed. Amanda had Moonbeam's green. "Are you planning to found an empire? I really don't think the world needs a new empire. Besides, power isn't all that. Look at me. I use my 'special skill' to rob ATMs and jewelry stores. Really noble, right?" Moonbeam's eyes widened. But Kayla ignored her and plowed on. "And look at Amanda. She's Superman-strong, yet she uses her power to be a super-powered thug, nothing more."

"Excuse me, I am *not* a thug," Amanda said.

Kayla nodded at the still-unconscious Daniel. "Tell that to

him." He'd started to moan and shift, but his eyes hadn't opened yet. "Getting more power isn't going to solve whatever personal issues you have. You're still going to be a messed-up dad and a horrible husband. Dad, please, think about it. Best case: It works and you're the one who gets the magic slam. Now you're an all-powerful murderer. Yay! Do you really think you'll be happy full of power stained with the blood of someone you used to love?"

Dad opened and then shut his mouth, and for an instant, Kayla thought she was reaching him. He was listening to her, which had to count for something. At last he said, "This is the only way to make things right."

"By killing someone you love? How's that right?"

"Father, don't listen to her," Amanda said. "This is your destiny. This is what we've worked so long and so hard for. This is our chance at greatness! Every great achievement requires a great sacrifice."

"What fortune cookie did you read that in?" Kayla asked. "Destroying someone you love doesn't sound like such a great achievement to me."

Lowering the knife a few inches, Dad covered Moonbeam's hand with his free hand. Kayla tensed, ready, though she wasn't sure what she was ready for. She didn't have a plan.

"Jack, listen to her," Moonbeam said softly.

"You're afraid," he said to Moonbeam. "But you don't have to be. Once we do this, you don't ever have to be afraid again. We'll have everything we ever wanted, the way it was supposed to be."

"Not true," Moonbeam said. "One of us will be dead."

"Oh, for God's sake, just do it!" Amanda cried. "I don't

understand why you're all even talking. If it would help, I'll shoot her." She swung the gun to point it at Kayla.

"Amanda, no!" Kayla's parents both rushed forward to the edge of the pool. Free from the knife, Evelyn raced out of the water to Daniel. She cradled him in his arms. She called his name, but he didn't wake.

"See?" Kayla said. "Amanda just proved my point. Thanks, sis. You *do* care about me, Dad. You care about your family! You stop this, and we could be a family again. You do this, and you lose that chance forever." She held her hand out toward her father. "You lost years with your wife. You lost my childhood. Do this, and you lose again. Stop, and maybe we can make things better. Now, we have a chance to begin again!"

Amanda scowled at her. "That is really screwed up."

For once, Kayla agreed with her sister. But she continued to smile hard, as if she thought reconciliation was possible, as if she ever wanted to see the psychopath who had threatened her mother again. As soon as she had Moonbeam safe, she was going to ensure they never saw him again. They were going to flee to the farthest reaches of the world and hide themselves more thoroughly than ever before. But for now, she smiled, as if she believed they could all be one big happy family, like the family in Mexico. "Please, Dad, haven't you lost enough?"

Moonbeam touched his arm. "Jack." She put a world of emotion into that one syllable. "You don't have to do this. We can find another way."

He stared at the knife in his hands as if seeing it anew.

"Are you serious?" Amanda asked. "Are you freaking serious? Because I did not do all of this, all the training, all the . . . everything, so you could be a coward at the last minute."

"Does she even know about the side effect?" Kayla asked. She turned to face Amanda. "Do you know if he completes this spell, we lose our powers? It doesn't summon new magic. It takes our magic and puts it into one of them."

Amanda's mouth dropped open. "You're lying."

"Tell her the truth," Moonbeam urged. "Why are you doing this? Why take this risk?"

He locked his eyes on Moonbeam. "I want to fix what we broke."

Kayla felt her jaw drop open. He wasn't doing this to make himself powerful? He *wanted* to take their power?

Amanda's voice was a shriek. "Dad?"

"You need to trust me," Jack said. "This is for the best."

Amanda began to sputter. Her face reddened. Kayla understood what she was feeling. Both of them had misjudged Dad. And Kayla wasn't sure this was any better. He was endangering her mother and Daniel's out of some messed-up sense of regret.

Jack looked at Kayla, then Amanda, then Daniel. "This will fix you. All three of you."

"But it won't," Moonbeam said gently. "It won't turn back the clock. Their power is part of them now. You can't take it from them. This isn't the way."

Kayla couldn't believe it was Moonbeam saying this. *Moonbeam.* The one who always made her hide her power. The one who made her pretend it wasn't part of her.

"This is the only way! It took me a long time to see that. A long time to see what the magic has . . . what *I* have . . . done to our daughter. To both our daughters and to Evelyn's son."

Moonbeam shook her head sadly. "It's too late."

"You're lying." Amanda's hands were shaking. The gun

wavered. "You're all lying! This is for more power! So you can fulfill your dreams! So we can make the world better, help the helpless, all of that, all the things you used to say! Not for taking *my* power! The spell grants magic; it doesn't take it!"

"Completing the spell will reallocate the magic, consolidating it into a single person," Evelyn said. "Or at least that's the theory, and it's supported by—"

Amanda swung the gun toward her. "Shut up. All of you, shut up."

"Amanda, put down the gun." Their father began to wade out of the water. Kayla held her breath. "I can explain. Years ago, Evelyn, your mother, and I cast a spell that we didn't understand and it had consequences we didn't—"

"I won't let you take it away from me. And if you're not in this for the magic . . . then I'll take yours too." Aiming the gun at Dad, Amanda squeezed the trigger.

26

The gun obliterated all other sound. Every bird fled. Every insect was silenced. But Kayla had reacted even faster. As Amanda squeezed the trigger, Kayla threw her mind at the bullet. As it exited the barrel, she knocked its tip. It veered off course and slammed into a tree on the opposite side of the swimming hole.

Moonbeam was screaming, but Kayla barely heard her. She felt as though every fiber in her body were vibrating. She clenched her hands into fists and held herself still. Ready.

Amanda fired again—this time, Kayla hit the bullet in the air before the sound even registered in her ears. The bullet ricocheted and embedded itself in the rocks. Walking forward toward her father, Amanda shot again, and Kayla plucked the third bullet out of the air. She let it fall to the ground.

Amanda pivoted and shot at Kayla.

Without any hesitation, Kayla smacked the bullet to the ground. She then lifted it up with her mind. It arched through the air and landed gently in her palm. "Enough, Amanda."

"You're really taking me on, little sis?" Laughing, Amanda tossed the gun into the bushes. "Okay, then, let's play."

"I'm not fighting you," Kayla said. "I just don't want you to shoot anyone." But Amanda wasn't listening. She lifted one of the tires out of the muck and flung it at Kayla as if it were no heavier than a Frisbee.

Kayla dove to the ground as her father charged out of the pool. He was followed closely by Moonbeam. Switching her attention to them, Amanda flicked her hands, and Dad flew across the water to land in the trees on the opposite side. Moonbeam flew after him, crashing down on top of him in a tangle of limbs. For good measure, Amanda also grabbed Evelyn and chucked her as well. She landed beside them. Using Amanda's distraction, Kayla scrambled behind the large rock that they'd first hidden behind. She'd need to fight smarter—

The rock shifted, wiggled like a loose tooth, and then rose into the air.

Crap, Kayla thought. She retreated fast and smacked backward into a pair of waiting arms. The world flashed white then green. Instantly, she was home in the garden. The torn-up bushes were in front of her, and the garden gnomes lay at her feet. She spun to face Daniel. "Take me back," she ordered.

"She's trying to kill you!" Daniel said.

"You jump our mothers out of there while she's distracted with me, *then* come back and save me." Out of the corner of her eye, she saw Queen Marguerite barrel out of the house.

"Did they start the spell?" the voodoo queen asked.

"Yes. There's blood on the stones. What do I do?"

"All of them?"

"Only two."

"Then it's not too late." Drawing a pouch out of her pocket, Queen Marguerite tossed it to Kayla. "Cleanse the blood off the stones with water and salt, then bring your mother safe to me. You hear me, girl?"

Catching it, Kayla said, "Now, Daniel."

And the world flashed. Instantly, they were back. This time, Daniel had deposited them behind a different, larger rock. *Clever boy*, Kayla thought. He was learning to be careful. About damn time.

Kayla peeked around the rock. Dad was on land, but Amanda, Evelyn, and Moonbeam were hip-deep in the water. Each held a stone. Amanda had a knife in her other hand.

The gun was floating in the air, aimed at Moonbeam's head.

Dad's eyes were fixed on the gun, but Moonbeam's were focused on the knife. Kayla thought of Queen Marguerite's relief that only two stones had blood. She had to act before the spell was complete.

Amanda might have brute strength, but Kayla had precision. *You can do this*, she told herself. She spotted one of the discharged bullets on the ground, lifted it up, and jammed it into the barrel of the gun. And then she waited for her moment.

On the edge of the pond, their father was pleading, "Don't do this! You could die! One in three chance." His face was contorted in anguish. Kayla tried to imagine what it would have been like to be raised by him. Had that twisted Amanda, or had she always been like this?

"And a one in three chance of true power."

"Amanda, don't—"

Without another word, Amanda sliced the palm of her own

hand with the knife. Ready, Kayla caught each drop of blood and veered them away from the stone. They landed in the water instead. "Not funny, Katydid!" Amanda called.

Kayla stayed hidden behind the rock. She focused on the water trickling down the rock face. She carried it in a steady stream toward the stones, washing the blood from Evelyn's and Moonbeam's stones. She then opened the pouch of salt and sent the grains flying toward the stones. The stream of grains split, some for each stone.

"You shouldn't have come back," Amanda said. A rusted car door rose out of the water and flew at the trees. It impacted and shattered only a few feet from Kayla. She kept the salt flying. "I know you're near. You're not as clever as you think. There aren't many places to hide."

Salt landed on the stones, mixing with the water, cleansing them.

A tree cracked and crashed on the other side of Kayla, and Kayla flinched. Other trees began to fall, one after another. Taking advantage of Evelyn's preoccupation, Daniel appeared in the water, clapped his hand on his mother's shoulder, and they both vanished—with Evelyn's stone.

"Amanda, please, don't!" Moonbeam said. "She's your sister."

"My sister's dead," Amanda said. "She died when you stole her from me!" Shoving, she knocked Moonbeam back. One of the tires flew toward Moonbeam and landed on her, pushing her down. Water closed over her face.

Kayla screamed. "Mom!" She burst out from behind the rock. "Amanda, stop it! Leave her alone. Come on, you know you really want to go for me."

Dad tried to yank the tire off Moonbeam, but Amanda was

holding it in place. He strained as he pulled, shouting at Amanda to release it.

Grabbing a bubble of air, Kayla forced it into the water. She pushed it through the water and into her mother's mouth. *Distract her*, Kayla thought, *and she'll let go.* Amanda couldn't hold multiple things at once—even the corpses in the catacombs had flown one at a time. "You hate that our father wants to change you. You hate that you aren't enough to make him happy. You hate that he kept looking for me even though he had you."

"You little—" Amanda reached out with her mind and grabbed the rocks on the cliff. In order to do this, as Kayla had hoped, she released her hold on the tire that was drowning Moonbeam. Moonbeam burst to the surface. Kayla's father reached for her, and Moonbeam lunged away—into Daniel's arms.

Moonbeam and Daniel vanished as Dad yelled.

Amanda didn't seem to notice. Tears streamed down her cheeks. She hurled rocks at Kayla. One of them clipped Kayla's shoulder as she tried to dive for cover. She cried out and fell to her knees. Several other rocks were hurtling toward her.

Kayla's father launched himself into Amanda, knocking her over. Her control over the rocks broke, and Kayla ducked as the other rocks smashed harmlessly around her. She popped up again to see that Amanda was crying harder—and hitting her father over and over again with her right fist. He was holding her back, and her fist landed only lightly on his chest.

Daniel appeared beside Kayla. "You all right?"

"I don't know whether to help him, or help her," Kayla said. She got to her feet and dusted off her knees. They ached from where she'd hit the ground, and her shoulder throbbed.

"Why not leave them to each other?"

Her father caught Amanda's wrist. She sagged against him, still crying, still clutching the third stone. Dad stroked her back and murmured to her as he looked up at Kayla. His eyes met hers.

"Okay, let's go," Kayla said to Daniel, and the world flashed around them.

27

Kayla blinked fast, trying to force her vision to steady so she could see where she was. She recognized the room in seconds: she was in Selena's house, specifically the media room. The TV was on, paused in the middle of a random car chase scene, and a bowl of edamame was on the coffee table. The shells were littered over the rug, as if they'd been spilled. Moonbeam and Daniel's mother were there, collapsed on a couch and wrapped in towels, their backs to Kayla and Daniel. In front of the TV, Selena was pacing back and forth.

"Smart," Kayla said softly. Neither Amanda nor Queen Marguerite knew Selena's house.

Selena rushed over to her. "Not smart. What if my parents come home early? What if your father comes here?"

Moonbeam jumped to her feet. "Kayla! You're alive!" Beside her, Daniel's mother twisted to see her and asked at the same time, "What happened? Is Jack all right?"

Talking over them in her loud-as-a-trumpet voice, Selena continued, "Why are they here? And why are there gobs of algae on my couch? Kayla, what is going on?"

Kayla faced her mother. She plucked the stone out of Moonbeam's hands. Moonbeam didn't resist. She reached her empty hands toward Kayla. "Kayla . . ."

"We'll talk later," Kayla told her mother. She asked Selena, "Do you have a sledgehammer? I want to destroy these puppies before they do any more damage." She waved the stone in the air for emphasis.

Clutching her stone to her chest, Evelyn stroked it as if it were a baby. "It won't work. They're indestructible. That's why they were split up in the first place."

"Excuse me if I don't believe you," Kayla said. "I've lost track of who's lying to me." She tried to take the stone. Evelyn tightened her grip. "Sorry, but I'm really not interested in arguing with you about this." Without a pause, Kayla lifted a dozen edamame shells with her mind and tossed them in Evelyn's face. Startled, Daniel's mother flinched and loosened her grip. Kayla snatched away the second stone. "Selena?"

"Sledgehammer's in the garage."

Dropping the towels, Evelyn shot to her feet. She lunged to take her stone back, but Kayla danced backward around the couch.

"How do we know we can trust you with the stones?" Evelyn cried.

Stepping forward, Daniel blocked her path, placing himself directly between Evelyn and Kayla. "Mother. Stop. You can trust Kayla. And me."

Evelyn touched his face lightly. "Oh Daniel, I know you mean well, but you don't understand. It's a complicated issue—"

"It's *not* complicated. The stones are evil."

"Powerful isn't automatically evil! Surely, you can't be so simplistic—"

"Sometimes there are shades of gray," Kayla said. "This is not one of those times." Carrying the two stones, Kayla strode out of the media room. Everyone chased after her.

"Kayla, we need to talk," Moonbeam said. "Your sister—"

"You have no idea what you're dealing with," Evelyn said at the same time. She tried to grab Kayla's arm again, but Kayla walked faster. Selena flanked her, forcing Evelyn to trail behind. Evelyn called, "Those stones are ancient artifacts of immense power—"

"Any chance of an explanation?" Selena asked Kayla. "Why are they here? How did you get two of the stones? What happened with your father? Are you okay?"

Before answering, Kayla glanced back at Evelyn. Daniel had begun arguing with her a few paces back. "Short summary: Turns out my dad didn't kill my sister, Amanda. She's alive. She's telekinetic like me, and a psychopath like him."

Evelyn interrupted. "Just because Jack—"

Ignoring her, Kayla continued. "I stopped the spell. Daniel got us out. But Amanda's pissed. She really, really wants the stones back. And Queen Marguerite is also pissed. She really, really wants the stones too—for different reasons, she says, but we're not sure we trust her anyway. So I'm going to destroy them myself and then go around and tell everyone to calm the hell down because it's over."

Moonbeam gasped. "You know Marguerite? Kayla, how do you know—"

At the same time, Selena said, "Your sister's *alive*? But I thought the whole reason you—"

"Yeah, my mom lied." Kayla charged up the stairs. Everyone thumped up the stairs behind her.

"I can explain," Moonbeam began.

Daniel's mother called, "She had reason. Your father wanted to—"

"My mother sent us to the voodoo queen," Daniel answered Moonbeam.

"Evelyn! Why?" Moonbeam cried. "And how did my Kayla—"

"You could have left a less cryptic note," Daniel told his mother. "If you'd just told us to go to Tikal in the first place—" Kayla reached the top of the stairs and strode through the hall toward the foyer.

Evelyn said, "You needed information she had—"

Moonbeam nearly stopped walking. "You've been to Tikal?"

"And Peru and Mexico and Spain," Selena supplied helpfully.

A housekeeper dropped a pile of laundry as they all marched by. Her jaw fell open but she didn't say a word. Kayla marched toward the front door without glancing at her. Sunlight streamed into the foyer, making all of this seem surreal. She couldn't have just been with her father and sister. Her sister couldn't have tried to shoot her and her father—but it had happened, all of it. And she was going to end it.

"So I was right? About Seville?" Selena said.

"One hundred percent brilliant," Kayla said. "I owe you."

"Damn straight."

"Which is why, when this is done, I am going to help you with Sam," Kayla said. "He likes you, and you like him, and everything else is crap."

Selena shook her head, slowing in a swath of sunlight in the foyer. Sun caught the crystal vase on the antique end table. "You don't understand. I can't. I'm not strong like you—"

Daniel interrupted. "Is this really what we're talking about right now? Her relationship drama? Can we please save it for later?" Passing them, he pushed the front door open and led the way outside. Everyone spilled out onto the marble steps.

Evelyn blinked up at the sky. "Palm trees? Where are we?"

"California," Moonbeam told her. "Evelyn, how could you involve my daughter? You know everything I did—"

"I had no choice," Evelyn said. "He found me—"

"Of course he found you!" Moonbeam said. "You didn't try to hide. You wrote papers. You gave talks. You did everything but hang a neon sign on your door saying 'I am still a witch.'"

"Sledgehammer?" Kayla asked Selena.

"With the other tools." Selena strode toward the garage. Hurrying to catch up, Kayla paced her. "Your sister is really alive? Are you sure she's not an imposter? Or a robot? Or someone who has been brainwashed to believe she's your sister but is really the lost duchess of Umbria? Not that there is a lost duchess of Umbria. I mean, there *could* be, but I picked it as an example."

"I hope she's not my sister," Kayla said. "She tried to shoot me. But she looks like she could be, and she has her laugh. Plus Moonbeam hasn't denied it."

"Oh, Kayla . . . ," Moonbeam began.

"Shoot you? Like with a gun?" Selena asked.

"No, with a cucumber. Yes, with a gun." Kayla spotted the tool bench on the opposite side of the garage, behind the Lamborghini. She surveyed the array of pristine tools. All of them looked fresh out of their packaging. Each was stowed in its own slot on a corkboard wall, an outline of the tool drawn around the hooks. She found the sledgehammer and hefted it off the wall. Her heart was beating so fast that it felt like it was a horse galloping inside her chest.

"I trusted you," Moonbeam said to Evelyn.

"We all trusted each other," Evelyn said. "You were the one who walked out on us. Jack wouldn't have lost it so badly if you'd been there to balance him."

"He lost it before I left. That's *why* I left. He only cared about power. He didn't care about us. When Amanda first showed signs of having power . . . You don't know what it was like. He was warping them. And I wasn't strong enough to stand up to him. He . . . hurt me when I tried, even though he swore he never would, that he wasn't like his parents, that everything would be different. Better. But it only got worse."

Passing them, Kayla carried the sledgehammer out of the garage. She laid one stone on the driveway, tucked the other in her pocket, and tried to swing the hammer. Her arms shook, and the hammer wobbled. Bracing herself, she tried again. She swung, and it cracked down.

The stone didn't shatter.

"I'll try," Daniel said. She handed the sledgehammer to him, and he slammed it down on the stone. No luck. He tried again. And again.

"Oh, good grief, let me," Selena said.

"I thought you said you weren't strong?" Daniel said.

"Emotionally. Psychologically. But I'm happy to hit things." Selena took the sledgehammer and swung. Same result, except that she shattered one of the driveway paving stones. "Oops."

"So what happened with Sam?" Kayla asked.

"I was going to do it. I was going to tell my parents this is what I want and they need to respect my choices, et cetera. I was all set to invite him over . . . but then they walked in, and I couldn't. So I sent him to you instead. Glad I did since they confiscated my phone afterward. Said 'that boy' was interfering with my studies." She hit again, harder.

Arms crossed, Evelyn watched them. "That will never work. The stones are indestructible. You clearly don't know what you're dealing with."

"You've done a lousy job of dealing with it so far, so I don't think you get a vote." Kayla tried again with the sledgehammer. Zero luck. The stone wasn't even dented. She wondered what the damn thing was made of, or if it was more magic. "But if you have a suggestion, I'd love to hear it."

"Travel to Mordor and drop it in a volcano?" Selena suggested.

"Or I could drop it in the ocean," Daniel said. "Maybe the Mariana Trench?"

Evelyn gasped. "You can't! These stones are priceless, unique pieces of history!"

Moonbeam objected too, simultaneously. "You can't guarantee they'll stay in the ocean. They could wash up somewhere. Some poor unsuspecting soul could find them, and his children would pay the price."

"Not if it's deep enough," Kayla said. She turned to Selena. "Selena, I'm sorry to ask, but . . ."

"But you need another favor? Ask away."

"I need you to make sure they don't leave, that they don't call anyone, that they don't do anything to make this worse." She pointed at Moonbeam and Evelyn.

"You don't trust them?" Selena asked.

"You don't trust me?" Moonbeam echoed.

Kayla gave her a look. "And that's such a shock?"

"Daniel, please, you can't do this," Evelyn begged. "These are ancient and powerful artifacts. They deserve to be studied, to be treasured, to be in a museum. These stones are a part of history! The pestilence stone—soon after it fell into the hands of Spanish explorers, smallpox spread. Coincidence or history? The mind stone—can it explain the similarities in cultures in different parts of the world? There's so much to be learned! Now that we have them, we can take care of them properly, ensure that they don't fall into the wrong hands."

"You *are* the wrong hands," Kayla shot at her.

Daniel shook his head. "You burned your notebook, but you still weren't able to prevent Kayla's father and sister from getting the stones and starting the spell. How do you expect to protect them now that they're no longer hidden?"

"We'll find a way! If we work together—"

A sudden thought occurred to Kayla, and she spoke before she considered the ramifications. "Did you help my father voluntarily?"

The question shocked everyone so much that they all turned to stare at Evelyn. She took a step back and bumped into Selena's BMW. "No! Of course not! How can you think that?"

"You're willing to 'work together' with us to save these stones," Kayla pointed out. "Why not with him?"

Evelyn looked outraged, offended, maybe a little frightened. "I didn't want the spell to happen! It's Russian roulette but with worse odds. I would never—"

"But you wanted the stones," Kayla pressed. "You told Daniel to find me and Queen Marguerite. You sent him on a quest for the stones. You could have simply given him a clue to where you were, and he could have rescued you or sent the police after you. If you wanted the stones to stay safe, then why not leave them exactly where they were?"

"Kayla has a point," Selena said. "Danny-boy has that handy teleporting trick. You could have used that to save you, easy-peasy." She wiggled her fingers in the air as if she were a stage magician. Kayla was surprised she didn't add a sound effect for good measure. "It would have been simpler and faster. Plus it would have kept Kayla and her mom out of it, leaving them nice and safe, which would have had the added benefit of leaving me nice and safe, which frankly I prefer."

Evelyn's eyes flicked from one person to the next, and then at the door.

In a quiet voice, Daniel asked, "Mom? Why did you leave such a cryptic note? Why didn't you tell me where to find you?"

"I didn't know where he'd take me."

Weak excuse, Kayla thought. "Yes, you did. You knew he'd go to Tikal. You wrote a paper on it. You knew, or at least suspected, that the map was there."

"He made me tell him!" Evelyn cried. "I didn't want to help him."

"Either way, whether you wanted to help him or were forced to, you knew you'd go to Tikal. So why not tell Daniel that? Why send him to Queen Marguerite? Why involve me?"

Evelyn opened her mouth.

Kayla cut her off before she could speak. "I think it's because you knew my father couldn't reach the map. My sister doesn't have that kind of precision. But I do. If you only wanted to be 'saved,' you needed Daniel. But if you wanted the stones . . . you needed me."

Evelyn appealed to Moonbeam. "You know that I never wanted Jack to start the spell. I wouldn't have risked the stones' falling into his hands."

"But if your plan worked, they weren't falling into his hands," Selena pointed out. "They were falling into your son's hands. And you trusted him to give them to you, after he 'saved' you from Kayla's father. Ooh, tricky! I vote for her as the mastermind. She could have contacted Kayla's father and started it all. Maybe she set all of this in motion!"

"You've been researching the stones all these years," Kayla said.

"This is absurd!" Evelyn said. "I burned my research! Daniel saw me. Tell them, Daniel. Why would I do that if I wanted the stones found?"

Daniel nodded. "I saw her burn the notebook. Kayla, I think you're way off base. I know you don't want to believe your father and sister are solely to blame—"

"I've thought my dad was evil my entire life," Kayla said. "Hardly about to start protecting his reputation now. I'm sorry, Daniel, but she could have burned the notebook to be sure that she was the only one who had the information."

"Very clever," Selena said, looking at Evelyn with admiration. "Since Kayla's dad couldn't get her research, he took her. Just like she planned."

Evelyn's face turned from pale to bright red. "Ridiculous! I didn't stage my own kidnapping. Daniel, you can't believe that. Who is this girl anyway? Why are you even listening to her?"

Selena put her hands on her hips. "I'm the one whose property you're trespassing on. Or your gracious hostess, depending on how you want to look at it." To Kayla, she said, "I'll keep them here."

Pivoting, Evelyn appealed to Moonbeam. "You can't possibly think—"

"Evelyn," Moonbeam said gently. "Jack would never have

known how to find the other stones if not for you. You were always the smart one, the straight-A student."

"You knew where the parchment was," Kayla said. "You mentioned it in one of your papers. You must have figured out it was only accessible to someone with telekinesis. You contacted my father, because you knew about Amanda. And once you realized that Amanda couldn't do it . . . you set in motion a plan to involve me."

Evelyn appealed to her son. "You can't believe this. It's not true. They're speculating wildly because they're scared. Please, say you believe me."

He swallowed hard. "I *want* to believe you. And if you tell me, if you swear, that none of this is true, that you didn't try to use me and to use Kayla, I will believe you." He held up his hand as Evelyn started to speak. "Tell me *after* the stones are gone. It won't mean anything if you say it now." He turned to Kayla. "Are you ready?"

Kayla nodded.

"Daniel!" Evelyn cried.

Stepping away from his mother, he said, "I'm sorry, Mom. I have to do this."

Selena patted Evelyn on the shoulder. "Why don't you come inside and relax while my friends fix the mess you made?" To Kayla, she said, "Go. Finish this."

Kayla nodded and scooped up the stone that was on the driveway. She put it in her pocket. The second stone was still in her other pocket. As she reached for Daniel's hand, Evelyn dove past Selena toward her. "No, you can't! I've worked too hard—"

Moonbeam caught her arm and whispered several melodious words. Evelyn's eyes rolled back. Her mouth gaped open, and her muscles seemed limp. She slumped against Moonbeam, and Moonbeam lowered her to the ground.

With a shout, Daniel surged forward. Dropping to his knees, he cradled his mother against his chest. "What did you do to her?"

"And how?" Kayla didn't know her mom could work magic like *that*.

"She's fine; she's asleep," Moonbeam said. "But without the right herbs, she'll stay asleep for only a few minutes at best."

"But you—"

"Go, Kayla, fix this. Make it right."

Kayla nodded. Reluctantly, Daniel lowered his mother down and backed away. Eyes fixed on his mother, he took Kayla's hand, and everything vanished.

28

Daniel's bedroom.

Kayla looked around the wreckage. "Why are we here?"

"I need images." Daniel climbed over the destroyed desk to a wall that used to be covered in maps and photos. He picked up several from the floor and pinned them back on the wall—the Eiffel Tower, the Grand Canyon, a waterfall, a cave, the Sahara. "Can't jump blind. Any ideas?"

Joining him, Kayla scanned the wall. She helped him pick photos off the floor. A few were crumpled. A couple were torn. She smoothed them out and wondered how long he'd been working on this wall. She'd discovered her power when she was eight years old, around the time that Amanda had died. Or not died. "How about here?" She showed him a picture of a volcano spewing lava. "Mordor isn't a bad idea. Worked for the hobbits. Even if the lava doesn't melt the stone, it would be difficult to retrieve. We could throw one stone into a volcano and drop the other in the ocean."

He nodded. "I know several lava lakes. Erta Ale in Ethiopia, Nyiragongo in the Congo, Kilauea in Hawaii, Mount Erebus in Antarctica, and Villarrica in Chile." He rattled them off as if they were as familiar to him as the shop names on State Street were to her. "Any preference?"

"Jump us to each of them. Don't tell me which is which. And then close your eyes. I'll toss a stone in one at random. That way, neither of us will know where it is and no one can ever get the information out of us." She hesitated. "Daniel, I'm sorry about—"

He cut her off. "Forget it. We have work to do."

The house flashed around them, and instantly Kayla's lungs felt squeezed and scorched as if she'd been filleted from the inside out. Smoke clogged the air, and the ground was split with lines of glowing red. He closed his eyes and waited.

She felt as if they'd stepped back to the dawn of time. Any second, a dinosaur would lumber out onto the bulbous rocks. Above, the sky was streaked with a smattering of stars. The moon had a line of smoke across it. It smelled like sulfur, and the sheer heat burned her tear ducts dry.

It was incredible.

"Do it or don't do it," Daniel said.

She took out one of the stones and pretended to throw it so he'd hear and feel the movement, but she didn't release it. She tucked it back in her pocket. "Next lake."

The world flashed.

The next lava lake glowed an angry red. It swirled deep in the center of a crater, and they were standing on the rim looking down at it. White smoke billowed up from it, and the walls of the crater were black lumps, all ash and volcanic rock. She saw stretches of mirrorlike black stone.

It was day here, and the blue sky contrasted with the red of the lava lake. The black stone reflected clouds and smoke as they billowed past. Her feet were cold, and the air tasted like ash.

Again, she pretended to throw. "Next," she said.

Third, a bubbling pit of orange and red. It writhed only a few feet from them. This time, she hurled the stone in. It landed silently, as if sucked in by the ooze. And then she guided the lava away, so that the stone would sink farther in and out of sight. It vanished into the orange, eaten by the fire that bubbled and burned. She put her empty hand back in her pocket and thought she should feel something—relief or regret—but instead she only watched the lava pop and writhe and thought, *So pretty.* "Next."

The fourth lava lake looked like a crescent moon set afire, or like an angry wound. It glowed through the rocks, and she thought it was like seeing inside a living body. The blood of the world flowed through these rocks. Here, the ground felt hot, as if the rock wanted to split beneath them and release more of the blood-colored lava. She pretended to throw again. A geyser of red shot up a few feet in front of them, and she stumbled back, holding on to Daniel's arm. "Next, hurry!"

And then the final lava lake. The lava oozed over the uneven rocks. It dripped like blood in thick, clogged rivulets. The ground felt warm but not hot under her feet, and a breeze blew over the air, carrying the smoke away. In the distance, she saw the ocean, so blue, so beautiful. They were on a mountainside, and beyond the field of lava were green trees. She heard birds calling to one another. One took flight, its orange feathers spread against the sky. She realized in this instant that she had just seen the world, or at least more of it than she'd ever expected to see.

"Are you done?" Daniel asked.

"Almost." She hesitated, drawing the moment out even longer. Then she put her hand in her empty pocket, drew it out, and pretended to throw. A breeze blew in, and the air tasted like ocean. She wondered if this was Hawaii, and then pushed the idea out of her head. She didn't want to guess where the stone was. It was better if she never knew. "Done."

They snapped back to Daniel's room.

"That worked well," Daniel said.

"That was incredible!" Kayla leaped into Daniel's arms and kissed him hard on the lips. He tumbled backward and landed, with her on him, on his bed. He started to laugh. Laughing, she rolled off him and jumped to her feet. She hadn't heard him laugh often enough. "Ocean next? Can you even do an ocean? It's not like it has landmarks."

He smiled. "That's the beauty of it. I won't know which ocean we're in. I'll picture waves surrounded by nothing but ocean. Horizon all around."

"Sounds beautiful," she agreed.

Standing up, he reached for her hands.

Kayla pulled back. "Wait! I am totally not dressed for being dumped in the middle of the ocean. Or for being eaten by sharks. How about we use a boat?"

"Please tell me you don't plan to steal a boat."

"Only a raft."

"Ahh, okay."

"Actually, I was thinking it was time to introduce you to a life in crime. Can you take us to State Street? I know an outdoor-sports store that would be perfect." She took his hands.

Without another word, Daniel hopped them to State Street. Kayla smiled at the familiar sight of the brick benches, the palm trees, the smoothie café. They'd appeared on a brick bench, in the midst of a pack of black-clad, heavily pierced teens.

"Hey," Daniel said.

"Hey," one of the teens replied.

"Were you here a minute ago?" a girl asked.

"Yeah," Daniel said. "Been here a while."

"Oh," the girl said.

"And now have to go. 'Bye!" Kayla flashed a smile at the girl, and then pulled Daniel up with her and sauntered toward the outdoor-sports store. She bypassed the clerk and headed for the window display. It had an orange inflatable raft with a mannequin in it in full fishing regalia. She picked up the mannequin and took it out of the raft.

The clerk bustled over. "Hey, what are you doing?"

Kayla looked over his shoulder and feigned astonishment. "Oh my goodness, what's happening to your cash register?" She pressed the Open button with her mind, and the drawer popped out. Cash flew out of the machine. Squawking, the cashier ran back to the counter and began catching the bills that darted over his head like crazed birds.

"Aren't you the one always telling me to be more careful?" Daniel asked.

Kayla shrugged. "Maybe you're rubbing off on me. Besides, Moonbeam and I will be leaving here, changing our names, and starting new lives soon anyway."

"Will you tell me your new name, or will you and your mother just disappear?"

"I . . . Let's finish this first, okay?" She sat down in the raft. Daniel joined her. He gripped her with one hand and the side of the raft with another. A second later, the store disappeared.

Kayla held on to the raft as wind and water crashed into them. Waves rose and fell. The sky overhead was mottled blue and purple and white. There was no sound other than the waves, water hitting itself. There was no land anywhere to be seen. Just blueness meeting the blue of the horizon in every direction.

She leaned over the side of the raft. "Ready?"

He leaned over next to her. The raft tilted. The water was only a few inches below her hands. "What if the current catches it and washes it to shore?" Daniel asked.

"I can guide it down. Not so different from moving raindrops, so long as I limit my focus to the immediate area around the stone. I think."

"Okay. Do it."

She opened her hand, and the stone plopped into the water. Concentrating, she shifted the water so that it sank faster, clearing a thin path for it to plummet down, down, down through the ocean.

She felt shapes in the water: plankton, tiny swift fish, large floating fish, whales. Current pushed against her, and she guided the stone around the flow so that it would keep falling and not be swept away. She concentrated on little bits of water at a time, easing it through the ocean. Spots of white speckled her vision as she reached farther and farther. She'd never done this distance before. Whichever ocean this was, it was damn deep.

At last the stone hit a cliff. She used the water to tip the stone off, and the stone fell into the abyss. It tumbled into the depths of the ocean, unimaginably deep. She lost all trace of it as it sank.

Kayla collapsed back into the raft. Stretching out, she lay there for a moment, feeling the sun, feeling the way the raft rose and fell on the open ocean. Her head ached. "It's done. Two stones, gone. Only one left. Good enough, right?"

Daniel stretched out beside her. Their fingers intertwined.

On their backs, they stared up at the sky as the ocean rolled under them, lifting them up and sinking them down.

"Are you really going to run away again?" Daniel asked.

"Yes."

"What about Selena? And your life in Santa Barbara? And me?"

She dodged the questions. "You don't live in Santa Barbara."

"So you will tell me who and where you are?"

Moonbeam always said that to truly hide, you have to cut all ties. She hadn't done that with her friend Evelyn, and look where it had led. Then again, could she really say good-bye to Daniel and Selena and everything she knew? "It would be nice if I had some grand plan to convince Dad and Amanda never to bother us again, but I don't see it happening." And Moonbeam would never agree anyway.

Daniel propped himself up on his elbow. He caressed her cheek as if memorizing the shape of her face. "We could improvise."

She blinked up at him. Sunlight was like a halo around his head, so bright that she could barely see his face. "Seriously?"

"Okay, you're right—we might want a better plan than that."

"How about you kiss me?" she suggested.

"I think I like that plan," he said gravely. Then he leaned over her and touched her lips with his. She closed her eyes and let the kiss wash over her. She heard the ocean around her, the only sound. His body was warm against hers. She wrapped her arms around his neck and kissed him back as if she never intended to stop.

∽ ∾

Lying curled against Daniel, Kayla listened to his heartbeat, the slap of the waves on the raft, and the wind. Overhead, the sky was streaked with rose-colored clouds and deep blue clouds that looked like smears of paint. In the west, the sun was sinking, and it looked like lava, melting into the ocean. In the east, the sky had already deepened to a rich blue.

"I don't want to go back," Daniel said.

"I don't want to be eaten by sharks, die of exposure, or get sunburned," Kayla said.

He was silent, as if considering those options. "Is that in any particular order?"

She smiled, then her smile faded. "You know they'll be worrying about us."

"Just a few more minutes."

They lay for a while as the sky continued to darken. A few stars poked through, then more. Every time she blinked she thought that more appeared, as if they were sneaking out during the instant that her eyes were shut. "What is it that you want to happen when we go back?" Kayla asked.

"Ideally, or realistically?"

"Ideally," she said.

Silence again. She could almost hear him thinking. She listened to the water hit the sides of the raft. She thought about how many miles of ocean were beneath them. Reaching down with her mind, she felt the water, the life under them. She felt so fragile and yet so eternal above all those little bits of life and away from absolutely anyone else.

"I want my mom to swear this wasn't her idea, that she didn't use me to find her stupid stones, that she didn't make me worry about her and risk myself and risk you because of her goddamn research. I want her to care about me more than her work. Just once. Ever since my dad died, it's been her work first, then me. I want her to see me as more than a tool she can use. How about you?"

Kayla considered it. "Well . . . For starters, it would be nice if my mom told me the truth, whatever it is. And it would be nice if my sister would stop trying to kill me and my parents. It would be great if we could be some kind of fully functional normal family again like that family in Mexico, but that's not going to happen, and honestly I'm not sure I'm comfortable having Cheerios in the morning next to two people who may or may not want to kill me or each other at any given moment." She thought about it longer as she stared up at the stars. "Yeah, I think that's what I want: I don't want to be afraid anymore. That's all."

"I don't think that's too much to ask," Daniel said.

And with those words, she decided that she was in love with him. She smiled up at the sky. "Neither do I." They fell into silence again.

More stars. So many more stars than she thought it possible for the sky to hold. At this rate, if more kept appearing, the sky would be as full of white light as the brightest desert noon. The Milky Way was a white cloud-like smudge across the sky. The western horizon continued to glow a deep amber until the dark blue-black spread to it. The ocean around them was black. Kayla stayed entwined with Daniel.

"How do we make it happen?" Daniel asked.

"No idea. My father's probably still determined to rid us and psycho-sister of our magic, so he probably wants the stones back. Our moms have probably escaped Selena and been caught again by Dad, Amanda, Queen Marguerite, or all three. They, plus Selena, are most likely being held hostage in exchange for the two stones that we just tossed away."

"Yeah, that's pretty likely. How about we simply don't go back?"

"You mean run away, you and me?" Kayla thought about that, really thought. With their powers, they could go anywhere and do anything. The possibilities were intoxicating. "That would be cowardly and selfish."

"Yeah, I know."

They both fell silent, staring up at the stars.

"Tempting, though," Daniel said.

"Very," Kayla agreed. "How about we make that plan B if all else fails?"

She imagined he was smiling in the darkness. She felt him shift beside her, turning to face her. "I like plan B," he said. "Do we have a plan A?"

"I think it would be nice if we could get everyone to sit calmly together and discuss everything like rational human beings."

"Wave a white flag and ask to talk?" He shook his head. She saw it as a shadow moving in the darkness. His whole face was a blur of shadows. "Never going to happen."

"Actually, I was thinking more along the lines of kidnap everyone, tie them up, and not let them out even to pee until they start acting like rational adults rather than four-year-olds throwing tantrums because someone else played with their favorite toy."

He laughed and then fell silent.

She stared up at the stars, trying to drink them in, as if she could absorb them for their strength. "Guess we'll have to go back and just see what's happened." The stars disappeared.

29

Selena's basement.

Hand in hand, Kayla and Daniel surveyed the empty media room. Edamame shells were still strewn over the carpet. The TV was off. "Still outside?" Kayla suggested.

They jumped to the driveway, where the sledgehammer lay on the cobblestones. Kayla felt her heart beat faster. She'd been right—Evelyn and Moonbeam were gone. They'd escaped, and Moonbeam could now be in even more danger . . . Kayla barged into the garage.

And found Evelyn wrapped up in duct tape. She was gagged with a dust cloth. Selena was perched on the hood of the Lamborghini, a wrench in her hands. Moonbeam was standing next to Evelyn with her arms crossed like a disappointed schoolteacher. Kayla skidded to a stop and stared, speechless.

"Mom!" Daniel cried. He rushed forward.

Moonbeam held up a hand to stop Daniel. "We can explain."

Sliding off the hood of the Lamborghini, Selena rushed to Kayla. "I did it! I really did it. I always thought I'd fall apart when the moment to act came, but I didn't fall apart. And my parents aren't due home yet, so double hooray!"

"She was magnificent," Moonbeam affirmed.

Kayla hugged Selena. "I'm proud of you. Not surprised, though. You're more than you think you are. Stronger than you think you are."

Selena rolled her eyes. "You *were* totally surprised. I saw you."

"Slightly surprised," Kayla admitted. Selena beamed and twirled the wrench in her hand like it was her new favorite accessory. "After all, you were sitting on the Lamb. You could have gotten smudges on it."

Selena laughed. She was sparkling even more than her sequined shirt. Kayla grinned at her and wondered what had caused this change.

Daniel was scowling. "This isn't funny. Why is my mother tied up? What happened?"

Selena waved the wrench to indicate Evelyn. "She had nefarious plans and was being all nefarious. After the spell wore off, she faked being still asleep. I caught her trying to call Kayla's sister and father, and I bashed her cell phone with the sledgehammer. She was planning to use Moonbeam to force you two to reveal where you'd hidden the stones."

Daniel paled. "Mom?"

Evelyn shook her head frantically, as if to proclaim her innocence.

"I'm sorry, Daniel," Moonbeam said. "But it's true. Selena and Kayla were right. Evelyn was the one who set this all in motion. She contacted my husband. She used you to involve my Kayla. She thought she could control everything and everyone to win the stones for herself. But she couldn't."

Pushing past Moonbeam, Daniel knelt in front of his mother and pulled off her gag. "Mom, is it true? Are they telling the truth?"

"Absolutely not," Evelyn said. "Untie me. There's been a misunderstanding. These people don't see the potential in those stones! The historical value is phenomenal. Daniel, you have to—"

Kayla reached with her mind, lifted the cloth out of Daniel's hands, and stuffed it back in his mother's mouth. "She played us all. You know that. Maybe she never meant to use the stones—I can believe that. But she wanted to find them, and she used us to do it."

Daniel ran his hands through his hair as if he wanted to tear it out. "But she burned her notebook!"

"So Jack and Amanda would need her," Moonbeam said. "I'm sorry, Daniel."

"And she let them trash our house!"

Evelyn squawked, her eyes wide.

"Maybe she didn't let them," Kayla guessed. "Maybe they did it because she wasn't cooperating. She's said over and over that she didn't want them to cast the spell."

Moonbeam nodded. "She didn't want to use the stones. After all, if they did, you'd lose your power and she'd risk death. She just wanted to have them. So she hid the knife, thinking that would stop Jack from casting the spell."

He took the gag out of his mother's mouth again. "Yes, the knife!" Evelyn said. "I gave it to you to keep it safe! I knew Jack wouldn't want to do the spell without the knife. He wanted to re-create everything about the original spell, so that meant the three original casters and the original knife. I thought if I hid it, it would keep him from casting the spell!"

Daniel studied her. "Then you admit you were planning this." His voice was even, emotionless, but Kayla saw the hurt in his eyes.

His mother must have seen it too. "I . . . I wasn't . . . Daniel, the stones would have guaranteed tenure. We'd have been permanently secure. That kind of security . . . You don't know what it was like, growing up like I did. Never knowing when you'd be hungry. Or hurt. Or alone. I didn't want that for you, for us."

"But you didn't have to do this!"

"After your father died . . . it was up to me. You, your future, it was all up to me. So I went back to what I knew. I figured the stones had done so much damage to your life that maybe I could use them to do some good. I was going to publish papers on them. Maybe write a book. Donate them to a museum so they'd be safe forever."

"She thought she could use Jack and Amanda. She underestimated them." Moonbeam looked sadly at Daniel. "Thankfully, she underestimated you too."

Daniel was silent.

"How about you take her home?" Kayla suggested. "You can have that conversation you've been wanting to have. And she'll be two thousand miles away from here."

He shook his head. "You might need me. Your father and sister are still out there."

"In Louisiana. Not here." Kayla took Daniel's hands and stepped between him and his mother so he'd have to look in her eyes and see that she meant it. "You wanted to save your mother. This is your chance. Take her home. Let her see what her so-called allies did to her house while she thought she controlled them. And tell her the truth about where the stones are. They're beyond anyone's reach now." Kayla thought that Evelyn might already know about the house, despite her surprised reaction. She could have staged it for Daniel's benefit, to keep him searching for the stones, to give him hope that it wasn't over. She could have even left the photo album untouched on purpose. Kayla didn't voice that suspicion out loud.

Leaning forward, Daniel kissed her. Kayla heard either Evelyn or Moonbeam gasp—she wasn't sure which it was. Maybe both. Self-conscious, she pulled away from the kiss.

"You're certain you'll be okay?" Daniel asked.

"I'll be fine. You take care of your family. I'll take care of mine."

"But I'll see you again, right? I can jump to wherever you go. Call you whatever new name you want. All I need is a picture, and I can find you."

Kayla smiled. "I'll send you a postcard." This time, she kissed him, and she ignored the others. She wove her hands together around his neck. His hands spread across her back. She drank in the taste of his lips, and she tried to memorize this feeling.

When they broke apart, he turned to Selena. "Thanks for everything. Sorry about nearly getting you in trouble, with the church thing."

Selena waved her hand as if dismissing him. "We're even. You did me a favor." She smiled brightly at him. "At least now I know I don't have the worst mother in the world."

Daniel winced. He then put his hand on his mother's shoulder, and with one last look at Kayla, he vanished. Kayla exhaled. She hoped sending him away was the smart choice. It did take care of Evelyn. Kayla trusted that he'd be able to keep her from contacting Dad and Amanda, at least until she and Moonbeam could flee.

It was time now to leave Santa Barbara, leave their lives, and start over again, before Dad and Amanda tracked them down. She opened her mouth to say this, but Moonbeam spoke first. "It's time for us to go home," Moonbeam said. "We have a lot to talk about as well."

"I don't think we *can* go home," Kayla said. "Home has Queen Marguerite, and I don't know if she's on our side or not. I think we have to run." Her heart twisted as she said it. She didn't want to start over, to be someone new, to hide again and fear again. But she didn't see any other option.

Moonbeam shook her head. "We don't need to run from Marguerite."

"We don't? But—"

Turning to Selena, Moonbeam asked, "One last favor? Can you take us home?"

"Gladly." Selena led the way to her car and jumped in. Moonbeam climbed into the front seat. Selena turned the car on, and the music blared.

"Do we have a plan?" Kayla called over the music.

"Yes!" Moonbeam shouted back.

Kayla hurriedly squeezed herself into the backseat. She strapped on the seat belt and leaned forward so Moonbeam could hear her. "What is it?"

"I'm going to give her what she wants!"

"She says she wants the stones so she can hide them! But I don't believe her. I think she wants to use them herself!"

"That's not what she really wants!" Moonbeam called back.

And then Selena peeled out of the garage, and it was impossible to hear what else Moonbeam said.

As they careened down the twisting driveway, the wind whipped into their faces. Kayla's hair battered her cheeks. It smelled as salty as the ocean, and in the distance, she saw the waves crash in sweeping lines of white foam. Beachgoers sunned and played and walked on the sand, and Kayla felt so distant from all of them.

She'd planned to spend her summer as one of them, lazing in the sun with Selena, maybe shoplifting here and there to hone her skills, not doing anything important or real or meaningful.

She kind of missed that summer that would never be. Thinking of the photos of her parents, she wondered if they missed their summers. She thought of her sister and wondered what kind of childhood she'd had. She imagined what her own childhood would have been like if Moonbeam had stayed, if she'd grown up with Dad and Amanda. And she was very, very grateful for Moonbeam.

Selena slid into a parking spot across from Kayla and Moonbeam's cottage. "Do you need me?" she asked. "Because I'm feeling heroically brave today."

"You've been wonderful, Selena," Moonbeam said, "but we'll take it from here."

Selena raised her eyebrows at Kayla, and Kayla nodded in agreement. "You are going to keep in touch with me, right?" Selena asked. "You've known me a lot longer than lover-boy."

Kayla hesitated. It would give her father a way to track them, if he suspected. Look how much trouble had come from Moonbeam keeping in touch with Evelyn. On the other hand, Dad didn't know Selena. "This isn't good-bye," she said firmly. She'd find a way to make it work, somehow. "Are you going to be okay? I mean, with your parents?"

She smiled, and Kayla saw tears in her eyes. "Actually, for once, yes." Pulling out her sunglasses, Selena put them on. "I think I'm going to visit a boy I know."

"Glad to hear it. And, Selena . . . You're the best friend anyone could have."

"I *am* the best. But no worries. You're the penultimate."

Waving, Selena drove away, and Kayla had the unsettling feeling that she wasn't ever going to see her again. Despite what she'd said, it had felt like a good-bye. Moonbeam put her hand lightly on Kayla's shoulder, as if she didn't know whether to comfort Kayla or not.

Together they crossed the street. Moonbeam moved to push the gate open, but Kayla caught her arm. "Are you sure about this?" Kayla asked.

To Kayla's surprise, Moonbeam smiled. "More sure than I've ever been about anything."

30

Side by side, they pushed through the gate and went into the garden. The garden was still a mess. A gnome had been knocked over. Its base was broken, revealing its hollow inside. It looked like a war victim. Clippings from the hack job that Kayla had done on the hedge still littered the lawn. The flowers had been half trampled. As Kayla and Moonbeam walked through the verdant wreckage, Kayla felt her palms sweat and her heart hammer in her chest.

Reaching with her mind, Kayla "felt" inside the house. There was a figure, about the size of the voodoo queen, within. "She's there," Kayla said softly.

"Alone?"

"I think so." Creeping up to the window, Kayla peered through into the kitchen. She reached with her mind to touch the scarves, sewing needles, and herbs, ready in case she needed them.

Seated at the kitchen table, Queen Marguerite shook a handful of bones. She spilled them on the table, squinted at them, and then scooped them up again. "I know you're there, fixer girl," she said without looking up. "You may as well come in and tell Queen Marguerite what happened."

Behind her, Moonbeam said in a trembling voice, "Marguerite?"

Dropping the bones, Queen Marguerite rushed out of the house. "Lorelei? Lorelei, you're alive!" She scooped up her skirts to run faster, and Moonbeam ran toward her.

Kayla stepped out of the way as the two women crashed into an embrace in the middle of the garden. Laughing, Marguerite pressed her cheek to Moonbeam's. Tears were pouring down their faces, and Moonbeam was laughing too.

"Um, okay, guess I'll just . . . Yeah." Kayla released her hold on the scarves and other items inside the house. It looked like she wouldn't be needing them. "So, I take it she's not an enemy?"

Marguerite stroked Moonbeam's cheeks and her hair. "Lorelei, oh, Lorelei, are you well? The spell . . . Did it complete? Tell me what happened."

Moonbeam smiled through her tears. "My Kayla saved me."

Queen Marguerite beckoned to Kayla. "Come here, child."

Kayla inched closer to them, and Queen Marguerite snaked out an arm and pulled Kayla into an embrace too. "What one destroys, the other heals," Marguerite said. "I knew it! Our little fixer!" She then pushed Kayla back at arm's length and studied her. Her other arm remained firmly around Moonbeam's shoulders. Clucking her tongue, she said, "You don't have the stones."

"Two of them are gone," Kayla said.

"Jack and Amanda have the third," Moonbeam said. "We left them back in Louisiana. Daniel has taken Evelyn home to Chicago. Oh, Marguerite, she was responsible for it all! She contacted

Jack. She led him to you. She set Daniel and Kayla on their path . . . She wanted the stones for herself. She was so blind to everything else that she even let slip to Jack where to find me, though she claimed it was an accident. Fact is, she betrayed me. And you."

Queen Marguerite comforted her, then turned to Kayla. "Exactly what do you mean 'two of them are gone'?" Her voice was casual but her eyes were intense.

Kayla described how she and Daniel hid the stones in a way that neither would know where they were. "They're beyond anyone's reach. Even yours."

Queen Marguerite stared at her for a long moment, and Kayla tensed, prepared to defend herself if she had to, then the queen tilted her head back and laughed loud and long. "Well played, my dear. Well played. Aren't you the clever one? Lorelei, you did something right here."

Kayla gaped at her. So she'd been telling the truth? All along, she really wanted the stones gone? She wondered if she should apologize for misjudging her.

"But not with my other daughter." Sighing, Moonbeam sank onto the bench. She knocked the broken gnome out of the way with her foot. "I did something very wrong there."

Sitting beside her, Marguerite patted Moonbeam's shoulder. "You did nothing wrong. You were faced with an impossible situation, and you did the best you could."

"I should have found a way to take her with me. Or I should have stayed, fought Jack—"

"At what cost?"

"Who's to say it wouldn't have been better than this cost? You didn't see her, Marguerite. She's damaged . . . and it's my fault."

"You saved yourself and Kayla."

"I should have come to you. But I thought more magic . . ."

"You were afraid. There's no shame in that. But you don't have to be afraid anymore."

Moonbeam leaned her head against Queen Marguerite's shoulder. Softly, Marguerite murmured to her as she stroked her hair, as if she were a child who had woken from a nightmare.

While they were preoccupied with each other, Kayla ducked into the house and grabbed her emergency backpack. She emerged and cleared her throat. "Moonbeam? I'm ready to leave whenever you are."

Moonbeam shook her head. "Not this time. No more hiding."

"Are you sure, Lorelei?" Marguerite asked.

"Yes, I'm sure." She smiled at the voodoo queen.

Kayla felt her jaw drop open. She thought about shaking her head to clear her ears, but she didn't doubt that she'd heard Moonbeam say those words. She just didn't understand what they meant. They sounded like nonsense syllables. "We aren't?"

"I abandoned my daughter once; I won't do it again."

"You didn't abandon me . . . Oh, you mean Amanda. Um, she tried to shoot me. You remember that part, right? And Dad. She fired several times."

"She needs help," Moonbeam said.

"Um, I don't think she wants it. Especially from you. No offense meant."

Moonbeam sat up straighter, as if good posture would give her courage. "I won't pretend it will be easy. But it's time to face my responsibilities."

"She's dangerous and unstable," Kayla pointed out. "You saw

her. It's not like you can give her a hug and make everything okay."

Queen Marguerite hugged Moonbeam's shoulders. "She might just need a little motherly love. Problem is, right now she won't listen to her mama. And she has the power to keep from having to listen."

Moonbeam nodded. "That's what I think. And that's why I need your help." She faced Queen Marguerite. "Old friend, will you help me?"

Kayla looked from Moonbeam to the queen and back again. The way they acted, the way they talked, had the weight of years behind it. She wondered what she didn't know about their past. Queen Marguerite had claimed they were friends, and Moonbeam had been so certain that she could appease the voodoo queen. Maybe they truly had been close.

"You know my help always comes with a price. Even for you, my dear," Queen Marguerite cautioned. "What do you have that I want?"

"Me," Moonbeam said simply.

Queen Marguerite seemed to freeze. She didn't speak. She didn't breathe.

"You want to pass your legacy on to someone. You haven't taken on an apprentice. You don't have an heir. Help me help my daughter Amanda, and I will come with you to New Orleans and be your legacy."

"Mom?" Kayla's voice came out as a squeak. She couldn't believe she was hearing this. "Do you know what you're saying? You hate magic! Why on earth would you volunteer to be the next voodoo queen?"

Moonbeam put her hand on Marguerite's hand. "Because I'm

done with hiding. Because magic is what I am meant to do. Look around you. I didn't give it up. I demanded that you do without it, but then I steeped us in tons of my magic. I couldn't even cut my ties to Evelyn, even though that endangered you. I've been lying to myself. I am what I am, and this is my fate. Isn't it, Your Majesty?"

There were tears again in Queen Marguerite's eyes.

"Will you help me heal my daughter?" Moonbeam asked her.

Speechless, Marguerite nodded.

Moonbeam threw her arms around the voodoo queen, and Marguerite hugged her back. They stayed that way for a long while. At last, Marguerite pulled back. She was smiling the most real smile that Kayla had ever seen on her face. She touched Moonbeam's cheek softly, tenderly. "At my age, I expected to be finishing journeys, not beginning them. Tell me where to find your wayward girl."

Moonbeam was smiling and crying too. Tears had smeared the makeup under her eyes. "You know that old swimming hole on the Beaumont land?"

"Of course. Used to skinny-dip there myself back in the day."

"That's where we did the spell."

Queen Marguerite laughed. "Two miles from my home. Right under my nose. Very well. I'll be back, with company. Be ready." And then she vanished, leaving Kayla and Moonbeam alone.

Kayla moved toward her. "Moonbeam . . ."

"Don't try to talk me out of this, Kayla."

"Actually, I was going to ask if you can use that sleeping spell on Amanda. It might be a nicer solution than just bashing her on the head, albeit less satisfying."

Moonbeam looked relieved. "I want to talk to her first, without her father's influence. I might be able to reach her, at least enough to convince her to try . . ."

"And if you can't? Sleeping spell, yes?"

"The spell will need to be stronger. If I only use words, it lasts a few minutes at best. But with herbs . . ." Jumping to her feet, Moonbeam scurried inside the house. Kayla trailed after her. Moonbeam beelined to her shelves and pulled out several kinds of herbs. She began to mix them, crushing them with a pestle. She then poured them into a shallow bowl and added oil. "The smoke from this will make her sleep until we're ready to wake her." She set a wick in it as if it were ordinary incense oil. Moonbeam lit a nearby candle. Her hands were shaking. She murmured words over it. "The wick will need to be lit. I don't know if—"

"I can do it," Kayla said.

"She has to inhale the smoke."

"I can make her do that," Kayla said.

Her mother studied her for a long moment. "Kayla . . . I don't know how to apologize for failing you so very badly."

"You didn't fail me," Kayla said automatically. Once the words were out of her mouth, she wasn't sure they were true. Moonbeam had lied for years.

Moonbeam blew out the match. The candle wreathed her face in a soft light. It made her look fragile. "I can't guarantee I'll be able to save your sister."

"That's okay. Really. She's kind of a psychopath."

Moonbeam positioned the candle on the counter near the oil. "But she's *my* psychopath. I owe it to Amanda to try. She blames me for leaving."

"She said she locked herself in the bathroom and screamed for Dad."

Moonbeam's eyes widened. "She told you that? It's true. It was either leave with you then, or lose the chance to leave at all. Still, I've replayed that day in my mind so many times. If I could have prevented her, or explained better . . . She was young. She didn't understand the consequences, not truly."

"For what it's worth, I don't blame you." That much was true. She was able to say the words easily.

"You don't? But I lied to you." Moonbeam's eyes were wide and so full of hope.

Kayla wanted to put her arms around her mother. But she didn't. Instead, she wet a paper towel and dabbed the smeared makeup under Moonbeam's eyes, cleaning her up. "You should have told me the truth sooner, but you weren't wrong to leave. I had a much better childhood with you than I would have had with Daddy Dearest. I would've turned out just like Amanda. You saved me from that. I know that's why you left. For me."

Moonbeam smiled, albeit sadly. "Kayla—"

"Your little psychopath is here." Kayla pointed out the window. Queen Marguerite stood between the bench and the gate. She was gripping Amanda by the arm. Shrugging her off, Amanda strode toward the house. Kayla felt her heart beat faster.

"Let me try to talk to her before you burn the oil," Moonbeam commanded.

"Fine. Talk fast."

Leaving the oil and candle, Moonbeam ran for the door. Kayla stepped onto the kitchen counter and out the window. She jumped off the window box. As she did, she grabbed with her mind for the stray leaves and twigs that littered the lawn. She aimed them at Amanda.

"Kayla, no, we talk *first!*" Moonbeam cried, bursting outside.

Kayla let the leaves and twigs drop.

Amanda picked up the bench with her mind and threw it at Kayla. It pinned her against the house. "Happy to talk. Tell me where the stones are."

"Gone," Kayla said. Glaring at her mother, she didn't move a muscle. "Daniel jumped me to multiple locations without telling me where he was. He closed his eyes so he wouldn't know where I dropped the stones. So no one knows where they are."

"You're lying," Amanda said. "No one would throw away that much power."

Moonbeam came toward her. Her hands were open, palms out, a soothing gesture, as if Amanda were a wild deer that Moonbeam wanted to feed. "*I* did. At great cost. At the cost of you."

"Don't talk to me," Amanda said. "You don't deserve to talk to me."

Hands still out, Moonbeam halted. "I'm your mother." Her voice was gentle, soothing, as if she wanted to break out in a lullaby. Kayla felt calmer hearing it. She reached with her mind toward the candle, ready to light the oil.

Amanda snorted. "You gave up that right when you left me behind."

"You chose to stay."

"I was a kid! You were trying to take me from my father, to destroy my family! You should have stayed." Amanda pointed at her, and wind bashed into Moonbeam, knocking her off her feet.

Pushing herself up, Moonbeam stood. "I couldn't stay, and you wouldn't leave. And then suddenly, it was done, and it was too late. Believe me, leaving you behind was the hardest thing I've ever done."

"Pretty words."

"He'd already won with you. I realized it when you screamed for him. You and he were a team. But when Katie began to show signs of her power . . ."

"I know. You had to 'save' Katie. It's always about the precious baby Katie."

Moonbeam stepped toward her again. "I missed you."

"Don't lie to me. How could you miss me? You had her."

Not moving from behind the bench, Kayla said, "*I* missed you. I missed my big sister. Remember how we used to play tea party with all my stuffed animals? Remember how you tried to teach me to read? We'd play school, and you taught me how to write a poem with lots of rhymes. You were the one who stood under me when I first started to climb trees. You were the one who taught me how to climb onto the roof. We used to sneak out and look at the stars at night. Do you remember that?"

"Of course I do," Amanda said. "But that was a long time ago, and it doesn't matter now. I'm not Dad. I'm not weak-minded or weak-willed. You are going to tell me where the stones are, whether you want to or not."

Queen Marguerite laughed lightly. "Oh, bless her heart, she still thinks she can win. Honey, you were outsmarted fair and square. Cut your losses and seek another way."

Spinning to face her, Amanda shot her a glare that was nearly as powerful as the wind. "You wanted those stones too. Are you telling me you're giving up? There's a limited number of places they could have jumped in the time they had. You and I, we can search them all. After all, it's still only two." She drew the third stone out of her pocket and held it up.

Queen Marguerite frowned at it. "That's a fake."

"What?" Amanda shrieked. She dropped the bench. It landed with a crash in front of Kayla, and the back of it cracked, a split right between the symbols for peace and tranquility. Amanda carried the stone into a patch of direct sun and twisted it in the air. Colors sparkled from deep within the black.

"I'm sorry, my girl, but you've been tricked. It's a fake."

Staying pressed against the house, Kayla eyed the bench. It could rise again at any time. Especially since Amanda was growing more and more angry. She kept a portion of her mind touching the flame and glanced at Moonbeam. Moonbeam shook her head.

"Do you mean to tell me the spell—" Amanda raged.

"Oh, the stone *was* real, and the spell would have worked. Someone would have died," Queen Marguerite said. "But this . . . is not real. It must have been switched."

Amanda lifted up the bench again, and this time the bench rotated as if she was planning to hit Kayla with it. "*You* did this! Where is it?"

Kayla held her hands up in front of her, knowing that wouldn't be enough to stop the bench if Amanda decided to throw it. "Not me. You've seen my power. I can't levitate much more than a pencil. Rocks are out of my league."

With a cry, Amanda threw the stone. It hit the house and fell on the grass. Rolling, it landed at Queen Marguerite's feet. The voodoo queen met Kayla's eyes. Slowly, she winked. Kayla looked at the stone. *It's real*, she thought. *She lied.*

Before Amanda could act again, Moonbeam stepped in front of her, between her and Kayla. "Amanda, look at me. Put down the bench."

Amanda glared at her and didn't lower the bench.

"Look at me, Amanda."

Crossing her arms, Amanda said, "I *am* looking at you."

"You know what I see when I look at you?" Moonbeam asked. "Me. I see me. You are exactly like I was when I was your age. All fire and no sense. I wanted to soar free. I wanted to be different and special and *safe*. I wanted to be so powerful that no one could ever hurt me or, more importantly, hurt the people I love." Reaching out, she stroked Amanda's hair. Amanda flinched back but didn't move away. "And in the end, I lost nearly everything that mattered to me. My husband. My home. You. My job. Myself. Even my own name."

"You didn't lose anything; you left."

"I lost," Moonbeam insisted, "in every way that mattered. Your father and his ambition would have destroyed us all. You were young. You didn't know what he was like. He was relentless, and I was weak. If I hadn't left . . . I had to become someone else to find out who I was."

Amanda pulled away. "You expect me to believe that? You were 'finding yourself'?"

"I'm sorry I left you. I'm sorry I wasn't there for so much of your childhood. I am truly, deeply, honestly sorry." Her eyes were wet, and her voice had so much sincerity in it that Kayla could almost taste it in the back of her throat.

Amanda seemed to hesitate. "I want . . ."

"What do you want?" Moonbeam's voice was gentle, motherly. "Tell me."

"I want you to never speak to me again."

"You don't mean that," Moonbeam said, taking her hands. "I'm your mother. I want to fix this, fix us. We have the chance to learn to be a family again." *Okay, now that is laying it on too thick*, Kayla thought. After all, Amanda had just tried to kill Dad, whom she purportedly loved.

Beyond them, Kayla noticed Queen Marguerite lowering herself onto the grass. She picked up the stone and then looked at Kayla, as if to make sure that Kayla was watching her. Hidden from Amanda by the folds of her billowy skirt, the queen fit the stone inside the broken garden gnome and then set the gnome upright.

Amanda turned back to Kayla. "I tried to shoot you. Are you on board with all this lovey-dovey forgiveness?"

Kayla shrugged. "Personally, I think you're a psychopath. Or sociopath. I don't really know the difference. Regardless of the diagnosis, I think you need years of therapy before we can have a normal relationship."

"Or you can come with me right now and we can be a team," Amanda said. She lowered the bench to the ground and took a step toward Kayla, her hand outstretched.

"Exactly what part of 'I think you're a psychopath' was unclear?"

Moonbeam shook her head. "Kayla, you aren't helping."

Amanda pivoted to glare at her. Kayla noticed that the hedges were trembling, as if the wind had increased, except that it hadn't. "At least she's being honest! At least she isn't trying to trick me!"

Kayla took that as a somewhat ironic cue. Reaching into the cottage with her mind, she drew the candle flame to the wick in the oil. It began to burn, and smoke tendriled up. She then yanked the prayer scarves out the window. Snaking them down the side of the cottage, she drew them over the lawn to just behind Amanda.

"Enough talking," Amanda said. The hedges shook harder.

Kayla agreed. Whether Moonbeam was ready or not, it was time. Kayla flew the scarves up around Amanda's eyes. As she clawed at them, Kayla guided the smoke out the window and toward Amanda's face.

The walls of the cottage began to shake, as if in an earthquake. *Crack.* Plaster split. Kayla fell to her knees, landing hard on the quaking grass, but she held the flame to the incense, keeping it from spilling, as she wafted the smoke into Amanda's mouth.

Both Moonbeam and Queen Marguerite began to chant.

The amulets around Moonbeam's neck began to glow, as well as the blue-eye necklace that Kayla wore. They were echoed by the protective stones that circled the house—each of them glowed with a soft, moonlike white light. Slowly, the earth began to steady. Kayla kept up the flow of smoke, forcing it into her sister's mouth and nose. She also kept the scarves over her eyes so Amanda couldn't see to attack.

Amanda's knees buckled.

She pitched forward as the earthquake died.

Moonbeam caught her. She sank to the ground with Amanda in her arms. The stones and the amulets ceased glowing. "My poor sweet baby," Moonbeam murmured.

The walls of the cottage were cracked. The roof had a split in it that traveled across the shingles. In the garden, all the chimes were strewn on the lawn, and the gate had been ripped from its hinges. Kayla continued to funnel the smoke into her sister's mouth until Queen Marguerite put her hand on Kayla's shoulder. "Enough," she said gently.

Reaching with her mind, Kayla snuffed the flame. The smoke died, and the wisps dissipated into the air. She released the scarves as well.

"I'm so sorry," Moonbeam said softly. She held Amanda for a moment more and then lowered her onto the grass. Amanda's chest rose and fell. The scarves had slipped from her closed eyes and lay loosely across her neck. Her mouth had fallen slightly open. She looked so peaceful.

Kayla liked her much better this way.

"You really think *she* can be part of a functional family?" Kayla asked.

"It will take work."

"Uh-huh."

"I may have pushed a bit too hard too fast."

"Did you honestly expect her to hug you and say 'I'll forgive you, let's go shopping for shoes and forget this ever happened— oh, and sorry about nearly shooting my father, drowning my mother, and trying to kill my sister in at least three different ways'?"

Moonbeam sighed. "Honestly, no. But it did distract her, and we've bought ourselves some time. For now, until we decide to wake her, it's over."

Queen Marguerite coughed lightly. "Not quite over yet. There's the little matter of your ex-husband. He might not like our plans for fixing his darling daughter."

"Then perhaps it's time for him and me to have a talk." Moonbeam drew herself straighter, and Kayla stared at her as if seeing her for the first time. She sounded so confident, and she looked so very strong and sure. "Kayla and I can handle him."

Kayla was fairly certain nothing could shock her anymore. "Mom?"

Moonbeam smiled at her, albeit sadly. "You're powerful. More powerful than I imagined. And I have been clipping your wings, keeping you caged, all those metaphors and more. I think it's time I trust you a little, don't you?"

Nodding slowly, Kayla didn't know what to say.

"Bring him here," Moonbeam ordered.

31

Kneeling next to Amanda, Moonbeam gently unwrapped the scarves that lay across her neck. Kayla joined her, took the strings of prayer scarves, and began to tie them around Amanda's wrists and ankles. "You don't need to . . . ," Moonbeam began.

Looking at her with her eyebrows raised, Kayla tightened the knots. "I thought you believed that magic is evil. Are you sure about this? You're sacrificing your future to help someone who doesn't want to be helped."

Moonbeam studied Kayla for a minute before speaking. "Do you remember when you were little how we used to play on the beach?"

"Sure. We used to go all the time."

"I'd make you wear sunscreen, and you hated it."

"Still hate the stuff. But at least the spray is quicker. Why are we talking about this?" Crossing the garden, Kayla uprighted the bench and put it back by the hedges. She picked up one of the broken chimes. It used to have a glass globe in the center. The globe was shattered all over the ground. She scooted the broken shards into a pile with her foot. "Shouldn't we be planning for Dad? Queen Marguerite will be back soon." Maybe she could use the shards of glass as a weapon. She tested lifting one into the air with her mind. It was light enough. Concentrating, she picked up several at once.

"You used to make sand castles, just using your mind, and I let you. You'd make these magnificently beautiful towers with arches and pillars. You'd use shells to be the knights and princesses, and we'd play for hours."

"You let me use magic? I don't remember that."

"It was beautiful, and you were so happy." Moonbeam pushed herself to her feet. "I've made mistakes, Kayla. And I intend to fix as many of them as I can."

Before Kayla could decide how she felt about this pronouncement, Queen Marguerite returned. This time she had Kayla's father. He dropped to his knees on the grass beside the unconscious Amanda.

"Amanda!" he cried. "Amanda, can you hear me? Are you okay, baby?" Scooping her into his arms, he cradled her against his chest. "What did you do to her?"

Moonbeam crossed her arms, looking more fierce than Kayla had ever seen her look. "The key question is, What did *you* do to her?"

"Well, I think you three have a lot to talk about," Queen Marguerite said brightly. "I'll be inside. Give a shout if you need him taken to Timbuktu." She headed for the house and opened the door. "Ooh, what a mess. I'll do a little cleanup while you three chat. I owe Kayla a cleaning." She ducked inside without waiting for a response.

Kayla held the shards of glass in midair, ready. If he so much as said one word of a spell, she'd make them fly. Crossing her arms, she waited to see what her parents would do.

Moonbeam knelt in front of him. "Oh, Jack."

"What did you do to her?" he demanded again.

"She's asleep." Moonbeam sighed heavily. "How did we come to this?"

"You left," he said.

Kayla walked closer, bringing the shards with her. "That was a rhetorical question. After seeing the result of your parenting style, I'm pretty convinced she had cause."

"Jack," Moonbeam said. "Remember when we were younger? We had all these plans to change the world. Protect the weak. Help the helpless."

"Of course I remember. You walked out on all of that."

"Don't lie to yourself, Jack. It stopped being about that long before I left. You wanted to mold our children into living weapons, not because it was right for them or because you wanted to help anyone. You wanted it for you, to prove you weren't that scared little boy anymore."

"They had power!"

"So? They were children who deserved childhoods."

Looking down at Amanda, he seemed to deflate. "It went wrong. I don't know where or when. I did my best. I swear I did. I only wanted her to live up to her potential, to be strong, to be someone no one could ever tear down. But Amanda . . ."

"Taking away her power isn't going to fix her. It isn't the power that's broken; it's her."

There were tears in his eyes. Actual tears. "I didn't mean to break her."

"But you did." Her voice was soft, kind. She looked up at Kayla. "Kayla, I am so very sorry. I should have told you the truth. At first, you were too young to understand. And then, I'd lied for so long that I didn't know how to tell you the truth."

"I'll forgive you eventually. But what do we do with him?"

"We don't do anything. *He* leaves us alone," Moonbeam said. There was steel in her voice, the same as when she'd grounded Kayla. "Won't you, Jack?"

"But Amanda needs me!"

"She needs anyone but you right now. You won't come near us ever again, Jack. Do you understand me? Don't seek us out. Don't find us. I intend to fix what you broke."

"Let me help," Jack said.

Firmly, Moonbeam said, "No. It's my turn now. Your idea of fixing things involves guns and knives. That doesn't work for me."

"I'll find you," Jack said. "I'll always find you. I still love you. After everything. We're meant to be together, Lorelei. We can work through this."

Kayla came closer to them. "See, you think that sounds romantic, but it's just crazy stalker talk. Moonbeam said no. So did I. We don't want you in our lives. And if we catch you near us . . . Scratch that, if *I* catch you . . ." She guided the shards of glass toward him, grazing his skin—not close enough to cut but close enough for him to feel the tickle of the sharp edges. "Amanda may have brute strength, but I have precision. And I'm much smarter than she is. You've pissed me off too many times already. Don't do it again."

"Are you threatening your own father?" her dad asked.

"Yes, absolutely. Weren't you listening? Honestly, I thought I was being pretty clear." Kayla looked at her mother. "You're threatening him too, right?"

"Yes, indeed." Moonbeam reached toward him. He flinched, instinctively turning his head away. She plucked several strands of his hair. "I will be making a doll with this. And not for your protection. I will use it if I have to." She tucked the hairs into the pocket of her dress.

"You wouldn't—"

"You went too far. You always do. But I'm done being afraid of you, Jack," Moonbeam said. "And I'm done with you." She called to Queen Marguerite. "You can take him away."

Queen Marguerite came outside, the door banging behind her. It half hung off the doorframe. The entire house was tilted, shifted off its foundation. It looked as if a stiff wind would blow it over. "Gladly! Where would you like me to take him?"

"Tikal," Kayla suggested. "Tell the archaeologists that he's the one who's responsible for the cave-in, and he's offered to pay for the damages to their national treasure."

"Delightful," Queen Marguerite said. "I like how your mind works, child."

"Wait, that's it?" Jack said. "You're sending me away just like that? No further discussion? But . . . I can change! I have already changed!"

"Oh, Jack, you haven't changed," Moonbeam said sadly. "You're still that little boy who's afraid his daddy will hurt him again. Only now, the monster you're afraid of is one you created, your own daughter."

His jaw clenched, and his face reddened. He opened his mouth to reply, but Moonbeam cut him off.

"You made your choices, and I made mine. We can't erase

what's happened between us, or what we've done. We have to live with it. And I choose not to live in fear anymore. Come for us again, and I won't flee. I will fight you."

"But my daughter—"

"Needs help," Moonbeam said. "You know I won't hurt her, Jack. I want to help her."

"You'll turn her against me! Like you turned Katie."

"You did that all by yourself," Kayla said. "You told Amanda to cause that cave-in, didn't you? And you left me in that tomb in Peru, not knowing whether Daniel would live or die, not knowing whether I'd survive. Then to top it off, you kidnapped my mother and Daniel's mother and were perfectly content to sacrifice either one of them because you thought you were right—you thought the stones would fix Amanda and grant you your dream all in one shot, never mind the price, which, by the way, would have affected me too. Did you ever even ask me if I wanted to lose my magic? It's part of me, who I am! Even if Moonbeam forgave you, I think I have plenty of my own reasons to decide you're evil."

Dad's face paled more with each word she said. "But I didn't think you—"

"Exactly. You didn't think of me. You thought of yourself. Your fear, your pain, your mistakes, your solutions. And this is the cost." Kayla looked at Queen Marguerite. "I'm done with this conversation. Please take him away."

Queen Marguerite sauntered over to him.

"Katie!" Dad cried.

"And for the last time, don't call me Katie. My name is Kayla."

Queen Marguerite laid her hand on his shoulder, and they vanished. "Good-bye, Jack," Moonbeam murmured. She slipped her hand into Kayla's.

Silence fell over the garden.

Lying on the grass at their feet, Amanda slept on.

∾ ᴄᴏ

Eventually, they had to deal with the house. Even if Moonbeam hadn't promised to move to New Orleans, it couldn't be home anymore. It was too broken. Several houses on the street were damaged in the "freak earthquake," as the news was calling it, but theirs was damaged the worst. Building inspectors came through and pronounced it uninhabitable. The police wrapped DO NOT CROSS tape over the door and windows. But after they all left and the reporters left and the street was quiet again, Kayla and Moonbeam went back in.

It was cracked in so many places that it creaked every time they walked through it. Taking turns, they darted in and retrieved items, spreading them out on the lawn. Side by side, they packed. They talked a little, off and on, about memories of the different items: a dreamcatcher that always hung in the kitchen window, a pair of flip-flops that Kayla loved but were broken, a scarf that Kayla had given Moonbeam for Mother's Day, a book of poetry that they'd traded back and forth—all the little things they'd accumulated in their life here. Half of the things they left lying on the ground. The other half they squeezed into boxes and suitcases.

When Moonbeam wasn't looking, Kayla tucked the broken garden gnome inside her emergency backpack. She then helped her mother wrap a few of the handmade mugs in scarves so they wouldn't break on the journey.

"Are you ready for a new adventure?" Moonbeam asked. "You'll like New Orleans."

"Until the last few days, I thought you'd never want to leave here."

"It was Moonbeam's home. It was never Lorelei's."

"Can you really go back to being her? You've been Moonbeam for a long time."

Moonbeam smiled. "I'd like to try."

"I'm still calling you Moonbeam."

"Not everything is going to change, Kayla."

Yes, it is, Kayla thought. And she couldn't decide if that made her happy or sad.

When Queen Marguerite returned, she made multiple trips: first Amanda, next Moonbeam, and then their belongings. Kayla helped load her up with various suitcases and boxes to bring to Moonbeam in New Orleans. As the sun sank, the pile of luggage dwindled, and soon there were only the things they'd decided to leave behind. Kayla sat down on the bench that her mother had painted and looked at the wrecked garden and broken house. The bench was broken as well, but it still held her fine.

When Queen Marguerite appeared again to take Kayla, Kayla didn't move. She tried to look calm, as if she were merely resting on the bench, but every muscle felt tense.

"I assume you aren't coming," the voodoo queen said as she picked up the final suitcase, full of various amulets and the remainder of Moonbeam's herbs.

"Not right away."

"Thought as much."

Kayla felt her muscles unclench. Queen Marguerite wasn't going to argue. Maybe she even understood. "Please tell Daniel that I'll be at the place we first met. And tell Moonbeam that I love her and not to worry."

"She'll worry anyway," Queen Marguerite said. "Do you have a plan for where you and the boy are going and what you're going to do?"

Kayla smiled. "I plan to improvise."

"Don't take too long, fixer girl. You're still needed."

Standing, Kayla shouldered her backpack, and she walked for the last time out the garden gate. No chimes rang—they were either broken or packed. The gate itself didn't close anymore. She didn't look back.

Seagulls cried overhead, and she heard the music from a half-dozen radios, playing over one another. She kept walking toward the ocean. After a while, she saw the blue between the palm trees. Closer, the sound of shouts, laughter, and the crash of waves all washed over her. Sticking to the sidewalk, Kayla strolled with the tourists past the beach volleyball courts, past the sunbathers, past the artists with their easels, past the vendors selling tourist junk, past the ice cream truck and the surreys. She reached the dolphin fountain and then headed up State Street.

It looked exactly as it always did. Tourists clustered at the cafés and restaurants, eating at outdoor tables. The black-clad teens panhandled and taunted people from the brick benches. She picked an unoccupied bench not too close to anyone and sat down.

Pulling out her phone, she called Selena.

Selena answered on the third ring. "Hey, girl, guess what? Sam's here. He's having dinner with my family tonight. In exchange for me not skipping any more classes, they've agreed not to be rude to him or to poison him or anything, which isn't exactly giving their blessing, but it's a start. Where are you? What happened with the voodoo queen? Are you okay?"

"Yeah, I think I really am." Kayla filled her in on everything that had happened.

"Come see me tomorrow. We'll go to the beach. You need a break."

"Not tomorrow."

"Soon?"

"Soon," Kayla promised.

"I will not accept living in New Orleans as an excuse not to hang out. Daniel knows how to find my house. You have him jump you here soon. We can double-date!"

"Sounds fun."

"Ooh, gotta go. Appetizer time. Can't miss crab cakes. Even for you."

Kayla said good-bye, then hung up. She was smiling as she tucked her phone back into her pocket and leaned back on the bench.

After a while, one of the teens—a girl—approached her. "Hey, aren't you the girl who was here before? The one who disappeared with that boy from the store window? How did you do that?"

"Magic." Kayla wiggled her fingers in the sign that Selena had invented.

"Really? Sweet."

"You should see what my mother can do." Kayla looked at her and smiled. "She's the next voodoo queen of New Orleans."

"Oh, so it was a trick?"

"Exactly. It was a publicity stunt for a store called Voodoo Spells and Charms."

The girl looked crestfallen. Slinking away, she rejoined her friends. Kayla felt them talking about her and, out of the corner of her eye, saw them pointing at her and watching. After a while, though, they lost interest. Eventually, they moved on. She was left alone.

The sun began to set. At the end of State Street, in front of the pier, the dolphin fountain was framed by a glow of liquid gold. Overhead, the sky was tinted rose. Still, Kayla sat, thinking and not thinking, her backpack on her lap.

As stars began to appear overhead, a boy sat next to her.

She smiled.

"Nice night," Daniel said.

"It's Santa Barbara. We specialize in nice nights."

"Live here long enough and you get used to it?"

"I think I've lived here long enough," Kayla said. "I'm ready to move on." She slipped her hand into his. His fingers closed around hers. She tilted her head to look at him. His eyes still looked like a storm over the ocean, but he was smiling at her. She smiled back. "I hear Paris is lovely this time of year."

On top of the Eiffel Tower, Kayla perched on a beam one level above the usual tourist platform. Daniel sat on one side of her; the garden gnome sat on the other. So far, no one had yelled at them to climb down. She didn't doubt there were people below wondering if they were safe up here.

She felt safer than she ever had.

"Are you okay with this height?" Kayla asked.

"Strangely, yes," Daniel said. He'd been clutching the beam with both hands, but he released it and exhaled. "At least something good came out of all this."

"Also, I'm getting to see Paris. And so is Jerome."

"Jerome?"

"Jerome the Gnome. I named him."

"Ahh. Can I ask why?"

"No," Kayla said.

Daniel didn't argue. He put his arm around her shoulders, and she leaned her head against his shoulder. His arm felt as comfortable as the warmest coat. From up here, Paris looked like a garden. Clusters of buildings were clumps of flowers, painted yellow and mauve by the rising sun. Cars and buses scooted between them like bees, and people scurried around them like ants. The Seine twisted through, sparkling in the dawn. In the distance, the sun rose up the face of a set of beautiful white domes and a tower. They glowed on top of a hill overlooking the city. She saw why hundreds of romantic movies were filmed here. She looked at Daniel.

He stared out over the city, but she didn't think he was looking at it. His eyes were fixed on the horizon beyond, and she thought his mind was thousands of miles away.

"Are you thinking about your mother?" Kayla asked.

A muscle in his jaw twitched, and his arm tightened around her. "Yes." *Stormy eyes*, she thought. He'd left Evelyn in Chicago, but Kayla could tell he hadn't really left her behind, any more than she had left Moonbeam, Amanda, or her father.

"Do you think she's going to cause more problems?" Kayla asked.

"Probably. But not right away. She doesn't want to disappoint me, she says. But I think she's only saying that because the stones are gone."

Kayla nodded. On the Seine, tour boats drifted through the smooth-as-glass water. She wondered how many people in this city were here only briefly, like them, and how many were thinking of people elsewhere. "Do you think my mother is safe with Amanda?"

"Certainly while Amanda's asleep. And she has Queen Marguerite with her for when she wakes. The two of them can handle her."

Kayla snorted. "She already destroyed the voodoo shop once."

"Hey, at least your mom is trying to have a relationship with her."

"You think I should be trying?"

"You? No. Your sister's a psychopath. I was talking about my mother and me, in an oblique way. She used me. She's always used me. Her work has always been more important. Your mother put you first. And now she's trying with Amanda. She may even succeed. Your mother is a determined woman. I think she genuinely regrets lying to you and wants to make everything right."

Kayla nodded. "I *am* going to forgive her. After we travel for a while." And she'd also go back to see Selena, frequently. Even if she had to live in New Orleans now, she wasn't giving up on an eight-year friendship. Given that she knew two teleporters, she shouldn't even have to take a plane. As Selena had said, there was no excuse not to hang out.

"I always did like plan B." Daniel lay back on the metal platform. Kayla lay with him and looked up through the metal bars toward the tip of the Eiffel Tower. The steel bars framed the lightening sky like a modern art installation with the sky as the canvas.

From below, she heard a shout in French, aimed at them. In a few minutes, one of the guards would be climbing up to fetch them. Maybe it was a sign they were done with Paris, for now.

Daniel shifted slightly, turning his head to look at Kayla. "Where to next? Rome? Cairo? Tokyo? Sydney?"

"Any interest in exploring an Egyptian tomb? Maybe we'll find another immensely dangerous magical artifact that long-lost family members will want to kill us for."

"Cairo it is."

And Paris vanished.

White. Blue. Then tan.

Lying on a rooftop, Kayla breathed in the dry desert air and a hundred spices she didn't recognize. Voices in a language she didn't know assailed her ears. She was looking up at a midday sun that bleached the sky.

Pushing herself up to sitting, she saw they were on a roof with a view of the Great Pyramids of Giza. Several high-rises, framed by palm trees, were in the foreground, and then beyond them the pyramids rose out of a sea of sand. A haze surrounded them, and the glare of the sun made Kayla's eyes tear. She shielded her eyes with her hand. "Amazing," she breathed.

"You know, I've seen this view at least a dozen times. This is the only time I've ever thought it was amazing." He touched her cheek and brushed a stray strand of hair behind her ear.

"You're just saying that because you want to kiss me."

"And because it's true. But also because I want to kiss you." He leaned closer.

"You should have kissed me in Paris. That was the romantic view."

"You don't like this view?"

"Of course I do. But it does make me think of mummies." And that made her think of the tomb in Peru, which made her think of her father again. She wondered if he'd left Guatemala and where he planned to go. "You know, for two people who didn't pack much, we brought a lot of baggage with us." Kayla inhaled, breathing in the spices and the car fumes and the chalky dust. "I have a proposal. For the next however-long-we-want, we don't talk or think about our families."

"So what do you propose we talk and think about?"

"Us, obviously."

"Are we an 'us'?" Daniel asked.

"Hope so, since we're traveling the world together. It's a bit too late to tell me you have another girlfriend in Paris and one in Peru. You don't, right?"

He kissed her, thoroughly and sweetly. She closed her eyes and breathed in the taste of him, mixed with the taste of the Cairo air. When they broke apart, they didn't move more than an inch from each other. Daniel touched his forehead to hers. "Only you. You stole my heart."

She groaned. "Tell me you didn't seriously go there with the cheesy thief reference."

"Afraid I did. Do you still love me?"

The breeze stopped, as if it were listening. Voices from the street below seemed hushed. It was as if, for a moment, the world had shrunk to only the two of them. "Still? I don't think I ever said I did."

"Then I'll say it first: I'm in love with you, Kayla. I love you."

Kayla stared into his eyes, so intensely fixed on her. "I think I love you too."

"Just 'think'?"

"Well, you're still an asshole."

"I'll try to change," he vowed.

She began to smile. "Don't. It's one of your finest attributes."

He smiled back. "Okay, then I accept your proposal: no thinking about any of our crazy relatives until we're finished seeing the world."

"Deal," she agreed. Leaning against him again, she kissed him. She'd leave the third stone somewhere around here, when

Daniel wasn't looking. Maybe she could convince him to swing by some uninhabited part of Siberia. Or she could drop it down a deep crevasse in Antarctica or bury it in the jungles of Madagascar . . .

There was no rush to decide. They still had a lot of world to see.

Acknowledgments

I love the question "If you could have any power, what would it be?" Over the years, I've given this a lot of thought. And I mean a *lot* of thought.

The true answer is that I'd want the power to keep everyone I love happy and healthy for all time. Also, to bring about world peace and to end world hunger. And the power to avoid saying anything stupid ever. But assuming all of those were off the table . . .

Not flight. I'm kind of afraid of heights, or at least afraid of flying into power lines. Not shape-shifting. With my luck, I'd change into a mouse, and my cat would eat me. Not weather control. Way too much responsibility. Not invisibility. People would constantly step on my feet. And run me over with cars. But telekinesis . . . That would be *awesome*.

And that's where this book began, simply playing with telekinesis. In fact, for a while, before this book had an actual title (or plot or characters or anything), I called it, in my notes, "Telekinesis Girl." So I'd like to begin by thanking everyone who ever asked me that question.

I'd also like to thank the people who made this book a reality: my fabulous agent, Andrea Somberg; my wonderful editor, Emily Easton; and all the fantastic people at Bloomsbury, including (but not limited to) Erica Barmash, Beth Eller, Courtney Griffin, Linette Kim, Cindy Loh, Lizzy Mason, Jenna Pocius, and Emily Ritter. If I could use telekinesis to send you all daily chocolates, I would.

Special thank-you to my mother, who answered my many random questions about the Maya and who taught me to love books in the first place (and, you know, gave birth to me and is all-around incredible); to my family and friends, who have loved and encouraged me from the beginning; and to my husband and children, who share my dreams and make my world magical every day. I love you all more than chocolate.